ADVANCED PRAISE

Wow! What a great story! It had me hooked from beginning to end. What a message it holds!

—Esther Wyngaarden, Retired Educator

The rich and captivating story line of *The Light Keeper* expertly leads the reader through an emotional journey that mirrors real life experiences. Moments of levity are intertwined with soul-wrenching events that draw the reader into the life and heart of the main character through struggles, joys and honest internal dialogue. The author's exemplary command of language enhances the richness, enjoyment, and faith-stretching impact of the book. An excellent read!

—Garry Schubert, Retired Educator

A riveting narrative, *The Light Keeper* delivers a timeless take on human nature and the joy of the Lord. The author digs deeply into questions of life and faith and, like the psalmists of old, does not shy away from revealing true human emotions. The protagonist's indomitable spirit has stayed with me, earning Dora a place among my favourite literary heroines and reminding me to take heart as I navigate the deep waters and dark valleys of my own life. Like Dora says, I am not alone.

—Victoria Sparrow, OCT, Educator

The Light Keeper is a beautiful historical novel that follows one woman's life journey as she discovers the heavenly treasures and lessons revealed through her suffering and struggles. It is much like each one of our stories as we learn to put God first in our lives. While I turned the pages, I found myself laughing and then crying and then laughing again. It was a book that I couldn't put down, keeping me up very late at night. I thoroughly enjoyed it.

—Patricia Kimmerly, Avid Reader

Dora's story of love and faith plays out over many years and is written with sensitivity and realism. Her life is one that holds wonder and a certain innocence tested over time. Her moments of simple prayer and leaps of faith feel real as does her journey of loss, sorrow and grief. The faith questions are present and honest as Dora moves through the many seasons of her life. I often speak of 'God moments', times when God whispers and the soul hears—one is moved and is often surprised. Dora knows such moments. Ms. Le Gresley's story of Dora will be appreciated by people of faith as well as others who question, doubt, and wonder.

—The Rev. Canon Gregory Physick, B.A., M. Div. Anglican Priest (Ret.),
Diocese of Toronto, Canada

In this well researched work, Katherine sensitively addresses the timeless issues of mental health, loss, and disappointment. These issues are likely to feel familiar, as may Dora's struggle to trust and surrender her wishes to God's plan. If you find yourself in need of hope and inspiration for your life journey you will want to read *The Light Keeper*!

—Sarah White, B.A.Sc., M.Sc., Registered Psychotherapist/Registered
Marriage & Family Therapist

An easy to read, fictional story based on the life of an ancestor who inspired the author to share insights into the joys and tragedies of a life lived in faith. Dora, whose name means "a gift from God" struggles with how to be the hands and feet, eyes and voice of the Jesus she loves and who calls her "Beloved". How does she honour her need to care for her family with her own loves, needs and ambitions? The reader is challenged and exposed to eternal questions such as "Why must this special person die?"; "What do you demand of me, Lord?"; and "How do I know what you want me to do?" The book resonates with the faith-filled articulate prose and poetry of the author and leaves the reader inspired and with much to ponder.

—Marion Saunders, B.A. D.Ed., Past National President,
Anglican Church Women of Canada

The Light Keeper is continuing evidence of Katherine's giftedness in the literary world. Descriptive use of the English language, faithfulness to the era in which the story evolves, and a passion to restore what was lost in the folds of time assures the reader that *The Light Keeper* is more than just a good read. Despite the disappointment, tragedy, and despair that penetrates the life of Dora Farncomb, her life choices and commitment leaves the reader pressed to evaluate their own commitment to God, to ask themselves if they would be willing to give up all that life and love seem to offer for the sole purpose of following His call. With what appears to be a great sacrifice from the human perspective, Dora made her choice, and although the tragedy of life intercepted countless times, she never questioned God's call on her life. Profoundly bold and challenging, Katherine has hit a grand slam!

—**Ruth Waring, author of** *Come Find Me,* *Then Came a Hush,* **and** *Harvest of Lies*

Katherine J. Le Gresley

THE
Light
KEEPER

THE LIGHT KEEPER
Copyright © 2022 by Katherine J. Le Gresley

All rights reserved. Neither this publication nor any part of this publication may be reproduced or transmitted in any form or by any means, electronic or mechanical, including photocopying, recording or any information storage and retrieval system, without permission in writing from the author.

This is a work of fiction. Names, characters, places and incidents either are the product of the author's imagination or are used fictitiously.

With special thanks to McLaughlin Library Archival and Special Collections at the University of Guelph, Ontario; Bishop Strachan School Museum and Archives; the Newcastle Village and District Historical Society Archives; and back issues of *The Canadian Statesman*, *The Newcastle Independent* and *Orono News*.

All scripture is taken from The King James Bible, public domain.

Printed in Canada

ISBN: 978-1-4866-2211-5
eBook ISBN: 978-1-4866-2212-2

Word Alive Press
119 De Baets Street Winnipeg, MB R2J 3R9
www.wordalivepress.ca

Cataloguing in Publication information can be obtained from Library and Archives Canada.

This book is written to the glory of God
in loving memory of my Great-Grandaunt
Dora Farncomb (1863 - 1938)

and is dedicated to my parents, Nancy and Farncomb Le Gresley.
With love beyond measure and gratitude beyond words—
I'll always be your little girl.

Dear Pat,
We can trust in God & not be afraid!
Katherine Isa. 12:2

Acknowledgements

This book has been many years in the making. From the seeds of family stories shared with me in my youth, to the letters and articles I unearthed in preparation for writing Dora's story, I have been deeply blessed to have had the privilege of getting to know my forebears in such a real way. How grateful I am that my family has kept these stories—tragic though many of them are—alive for each new generation to learn from and embrace. I am particularly thankful for my dear cousin Marjorie, though we never had the chance to meet, who gifted my parents with two of Dora's books as a wedding gift. Those cherished volumes were my first introduction to the Great-Grandaunt I now hold so dear.

Writing Dora's story has been such an adventure! In the process, I have had the pleasure of meeting long-lost relatives like Marjorie's grandniece, my cousin Mary, and of learning of other family members with whom I have not yet had the delight of connecting. I also had the joy of scouring mountains of fascinating first-hand information, thanks to the members of my family who saw fit to donate collections of personal letters, family documents, and other items of historical interest to the Newcastle Village and District Historical Society. I will forever be thankful for their foresight.

As with any work of historical fiction, years of research have gone into making Dora's story as accurate as possible. The folks at the University of Guelph McLaughlin Library Archival and Special Collections department provided access to one hundred years' worth of *The Farmer's Advocate and Home Magazine*, including a wealth of interesting articles and advertisements written during Dora's lifetime, as well as all of Dora's articles. The women in charge of The Bishop Strachan Schools' Old Girls' Museum and Archives went out of their way to respond to my emails and search school records to provide invaluable information on Dora, as well as facts about the running of their school during the time Dora attended. They even sent me a copy of her school photo! The men and women who run the Newcastle Village and District Historical Society were another source of meaningful information. Always helpful and welcoming, they patiently answered my questions and provided me with a treasure trove of interesting details as I searched through our family archives. How thankful I am that you have preserved so much of our family's history for us! I would also like to thank the interpreters at Lang Pioneer Village located in Keene, Ontario. Their patience in answering questions, and the knowledgeable responses they provided, helped bring Dora's world to life. I especially appreciated their special presentations on love, death, and Christmas in the late nineteenth century.

I cannot even begin to count the people who contributed to the writing of this book. To my friends at McDonalds—where I wrote most of Dora's story over breakfast in the hours before my workday began—your interest and encouragement motivated me to keep focussed and helped me to press on when the pressures of life bid me set my writing aside. I wanted to name my characters after you guys, honest, I did, but… maybe next time?

To the women in my writers' group—Ruth, Esther, Donna, Kathy—while we may not have been able to meet as regularly in the last couple of years as we would have liked, the patience you showed as I jumped from scene to scene, never quite telling the whole story, has not been forgotten. Your solid encouragement and honest critique have helped to make this story the best that it can be.

To those who read my manuscript before publication—Canon Greg, Cynthia, Ruth, Esther, Garry, Sarah, Trish, Marion—thank you. Your feedback was so appreciated. To Sara who painstakingly combed through each page to catch my errors and help make this book shine, and to Victoria who did that final whirlwind proof when the editing was complete to be sure that no errors had been missed, no words of thanks could ever be enough. And to Jen and the team at Word Alive Press, your confidence in this story has meant so much to me. How I appreciate the expertise and work you have put into bringing this work to completion.

Dora has played a big role in my life over the past six or seven years, and now it is time to share her with you, my readers. May God bless you as you consider Dora's story. May He use it to challenge and comfort and grow you in Him, even as He has used it to do those same things in my life. Like Dora, may we wholeheartedly embrace the mission He has given each one of us as we go about the work He has purposed for us to do. Look up and behold His face!

Soli Deo Gloria

https://www.facebook.com/katherinejlegresley

Prologue

AUGUST 24, 1903

I clung to the back of my mother's settee, my knuckles white as the fur of the mighty polar bear I'd read about in my brother's *National Geographic* magazine. Why I should notice such a thing when the billows of life crashed around me, threatening to sweep me off my feet, I cannot say, yet I could not pull my eyes away. White and waxy and unnatural my fingers looked, standing in such stark contrast to the rose-patterned tapestry beneath them. Who could have guessed that a person's knuckles could turn so white?

I tightened my grip, a curtain of black hovering at the edge of my consciousness, and my body swayed. I had to be strong—my family needed me. "Please God…" The whispered words rushed past my lips before I could stop them, and I swallowed hard. My mouth felt as though it was coated in sawdust. "… not again."

Surveying the room, I choked back a sob. My brother John sat at the far end of the settee, rocking his dear wife, Jane, as she wailed in his arms, her face buried in her hands. "Charles… Jackie. No-o-o-o-o-o." Her keening wails ripped at my heart, slashing at the edges of an old wound. With a pain so intense I thought I would die, the dungeons of my heart broke open and searing memories gushed forth—memories I would just as soon forget; memories I had spent years trying to suppress—and I fell to the floor in a heap.

When I came to, I was surrounded by a knot of anxious faces staring into my own. As usual, Mother was the first to respond. Her hand trembled as she ran a wrinkled knuckle down my cheek, her watery eyes gazing into mine. "Dora…" She stopped, her face contorted in pain, her voice strangled by grief. Thrusting her arms around my quivering shoulders, she pressed me to her bosom, enveloping me in a fierce embrace. Her heart beat against my chest, drumming in time to my own, and a precarious peace descended upon me. We were going to be okay.

With an unladylike sniff, I loosed my death grip on Mother's neck and rocked back to look her in the eyes, a quiet knowing passing between us. We had been here before and survived. Life had been forever altered, but it had not come to an end. With the slightest dip of her head, Mother accepted my brother Alfred's hand and he helped us both to our feet. If only Father were here to guide us as he had that day so long ago. In his absence, I looked to Alfred and laid my head upon his shoulder.

"Weeping may endure for a night," he rasped, quoting the scriptures of which Father had been so fond, "but joy cometh in the morning, Dora. This, too, shall pass." His voice faded with each word. Patting my shoulder, he led me to the overstuffed chair by the fireplace. I tried to be strong, tried to resurrect a smile, but the pressure building behind my eyes would not be ignored, and the tears I fought so hard to restrain burst forth. The nights were getting longer—morning would be a long way off.

Part I

Chapter 1

EBOR HOUSE, NEWCASTLE
JULY 1878

"Aww, Charlie..." I tossed a glance heavenward and gritted my teeth. "Tell me it isn't so. Tell me you didn't just say what I think you said." With the slightest tuck of his chin, Charlie peered at me from beneath raised brows, a cherubic smile lighting his face. *Little brothers.* "You know Father is never going to allow it." I grabbed the scroll-shaped finial topping the final post of the banister and moved to push past the curly-haired imp blocking my way.

"But Dora..." Determined to avoid the big, brown eyes staring up into mine, I averted my gaze. Charlie was nothing, if not a charmer. "What could I do?" His voice cracked. "He is, after all, one of God's little creatures, is he not? It is our duty to care for him."

I flopped onto the nearest step, corralling every ounce of patience my fifteen years could muster. *Of all the ridiculous things.* "Char-lie..." With only three years between us, he should have known better. "It is a dog. A mangy, old mutt."

"Oh, but he isn't old, Dora." Charlie lunged forward, landing on his knees on the floor below me. "I'm certain he is still a pup." He pumped his head up and down, his eyes never leaving mine. I scowled at his obvious attempt to manipulate my emotions and crossed my arms in front of my chest. I never could say no to that boy. "Just take a look?" He cocked his head innocently and shrugged. "Then if you are able to turn him out to starve to death, you can."

Honestly. "All right. All right." I raised both hands in surrender. "Where is he?"

Charlie jumped to his feet and scooted past me. "He's upstairs in my room." Rolling my eyes, I pulled myself to my feet and trudged up the stairs behind him, ignoring the triumphant grin he aimed my way. "You're going to love him, Dora. I promise."

"Yeah." I tried to sound cross. "Like I love *you*?" A soft whine wheezed from beneath the door of the chamber opposite mine, and I eyed my brother expectantly.

"Wha-at?" His shoulders drooped as he fell against the door. "So he sounds a little pathetic. That doesn't mean he is. His name is Samson."

Samson. The strong-man. I pinched my lips shut before I could say anything I would regret and let out a long, slow breath. "Could we get on with this please?"

A wet, snuffly nose greeted us the moment Charlie pushed the door open and I stiffened, willing myself to remain aloof. Father would eat baked worms before he let Charlie keep this… this creature. I entered the room slowly and dropped onto the bed, loathing the words I knew I had to say, words that were sure to extinguish the glorious light of hope that sparkled in my brother's eyes. If only I wasn't the one who had to squelch his dreams.

The quiet clatter of untrimmed claws distracted me from my thoughts as a filthy mutt made its way across the floorboards, its fur matted and laced with burrs. With a groan, I covered my face with my hands. Maybe if I didn't look. But it was no use. A furry head bumped my elbow before coming to rest upon my knee whilst a thick, shaggy tail thumped hopefully against my foot. I inched my eyes open to see a pair of big, brown eyes gazing trustingly into mine and I sighed. *Just like Charlie's.* "Okay, little brother, you win." I ruffled the fur between the dog's ears and pushed myself up from the bed, desperately striving to quash the grin that threatened to undo me. "So, what is the plan? How do you propose we convince Father to let you keep this dog?"

Chapter 2

Pressing my eye to the keyhole, I peered around the kitchen. Anna, our oldest servant and beloved kitchen mistress, stood at the far end of the centre board kneading a lump of dough, while our young housemaid, Betsy, sat peeling potatoes at a table in the corner. I looked over my shoulder at my brother and shook my head. Getting both maids out of the kitchen at the peak of dinner hour preparations was sure to be more of a challenge than we had anticipated, but it had to be done. If there was any hope of Father letting us keep that silly mutt, Charlie had to get it out the door for a bath somehow. The question was how to do it without alerting the whole household to the presence of our new four-legged friend.

Squaring my shoulders, I winked at my brother and pushed my way through the kitchen door. "Good afternoon, Anna." I twisted a finger around the long French braid draped over my shoulder and smiled sweetly. "Do you suppose Betsy might be spared to help me gather some flowers for the dinner table?" Pinching a piece of abandoned dough from the board, I headed toward the young maid in the corner. My, but her fingers flew!

Anna brushed a floury hand across her forehead and stooped to slip a pan of biscuits into the oven. "Betsy will be pleased to help you gather flowers once Master Frederick's dinner has been served, Miss Dora." Straightening, she eyed the wood bin in the corner. "Betsy dear, come stoke the fire 'fore these biscuits come out half raw."

Darn.

"Yes, mem." Betsy tossed the last potato into the pot on the table and hurried over to the stove. Easing the rear burner from its place, she slid two apple logs into the fire and replaced the heavy lid.

Seizing the opportunity, I cleared my throat. "Betsy would do well to kindle a fire in the conservatory before Father arrives, also. Do you not agree, Anna?" I schooled my features, feigning nonchalance. "It has been unseasonably cool lately, and the evening air can get quite chilly." The kitchen mistress scowled at the young maid and blinked her assent. *It worked! One down, one to go.*

"Is there anything else, Miss Dora?"

"As a matter of fact, there is, Anna." I tapped a finger on my chin, wracking my brain for a plausible task that would take her out of the kitchen, if only for a few minutes. "Did *The Farmer's Advocate* happen to arrive today?"

"Yes."

"Wonderful!" I clasped my hands against my chest. "Would you mind fetching it for me, please, Anna? I am most eager to see if Miss Minnie May has responded to the letter I sent her last month."

The moment Anna left the room, I ushered Charlie and his canine friend through the rear door of the kitchen and onto the back porch. It would have been so much easier if we could have simply gone out the front door, but it wasn't worth the risk. Mother would be sure to ask questions if she heard the front door open in the middle of the afternoon. "This better be worth it," I whispered.

"It will be." His eyes danced as he struggled to corral the playful pup in his arms. "You'll see."

"I had better." I huffed, turning just in time to see Anna bustle into the kitchen with the magazine I had left in the conservatory.

"You had better what, Miss Dora?" Her eyebrows rose as she handed me the periodical.

"Why, I had better… see what Miss Minnie May has to say in her column." Grinning, I held the magazine aloft and disappeared through the kitchen door. If Mother caught wind of what I had just done, she would confine me to my chamber for a month.

Chapter 3

The grandfather clock in the entrance way chimed seven, and my stomach rumbled in response. With a final glance in the mirror, I smoothed the wrinkles from my skirt and hurried down the stairs, anxious to make it to the dinner table before Mother and Father arrived. Punctuality was, after all, the hallmark of respect. That's what Father always said, anyway. The clock's final bong still echoing in my ears, I slid behind my chair, grateful to see the two empty spaces at the ends of the table. *I made it.* My three brothers were already stationed behind their seats—Johnny on my right, Alfred across the table from him, and Charlie opposite me.

"You look lovely tonight, Dora." The consummate gentleman, Alfred abandoned his conversation with Johnny as soon as I entered the room and turned his attention to me. "You are looking mighty grown up these days, oh sister of mine."

What a joy it was to have him home from medical school. "Why thank you, kind sir." I fluttered my hand before my chest and dipped a curtsy, imbuing each word with the sophistication of a queen. A childlike giggle escaped my lips and laughter swelled around the table as Mother and Father swept in. Mortified, I scrambled into my chair as soon as they were seated, hiding my burning cheeks behind a napkin.

Father surveyed the sight before him, his booming laugh only adding to my brothers' merriment. "Ah yes, it is good to be home. A cheerful heart doeth good, like medicine," he quoted. "Is that not so, Alfred?" He looked pointedly at my brother. "Have they not taught you that in medical school?" Alfred pursed his lips and folded his hands in his lap. This was one of Father's favourite topics. "Few things do a man's heart more good than a happy home, son," Father continued. If I had a penny for every time he had expounded upon the wonders of a joy-filled home, I would be the richest girl in the village. "As a doctor, you ought to know that. A merry heart lightens the load of a long, hard day and buoys the weary soul when the tempests rage. It shelters the spirit when the billows of life threaten to overwhelm and restores lost perspective like nothing else can. Truly, there is nothing more soothing to the despairing heart than a family whose foundation is unity and joy."

I shifted on my seat, willing my hungry belly to cease its angry roar as Father went on. "Yet, it is a highly undervalued commodity these days, I am afraid—one this world would do well to embrace far more heartily—one I hope you will never toss aside." Sermon complete, he raised his eyes heavenward and bowed his heart in prayer. "Thank you, Holy Father, for this happy home and bless the food which nourisheth us." A spirited *amen* erupted from the end of the table, setting us all to giggling yet again.

"Hungry, Charlie?" Johnny asked.

"Starving!" Charlie heaped a mound of mashed potatoes onto his plate and reached for the roasted hen. My thoughts leapt to Samson. His big, trusting eyes, so like my brother's, had etched themselves into my memory. *I hope Charlie found him some food.* I glanced across the table, hoping to catch my brother's eye, but, true to form, nothing short of a band of marauding pirates could have distracted him from the sumptuous fare before us.

"I got a letter from young Master Wellman today," Father announced. Every head turned to face him, eager for the day's news. Except Charlie's. Father laid his fork on the side of his plate and cleared his throat. "It seems that Matthew begins his final year of seminary in the fall and wishes to know if there might be an opening in his home parish for him to complete his internship." I leaned forward, eager to hear more. "He seemed particularly interested in finding out how you are doing, Dora."

"Indeed." Alfred waggled his brows at me, his eyes twinkling, and my heart skipped a beat.

Father winked at Mother then pinned his gaze upon me. "Perhaps you should write the young man a letter."

Fidgeting in my seat, I struggled to maintain a vestige of decorum. "Me?" I squeaked. "Write Mattie a letter? Why, I could nev—" A wave of laughter erupted around the table and I fell silent, realizing my blunder.

"Oh ho!" Father rumbled. "So it is *Mattie* now, is it?"

"Dora and Mattie, sitting in a tree…" Johnny's playful jibe was cut short by a gleeful howl from Charlie and my stony façade began to crack. With a sigh, I raised my eyes heavenward. Was nothing sacred?

Chapter 4

JULY 18, 1878

My Dear Mr. Wellman,

Greetings to you on this most lovely evening. You cannot imagine my joy when Father informed me that you are hoping to complete your final internship here at St. George's in the new year. It seems like such a long time since I have seen you, Mattie. I do hope you can make the required arrangements quickly. It would be good to have you home again.

    Things are going well here. Alfred is home for a few weeks for summer furlough, but is due to return to school again soon. He graduates from medical college in the spring, after which he plans to continue his studies somewhere in England. It is his desire to become a specialist in women's and children's medicine. His alma mater is most proud of him, he being the first Trinity graduate to secure a medical degree.

    Johnny will no doubt be glad to be out from under Alfred's shadow when he moves on to seminary in the fall. He asked me to send you his greetings and tell you that he would love to have a chat with you before the semester begins. I think he is rather nervous about starting a new school, although I am sure he would never admit to it. I imagine that he will make a very fine minister. If you could spare a few minutes to speak with him, I know it would be appreciated. A goodly dose of reassurance would do my brother more good than you could imagine. That brother, anyway.

As for Charlie... what can I say? He found a stray pup today, and is, at this very moment, trying to convince Father that he should be allowed to keep the pathetic little beast. Knowing Charlie, he will succeed, although I cannot begin to fathom how. I do not believe I am the only one in this family who cannot say no to my little brother, though. He simply exudes charm—he and the dog both. He named the little beast Samson, if you can believe it. Samson! Maybe after Delilah got a hold of him. I can only imagine what Anna will have to say if Father lets Charlie keep the thing.

Well, I am quickly running out of space. Father and Mother send their love and bid you drop by for a visit. As soon as Father can make the necessary arrangements for your internship, he will contact you. My love and prayers go with you, dear Mattie.

Affectionately,
Your Dora-girl

Replacing the pen in its pot, I sprinkled a light layer of sand over the finished letter and rummaged through my desk drawer for an envelope to address.

Mr. Matthew Wellman
Trinity College, Toronto

With a final flourish, I folded the fragile paper and tucked it into the envelope. I considered misting it with the lavender toilet water Alfred had given me for Christmas, but thought better of it. Mother would be sure to smell it and, no doubt, think it scandalous. After all, I wasn't his sweetheart—yet. A light tap on the door startled me and I rose, hiding the letter in the folds of my skirt.

"Did you finish your letter?" My mother's voice held a suppressed enthusiasm I had not anticipated.

Sheepishly, I pulled the envelope from my skirt and nodded. "I was about to seal it."

"Then I am not too late." Mother strode into the room. "Did you tell our Mr. Wellman that your father will be in touch?" Again, I nodded. "Good. Did you invite him to come for a visit?"

"Yes." I lifted the flap on the envelope and raised it to my lips, but Mother stretched out a hand, stopping me.

"Not so quickly, Dora." The corners of her eyes crinkled as she stepped closer. "Did you remember to mist it with some of that lovely toilet water your brother gave you?" she whispered.

"Mother!" My jaw dropped in a most unladylike show of surprise. "Do you not think that rather scandalous?"

She waved her hand dismissively and lowered her chin. "What could be scandalous about a young woman sending her sweetheart a perfumed letter?"

"But Mother…" I could hardly believe we were having this conversation. "I am not his sweetheart."

"Are you not?" She cocked her head. "Are you certain?"

"Of course I am certain. He is my friend. I—"

"Did your father happen to mention to you that our young Mr. Wellman has asked for permission to court you?" My breath caught in my throat and I turned, pressing the letter to my bosom. "That young man has doted upon you since the day you were born, dear. A finer beau you could not find."

"He actually asked Father for permission to court me?" A dream-like quality crept into my voice and I cleared my throat. "But I still have three whole years of schooling left before my education is complete. Such things simply are not done. I mean—"

"I know exactly what you mean, dear." My mother laid a hand upon my shoulder and turned me to face her once again. "You mean that it is the fulfillment of a dream beyond all imagination—a dream you would never dare to voice, the most cherished hope of that ever-loving heart of yours." She tapped my chest with her finger as she said the final words and I nodded, awed that my mother should understand so completely the deepest caverns of my heart. "I know that the timing of this is a little unorthodox, dear, but your father and I have had our sights set upon a union between the two of you since the day you first met. With our dear Matthew's entrance into the Anglican priesthood imminent, we would not want him to get away." She winked playfully at my slack-jawed response. "We will not formally announce your courtship until your schooling is complete, of course, lest wagging tongues call into question your purity. There is however, nothing to say that you cannot begin to deepen your friendship with him in the meantime, knowing as we do that his intention is to take you as his bride as soon as your father will allow it. So now…" All business, Mother crossed the room and scanned the top of my bureau. "Where do you keep that lovely toilet water of yours?"

Joining her, I selected a small glass bottle from a tray and squeezed the atomizer to release a mist of aromatic bliss into the air. Sharing a secret smile, Mother reached for the letter and removed it from the envelope, spreading it gently on the top of the dresser while I gave the little bulb another squeeze. We watched in silence as the tiny droplets settled over the paper. No doubt Mother was imagining, as was I, the look on Mattie's face when he slit the envelope and got a whiff of what was inside. Our eyes met and I leaned in to kiss her cheek.

"Good night, Dora," she whispered, drawing me into her warm embrace. "Sweet dreams."

Chapter 5

Those were the golden days. The boys spent their mornings helping Father at the harbour and their afternoons swimming in the lake. I spent mine sewing the skirts and blouses I would need for the upcoming school year. Tail forever wagging, Samson followed Charlie wherever he went until Father finally gave in and accepted him as part of the family. Truth be told, I rather think Father wanted the dog every bit as much as Charlie did, not that he would ever admit it. Yet, when he thought no one was looking, he treated that dog like a member of the family and never missed an opportunity to run his fingers through its shaggy fur.

Come evening, though, Samson was mine. After supper, when we retired to the conservatory for tea, Samson would follow me to the pianoforte and sit at my feet where he would howl away as I played until everyone—including Father—laughed so hard the tears ran down his face. That dog brought more laughter into our home than anything else ever could—except perhaps Charlie. Like master, like dog, I suppose.

When Mattie arrived in the first week of August to finalize arrangements with the rector, I thought I might burst. Though he spent most of his days with my brothers, I cherished each precious moment I found myself in his company, whether visiting in the parlour or relaxing on the front porch or strolling along the banks of the mill pond. Most memorable of all, however, was the day he called upon me in his father's carriage. I marvelled when Father granted me permission to accompany Mattie to a birthday tea in honour of his great-grandmother who lived a mile or two past Scott's Corners.

Of course, it would be unseemly for two young people to travel alone, and my older brothers were otherwise occupied, so Father released Anna from her regular chores to chaperone. The one-and-a-half-hour drive flew by as Mattie regaled us with story after story of his great-grandmother's youthful hijinks. She was obviously a woman worth knowing.

• • •

"Aha!" Great Grandma Josephine announced when Mattie introduced us. "You must be the one whom our dear Matthew has decided to marry." Heat rushed to my face as she pinned me with her eyes, but I tried not to fidget. I must have passed the test—whatever it happened to be—because the next moment, a toothless grin melted her features and she leaned forward, slapping her knee. "He is a handsome young devil, is he not?"

"Grandma Josephine!" Matthew's mother glanced apologetically my way then turned to the wrinkled old woman whose rattling laugh had captured the attention of every guest in the yard.

Mattie stood still as the grave, his eyes fixed forward, his ears red as a cherry lollipop. "Come, Dora." His words were clipped, his voice pinched, quite unlike the amiable and easy-going young man with whom I had arrived. "It is time for us to go." He held his arm out stiffly and I slid my hand obediently into the crook of his elbow, suddenly dreading the drive home.

A heavy silence attended his every move as Mattie helped Anna and me into the carriage and took the reins. This could be a very, very long drive. The hollow clopping of the horse's hooves drummed in the stillness, and I shut my eyes, desperate to make sense of the afternoon's events. The party had barely begun and we were already on our way home? *Father God, what just happened? Is it really true? Has Mattie told his family that we are to be wed?* We hit a bump in the road and my eyes flickered open. Mattie grimaced and slapped the reins across the horse's rump, urging it to a trot. We hadn't even left Scott's Corners yet.

Mile after mile passed without a word. "It is a lovely day for a ride," I finally managed. No response. A fly buzzed around my head and I waved it away. "Did you have an opportunity to speak with Johnny about seminary life yet?" Still no response. The shadows lengthened as we bumped along the Danforth Road. Odd how the passage of time could vary so.

Mattie shifted in his seat, his face drawn. Why did he not speak? I scoured my memory of the afternoon's events. Surely his great-grandmother's careless words could be dismissed as the ravings of an old woman. Had my response to her announcement somehow upset him? I dared a surreptitious glance in his direction and noted a subtle change in his demeanor. My breathing stilled as his hand darted onto my lap and closed around mine. Sliding it onto the bench between us, he hid it in the folds of my skirt, his strong, gentle fingers squeezing mine. Now this was progress.

Emboldened by his forwardness, I dared another peek in his direction. His eyes remained fixed upon the road ahead, but a boyish grin now played at the corners of his mouth. Suppressing a smile of my own, I relaxed into the cushions, directing my gaze forward as he ran his thumb along my wrist. Perhaps there was hope for us after all. Awkwardness forgotten, the miles sped by with Anna dozing in the back, quite unmindful of her duties. But I wouldn't tell.

Father and the boys were returning from their day's work when Mattie finally lifted me from the carriage onto the hard-packed turnabout. He paused before releasing my waist and leaned in close, his breath warm against my ear. "I love you, Dora-girl," he whispered. He caught my eye and winked then lifted my hand to his lips, placing a tender kiss at the base of my ring finger. "Perhaps Great Grandma Josephine is onto something."

Chapter 6

ONE YEAR LATER
JULY 23, 1879

The aroma of roasting pheasant wafted through the house, alerting me to the hour. Mattie would be here before I was ready to receive him if I didn't hurry. My fingers trembled as I fastened the lovely blue cameo Grandmother had given me for my birthday around my neck, my heart dancing at the thought of the miniature portrait hidden within. Curling my hand around the locket, I twirled across the room, imagining the day when Mattie would finally ask me to marry him. Perhaps that day would be today. I was, after all, sixteen now. Young as that was to accept a betrothal, it certainly was not unheard of, though the fact that I still had two years of schooling to complete would raise more than a few brows.

Still, Marla King was already married by the time she was my age, and Phoebe Welks had been betrothed for nigh unto a year. Caroline Simms even had a baby, though few acknowledged the young mite. "There is a reason I do not approve of bundling," Mother always said whenever the topic arose—whatever that was supposed to mean. Perhaps Caroline wasn't the best example to cite should Father need encouragement to allow Mattie and me to be joined in matrimony.

A ringing knock sounded in the hallway below, and I rushed to the looking glass. That would be him. I drew a hand to my waist, desperate to calm the jitterbugs dancing in my belly. Betsy had outdone herself, curling each strand of my stubborn, mousey-blonde hair and arranging it into a lovely updo, so different from the French braid I wore every day. I twined an errant ringlet around my forefinger, admiring the effect. *Like a princess awaiting her prince...* I clasped my hands in front of me and inclined my head with a demure smile as I had often seen Mother do when Father entered the room. *No... like a woman adorned for her husband.* My locket rested upon the creamy satin of my blouse, glittering in the shaft of sunlight slanting through the window. Mattie couldn't help but notice it. *I wonder if he will guess that there is a picture of him inside.*

Footsteps sounded on the stairs, and I turned to find Betsy staring at me. "He's here, Miss Dor..." Her eyes trailed down the length of my dress before she remembered herself. "Master Matthew, I mean." Lowering her chin, she caught her bottom lip between her teeth. "You look lovely, Miss Dora. Shall I have him wait for you in the parlour?"

A bubble of excitement burst within me. "Please do," I responded. "Tell him that I shall be down directly." Returning to the mirror, I brushed a stray hair from my skirt and pinched my cheeks lightly, smiling at the rosy blush that ensued. Heaven forbid I should keep Mattie waiting.

My feet barely making a sound, I floated down the spiral staircase, eager to see the man I hoped to soon call my betrothed. *Mrs. Mattie Wellman.* I stopped, my heart caressing each syllable. *No... I* scrunched my nose. *Not Mattie... Matthew. Mrs.* Matthew *Wellman.* My smile broadened with every step. Why else would he formally request an invitation to our table?

The moment I saw him, his elbow leaning upon the marble mantelpiece, his hand clenched beneath his nose, I knew something was desperately amiss. "Mattie?" Instantly alert, he jerked to attention as I stepped into the room. A chill shivered up my spine at the dark circles shadowing his eyes. *What is going on?* His Adam's apple bobbed and he opened his mouth as if to speak, but no words came. "Mattie, what's wrong?" My heart beat wildly in my chest. *Has somebody died?* "Mattie, you're frightening me. What is it?"

His eyes met mine and he swallowed hard. "We have to talk." He offered me his arm and gestured to the door. "Walk with me?"

I glanced over my shoulder, surprised to find us very much alone. Though I knew I ought not to go walking with him without a chaperone, I had to know what was wrong. Surely Mother and Father would understand. Slipping my arm through his, I nodded, comforted by the familiarity of his touch as my mind raced from one tragic scenario to the next, each more grievous than the one before. *Can he have failed his final examinations and been expelled from the priesthood? Has one of his friends taken ill or run into some sort of trouble? Perhaps his father...* Choking back questions, I walked by his side, hardly daring to breathe as I waited for him to speak. The grass crunched beneath our feet—sharp, brittle, fragile. Like my heart. It had been weeks since it had rained, and the crippling heat of summer had left the land barren and parched. *Perhaps there's been a fire and...* It took every vestige of determination I had to harness the ludicrous thoughts that fueled my anxiety. Some things simply could not be rushed.

The grass along the banks of the millpond, like the willows that shaded it, was lush and green, its roots nourished by the life-giving water. Mattie's steps slowed as we neared the old weeping willow that marked the northern-most end of the little lake and he ducked beneath its swaying boughs. *The Thinking Tree.* A favourite haunt since the time I was a child, I had retreated into its shade whenever I needed space to think and pray. Another shiver tingled up my spine as Mattie pulled me to the ground beside him and slipped his arm around my shoulders. Whatever he had to tell me, it couldn't be good.

Silence hung between us like a cloud. Heavy. Dark. Ominous. Shifting slightly, I drew my feet beneath my skirt. Mattie pulled me closer to his side, a great shuddering breath rocking his shoulders. "Dora, I…" His voice broke and he cleared his throat. "Dora, I came here tonight—at least, I had planned to come here tonight—to ask you… to ask you to marry me, but…"

But. So small a word, yet it had such a terrifying ring to it. "But? But what, Mattie?" The tremor in my voice was a mere shadow of the quake that shook the foundations of my being.

"But, Dora, I cannot do it." His eyes welled as he rushed on, his words clanging in my ears like cymbals. I looked away, unable to meet his gaze. "You have to believe me, Dora," he pleaded. "I want nothing more than for you to be my wife, but…"

That word again. I pressed my lips together. *Breathe in; breathe out; breathe in; breathe out.*

Mattie let his arm fall from my shoulders and pushed himself to his feet, pacing like a caged lion. Raking a hand through his hair, he rolled his eyes toward the heavens. "Oh, Dora…" He fell to his knees by my side, capturing both of my hands in his, entreating me to understand. "Have you ever heard God speak to you?" He paused, his eyes spearing into mine. "I mean, really speak… directly to you?" His question hung in the air between us, a sense of awe replacing the pall of grief that had entombed his voice.

"Heard God speak?" I repeated. "To me?" Freeing my hands from his, I pressed my fingers to my temples. *God? Speak to me? I suppose He could—if He wanted to. But* had *He?* I lifted my shoulder and blew a strand of hair from my face. "I am assuming that you have."

He nodded vigorously. "Last night. In a dream. Like when he spoke to Joseph."

I forced myself to remain silent and focus on his words, though everything within me yearned to resist. *A dream?*

"He showed me an image of a place far across the globe, where the people were enslaved, not by the bonds of man, but by something far more sinister—though what it was, I could not tell. Their anguished wails touched a place deep within me and I lunged toward them, only to find a great ocean separating us. As their cries escalated, I waded into the churning waters, anxious to ease their suffering, but the waves overwhelmed me and I nearly drowned."

Consumed by the story, I leaned forward, my stomach roiling. *Surely he doesn't believe those people are real.*

He squeezed my fingers gently and lowered his eyes. "Out of nowhere, a pair of hands appeared. They were strong and calloused, marred front and back by a white, waxy scar."

My eyes widened. "Jesus?"

Mattie nodded and a slow smile curved his lips. "With one hand, He lifted me from the swirling waves. With the other, He pointed to a ship breaking the horizon as it steamed toward a teaming quay. 'Go to them, beloved,' He said. 'Be My hands, My feet, My voice to the people in the land you call Tarapacá; free them from their bonds.'"

Tarapacá? Wasn't that in South America?

"A series of images played across my mind of me bringing food and water to shrunken prisoners, holding a cloth to the forehead of a shivering child, tending the sores of a wizened old man, anointing the head of a soldier."

As Mattie spoke, vivid pictures emblazoned themselves deep in my heart and my breath quickened. Surely this was a sign from God.

"As the final image faded, urgent voices crowded in upon me: 'Please come quickly.' 'Do not delay.' 'We need you.' 'We need you.' 'We need you.' But when the final voice gave way to silence, instead of leaping to their rescue, I turned to my Lord, a suffocating fear clawing its way up my spine. 'But what about Dora?' I cried, my voice seizing in my throat. 'I didn't see her in even one of the images You showed me.'"

Catapulted back to reality, I withdrew my hands from his and threw myself backward. *I wasn't in the dream? Surely that doesn't mean...*

I tore at the grass with my fingers as Mattie continued, his voice trembling. "'The mission I have called you to is for you alone, beloved,' Jesus replied. His voice was sad, yet firm, and His eyes glistened with unshed tears. Not wanting to hear more, I turned away, but He placed His palm upon my shoulder and drew me back. 'It is a difficult mission I entrust to you, Matthew,' He said, 'a mission filled with dangers you cannot yet foresee. You will not be able to embrace the calling I have placed upon you if you must care for another.'"

My eyes met Mattie's. Reaching for a strand of my hair, he twirled it around his forefinger, smoothing its glossy strands against his thumb. Twice he opened his mouth as if to speak, but when no sound came out, he clamped it shut again. Finally, thrusting himself onto his back by my side, he squeezed his eyes shut and pressed on. "My heart broke at His words and I grabbed His robe, shaking Him as if He were a child. 'But I love her!' I railed. 'You, of all people, should understand that.'" Mattie paused but a moment, his chin quivering. "A tear tumbled from our Lord's eye, and His voice grew quiet. 'I do, beloved. More than you know.'" Mattie rolled onto his side and propped himself up on his elbow.

"'I have called her also, Matthew,' Jesus continued, 'though to a mission much closer to home. A mission for which I have been preparing her from the day she was conceived in her mother's womb. A mission that will impact many lives for generations to come.' I wanted to argue with Him, to shout, 'But Your Word says that it is not good for man to be alone,' but before the words could leave my mouth, He drew me to Himself and whispered, 'You are right, beloved, but you will not be alone, for I promise that I shall be with you. Every moment of every day—no matter where you are, no matter what you do. And I will be with Dora also, for neither is it good for woman to be alone.' He blinked His eyes slowly, meaningfully, and I awoke, my heart hammering in my chest, my mind whirling with images I could not forget."

Mattie lapsed into silence as I searched for something to say in response to his disclosure. The shrill call of a Cooper's hawk split the air, giving voice to the cry of my heart, and a flash of mottled white stirred in the branches above us, but still no words came. At last Mattie spoke again, his voice so soft, I could barely hear it. "I told you earlier that I wanted nothing more than for you to be my wife, Dora, but that isn't quite true."

I dabbed my cheek with my handkerchief and waited for him to continue.

"There *is* something I want more. One thing." He pushed himself into a sitting position, pulling me with him as his voice grew stronger. "I want to submit myself to our Lord, who sacrificed so much on our behalf, and follow Him wherever He leads. I want to see His smile and hear Him say, 'Well done, thou good and faithful servant.' I want to be the man He created me to be when *I* was first conceived in my mother's womb."

With each proclamation, the waves of tension buffeting my soul began to recede. Those were the things I wanted, too. Exactly. "I just wish it didn't have to hurt so much," he added.

A mirthless laugh escaped me as I melted into his embrace. "Me too."

Chapter 7

Our much anticipated dinner turned out to be a most solemn affair. Though nobody knew the source of our grief, our red-rimmed eyes and subdued manner told a story even Charlie couldn't miss. "Come, let us retire to the conservatory," Father announced as he deposited his napkin on his plate. "Betsy will bring us our tea in there."

I breathed a sigh of relief, knowing the evening would soon be over. Barely had I taken my place on the settee beside Mother, though, when Samson bounded toward me and nudged my knee, his tail wagging in expectation. My teacup rattled on its saucer. *I can't play tonight; I just want this night to be over.* A sharp bark brought my attention back to the creature pawing at my knee. *Dumb dog.* As soon as I looked his way, he pranced toward the pianoforte and back, barely able to contain himself.

"I believe our Samson wishes to sing." Father's words brimmed with mirth, cracking the tension in the room.

I eyed him warily. *When does the silly mutt not want to sing?* Surely Father wouldn't—

"Play for us, Dora," he implored. "There is nothing like music to soothe the aching heart." Mattie shifted in his seat. Doubtless, he yearned for this night to end also. "How about that lovely little love song you play so well?" Father added. "The one by Beethoven."

Für Elise. My heart skipped a beat. *Father's favourite... Mattie's, too.* As legend had it, the great composer had penned it for Therese, the uncontested love of his life, though his affections were sadly unrequited. I set my teacup on the table and rose, clenching my hands in a desperate attempt to still their trembling. Was it not enough that Father had called me to play on this most dreadful evening? Whyever did he have to request that particular song?

With practised ease, I took my place at the pianoforte, smoothing my skirt around me as Samson pranced in place at my feet. My fingers stumbled on the keys as the opening notes bled from my heart and my eyes blurred, but there was no stopping now. It was a good thing I had the piece memorized.

∙ ∙ ∙

The final note still reverberating in the air, I drew my hands to my cheeks, embarrassed by the flow of tears raining from my eyes. Would this night never end? Heedless of the decorum my parents had engrained in me since I was a child, I leapt from the stool and fled the room, taking refuge in the quiet alcove in the corridor outside the kitchen. My temples throbbed mercilessly as I strove to regain control. *Why, God? Why must it end this way? Why must Mattie leave me behind?* Leaning my head against the wall, I lifted my handkerchief to blow my nose.

"Dora..." Father's voice floated down the corridor and I fought the urge to hide. "Our visitor wishes to bid you farewell."

Farewell. Adieu. Until we meet again. Why not be honest? He didn't wish to bid me farewell. The term was *goodbye*. Good. Bye. The. End. My head reeled and I slumped against the wall, barely catching myself before I fell. How was I supposed to bid goodbye to the only man—"

"Dora?"

My pulse quickened at the sound of Mattie's voice. Would I ever again hear my name whispered with such longing, such devotion, such despair?

"Please, Dora—"

His hand cupped my elbow. I lurched backward, pushing myself against the wall before I succumbed to the urge to fall into his arms. "I can-not..." My words were stilted, my voice thick. Undaunted, he closed the space between us, his arms inviting me to lose myself in his embrace, but I faltered, shaking my head. "I can't do it, Mattie. I cannot say goodbye."

His eyes shimmered in the lamplight as he reached for my hand and raised it to his lips. "Nor can I, beloved," he murmured. "My heart will always be yours. You do know that, don't you?"

Motionless, I watched as he turned my hand over and pressed an intricately carved love spoon into my palm, curling my fingers tightly around it. "Here. I made it for you, though I hadn't planned for it to be a parting gift. Go with God, my Dora-girl." His voice broke as he said my name. Leaning forward, he brushed his lips against my cheek and then he was gone.

For a moment, I entertained the idea of running after him—surely this was naught but a bad dream—but little good it would do if I did. *A calling. From God, no less. For both of us.* I sniffed back a tear and stumbled to the foot of the stairs, ignoring the sympathetic looks of my family. *Not really, Mattie. God may have called you, but what about me? You say that He has called me too, but to what? I always thought He had called me to be yours.*

Chapter 8

Darkness surrounded me as I tossed from one side of the bed to the other, the dying embers of the fire all but extinguished. Abandoning my sodden pillow, I grabbed the blanket from the chair by the fire and crept down the stairs. Samson lifted his nose from his paws and whined as I passed his sleeping spot beside the grandfather clock. "All is well, Sammy," I whispered. "Go back to sleep."

If only I could follow my own advice. The door creaked as I opened it and I froze, certain that I had awakened the entire household. One second passed. Then two. When all remained quiet, I slipped out into the night. Closing the door behind me, I crept onto the porch and lowered myself into the old wicker rocker. Though the stars had all but disappeared, the morning star yet shone, a luminous globe in the steely-blue greyness of the pre-dawn sky. *Venus, the queen of love, the bright morning star—a beacon of hope to herald the coming of the day.* "You really are with me, Jesus, aren't you?" The words slid from my lips unbidden and an unexpected peace enveloped my soul. Snugging the blanket more tightly around my shoulders, I closed my eyes, lulled by the gentle warbling of a sparrow's morning serenade. *Right here. Right now. Promise me You will never leave me.*

• • •

The warming rays of the sun caressed my face and I stirred, the fraying hem of a dream fluttering just beyond reach. "Jesus…" I murmured. A welcome breeze ruffled my hair and my eyes flickered open. For a moment, I stared at the vista before me, puzzled that I should find myself on the front porch—in my nightdress, no less.

"Sleep well?"

How long Mother had been there, I could only guess. I yawned and snuggled further into the chair. "Um-hmm. What time is it?"

"Just past two," she responded, patting my arm. "I must say, you certainly caused a commotion this morning when Betsy went to awaken you and you were nowhere to be found."

I gasped, imagining the scene. "I–I couldn't sleep. I didn't intend to worry anyone."

"I am surprised you didn't awaken to your father's bellow when he found you on his way to the office." Mother's eyes twinkled as she recalled the morning's events. "He would have carried you right upstairs and put you to bed himself, had I not forbidden it."

Sleepiness forgotten, I bolted upright, my hand flying to my chest. The last time Father had carried me to bed, I was seven years old. We had spent the whole day at Cousin Hannah's house in Scott's Corners, and I had fallen asleep on the way home. My older brothers, thinking it terribly amusing, had teased me for months afterward. I had determined then and there that it would never happen again. And it hadn't. Until today. I would never have heard the end of it had Father carried me to my bed this morning.

"I suppose I ought to be thankful that no visitors called," I managed, my eyes fixed upon the pitted cement beyond my slippered toe. When an immediate affirmation was not forthcoming, I drew my head up sharply, demanding a response.

"It was no one, really..." Mother braced herself on the side of the chair and pushed herself to her feet. "Only Matthew. He came by to be sure that you were all right before he left for Toronto."

A familiar pressure built behind my eyes, and I raised a hand to rub my forehead. "Why did you not awaken me?"

"He would not have it, dear." She shook her head slowly and helped me from my chair. "While it was obvious he grieved, his face brightened when he saw you, and a softness crept into his features. 'Our Lord is faithful, Mrs. Farncomb,' he announced. 'How quick I am to doubt.' His eyes strayed and he gazed upon your face, studying it as if he might never see it again. 'He is here, and she is at peace. How faithless of me to worry.'"

Mother's hand squeezed mine, but the gesture did little to ease the ache in my heart. "Without another word, he bent to lay the sweetest of kisses upon your brow, then stumbled from the porch, his shoulders quivering as he made his way to the road." She fumbled in her pocket for a moment before producing a small, ivory envelope. "He bid me give you this." She placed the envelope into my hand and reached for the door. "I shall ask Anna to prepare you a tray. You must be famished; you barely ate a thing at supper last night."

As if on cue, my stomach rumbled. "Thank you, Mother. That would be lovely."

Alone on the porch, I turned the envelope over and ran my finger across the two lone words centred on the front. *Miss Farncomb*. Swallowing hard, I sank back into the chair, anxious to open the letter, though I feared the words I would find within. Yet what good could it do me to hide from them? Wiggling a fingernail beneath the corner of the flap, I pried the paper apart, careful to preserve each fragile corner. Now to see what was inside. For a moment, I clasped the precious missive to my breast, paralyzed by the conflicting emotions warring within me. What could Mattie possibly have to tell me that had not already been said? Had he not, indeed, said all there was to say? With a sudden burst of determination, I thrust my hand into the envelope and retrieved the folded paper.

July 24, 1879

My Dear, Dear Miss Farncomb,

I have not ceased to think of you since the moment we parted. I close my eyes and you are there, your eyes brimming with sorrow I cannot erase, your voice pinched by words your heart is not prepared to utter. I wonder if either of us shall ever be whole again.

Oh, my beloved, I cannot bear the thought that you should hate me for the pain my love has visited upon you, or worse yet, that you should walk away from our Lord out of anger or despair. Lonely are the roads He has called us both to travel, and the sacrifice He requires of us is greater than I could ever have imagined. Yet it is not greater than His. I must keep reminding myself of that.

I do not understand why He has separated us like this, Dora, but were it not for some greater good of which we may never know, He would not keep us apart. Of this, I am more certain than ever. We must trust Him, beloved. I wish I had the words to comfort you—and myself—but I do not. God alone knows our sorrow and that is enough. At least, that is what I keep telling myself. "His grace is sufficient... His grace is sufficient." Sometimes He feels so near, but then, it is like He has disappeared on the wind. He promises that He will be with us both—and I believe Him—but there are times when I feel so very much alone. Like now. My ship weighs anchor from Toronto Harbour on Tuesday, and I wonder how I shall keep from crumbling beneath the millstones of fear and grief that hang about my neck. I shall prevail—of that I also am certain—yet I know not how. "Peace," He whispers to my heart, "I am with you. I will not go back on my word." Yet, as quickly as that peace enfolds me, it disappears.

"I will trust in You and not be afraid," my heart cries in response, but I am afraid, Dora. Very afraid. Afraid for you, afraid for me. Afraid of the sorrow and sacrifice before us that our eyes cannot yet see. Terrified. And yet, there is a peace. A peace I cannot even begin to understand myself, let alone describe to another. He is here, and He, too, grieves. He will not leave us desolate. We must take heart, my Dora-girl, and remind ourselves often of that truth. We can trust Him.

There is one last thing I must tell you, my love. While I would never expect you to reciprocate, I want you to know that, in my heart, you are already my wife and there will not be another. Whether or not you one day marry, and whether or not I ever see you again in this life, I will always remain your Mattie. It is not ours to understand why the Almighty has seen fit to link our hearts like this, but the bond He has given us cannot be undone. Nor could I wish that it were.

    I love you, my Dora-girl. Cling to what you know is true: He loves us, He understands our pain, and He has not left us alone, no matter how it may seem to these earth-bound eyes of ours. Be still and rest, beloved, for He is God. We may not understand, but He does. May our trust in Him never be found wanting. I will pray for you every day and will write whenever I can. We are in God's hands, Dora. Both of us. When I forget, I bid you remind me, and I shall do likewise for you. Know you are forever in my heart.

Love,
Mattie

Chapter 9

AUGUST 17, 1879

Suppressing an unbecoming comment, I set my stitching aside and rested my head against the back of the chair. School would soon be in session. I rubbed my eyes, troubled by the constant ache that throbbed behind my temples, but even more so, by the ever-present darkness that threatened to overwhelm my spirit. "Jesus..." I breathed. My eyes snapped open and I glanced around the room, relieved to find myself alone. "Jesus, where are You?" Silence.

A spark snapped in the grate and, with it, the fragile wall that housed the resentment I hid deep within my heart. "I need You. You promised that You would be with me." I cringed at the accusation colouring my words, yet I couldn't stop myself. "You have snatched from me almost everything I hold dear—the man I love... our dreams for the future... my life as I know it... You have taken it all. You cannot take Yourself from me, also!" Stifling a cry, I slapped my hands to my mouth, alarmed by the ferocity behind my demands, not to mention my boldness in voicing them. My breath came in quick, shallow gasps and my eyes flickered about the room as I waited for the wrath of God to consume me. "I–I did not mean to... I mean... I–I... I humbly confess my sin of—"

Be still, beloved.

My head jerked up. The words, though whispered deep within my heart, seemed almost audible.

I am here.

The tightness in my chest gave way as the breath of Heaven filled me. Was this what it was like for Moses when God spoke with him face to face? Falling to my knees, I basked in the unearthly peace that blanketed my soul—a peace I had not known since the morning Mattie had left for Tarapacá, a peace I had feared might never again be mine. For the first time in weeks, I felt a song stir within me. But the barest flicker of joy, it lapped at the edges of my soul like a long, lost friend, bidding my spirit soar.

The pianoforte beckoned from across the room and my heart fluttered to life. I hadn't played once since the night Mattie left. Legs shaking, I crossed to the beloved instrument and settled myself on the stool. How could I have let it go for so long? Closing my eyes, I gently stroked the keys, sighing as the rigidness in my body gave way. *Glory. Pure glory.* I blinked back a tear as the first heart-rending strains of *Für Elise* drifted through the house, a soul-stirring tale of death and rebirth, the love song of a grieving heart. Only it wasn't for Mattie this time.

Chapter 10

SEPTEMBER 1, 1879

The carriage lurched as the horse stumbled into motion. Leaning out the window, I raised my hand to wave as my parents shrank into the distance. Ten weeks suddenly seemed a very long time. I drew my head back and loosened my bonnet, letting it fall to my shoulders. *Too long.* Brushing the thought aside, I considered the ride ahead. *Nine long hours on the road.* I shifted in my seat as the horses gained speed, my hands fidgeting on my knees.

"I see y'er off t'school agin, Miss Farncomb." The coachman glanced at me over his shoulder then turned to slap the reins lightly against the horse's rump. "Come now, Sadie-girl, ye cin go faster dan'at."

I smiled at the gentle way he spoke to his mare, as though she were his child and not his work horse. "Yes, Mr. Thackery. The Michaelmas term begins in two days and the head mistress insists that all of her girls be settled in at least one day before classes commence."

"Well, 'twouldn't do t'be late then. Them school marms be right strict 'bout things like that, I hear." I nodded, forgetting that his eyes were trained on the road ahead. "So… y'be lookin' forwart t'the term ahead?"

"I suppose."

"Why y'ain't soundin' perticalerly enthusiastic there, Miss Farncomb. It couldna be that ye don' like school, could it? I thought that all young ladies liked school." He slowed the horse, directing the carriage toward the shoulder to avoid a series of ankle-deep holes. "Why, my Dolly—loverly lass that she is—begs me 'most ev'ry day to let 'er go t'school. But alas, ev'ry penny counts, as they say, an' it jist ain't t'be, I'm 'fraid.

"It's not that I don't like school, Mr. Thackery." I paused, searching for words. "I am most thankful for the opportunity to attend. It's just that…" *Just that what?* My gaze drifted out the window of the coach. How was I supposed to explain to a man the trepidation I felt about facing the girls in my form when the conversation turned, as it invariably did, to the topic of the men in our lives? I slumped against the backboard, staring at the stately birches that lined the road. The girls would all be expecting news of a coming betrothal after I accidentally let slip a story or two about Mattie last term. Some might even have news of their own to share, though of what I could only imagine. Regardless, they would surely be anxious to gossip about the eligible young men in their social circles. Whatever was I going to tell them?

Father's parting words clanged between my ears and I cringed. *I know that you love our dear Mr. Wellman, Dora, but he is not the only eligible young man in the village. Why, just yesterday another came asking permission to court you when your schooling is complete. It has been two months since Matthew left for South America, and he made it very clear that he had no intention of returning. Perhaps it is time to consider another offer.*

Mr. Thackery wouldn't understand my social angst any more than Father understood my refusal to entertain other suitors. What man could? Except, of course, Mattie. He understood. And Jesus. But He didn't count.

Why do I not count?

Instantly alert, I straightened in my seat, drawing a hand to my breast. *Jesus? Is that You?*

Why do I not count, Dora?

Was that a tinge of sadness I sensed lurking behind those words? *You do count. I only meant…* I stumbled over my thoughts, not entirely certain of what I had meant. *It's just that You aren't exactly here.*

But I am here.

I fidgeted with my wrap, the rhythmic clopping of the horse's hooves marking the time as I strove to unravel the tangled web of thoughts knotted within me. *I know You are here, Jesus.* A familiar stillness descended upon me and I exhaled slowly. *And I know that You understand. I just, well, I guess the fact that I cannot hear You with my ears or touch You with my hands makes me forget sometimes how very real You are.* There. I had said it. *You are real, aren't You, Jesus? I mean… that really is Your voice I'm hearing, isn't it? Please tell me You aren't some sort of grand delusion conjured up by my grieving heart.* A gentle breeze caressed my cheek, and I could have sworn I heard an appreciative chuckle.

Would it matter if I was?

I pondered that for a moment, waffling in my response. Of course it mattered if He was real. Still, if He but lived in my imagination—

If I am not real, then a lot of people suffer from the same grand delusion.

• • •

Shortly after passing through Prestonvale, the carriage creaked to a stop across from the smithy in Oshawa. "Why, i'looks like ye be havin' some comp'ny on yer ride t'school, Miss Farncomb."

I strained to see out the far window and suppressed a groan. *Another passenger. So much for a quiet ride.* Tucking a strand of hair behind my ear, I smoothed my braid down my shoulder and tightened the bow. It wouldn't do to appear as disheveled on the outside as I felt on the inside. Mr. Thackery's thick baritone caught my ear and I smiled. I couldn't help but like the man.

"O'course, mem. I pride m'self in takin' exter guid care o'm'passengers. I'll 'ave yer gran'daughter at the school safe 'n sound long afore nightfall. Ye cin count on it."

Granddaughter? School? I edged forward. With only one school for girls in the vicinity of York, we had to be headed to the same place. The door opened slowly and a dainty boot stepped across the threshold.

"Miss Farncomb, 'tis m'pleasure t'interduce—"

"Emily!" I shouted, lunging toward the willowy figure entering the coach. "What are you doing so far from home?"

"Dora?"

"Well now, would ye luik at that. I'seems no interductions be needed after all." Mr. Thackery's eyes crinkled and he winked as he closed the carriage door. "Now sit ye doon, ladies. We'd best be on'r way." Poking his head through the window, he looked pointedly at the bench. "We'd better be a moseyin' 'fore th'sun gets any higher. That school o'yers be a long way off yet."

Chapter 11

BISHOP STRACHAN SCHOOL FOR GIRLS, TORONTO
SEPTEMBER 3, 1879

"As our esteemed Mrs. Thomson was wont to say, 'Remember girls, you are not going home to be selfish butterflies of fashion. The Bishop Strachan School has been endeavouring to fit you to become useful and courageous women. I believe you will yet see our universities open to women. Work out your freedom, girls! Knowledge is now no more a fountain seal'd; drink deep.'"

My gaze swept the chapel as Lady Principal Grier droned on. Sixty or so girls filled the pews on the east side of the nave, their heads bobbing earnestly with the head mistress's every word. Was that how I had looked my first year—before the reality of life had wrenched from me my dreams and hurled them beneath my feet? When the dawning of a new day still held the promise of a future more glorious than I could possibly imagine? *Was that really only last year?*

"Oh God," I whimpered. "Can Your will not be done another w—" A hand touched mine and I looked down, surprised to find Emily's fingers folded around my own. I glanced down the pew. Had anyone else noticed my distress? If they had, they certainly didn't show it. Breathing a prayer of thanksgiving, I fixed my gaze once more upon Miss Grier.

"It is important that our girls not forget," she intoned.

Forget? Forget what? How very many things I wished I could forget. Drawing my handkerchief from my sleeve, I dabbed it beneath my nose, only dimly registering that the chapel had stilled. *Why God? Why can I not be with Mattie? I could help him with his work. I could minister to the women and children. Surely there are some of those in Tarapacá. I could be his help meet—*

You are needed here, beloved.

I jerked my head up to peer around the nave, surprised to find it empty. *Was that You, God?* My eyes lurched from place to place, finally coming to rest on the arches above my head. *I mean—*

"Miss Farncomb?"

I jumped to my feet, sending my prayer book skidding beneath the next pew. "Miss Grier. I..." Clenching the wooden bench in front of me, I searched for the words to continue. "I–I am afraid that I let my mind wander, ma'am, and missed the call to dismiss."

"I can see that," she countered. Silence stretched between us as I bent to fetch my Book of Common Prayer. "Are you ill, Miss Farncomb?"

I swallowed the urge to lie and shook my head. "No, Miss Grier. Not in body, at least."

"You speak wisely," she said. I pressed my fingers to my lips, desperate to still their quivering. "You know, Miss Farncomb, illness comes in many forms. Sickness of heart can be every bit as debilitating as sickness of the body." My eyes pooled, sending a fiery stream of tears gushing down my cheeks as her compassionate words found their way into my heart. "Come, Dora. Sit." She patted the pew beside her. "I think you and I need to have a talk."

A heavy groan rumbled through me as I collapsed onto the pew, hiding my face in my hands. What was wrong with me? I hadn't cried like this since—since I was five years old and accidentally smashed my new china doll on the rocks beneath the lighthouse. *Decorum, Dora,* I chided myself, mimicking my father's sternest voice. Barely containing the wail that clamoured for release, I dug my fingers into my scalp and strove to compose myself, painfully aware of the figure beside me.

A diminutive woman, Miss Grier sat perched upon the edge of the pew, her hands clasped in supplication, her head bowed as if in prayer. The usual sternness in her features had softened, and I thought perhaps she wept, though I couldn't be sure. Stern as she could be, there was a reason we girls all thought of her with such fondness. Could anyone help but love her? A bell sounded from somewhere far down the hall, and she looked up.

"Forgive me, Miss Grier," I whispered. Unable to hold her gaze, I shifted my focus to the door. "I should probably be going to class now." I made a show of gathering my books, but was arrested by her hand on my forearm.

"No, Dora. Wait. A woman must not deny her emotions, no matter how inconvenient they may be. Nor ought she to bury her burdens so deeply within her that no other may unearth them. Talk to me, child. Tell me what troubles you. A burden shared is no less a burden, but it is made easier to bear."

Fearing the swell of emotion building within me, I closed my eyes and drew a long, slow breath, holding it until the trembling in my heart began to still. "Miss Grier," I swallowed the fear urging me to caution and rushed on. "How did you know that God had called you to be a lady principal? I mean, did He... did He speak to you in some way, or–or appear to you in a dream, or..." My voice trailed off as the foolishness of my words took root. What was Miss Grier supposed to make of a question like that?

"That is quite the question, Dora." She hooked her forefinger around her chin, studying me intently. "Suppose I ask you a question before I respond. Do you think that God is calling you to do something?"

Burying my head once more in my hands, I wagged it slowly from side to side, searching for an answer. "No… I mean… yes… I mean—I really need to go." I stood quickly and stepped into the aisle. "I just needed a few minutes to compose myself. Thank you for your time, Miss Grier. I apologize for troubling you with my musings."

Before she could respond, I scurried across the nave and into the corridor, praying she wouldn't follow. Now to figure out where the rest of my form had disappeared to. The only thing worse than baring my heart to my classmates was trying to explain it to our lady principal, kind though she be. It was hard enough to confide in my own mother.

Chapter 12

SEPTEMBER 12, 1879

Intermittent laughter emanated from our dorm room amid the babble of youthful voices. Instead of being drawn to join in on the fun, though, I found myself shrinking into the shadows, seeking a way of escape. Was it that the carefree jubilance of my classmates emphasized the melancholy spirit eclipsing my joy, or was there something less troubling at work? Perhaps I was overly tired, or maybe I was simply growing up. Regardless, the frivolity of the other girls irked me.

"Are you coming in, Dora?"

Emily—dear, sweet Emily. A wave of gleeful tittering drew my eye to the gaggle of girls sharing secrets by the fire. It crossed my mind that I might be the object of their amusement, but I banished the thought as quickly as it came. Of course I wasn't. They didn't know of my sorrow; I hadn't even told Emily. I reached out a hand to steady myself on the doorframe, fighting the urge to flee. "Not tonight, Emily." Pins and needles raced up my legs as I strove to steady my voice. "I think I shall retire to the garden for a quiet stroll instead." With measured calmness, I stepped past the door, relieved when no footsteps pursued.

The first stars of evening greeted me as I stepped over the threshold. Starlight, crickets, the fragrant medley of autumn blooms—could anything be more glorious? The door swung closed behind me as I drank in the quietness of the evening, the tension of the day bleeding from my soul. The earthy aroma of the garden reminded me of home, and I swallowed hard. *Less than two weeks and I'm already homesick.* I cringed at the thought of the term ahead. *Eight more weeks.* It felt like forever.

Movement on the path ahead of me caught my eye, and I bent to see a tiny garden toad, no larger than my father's thumbnail, hopping toward the safety of a prickly barberry bush. "All is well, little toad," I coaxed. I crouched down, opening my hand before it. "You're safe with me. I'm not out to hurt you."

You are safe with Me too, Dora.

I jumped at the unexpected voice penetrating my thoughts—a voice so real, I could have sworn I had heard it with my ears, though I knew I had not.

I am not out to hurt you either, beloved. You need to remember that. I sank to a nearby bench, overwhelmed by the tenderness engulfing each word. *I only want the best for you.*

A gentle breeze fanned my face and I stood, welcoming its embrace. Laying aside the heaviness that had brought me to the garden in the first place, I raised my hands to the heavens, basking in the presence of my Creator and reveling in the peace that enfolded me. "I know," I whispered, "and I trust You. It is just so hard. It's as though You have asked me to sacrifice everything."

Not everything, dear one.

A door opened behind me, casting a pale glow across the path. Could I never escape? Perhaps if I stood very still… Hurried footsteps scattered the gravel as they hastened toward me and I lowered my arms, bracing myself for the company I had hoped to avoid. *If only I could be like you, little toad, safely hidden beneath the barberry.*

"Miss Farncomb?"

"Yes, Lydia?" I turned toward the breathless young woman approaching me. "What is it?"

"Miss Farncomb…" She raised a hand to her chest and drew in a stuttering breath. "I came… I mean… Miss Grier sent me to fetch you. She told me to bring you to her office without delay."

Miss Grier wants me? With a final glance at the bush, I nodded and followed Lydia toward the open door. "Did she happen to share with you the reason for her summons?"

"I'm afraid not, Miss Farncomb, but a most handsome young man waits in her office with her." Lydia looked away quickly, as if caught in the act of some terrible sin.

"A handsome young man?"

"Oh, yes!" Her eyes sparkled in the lamplight as we stepped into the corridor. Lifting a hand to my face, I tried to hide my smile. "He is broad-shouldered and tall with golden-red hair and the barest hint of a beard." She clasped her hands in front of her chest. "And his eyes…"

I wracked my brain for someone I knew matching her description, but could think of no one. It certainly wasn't Mattie. While he was broad-shouldered and tall, and I supposed that he could have sprouted a beard, the golden-red hair presented a problem. Mattie's hair was curly and brown, the colour of freshly-husked chestnuts.

An image of Mattie standing on the deck of a ship filled my mind, and my heart skipped a beat. The wind whipped his chestnut curls around his face as he pointed exuberantly at something I could not see. If only I was there to share his joy.

"Miss Farncomb?" The vision vanished as quickly as it had come. "Are you not feeling well?"

Embarrassed, I cleared my throat and quickened my pace. "I am feeling fine, thank you, Lydia. I was only trying to place the young man of whom you spoke. I do not believe I know him."

"I'm sorry I cannot be of more help, Miss, but I did not hear his name."

"There is no need to concern yourself, Lydie. We are sure to find out soon enough." A wave of foreboding trembled through my belly and my heart raced. Why would a strange man come calling at this time of night, and what could it possibly have to do with me?

Chapter 13

MISS GRIER'S OFFICE

Tap. Tap. Tap.

The muffled voices on the other side of the door ceased abruptly as the heavy oak slab creaked open. "Dora, come in." The familiarity in Miss Grier's greeting confused me, but even more perplexing was the stoic figure that stood by her desk. Manners forgotten, I burst into the room and hurtled toward my brother. "Alfred, what are you doing here?" Gone was the teasing smile I knew so well. His eyes, ever so full of joy, seemed dark, lifeless, almost haunted. Skidding to a halt, I gulped back a cry. "Alfred?" He blinked as if stunned, and I clamped my fingers around his forearms, shaking him with every ounce of strength I could muster. "Talk to me, Alfred," I demanded. "What is going on?"

"Miss Farncomb, compose yourself."

Dimly aware of Miss Grier's voice calling my name, I forced my hands to my sides, mortified by my unseemly conduct. I moved to back away, but my legs felt like over-cooked asparagus, and my knees buckled beneath me.

"I've got you, Dora." Quicker than a breath, my brother shot out his arms to catch me. "You need to be strong."

I clamped my teeth on the edge of my tongue and drew my lips into a hard moue, as Mother had so deftly taught me. *Strong? Me?* I glanced at Miss Grier. Head bowed and fingers laced, she looked as if she was having almost as difficult a time as I in maintaining her composure. *God, help me!*

"A telegram came for me today. We are needed at home." My brother's clipped words intruded upon my thoughts. "We must leave immediately. Miss Grier has sent for Emily to pack your bags. She will meet us at the carriage." Without another word, Alfred ushered me toward the door. "Thank you, Miss Grier. We will be in touch."

"Wait!" I stopped, refusing to leave without more. "What's happened? You have to tell me," I pleaded. I whirled around, gripping his forearms once more. "I need to know, Alfred. Let me see the telegram."

One second passed, then two. Alfred shrank beneath the intensity of my gaze, but I had to know. Three seconds... four... five. With a heavy sigh, he reached into his jacket pocket and drew out a thin piece of folded paper. My fingers trembled as I unfolded it.

> Alfred Farncomb, Trinity Medical School, Toronto
> Come home immediately bring Dora STOP accident STOP Charles missing
> Frederick Farncomb, Esquire, Ebor House, Newcastle

The words swam across the page. *Charlie? Missing?* I lifted a hand to my mouth. *Not missing… gone. Passed on. Dead.* The horrifying certainty clanged within me, reverberating through my soul. With a curt nod, I folded the paper and handed it back to Alfred. Now was not the time to make a scene. We had to get home.

Resolve stiffened within me as I strode toward the door. Was this the mission to which God had called me—the reason that Mattie and I could not be wed? The thought of how close I had come to being halfway around the world alarmed me. It was bad enough that I was here. Squaring my shoulders, I grasped the doorknob and cleared my throat. "We'd better be on our way."

Chapter 14

The pounding of the horse's hooves drummed in my ears as we jolted along the deserted streets. *Almighty God, Holy Father—don't let Charlie be dead. Please, please don't let Charlie be dead.* Why could I not shake the feeling that my little brother was no longer with us? Alfred flicked the reins, urging the horse to increase its pace. His unaccustomed silence unnerved me. "Charlie's dead, isn't he," I stated, my voice almost as lifeless as I felt. I fixed my eyes on the road ahead, unable to bear the grief I knew I would see in Alfred's eyes.

"We don't know that, Dora." He reached for my hand and curled his fingers around mine. "Foolish is the man who leaps to conclude that which he does not know." His voice, too, lacked its usual inflection, dulled by the pall of hopelessness hanging over us both. He also feared the worst—or so it would appear. I had never seen Alfred like this. Next to Father, he had always been the invulnerable one—steady, unrockable, totally in control—no matter what the situation. Braving a glance his way, I cringed at his careworn features. Back rigid and face set, he reminded me of a little boy about to meet the rod of his father. Though determined to meet his fate with the dignity and strength of a man, vulnerability enveloped him like a cloak, for the terrified child within couldn't quite maintain the façade.

I gave his fingers a reassuring squeeze. "It's going to be all right, Alfred," I whispered. He blinked twice and cleared his throat, but said nothing. "We will get through this together, big brother. God is with us—no matter what we might be called to endure." My eyes pooled, and a single tear blazed a pathway down the side of my nose. "And He is with Charlie, too—wherever he might be." The image of a tiny toad hopping into the bushes played across my mind. "God Himself will see us through the storm. We can trust Him."

"Even if Charlie is dead, Dora?"

For some reason, Alfred's words stung. Next to him, I was barely more than a child. What knew I of such things? My cheeks warmed at my presumption in citing such platitudes. He must think me positively infantile. *But they aren't platitudes* my mind shouted; *they are truths. Truths!* The little toad I had watched earlier hopped through my thoughts once more and disappeared beneath a shapeless shadow.

Will you trust Me, Dora? I pressed my lips together, lifting my face to the heavens. *Even if I take Charlie home?*

A weary groan ripped from deep within my soul, and my eyes squeezed shut of their own accord. If God was the God He claimed to be, and if He loved me as truly as He said He did, was I not beholden to Him to accept the good and the bad of life from His hand, as Job so pointedly put it, and trust that He was not out to destroy me? Was that not, after all, the message of the little toad? Odd that He should have revealed that to me when He did.

I shifted in my seat. Alfred awaited my answer—both of them did. "Even if Charlie dies." My voice cracked on the final word, but the decisive tone of my pronouncement surprised even me. Awed by the sudden sense of peace that washed over me, I breathed freely for the first time since Lydia had fetched me. A muscle jerked in Alfred's jaw and his Adam's apple bobbed. He didn't look convinced. My heart pounded to the beat of the horse's hooves, my mind awhirl with the immensity of my bold proclamation. *Even if... Even if... Even if... Did I really know what I was saying?*

The horse slowed as we approached Station Street. "What time does the train leave?"

Alfred lifted a shoulder in a half-hearted shrug. "I guess we'll find out soon. I didn't take time to check the schedule." He cast a wry glance my way. "I had other things on my mind."

The carriage rolled to a stop before the livery where a young man in a grubby apron greeted us. "Welcome to Union Station, sir. May I stable your horse for you?"

Alfred dug into his pocket and produced two green-edged copper coins. "Yes, please. A groom will be by in the morning from Trinity Medical School to collect the rig."

The stable hand dipped his head as he pocketed the coins. "I'll see that it is ready, sir. In the meantime, you and the young lady can leave your trunks with me and I'll see that they're delivered to the baggage room."

"That would be most helpful." Alfred shook the young man's hand then turned to help me from the carriage.

Slipping my hand into the crook of his arm, I followed him across the street toward the entrance, thankful that the daytime bustle of the station had long quieted. I waited by the door of the ticket lobby while Alfred stepped into the queue. A handful of people roamed the edges of the room, but only one patron stood before him. *At least we won't have to wait long.* I eyed the bench opposite the door, an overwhelming weariness sweeping over me. The clock on the wall above it read nine forty-two. No wonder I felt so tired. Back at school, I would have been tucked securely into my bed by now; I might even have been asleep. After a long day of classes, most of us sank into slumber as soon as the final bell rang, and I had a reputation for being among the first to succumb to my exhaustion. Not that I thought I would be able to sleep now. Too many anxious thoughts warred within me to do that.

"Are you all right, Dora?"

I started at the sound of my brother's voice. "Goodness! I didn't see you approach. Did you get the tickets?" He nodded, but something about his demeanor belied the good news. "Well?" I prodded. "When do we board?"

He cleared his throat and looked at the floor. "Tomorrow... at dawn. Six forty-five."

"Tomorrow? We have to wait until tomorrow?"

His eyes rose, boring into mine. "I know." Compassion edged each word, and I caught a glimpse of the comfort he must bring to his patients. "I am as disheartened by the need to wait as you must be, but the final eastbound train of the day departed the station almost an hour ago. There will not be another until the morning, and we are fortunate that there is room for us on it. There were but four empty seats."

Heat filled my face and I hung my head. "You're right, Alfred." I reached for his arm and tried to smile. "What shall we do while we wait?"

He hooked his hand around the back of his neck and looked away. "Therein lies another problem, oh sister of mine." His hand fell as a heavy sigh shuddered from his lips. "I would take you to an inn, but the tickets cost more than I anticipated. We shall have to wait here, I'm afraid."

Somehow the ludicrousness of it all struck my funny bone, and a half-stifled snort escaped me. Mortified, I clapped a hand to my mouth, but it was too late. Alfred erupted in a gale of laughter and drew me into his arms. How good it felt to laugh—it had been such a long time. Yet, as the laughter of the moment subsided, a deep sorrow rushed in to take its place. What a day this had been.

Alfred loosened his grip on me and we drew apart. "Come. I will escort you to the ladies' waiting room."

His eyes glistened in the lamplight as I took his arm. "We can trust Him, Alfred," I whispered, leaning in close, "even if—"

"Though He slay me, yet will I trust in him?" he murmured.

For the first time, I caught a glimpse of the depth of pain etching the familiar words of Job—and the faith that prompted them. Did I really have that kind of faith? We stopped at the doorway to the ladies' waiting room and I buried my face in Alfred's sleeve. If only there was a place we could wait together. "Rest well, big brother. I fear that we shall need all of our strength to cope with the day that lies ahead." I reached up to press a kiss to his cheek before disengaging myself from his arm and slipping through the door. *Would that I could take my own advice.*

Chapter 15

NEWCASTLE

Steam hissed from the engine as the great iron horse squealed to a halt. Eyes darting from seat to seat, a burly conductor hustled down the aisle, his clipped voice announcing our destination. "Newcastle Station. Newcastle Station. This stop." Alfred rose stiffly from his seat and offered his hand as I manoeuvered myself to my feet and down the aisle. Stomach churning, I stepped onto the platform and headed toward the familiar wooden building while Alfred waited for the lone porter to load our baggage onto a handcart. Old Henry had been the chief, and only, porter at the Newcastle station for as long as I could remember. Ever friendly and remarkably efficient, he eagerly saw to the comfort of his passengers as he carted their belongings to and from the train. I glanced over my shoulder at the two men, troubled by the porter's uncharacteristic silence and obvious refusal to meet Alfred's eyes.

Before I could think too much about it, though, a familiar figure emerged from behind the station house, and I hurried to intercept him. "Johnny!" I cried. The man stopped mid-stride and bowed his head as if praying for strength. Not a good sign. *First Henry, now...* Rushing to his side, I reached for Johnny's arm, dimly aware that Alfred shadowed my every move. "Johnny—what's happened? Is everything all right? Has Charlie been found? Is he well?"

"Be still, Dora." At the sound of Alfred's voice, I fell silent, my questions forgotten. My brothers' eyes locked in unspoken communication, and for the first time, I noticed Johnny's pale face and swollen eyes. He could have been mistaken for a beggar in his rumpled clothes, and he looked like he hadn't slept in a week. The hope of a happy resolution evaporated before it could even take shape. Though it was hardly necessary, Alfred ushered us to a quiet place at the edge of the platform and motioned for me to sit on a nearby bench. "Tell us, John. We need to know," he said.

"It was an accident... They–they were bathing... just Charlie and a bunch of his friends, like a thousand times before..."

I drew in a long, shaky breath, anxious for him to continue, yet terrified to hear the rest.

"Then the wind came up and the current changed course. It wasn't until they climbed out on the pier that they realized Charlie was missing... Charlie and Theodore Wilson both..."

I raised my head, my brows knit. "Theodore is also missing?"

Johnny nodded, his eyes fixed on a place more distant than eye could see. "They are still searching for their bodies."

Their bodies. The words clanged in my head, meaningless and out of place. It couldn't be true. "Oh, Charlie..." I murmured.

"Always hankerin' to be the centre of attention," Alfred added. He rubbed his hand against his beard and shook his head, his rueful smile mirroring dear Charlie's most mischievous grin.

Resting my head against Alfred's arm, I blinked back a tear. "I suppose he got what he wanted."

Ever the big brother, Alfred drew me to my feet and settled his hand on the small of my back, pressing me toward Johnny. "John, you take Dora to the carriage while I fetch our bags. It's time we got home. Mother will want us close by, and perhaps there will be something we can do to help."

Chapter 16

The door swung inward, hardly making a sound. Heart thudding, I paused on the threshold, afraid to move forward, yet knowing there could be no return. Everything seemed so different from how I had left it a mere two weeks ago. The cheerful banter of the servants had been replaced by silence, the busyness of the day's routine abandoned. Heavy drapes pulled tightly over the arched windows banished the morning light and with it the welcome warmth of the sun. The house felt like a tomb. My footsteps echoed on the hardwood floor as I stepped toward the parlour, my legs weakening with every step until I was sure they would hold me no longer. *Only two or three more feet.* Hushed voices filtered into the foyer, and I strained to make out the words.

"Yes... early this morning... under the pier. Will be here to measure this morn... no need for a wake." My stomach clenched. *Will be here to measure this morning? No need for a wake?* I inched closer. *He's really gone—they found his body.* A low moan intruded upon my thoughts, and I lurched forward, my eyes lighting upon a black-shrouded figure perched on the edge of the divan. *Mother.* Elbows resting upon her knees, she buried her face in her hands, her shoulders quivering. I choked back a sob. *Oh God, what do I do? Charlie is dead.* Barely able to breathe, I swallowed the lump in my throat and rushed to Mother's side. Throwing myself at her feet, I slid my arms around her waist and pressed my head into her lap, relieved when she straightened and brought her hand to rest upon my back.

"Oh, my Dora..." Her fingers trembled as she ran them through my hair, the familiar action soothing us both.

"I'm here, Mother," I whispered. I lifted my head to peer into her eyes, desperate to calm the churning darkness wrestling in their depths. "We will get through this together, no matter what may befall." Pulling myself up onto the divan, I drew her into a tight embrace. "God *is* with us, even in this. He has not abandoned us." My voice broke and I paused lest the grief clutching my heart find release. Above all else, I needed to remain strong.

An unexpected brightness pierced the darkness of the room and I jerked my head toward its source. Johnny stood by the window, his hand still grasping the heavy drapes as he drew them away from the glass. Closing my eyes, I leaned into the light, my chest expanding as if the luminescent rays contained the breath of life. While I understood the tradition of closing the drapes to signify the darkness of the soul in times of grief, the idea of banishing the light in the midst of life's greatest darkness made no sense to me at all.

A hush fell upon the room as an ethereal sense of peace descended upon us. Mother drew one long, slow breath after another, and the wildness in her eyes began to dissipate. She rose—as if from the grave herself—and crossed the room, an aura of acceptance surrounding her every move. Opening her arms to Father, she drew his head down to rest upon her shoulder. "It is as Dora said, my love…" Her words, though quiet, shivered through me. "God is with us, Frederick; He has not abandoned us. Charlie is in His hands now—as are we all." Freeing herself from Father's embrace, she looked pointedly around the room. "Alfred, you and John go with your father and Mr. Fairbank here to make arrangements with the rector while Dora and I assemble suitable mourning attire for everyone. I will have Anna and Betsy see to the house and prepare refreshments for those who come to offer their condolences after the funeral. The rector will be anxious to see to the burial as soon as possible, I expect."

With the confidence of a woman accustomed to being obeyed, she strode from the room. The paralysis of grief had been broken, and there was much to do. Hurrying after her, I scurried up the stairs and into my bedchamber. Betsy sat by the fire, feverishly stitching the folds of black taffeta spilling from her lap while Mother stood by the bureau with Anna, outlining the tasks for which the two servants were responsible.

Anna nodded curtly and headed for the door. "Come, Betsy. Mistress Jane and Miss Dora will take care of the mourning attire. We must prepare for visitors."

"Yes, mem." Betsy stood, placed the pile of fabric on the chair, and headed toward the door. She nodded as she passed, her glassy eyes not quite able to meet my own.

Forcing a smile, I placed my hand upon her shoulder and gave her a gentle squeeze. "All will be well, Betsy. You'll see." Tears spilled down her cheeks as she rushed from the room. Everyone loved Charlie. Everyone. I blinked rapidly to clear my vision and turned my attention to the abandoned pile of taffeta. *Oh Charlie. Did you have to go and die on us? I look wretched in black.* I could almost hear his boyish chortle in response. *Well, I do, you know.*

Chapter 17

Samson sniffed at my feet then gave his tail a half-hearted wag before plopping himself once more beside Charlie's chair. He laid his snout on his outstretched paws then gazed up at me with those big, trusting eyes of his and whimpered.

"I know, Samson. I miss him, too." I bent to stroke his matted fur. "Why don't you come and sit beside me?" I patted my leg, urging him to follow, but he wouldn't budge from his spot. He knew who his master was; that one-track doggy brain of his just hadn't figured out that the one he adored was not coming home.

Alfred shook his head as I slid into my chair. "I tried, too. Dumb dog."

"Not so dumb, if you ask me." Johnny inclined his head toward the mutt. "Word has it he spent the whole night nosing about the pier in search of his master."

I picked up my napkin and spread it over my knees. "I wonder if he knows."

"Oh, he knows." I turned at the sound of Father's voice. Alfred and Johnny scrambled to their feet as Mother entered the dining room on Father's arm. "At least, he knows that *something* is up. He knows that his master has disappeared." Father motioned toward the table. "Come, sit. It's time to eat."

Father's words melted into silence as Betsy served the soup. I spooned the savoury broth into my mouth and forced myself to swallow. Odd, how grief could sour the taste buds so. After only a few spoonfuls, I pushed the bowl away and folded my hands in my lap. It appeared that no one had much of an appetite this afternoon. Father dabbed his napkin against his upper lip and pushed his chair back from the table. "The funeral procession will leave the house at three; the mourners will arrive at quarter to." With that, he rose from the table, extending his arm toward Mother. "Come, my love. We must talk."

• • •

The quiet hum of conversation buzzed around me like a troublesome gnat.

"What a shame that you should lose your brother to such a cruel death." Mrs. Simons tsked.

"Yes," I responded, not knowing what else to say. Would that I hadn't had to lose him at all. At least it was a blessing that we only had to deal with one family of well-wishers at a time.

"How sad that he was taken at such a tender age, dear. He had such a promising future ahead of him." *Mr. Jones, our grade school teacher.*

"Yes, sir. He was a very talented young man." *Honestly. What else am I supposed to say? That he drove me crazy every day but had a heart of gold bigger than this grand dominion we call home?*

Gradually the parade of guests and the well-meaning torture they visited upon us melded into one in my mind.

"No one could make me smile like that little brother of yours. He was a right fine young lad, he was."

"Pity... such a pity. Alas! The good Lord always does take the best."

I nodded politely to each would-be comforter and murmured a response I hoped might be fitting.

"Poor, dear girl," one woman mumbled as she headed toward the door on the arm of her husband. "She looks like she hasn't slept in days."

Wonderful. And how, exactly, do you expect me to look? Pushing away my impatience, I scanned the room for a means of escape. Mother's eyes met mine and she inclined her head encouragingly. While the steady stream of mourners had largely dwindled, the few that remained would keep us on our feet for at least an hour yet. Propriety dictated that I welcome each guest by name and share with her a piece of my grief, but I eyed the parlor door instead. Surely nobody would notice if I slipped up to my chamber for a few minutes of peace—or, better yet, out to the orchard for a breath of fresh air. I glanced at my mother. Even from the back, she looked frail and worn. How could I even think of abandoning her now?

Approaching from behind, I slipped my arm around her waist and directed her to the divan. "Sit, Mother, while I get you some tea. Mrs. Hesslin, is there anything I can get for you?" A fleeting smile. A single tear. They were all Mother had left to offer, but my heart soared in response. Pride shone in her eyes as she turned once more to her guest, renewed vigour infusing her voice. *A burden shared...* The words of Lady Principal Grier rippled through me, affirming my choice. If God had called me to bolster my family through this time of grief, that is exactly what I would do. No matter what the cost.

Chapter 18

Silence. At last. With a noisy yawn, I collapsed into bed and pulled the covers up to my chin, the mattress cradling me like a child in the arms of her mother. I had navigated many a difficult day in my time, but none more agonizing than this. My eyes slid shut. Sleep would come quickly tonight. Rolling onto my side, I bunched the pillow beneath my head and surrendered to the weight of exhaustion squeezing the life from my soul. My breath slowed as the cares of the day fell away, but instead of being enveloped by the welcome oblivion of slumber, I found myself thrust into the midst of a raging storm. A gust of wind enveloped me and a peal of thunder rent the skies as the darkness fled in a flurry of blinding light.

Clapping my hands to my ears, I ran barefoot over the jagged rocks at the base of the lighthouse, heedless of the driving rain pelting from the heavens. The wind intensified, whipping my sodden nightdress around my ankles and loosening my hair from its braid. Still, I sped on, desperately searching the darkness, though for what, I knew not. Waves buffeted the shoreline and crashed around my feet as I scanned the raging waters. There it was! My heart churned in my chest. A hand appeared from the depths—grasping, reaching, flailing the air—then a head. I opened my mouth to scream, but try as I might, no sound came out.

Throwing off the covers entwining my limbs, I bolted upright in bed, gasping for breath. I palmed the wetness from my cheeks and peered around the room, confused. That was a dream I could just as soon have done without. An ember snapped in the grate. *What time is it?* Sliding my feet over the edge of the bed, I felt for my slippers. Tired as I was, the prospect of closing my eyes again sent chills up my spine. Careful to avoid the creaky floorboard at the foot of the bed, I crept across the room to the fireplace. Was I the only one who couldn't sleep? I stirred the embers and added a stick or two of kindling, then blew gently at its base until a flame burst from the ashes. *Though he were dead, yet shall he live.* The words from my brother's interment thundered through me and I sniffed back a fresh onslaught of tears. *Yes, he will live—I* know *he will live—but I want him to live here with us. I'm not ready for You to call him home."*

Will you ever be ready for that, beloved?

I hung my head. The little blaze heightened, dancing in the darkened room, and I bent to add another log. How was I ever going to live without my little brother? My thoughts turned to Mattie as I lit a taper and carried it over to my writing desk. Pulling a piece of paper from the drawer, I smoothed my hand across it and uncorked the jar of ink. *Oh, Mattie… if only you were here.* I dipped my pen and waited for the ink to fill its crevices. I should write him a letter. Charlie was his friend. Somebody needed to tell him.

September 15, 1879

My Dear Mr. Wellman,

Who would have known? Whoever could have imagined? My heart pounds when I think of the tragedy this day has brought, and I can hardly suppress the wail that claws its way up my throat. It is Charlie—my little brother. Alas! I can hardly bear the thought, let alone the reality of all that has come to pass. He is gone, Mattie! Gone. Just like that. Dead. Drowned in the harbour in Newcastle Friday afternoon. I feel like I have been plunged into the midst of a nightmare and I keep expecting to awaken in my dorm room relieved to find it naught but a dream, yet nothing I do can rouse me from the horror. It is real. Charlie is gone, and there is not one thing that I can do about it. My beloved Charlie—my playmate, my confidante, my brother—is gone and nothing will ever be the same again. I am scared, Mattie. Whatever am I going to do without him?

Affectionately,
Your Dora-girl

Chapter 19

OCTOBER 2, 1879

Water lapped against the pebbled bank of the millpond, a soothing counterpoint to the discordant thoughts whirling within me. Barely two weeks had passed since Charlie left us, yet somehow it felt like a lifetime.

"So this is where you have been hiding yourself."

"Father! What are you doing here?" Jumping to my feet, I swept a smattering of leaves from the grass with my foot and shifted to make room for him at the base of the old weeping willow.

"You always did love this place." He folded his long legs beneath him and leaned back against the tree, patting the ground beside him. A handful of grey hairs streaked his reddish-blond beard. Odd that I had never noticed them before. Perhaps they'd grown as a result of his grief.

Taking him up on his unspoken invitation, I settled myself on the grass by his side. A gentle breeze rustled the treetops, sending a rain of shrivelled leaves showering down upon us. The burden of my own grief was bad enough; I couldn't begin to imagine the pain wracking *his* soul. I closed my eyes and turned to face the breeze, reveling in the softness of its silken caress. *Thank You, Jesus. I needed to know that You are here.* Turning back to Father, I examined his every move, anxious to know why he had come. Though comforted by his presence, I couldn't remember the last time the two of us had been alone like this.

Father plucked a fallen willow wand from his jacket and set it on the ground between us. "Your mother is worried about you, you know. She fears all this time on your own might not be good for you."

Folding my hands on my lap, I lowered my head, grappling with the urge to share my heart. "But I am not alone, Father." I lifted my eyes to judge his response. When not a muscle twitched to betray his thoughts, I rushed on, an urgent need for him to understand compelling me to speak. "I am not alone because Jesus is with me. I mean, as bleak as these days may feel, He has not abandoned us." Father's face contorted and his lower lip quivered. "You must believe that, Father. Were it not for His presence, I'm sure I would die of grief."

"You do not know how much I wish I had your faith, Dora."

Silence rested between us as I strove to find the words that would free his heart to trust. Laying my head upon his shoulder, I reached for his hand. "Faith is not something we feel, Father. You know that. Isn't it you who always tells me that emotion rarely keeps company with truth?" His head sagged against his chest and I thought I felt a teardrop roll across my knuckles. "Faith is a choice we make to trust when we do not understand, when the world around us screams that God is not in control." His shoulders trembled and I pressed a kiss to his cheek. "God is with us, Father. Your heart is broken right now and cannot hold on to that truth, but that doesn't make it any less real." I paused, willing myself to stay strong, yet painfully aware of the way our roles had been reversed. "Until you can bear it once more for yourself, perhaps I can be the keeper of the Light for us both."

He loosed his hand from mine and drew me into a tearful embrace. "Hmm… the keeper of the Light. The Light Keeper." He closed his eyes and inhaled deeply. "We named you well, Dora-girl. You are truly a gift from God."

The breeze picked up, cradling us in the embrace of our Creator and a familiar peace invaded my soul. Father must have felt it, too, for his chest expanded and his body relaxed into mine as slow, deep breaths replaced the erratic puffs of moments before. "See, Father?" Awe fought with exultation as I strove to still my galloping heart. "He is here; He has not left us." I drew away and rose to my feet, throwing my arms into the air. *Thank You, Jesus. Thank You. Open Father's eyes to see You at work and his heart to rest in Your presence.* I spun in ever-widening circles as the wind gusted around me, lost in the embrace of the Almighty.

At last, the breeze abated, and I dropped my arms to my sides. Remembering Father, I dashed away the tears that bathed my face, wishing I could do something to hide my flaming cheeks. I contemplated him sheepishly, surprised to see a hint of joy emanating from his eyes. "He is here, Father," I repeated.

"I believe you," came his quiet reply. I took his hands in mine and pulled him to his feet, amused by the way he grunted as he rose. "I am getting too old for this, my Dora-girl."

"Too old for what?" I teased.

He looked at me askance and grimaced. "For *all* of it."

I nodded, touched by his honest response, and looped my hand around his elbow. "Did Mother really send you out here to find me?"

"Yes." The leaves crunched beneath our feet as we crossed the grassy sward. "We have something we need to talk to you about."

My stomach plummeted at the seriousness in his tone. "Then we must hurry. We wouldn't want to keep Mother waiting." I shuddered at the forced brightness that coloured my words, knowing it wouldn't have fooled a child.

Father's eyes met mine and he smoothed his beard with his hand, barely covering the ghost of a smile. "All will be well, my dear. He is here, remember?"

Chapter 20

"So, I am not going back to school?" I glanced from Father to Mother, hardly daring to believe my ears. As much as I desired to resume my studies, much of the term had already passed and it would be difficult to catch up on the work I had missed. Besides, I needed to be close to my family. When Alfred and Johnny had left to return to Toronto, I had felt as if the crumbling ruins of my life had been ground into dust and borne away on the wind. I couldn't begin to imagine being without Mother and Father as well.

"It is for the best, dear," Mother soothed. She peered at Father then returned her attention to me. "For all of us. You don't mind terribly, do you, Dora? We promise that you shall return for final form, and we will do everything we can in the meantime to see that you do not fall behind."

The undeniable plea in her voice caught at my heart. I nodded, not wishing to appear too eager. "Of course not, Mother. It hadn't even crossed my mind to return this year. I would prefer to stay here if that is all right with you."

Without a word, Father crossed the room, laid a kiss upon my head, and disappeared out the door. Mother's heavy mourning gown rustled as she rose to follow. "The Ladies' Sewing Circle begins in a little over an hour. Will you accompany me, dear?"

My heart skipped a beat. All the ladies of the parish would be there, and every one of them would want to talk about Charlie. I bit back a sour response and tried to smile. Mother reached over to tuck an errant lock of hair behind my ear and nodded. "It will never get any easier, I'm afraid, but it is something we both need to do. The sooner, no doubt, the better."

"Perhaps if we do it together, it will be easier." I scooped up our sewing baskets from their place beside the pianoforte.

Mother stepped into the hall. "Anna, could you please bring our wraps?" Hurried footsteps echoed on the stairs, heralding the arrival of our cloaks. "Thank you, Anna." Mother turned around to receive the woolen cape the older woman draped over her shoulders. "I think I should like to walk this afternoon, Dora. The fresh air will do us good."

Chapter 21

DECEMBER 24, 1879

Samson thumped his tail on the floor, scattering paper cones and scraps of cloth from one end of the room to the other. "Oh Samson." *What a mess.* At the sound of his name, the dog's hind end popped from the floor, his whole body wriggling with the force of unrestrained joy. A chorus of happy barks filled the room as he bounced in place, his big, brown eyes staring expectantly into mine. Why did he have to remind me so much of Charlie?

A familiar lump swelled in my throat, but I willed it away, refusing to let the tears flow. "Go see Anna in the kitchen. Maybe she'll give you a bone to chew." His tongue lolled from the side of his mouth as he dropped his head onto his paws, his eyes never leaving mine. "Sam–son," I repeated. Exhaling slowly, I wagged my head at the exuberant pup. "What am I going to do with you?" I bent to scratch him behind the ears, but in a trice, I was on the floor, his hairy legs straddling my chest as he eagerly lapped at my face. "Char…" Like the bursting of a bubble, my laughter turned to tears, and I pushed myself into a sitting position. Sensing my distress, Samson stopped his frenzied play and pressed against me, whimpering. Would the mourning never come to an end? Wrapping my arms around the crazy mutt, I rubbed my face into his silky fur.

"Dora, what is the meaning of all that racket?" Heavy footfalls accompanied the stern words as Mother approached the conservatory door, but the annoyance etching her approach faded when she saw the scene before her. "What happened?" she gasped. Her eyes widened, darting from me to the dog and back again before taking inventory of the room.

Still ready to play, Samson bounded toward the door and skidded to a halt at Mother's feet, his tail beating the air. What could I say? I lifted my hands and shrugged. "It seems that Samson wanted to play."

Mother looked pointedly at the disarray, then pinned me with the glare usually reserved for Charlie. "Well, it seems to me, young lady, that you have a mighty big mess to clean up."

"Yes, Mother."

"And as for you…" Mother's voice took on a hardness rarely heard as she directed her attention to the dog. His tail quivered to a stop and he tucked it between his legs as he lowered his belly to the floor. "Don't you give me those puppy dog eyes." She stepped backward and thrust her finger toward the clock in the hall. "Go to your bed. Now." Spinning on her heel, she strode toward the kitchen. "It seems Samson wanted to play."

•••

With a flourish, I tied the final ribbon onto the tree and stood back to admire my handiwork. The silvery cones I had painstakingly prepared in the morning—now laden with nuts and raisins—hung from every bough, glinting in the light of the lamp, but it was Betsy's famous gingerbread stars that drew my eye. Intricately cut and decorated with care, they had always been my favourite. Charlie's, too. Next to the popcorn garlands, that is. He'd had a fetish for those I would never understand.

The clock chimed five and I hurried from the room. Father would soon be back with the boys. With no time to lose, I ran to my chamber and pulled my stash of presents from beneath the bed. A carefully embroidered apron for Mother, a set of monogrammed handkerchiefs for Father, mufflers for Alfred and Johnny, a tatted lavender sachet for Anna, a lacy cap for Betsy to wear to church on Sundays. My fingers brushed against a final gift nestled in the bottom of the box, and my breath caught. I caressed the soft cotton wrapping as if the act itself could restore to me the one for whom it was made. Charlie had begged Father for a slingshot for almost as long as I could remember, but now that he was to be given one of his own, he would never have the chance to enjoy it. "You would have loved it, Charlie."

"Miss Dora?"

Yanking my hands from the box, I hurriedly replaced the lid and shoved the chest beneath the bed. "Yes, Betsy?" I cringed at the harshness in my voice as I rose from my knees, heat flooding my face.

"Are you well, Miss Dora?"

"Of course I am well, Betsy. You just startled me." I bent to gather the gifts from my bed.

"Why don't you let me take those down to the tree for you while you change for supper?" Without waiting for an answer, Betsy loaded the gifts into her arms and headed for the door. "Your Father will return with your brothers before the hour is up, and your aunt and uncle are due at any moment. Mistress Jane wishes to have you by her side when they arrive."

"Wait! You mustn't forget these." Rushing to my knitting basket, I pulled out three more gifts yet to be wrapped. A pair of socks for Uncle William, an embroidered handkerchief for Aunt Mary, and a small bottle of Alfred's favourite perfume for Cousin Hannah. "Will you please see that these get wrapped for me, Betsy?"

Gathering them into her empty hand, Betsy slipped from the room. "Do hurry, Miss Dora," she called over her shoulder. "You know your mother abhors tardiness every bit as much as your father does."

Chapter 22

Charlie's empty chair stared at me from across the table, an unwelcome intruder into the evening's festivities, yet at the same time, a beloved guest.

"I miss him, too."

Flustered, I jerked my eyes away from the chair as Cousin Hannah's whispered words penetrated the fog of grief enshrouding my spirit. Resplendent in a robe of deepest scarlet, she sat between Alfred and me, her brows raised in compassion, the perfect picture of composure. Unlike me. Acknowledging her kindness with a crooked smile, I turned my attention to my plate and forked a morsel of creamed potato into my mouth. My stomach churned. It tasted like ashes. Feigning great interest, I moved one forkful of food after another from one place on my plate to the next, occasionally lifting one to my mouth before returning it to my plate untouched.

"So, Frederick, how go things down at the harbor these days? Any interesting new arrivals?" Uncle William asked.

"Well, now, just the other day, Mrs. Coxwell from out Orono way received a lovely Persian rug from her brother in England," Father responded.

"I wager that was something—"

I glared around the table. How could they all be carrying on as if nothing was amiss? Had they not noticed the empty chair? Were they completely oblivious to the woebegone mutt lying beneath it? Did they forget that someone was missing? Pressure built behind my eyes, but I blinked it away, refusing to give in to its pull. I choked down a bit of carrot and a tiny bite of roast beef dipped in gravy. It all tasted the same.

"Are you finished, Miss Dora?"

Startled from my thoughts, I nodded, noticing for the first time that all the plates had been cleared save mine. "Yes, Betsy." I folded my hands on my lap and tried to sound cheery. "Thank you."

"And Dora…" Uncle William leaned back in his chair and closed his hands over his ample belly. "Have you heard anything from that young minister friend of yours lately?"

My stomach lurched and I snatched my napkin to my lips, afraid I might retch. I grasped for something—anything—to say, but it was as if a shroud had been drawn around my mind.

"Oh, our Mr. Wellman keeps contact with all of us when he can," Johnny piped in, as if the question had been directed his way. I studied the table before me, forcing my breath to slow. What would I do without Johnny? "He's moved to Tarapacá, you know. He indicates that he is in an area of some unrest, what with the War of the Pacific and all." Johnny paused to clear his throat. "War is a terrible thing."

"That it is." Uncle William wadded his napkin in his hand and wagged his head reprovingly. "You know, my father's father fought in the War of 1812. A horrible ordeal that was, with Britain's reluctance to give up its prize and America's refusal to bow to her rule. Why…"

His voice droned on and I lost track of what he was saying. Betsy entered the room with a beautifully sculpted plum pudding bathed in rum. Setting it before Father, she moved to the sideboard where Anna busily served the tea. As giver of the feast, Father relished the job of dishing out the much-anticipated Christmas pudding. Anna's skill in the kitchen was appreciated by everyone who had the good fortune of sampling her wares. I spooned a few crumbs into my mouth and dutifully joined in the chorus of praise lauding the cook.

Pride lit Anna's countenance as she drew her hand to her chest and dipped a curtsy. "I am glad it meets with your approval."

I smiled in spite of my turmoil and forced myself to eat. Anna would be mortified if I sent my portion to the kitchen untouched.

"Remember last Christmas when Anna presented Charlie with his plum pudding?" Alfred raised his left eyebrow, barely suppressing a smile.

Scrambling from his seat, Johnny affected a childlike pose, his thumb poised above his bowl. "Little Jack Horner sat in a corner eating his Christmas pie." Hannah giggled. "He stuck in his thumb, and pulled out a plum…" With great ceremony, Johnny thrust his thumb into the pudding. His brow wrinkled as he rooted around for the prize. "And pulled out a plum," he repeated. Obviously exasperated, he poked his forefinger into the cake beside his thumb and triumphantly pulled out a wrinkled prune.

"And said, 'what a good boy am I!'" Father and Alfred joined Johnny on the final line of the rhyme before dissolving into laughter. Even I had to smile at the bittersweet memory. Johnny popped the sweet treat into his mouth and smacked his lips appreciatively. Among all those present, only Mother seemed as wounded as I felt, waving a hand dismissively at her younger son and dabbing a handkerchief to her eye. There was no escaping the memories—or the mourning they begat. Charlie's love for Christmas was synonymous with the season. Every time I chanced to look upon his chair, I somehow expected to see him there, carrying on as only he could, charming the room with his presence.

Father stood, officially ending the Christmas Eve feast. "And with that, my dear ones, let us retire to the tree. Our Charlie would want it no other way."

Alfred helped Hannah and me to our feet. Extending an arm to each of us, he escorted us across the hall and into the conservatory. A golden halo wreathed the top of each candle I had so carefully clipped to the tree that afternoon. With the lamps turned down low and the fire burning merrily on the hearth, the room seemed almost magical. Betsy had been busy. I withdrew my hand from Alfred's elbow and settled on the divan beside Mother. She reached out a hand to squeeze mine, then buried it back in the folds of her skirt, her eyes staring straight ahead, her mouth set in a stern line. I recognized the look. I'd been practicing it all night myself as I strove to keep my emotions from overflowing the boundaries of decorum.

Unlike the excited chatter that usually accompanied our time around the tree, a solemn quietness filled the room. *Oh God, I can't do this. It's too hard. It hurts too much. Why did you have to take Charlie?* I contemplated the strained faces around the tree. *Look at us. Nobody knows what to say or what to do. Even Father looks as if he is having trouble containing his grief. It's simply too hard to bear. Remove from us this c...* I squeezed my eyes shut, overcome by shame. Was the cup of sorrow our Lord Himself bore not much greater than this?

Lean on me, beloved. The words, so lacking in condemnation, washed over my soul. I swallowed hard and took a shaky breath. *Remember that little toad, dear one? The bush it hopped into provided safety, but it was thorny and dense and tore deeply into the toad's delicate skin with every move the frightened creature made. It was the path that toad needed to take, but it took the dear little beast many days of suffering to recover.*

My brows knit and I opened my mouth to speak, but shut it again without uttering a word. Silly as it was, I cared about that little toad, perhaps because a part of me *was* that toad. *What happened to it?*

The toad made it to the other side, and in time, it recovered. And as it did, that little toad grew, beloved, until you would hardly guess it to be the same little creature you watched hop into that bush.

"And this pretty little package is for you, Dora." I jerked my head up at the sound of my name. Father bent to kiss my cheek and handed me a small velvet box wrapped in a scrap of white chiffon and tied with a red ribbon. "It is from your mother and me."

I fumbled with the wrapping, my fingers trembling. "Thank you, Father. Thank you, Mother." I infused my voice with what I deemed a suitable level of enthusiasm and smiled bravely. Firsts were always the hardest.

• • •

The creak of a floorboard. A soft knock at the door. A whisper of voices. "Dora? Are you awake?" Rising from my seat by the fire, I shuffled across my chamber and opened the door only to find my nocturnal guests had already turned to leave.

"Mother? Father? Is everything well?" They spun as one. There was something odd in the way they approached, though I couldn't identify exactly what it was. Guilt? Uncertainty? Trepidation? Father shifted a clumsily wrapped package from one arm to the other and cleared his throat.

"There is no need to be alarmed, dear." He glanced at Mother. "We have another gift for you."

"We thought you might wish to open this one in the privacy of your own chamber, though," Mother added.

My eyes flickered to the package Father offered me. The brown wrapping was coarsely folded and bound by a piece of twine tied in a lopsided bow. "It's from Charlie." Even as Father said the words, my eyes welled. I took the parcel in my hands and hugged it to my chest, caressing it as if it were Charlie himself. "He worked long and hard on this project; he wanted it to be special." Father's words resonated deep within me. "He began it the day after Matthew gave you his betrothal spoon. He wanted you to have a special place to keep it."

So like Charlie, always so thoughtful and giving and kind.

"He finished it the day before the accident."

Father's voice broke and Mother took over. "He knew that if he didn't finish it before heading off to school, it wouldn't be finished for Christmas, so he worked night and day to get it done. I had never seen him work so hard on anything as he did on that gift."

My fingers itched to pull the string and tear away the crumpled paper, revealing the treasure within, but somehow I couldn't bring myself to do it. Charlie's hands had touched this paper. His fingers had tied the bow. As irrational as it was, as soon as I undid that package, I would lose a part of Charlie that could never be recovered.

"Goodnight, dear." Mother leaned in to press a kiss to my cheek while Father gathered me into his arms. "Don't stay up too late."

• • •

The fire had long died, yet still I sat, Charlie's unopened gift cradled on my lap. The distant chime of the hall clock heralded the passing of another hour and I shivered. I couldn't sit here forever. Charlie would be appalled at my unwillingness to open his gift. I could hear him even now: *Come on, Dora, open it! Who cares about the wrapping? It's what's inside that matters. Open it!*

My fingers trembled as I grasped the twine and pulled. Charlie was right; a gift left unopened was a blessing unreceived and an unconscionable affront to the heart of the giver. My fingers stilled as the paper fell away. Somewhere in that was a lesson. My attention shifted to the smooth maple box resting on my knees. I moved it closer to the lamp and turned up the flame to examine the intricate carving that framed the lid.

Obviously Mother wasn't the only artist in the family. I had known that Charlie was a skilled woodworker, but this? The flowering vine he had carved around the perimeter of the box was exquisite, its detail so vivid it seemed almost lifelike. I ran a finger lightly along its ridges, admiring the handiwork. I could only imagine the amount of time he had invested to get it just so. A fleeting image of Charlie arriving at the table one day sporting a hand dotted with plasters came to mind. I had wondered at the time how our Charlie, always prepared to capitalize upon even the smallest of stories, had remained so uncharacteristically vague on what had happened. "Oh, I got a few scratches, that's all." He had shrugged and gone back to eating as if he hadn't seen food in a month. *A few scratches. Oh, Charlie.*

I fumbled with the clasp and lifted the lid. The inside of the box was lined with deep blue velvet, the colour of the sky at twilight. Soft, fine, luxurious. Wherever did Charlie find such beautiful fabric? I fished out the little card nestled in the corner of the box. *To My Favourite Sister.* I chuckled at the long-standing joke. Good old Charlie. *I made this for you because every lady should have a special place to keep her treasures. I hope that you like it.* I pressed my handkerchief to my eyes and drew in a steadying breath. *You are the best elder sister I could ever have asked for. Merry Christmas. With love from your favourite younger brother.*

My eyes wandered to the pen and ink drawing that decorated the corner of the card. A bushy-tailed squirrel sat on a ragged stump near the edge of a garden, surveying his kingdom as he gnawed on a stray nut. It looked so real, I almost thought I saw its tail twitch. Yet, it was the tiny toad peeking from between the clumps of grass growing at the base of the stump that transfixed me. Barely big enough to be seen, its eyes seemed to peer straight into my soul. I blinked, examining the picture more closely, careful to keep my tears from blurring the ink. Wherever would Charlie have found a card like this? It was as if he had known, but he couldn't have. Could he? I turned the card over in my hands, rubbing it gently between my fingers. This had been one of the last things my brother's hands had touched.

"Thank you, Charlie," I whispered, pressing the little card to my bosom. "I will treasure it always." I set the card into the box, reverently adding Mattie's spoon and the locket my grandmother had given me for my birthday. *Blessed Christmas, little brother. I miss you.* Arranging the beautifully carved box on the bureau, I crawled into bed exhausted, moments before the clock struck three. The last thing I saw as I dropped off to sleep was the image of a woodland scene like the picture on Charlie's card. The toad had emerged from its hiding place and hopped timidly toward the garden. Peace descended upon me as I watched the little toad and my eyes slid shut. *God sees the little sparrow fall...* The words of the beloved hymn floated through my mind and I sighed. *He sees the little hoppy toad, too.*

Chapter 23

MAY 14, 1880

My Dear Mr. Wellman,

I hope this letter finds you well. It seems as if a lifetime has passed since I saw you last. How are you doing, dear Mattie? Are you adjusting any better to the increased altitude? I can only imagine the challenges of living in a land where the air is too thin to properly fill the lungs.

The days creep by slowly here. Alfred left for Nice last week to continue his studies under Dr. Charles West, founder of the Great Ormand Street Children's Hospital in London. It seems there is also a second doctor—Dr. Breuer, I believe—who is developing some interesting theories on women's health that Alfred wishes to investigate. It all sounds rather foreign to me, I am afraid, but Alfred is the doctor, so I suppose he knows best. As for Johnny, the seminary, as you can imagine, claims most of his time. He has not darkened the door of Ebor House since the day after Christmas and I expect we will not see him again for some time yet. The daily routine, though still awkward at times, has returned, and I find myself rather at loose ends. Father has immersed himself in his work and Mother in the running of the household. She has redoubled her efforts to visit the poorer folk of the parish and minister to them however she may, and has taken charge of the ladies' sewing circle at church. She has dubbed it the Marthas and has been very creative in finding ways in which they can minister. New ladies are being added to their number every week, it seems.

I was so sure when Charlie died that I had finally found my calling in ministering to my family and holding in trust for them the strength and security of our Lord, but now I am not so sure. They do not need me anymore, Mattie. Life has resumed, and I no longer know what it is that God has called me to do. Oddly enough, Charlie's friends have begun to seek me out at church lately, as if I were in some way a big sister to them all. Canon O'Conner, having noted their interest, asked me to fill in for Mrs. Barrett when she fell ill a few weeks ago, so I have been teaching their Sunday school class for nigh unto a month. Perhaps that explains their growing attachment. Yet still, I confess I am a little confused by the deep connection I feel to these young men. I had a fleeting thought that perhaps God was calling me to minister to them in Charlie's stead, but it cannot be, can it, Mattie? The very idea of a young woman deigning to shepherd a group of young men scarcely two to three years her junior is tantamount to blasphemy, yet somehow it feels so right.

My ruminations are all rather moot, though, I suppose. Michaelmas Term will be upon us in three short months and I shall be headed off to school again. Besides, Mrs. Barrett is expected to return to her post next week. I only wish that God would make clear to me what He is calling me to do. It is as if I were playing a game of hide and seek. Forever It, I blunder from place to place, ever seeking, yet never finding. Like the child who happens upon a patch of fools' gold, I believe I have found the treasure, only to realize it is but a mirage. Why will He not simply tell me, Mattie, like He told you? Why must I be left to flounder, knowing He has a purpose for my life yet never privy to what that purpose might be. Why, Mattie? I will do what He asks, but I cannot read His mind.

    I gasp as I read the words I have just penned, appalled by my brazenness. It is a wonder God does not squish me like a gnat. I am far too demanding and impatient for my own good. I know that He will reveal His will when the time is right, but waiting is so very difficult. Pray for me, Mattie, that I shall be able to wait patiently and recognize His call when it comes.

    I pray for you often, my love. We do not get much word of the war Chile wages against Bolivia and Peru around here, but your safety in the midst of it is never far from my mind. Keep well, my love.

Affectionately,
Your Dora-girl

Chapter 24

BISHOP STRACHAN SCHOOL FOR GIRLS
OCTOBER 29, 1880

"Miss Farncomb." A hand squeezed my shoulder and I raised my head, alarmed to find myself the sole student in the classroom. "Miss Forsythe!" Snapping my book shut, I exploded to my feet.

"There, there, Miss Farncomb. No need for alarm. Do sit. I wondered if I might have a word with you." Ever so slowly, I resumed my seat, folding my hands on the desk before me and coaxing my galloping heart to still its frantic pace.

"You seem to be enjoying Lord Tennyson's book of poems," she began, motioning to the book on the desk before me. I nodded, braving a surreptitious glance around the room. *Where did everybody go?* "You must have been contemplating an extraordinary passage. The dismissal bell rang almost ten minutes ago." Miss Forsythe pointed to the book. "What were you reading?"

I missed dismissal? I vaguely recalled hearing a bell, but couldn't quite place when. "I–it is a poem called *St. Agnes' Eve*. Have you ever read it?"

Now it was Miss Forsythe's turn to nod. "It is a beautiful poem." Her voice softened and a look of wistful longing crept across her face as she repeated the final lines: "The sabbaths of Eternity, One sabbath deep and wide— A light upon the shining sea— The Bridegroom with his bride..." Her words faded into silence. A moment passed before either of us dared to speak. "It certainly leaves one thinking, does it not?" Miss Forsythe gave a half laugh and swept a lock of hair behind her ear. Perhaps she was younger and more sensitive than I supposed. "Thinking *and* yearning."

"I think..." I struggled to put my thoughts into words, yet I couldn't keep them inside. "That is, when I read this poem, I think I understand why Mr. Wellman and I could not marry."

"Oh?" Miss Forsythe tilted her head. By now, the whole school had heard my tales of woe, though I had revealed them to no one.

"I... I am already betrothed to Another." Running a fingertip across the empty space at the base of my ring finger, I closed my eyes, steeling myself to continue. "I am betrothed to Him." I pointed a finger heavenward.

"To the Bridegroom." Miss Forsythe placed her hand over mine and squeezed. "It is a wonderful thing to be betrothed to the Creator of the universe, Dora—more wonderful than words can tell. It's a call unlike any other, but it is not an easy one. It can be a lonely path we tread, and yet…"

I looked up as her voice trailed off, astounded by the beauty lighting her countenance. "You mean, despite the fact that Mr. Wellman and I shall never wed, there is hope?" I couldn't suppress the grin playing at the corner of my lips.

"Oh yes, Dora." She returned my playful smile with a wink. "There most certainly is hope. Hope far greater than these earth-bound hearts of ours can yet conceive."

A bubble of joy—the first I had felt in a very long time—escaped my soul and chased its way into my heart. As if a great load had been lifted, I tipped my head back, drinking in air.

"So—is this the poem you have chosen to analyze?"

In the blink of an eye, the bubble popped. "Yes, ma'am." I swallowed hard, puzzled by the pressure building behind my eyes.

"Wonderful. It's one of my favourites. I shall be looking forward to reading your paper." With a final squeeze, she loosed my hand and straightened in her seat. "Which brings me to what I really wished to speak to you about this morning."

My stomach plummeted as the wall of professionalism between teacher and student fell back into place. What could Miss Forsythe possibly wish to speak to me about? I clasped my hands tightly on my lap, fighting the temptation to speak.

"It seems to me, Dora, that in spite of the tragedies which have befallen you—or perhaps because of them—God has given you a great gift."

"A gift?" I propped my elbow on the desk, anxious to hear more. "What kind of gift?"

"A gift for ministering to God's people through the written word." When I did not respond, she continued. "A gift for writing."

Words failed me. I fidgeted in my seat, trying to think of something to say.

"It is a magnificent gift, Dora. My heart is blessed whenever I read your work, and I often find myself challenged by your words."

I fingered the composition book before me. It was true that I enjoyed writing, but a gift? Was that not a little presumptuous?

"You have a way of expressing yourself in writing that few young ladies share, and I would like to see you develop that skill further." Miss Forsythe raised her eyebrows. "Now, as you know, Miss Grier is also quite a writer. If I could arrange a few private mentoring sessions with her, would you be interested? We must not let the gifts God has bestowed upon us for the good of His people go to waste."

I nodded slowly, still trying to process the idea that God had given me the gift of the written word. My writing was not particularly magical. It was ordinary writing, no different from everyone else's, but still…"

"Splendid!" Miss Forsythe clapped her hands and rose. "I shall speak to Miss Grier this afternoon and let you know when your first session will be."

Without waiting for a response, she strode from the room and disappeared down the corridor, leaving me to figure out what had just happened. Could this be the answer for which I had so long awaited? Could writing be the call God was impressing upon my heart? *If only Mattie was here. My dear, dear Mattie. It has been so long since I have heard from you. Holy Father, keep him safe in the midst of the war. Please, please keep him safe. I don't think I could bear it if something happened to him.*

Chapter 25

FEBRUARY 23, 1881

Dearest Miss Farncomb,

I hope this letter finds you well. Sadly, many moons will come and go before you actually hold it in your hands, but there is naught that I can do to change that. Postal service is notoriously sporadic in these parts, particularly since the Chilean army has headquartered itself in the only accessible port city in the region. Trips into Iquique are few and come with significant risk. Crossing the desert is, in itself, a difficult task; but the threat of attack makes it particularly daunting. Would that this war would end soon!

So how are you doing, Dora-girl? You will surely be well into your final term by the time this reaches you. If I could impress upon you but one thing, it would be: Do not be anxious about the call God has placed upon your life. It is His call and He will make it clear to you when He sees fit. Do not try to rush Him, beloved. Remember that He is ever at work, preparing us for the mission He calls us to. If I have learned anything over these months in Tarapacá, it is this. His timing is impeccable and His plans beyond any our finite minds could devise.

Be patient and wait on Him, beloved. Do not try to force His hand or figure it out on your own. Let Him be God. More often than not, His call comes to us in the ordinary happenstances of our daily lives. So, my Dora-girl, I implore you: Do the ordinary things He places before you each day in service to Him and respond to the needs He impresses upon your heart with loyalty and love. If He desires for you to do something extraordinary, trust Him to reveal it to you. He will, you know. I promise.

Well, beloved, time is short and I must close. My heart brims with the desire to be by your side, and it saddens me to know this cannot be. Despite a nasty bout with fever during the winter, I am well. The men of the village are finally beginning to accept me, and I am gradually learning the language. The need here is great and it is difficult for the people to trust a foreigner, but the love of Jesus prevails. It seems they all figured that I would be gone long ago!

Be sure to extend my greetings to your parents, Dora. You are never far from my thoughts and I pray for you every day. Study well and remember to cast all your cares upon Him for He alone will never fail you.

Love,
Mattie

For the hundredth time, I ran my finger across his name. *How did he get to be so wise?* Oceans might separate us in time and space, but nothing could separate our hearts. He always did know exactly what to say to strengthen my soul and bring reason to the madness. *Do the ordinary things He places before you each day.* It seemed so simple when he said it like that. *The ordinary things.*

I reached for the novel on my writing desk and thumbed through the pages. *The Seaboard Parish* by George MacDonald. The great Scottish bard had a way with words that few authors shared. There it was. "What God may hereafter require of you, you must not give yourself the least trouble about. Everything He gives you to do, you must do as well as ever you can, and that is the best possible preparation for what He may want you to do next. If people would but do what they have to do, they would always find themselves ready for what came next." *Mattie would love this!*

I drew my pen from the ink and pulled out a piece of paper.

April 29, 1881

My Dear Mr. Wellman...

Chapter 26

"The words you use are lovely, Dora, but they must not detract from the message you wish to convey." I bit my tongue, restraining the quick retort that sprang to my lips. Miss Grier, kind and dear as she was, could be as tenacious as a bull. Maybe more so. "A good writer never sacrifices clarity for the sake of beauty."

I scanned the page before me. Where had I gone wrong this time?

"Perhaps you should consider removing a sentence or two," she prodded. "In a multitude of words comes misunderstanding. Remember, unnecessary explanation demeans the reader and dulls his ability to understand." I nodded dutifully and turned my attention back to my work. "How be you do a little editing and we will look at it again next week."

I returned the pen to my desk and gathered my books. Had I realized how grueling these lessons would be, I might never have agreed to them. "Thank you, Miss Grier." I dipped my head in her direction and started for the door.

"Do not be discouraged, Dora." Her chair scraped against the hardwood floor as she pushed away from her desk. "You have been given a gift; the ability to use it well will come with maturity and practice. The honing process is rarely fun."

"Yes, ma'am." I dipped my head again and kept walking. *Maturity and practice.* Try as I might, I couldn't restrain the sigh of dismay that threatened to deflate my every hope. *I thought I already was using it well.*

Painfully aware of the self-pity that coloured my attitude, I squared my shoulders and lifted my head, ignoring the heaviness of my limbs as I strode toward the dormitory. At least most of the girls would be elsewhere, enjoying a few minutes of leisure before the call to dinner. *What am I missing, Jesus? Why does everything I do have to be so difficult?* I set my books on my desk and sank onto the bed, burying my face in my hands. *What a day.* Throwing myself backward, I rubbed my eyes, my mind drifting to the letter I had sent out in the morning post. I had read it so many times, I almost had it memorized.

My Dear Mr. Wellman,

It was with much relief that I received your last letter. It is too bad that the postal service between us is so interminably slow, what with the war and all. Would that the conflict be resolved soon. I hope this letter gets to you safely and without delay. I am pleased to hear that the people of the region have finally started to accept you. While your grasp of the language is, no doubt, rudimentary, the love and faithfulness that so define your character need no language to convey. That, above all else, will draw them to the Light.

    I have been thinking a lot about what you said in your last letter about God's call being in the ordinary things we do each day. It reminded me of something George MacDonald wrote in his book, The Seaboard Parish. If you have not read it, I am sure you would enjoy it. In it, the opening character reminds his daughter that she must not look to what God may call her to do in the future. Instead, she must do the things God places before her each day with all her heart, for they are the best preparation for all He has in store for her.

    And so I dedicate myself to being the hands and heart of God to all I meet each day and doing His will in every circumstance He places before me. I cannot help but feel as if there is something more to which I have been called, though. The very thought seems horribly presumptuous, and I have prayed earnestly that God would purge me of the pride that should beget such impertinence. Still, I cannot shake the certainty that there is more that He requires of *me—despite the fact that He seems none too willing to reveal what that might be. Miss Forsythe believes God may be calling me to write, but I remain unconvinced. I may enjoy writing, and she may see in me some talent, but my tutoring sessions with Miss Grier have been less than encouraging.*

Alas, such things are too lofty for me to figure out, so I shall leave them in the capable hands of our Father. "Do not worry about tomorrow," our Lord instructs us. He will place before me the doors He wishes for me to open. Is that not what you would say were you here, Mattie dear?

"There you are, Dora! I've been looking all over for you." Emily poked her head around the door and drew in her chin, her look demanding an explanation.

"I just returned from my writing session with Miss Grier." I paused, knowing my response was insufficient, yet not knowing what else to say. "I needed some time alone," I added quickly.

Emily sailed across the room and sat on the edge of the bed next to mine, her knees almost touching my own. "Those sessions are not turning out to be all that you had hoped, are they?"

I shrugged dully. "It's just that—"

"Just that what?"

"Oh, I don't know…" I flopped onto the bed and stared at the cracked plaster on the ceiling. "It seems that, no matter how hard I try, I cannot satisfy Miss Grier. It is as if her definition of good writing and my definition of good writing cannot possibly be reconciled." I pushed myself up onto my elbows. Emily frowned and scooted closer to the edge of the bed. "Much as it pains me to say, Emily, Miss Forsythe was wrong. I don't have what it takes to be a writer."

"Oh, but you do!" Emily cried. "Your talent for writing is obvious to everyone."

"Not to Miss Grier."

"Are you certain? Miss Grier loves each one of us and has always dedicated herself to getting the very best from her students. She wouldn't push you so hard if she didn't think you had it in you." A fire lit Emily's eyes as she stood and pulled me abruptly to my feet. "She just doesn't want to praise you too much lest pride take root in your heart. You know how she is when it comes to things like that."

The supper bell rang, relieving me of the need to respond. If only Emily's assessment was correct.

Chapter 27

JUNE 25, 1881

The chapel felt crowded, though there could scarcely have been seventy souls filling the pews behind me. Fidgeting with the lace on the edge of my handkerchief, I fought the urge to turn around. Why I should be so on edge escaped me. It wasn't as if I was getting one of the awards. Smoothing my dress across my knees, I picked at a little ball of fluff clinging to the heavy fabric. The sooner this service was over…

I grasped the pew beneath me, intensely aware of Father's eyes boring into the back of my head. If only I could rush to his side and feel his arms close around me. Suppressing a sigh, I ran my toe along the edge of the kneeling bench. I would simply have to wait until the prize giving ceremony was over. Besides, I knew the pride I would see glistening in his eyes would only serve to stir my own emotions. While I had known that Mother and Father would be attending my final end of year ceremony, I had been surprised to see Johnny by their side when I entered with my class. Him *and* Cousin Hannah. The significance of her attendance needled my curiosity. Alfred had obviously been sweet on her for years, but the fact that she would come to my awards ceremony in Alfred's place signaled a definite new step in their relationship. Could it be that they were contemplating marriage? Charlie would have had a heyday with that one.

My smile faded as quickly as it had come. The only one missing on this day was Charlie—and Mattie, of course. I swallowed the lump in my throat and opened my prayer book to the Prayer of Saint Chrysostom then slammed it shut before reaching the end. What had I been thinking? A hand lit on my own and I realized I was trembling. At least I was among friends.

"Good afternoon, ladies and gentlemen." Emily withdrew her hand and I straightened in my seat, grateful for the interruption. Miss Grier stood on the steps to the chancel, her arms extended in welcome. "It is my pleasure this afternoon to welcome each of you to our 1881 Prize Giving. Our girls have worked hard this year, and I know I speak for them in saying it is a delight to share this special time with you, their family and friends. I cannot tell you how proud I am of our young ladies."

An errant ray of afternoon sun found its way through the stained glass window behind her, sending a shaft of warm, red light across the altar. *Focus,*

Dora, I chided myself, yet no matter how hard I endeavoured to corral my thoughts, I was unable. My school days were over; the next step in the great journey of life lay before me and I still didn't have any idea of what the illusive mission was to which Mattie claimed I had been called. *What next, Jesus? Will you ever see fit to reveal it to me?*

An elbow nudged my ribs, snatching me from my wandering thoughts, and I peered at Emily. "Go!" she whispered, jerking her head toward the pulpit. I glanced at the front of the church then back to Emily, my breath catching in my throat. Her teeth were set in an odd kind of smile, her eyebrows raised as if willing me to understand. "Go!" she mouthed once more. "Now!"

Miss Grier's voice penetrated my senses and I rose, as if in a dream, to make my way to the front. "Miss Farncomb is a young woman who has forged her way through great personal tragedy to get to this place today. Her grace and faith in the face of tribulation has won her the favour of all. She truly takes delight in our Lord and seeks in all her ways to serve and honour Him. It is for her devotion to Him, as well as her knowledge and understanding of the Holy Scriptures, that she has been chosen as the recipient of this year's First Religious Subjects Prize. Her knowledge of, and memory for, the Scriptures surpasses that of most young men and women in our churches today, and her determination to follow in the ways of our Lord would put many of us to shame."

My cheeks burned as I took the final step to the base of the pulpit, my eyes firmly glued to the floor in front of my feet. "It is, therefore, with great pleasure that I present Miss Dorathea Farncomb, recipient of the First Religious Subjects Prize of 1881." Miss Grier descended the steps from the pulpit and shook my hand as she handed me a lovely leather-bound prayer book engraved with a large golden cross.

"Th-thank you, Miss Grier." I lifted my eyes to meet hers and tried to return her smile.

"Do you know what your name means, Dora?" She inclined her head close to mine as she turned me toward the congregation, her whisper brushing against my ear like a gentle breeze. "It means *gift from God*, and that is exactly what you have been to me. With all my heart, I thank you for being such a blessing to this old heart of mine."

Speechless, I gazed into her eyes, amazed to find them as glassy as my own. As the clapping subsided, I slipped down the aisle to my seat, my legs as wobbly as willow wands in spring. My head swam as I neared my seat. *Only a few more steps.* I reached out a hand to steady myself and a familiar hand grasped mine, pulling me into the pew. *What just happened?* Emily squeezed my hand as Bishop Sweatman began to read from *The Book of Common Prayer* and I bowed my head.

"Dearly beloved brethren, the Scripture moveth us in sundry places to acknowledge and confess our manifold sins and wickedness..."

My breathing slowed as the familiar cadences washed over me and my heart's fevered gallop gradually ceased. Fingers tingling, I leafed through the gilt-edged pages of my new prayer book, trying to locate the Evensong service. Never in my life had I held such a beautiful book in my hands. I forced myself to attend to Bishop Sweatman's every word as I scrambled to my feet for the Magnificat. "My soul doth magnify the Lord and my spirit hath rejoiced in God my Saviour. For he hath regarded the lowliness of his hand-maiden. For behold, from henceforth all generations shall call me blessed. For he that is mighty hath magnified me and holy is His Name..." My voice trailed off as the rest of the congregants sang on.

For He that is mighty hath magnified me. I lifted my eyes heavenward, my soul a-flutter. Though I had sung those words countless times over my eighteen-year sojourn, never had they quickened my senses as they did today. I marvelled at the glory of those eight simple words and the comfort Mary must have taken from them—the comfort I myself felt, for He that is holy had magnified me also. *Holy, holy, holy is Your name,* my heart breathed. *The whole earth is full of Your glory!*

As if a great burden had been lifted, I straightened, knowing I deserved not the honour bestowed upon me, yet keenly feeling the divine hand of blessing from which it came hovering over me. *Oh God.* I fell to my knees and let the tears flow. *You know the turmoil of my heart—not to mention the willfulness of my spirit—yet still You choose to honour me. Why, Jesus? Why? I feel like such a hypocrite.*

Do you suppose that Mary felt any differently?

Now there was a thought I had never considered. *Mary. The mother of our Lord.* Of course, she was different—or was she? Was she not every bit as human as I? Could it be that she, too, felt unworthy? She must have. How else would she have felt? Yet, could she truly have felt as unworthy as...

"The grace of our Lord Jesus Christ, and the love of God, and the fellowship of the Holy Ghost, be with us all evermore. Amen." The murmuring of the congregation penetrated my mind as the words of the final blessing echoed through the nave. Rising with my classmates, I gathered my prayer books and filed out of the chapel. The reverent calm that had enfolded us throughout the ceremony disappeared as soon as we hit the receiving room across the hall where excited voices exploded around me, jarring me from my contemplations. Before

I knew it, an ever-changing knot of well-wishers—most of whom I knew little, if at all—congregated around me, congratulating me on my accomplishments.

"How nice it is to meet you, dear. My darling Katie is mighty blessed to be able to call you her friend."

"'Twas a glowing tribute Miss Grier awarded you, Miss Farncomb. My young Lettie could learn a thing or two from you, I daresay."

Well trained in the art of cordiality, I smiled and nodded politely, though my heart cringed, repulsed by the shallow assumptions of my admirers. They didn't know me; they had no idea. They had heard Miss Grier's words of praise and imagined me to be some sort of super-saint who could do no wrong. If only they knew.

"Miss Farncomb!"

Another one. I turned a sunny smile on the portly woman hurtling toward me. "What a delight it is to finally meet you! Our Caroline has always spoken so glowingly of you, and now we know why." She clasped her hands against her chest and looked pointedly at the man beside her.

"Good evening, Miss Farncomb." His voice was calm, quiet, cultured. Like Father's. Inclining his head toward me, he enveloped my hand in his. "Perhaps you could come and visit Caroline for a week or two sometime in the summer. I am certain she would be thrilled to spend time with you outside of school."

"I shall have to see how things go, Mr. Phillips." I dipped my head in assent, my mind churning for a diplomatic response. "I do not yet know where God's hand will lead." Caroline and I weren't friends. Not really. Acquaintances, yes, but friends? I glanced toward the door as Caroline's parents headed toward the refreshment table, relieved to see Father pressing his way through the crowd. Perhaps he would rescue me from the congregation of admirers I seemed to have attracted. As soon as our eyes met, my irritation abated. Hitching my skirt in a most unladylike fashion, I hurried toward him, excusing myself as I made my way across the room. Did a girl ever outgrow her need for her daddy?

Never.

I laughed aloud at the cherished reminder. *No, I could never outgrow my need for You either, could I?*

The cares of the day melted away as I fell into Father's embrace. "I am so proud of you," he whispered, his breath tickling my ear. He pulled back to look me in the eyes, and his bushy eyebrows twitched. Was he laughing at me? "You may not be the saintly creature Miss Grier made you out to be, my girl, but God does have His hand upon you. Of that, I am certain. Your mother and I couldn't be more proud. But don't tell *her* that I told you that," he added in a conspiratorial whisper. "She would be rightly horrified, lest you were to become vain." He drew his head back and winked.

"I shall endeavour to remain humble, Father." I put a hand on my hip and waved the other loftily in the air, affecting the haughtiest voice I could muster. "But it shall be difficult."

He nodded gravely, though his moustache danced, and I fell into his arms once more, hoping nobody noticed my giggle. "Difficult, or *impossible?*" he whispered, his voice rumbling with suppressed laughter.

"Fa-ther!" I pushed him away playfully, my mouth agape. I had forgotten how it used to be between us... before Charlie's passing forced us all to grow up. How I missed these moments of playful banter. It had been a long time.

"Ahem."

Ever so slowly, I turned, my head lowered in anticipation of Mother's disapproving glare. That she frowned upon such public displays of affection, I well knew; I didn't need to be reminded. "Mother, I was wondering where you had gotten to."

Her misty-eyed smile baffled me, but no more than her quiet whisper as she drew me into her warm embrace. "I'm so proud of you, Dora. So very proud."

I squeezed her shoulders, burying my face in the folds of her gown. Tears pricked the backs of my eyes, and I struggled to suppress the unexpected surge of emotion threatening to overwhelm me. She was proud of me. My mother. Proud of me. And she had actually told me so.

"I love you," I whispered. Our eyes met and I leaned in to kiss her cheek.

"God has a plan for you, beyond any this feeble mind of mine can conceive, dear." She glanced at my father and he nodded. "I am certain of it. I can't wait to see that plan unfold as you step beyond these walls. You are such a blessing to us."

A blessing. There was that word again. First from the mouth of Miss Grier, now from Mother. *A blessing? Is that what You have called me to be, Jesus?* "Thank you," I murmured, uncertain of what else to say. Perhaps that was the call God had placed upon my life, but if it was, I had no idea of how to accomplish such a task. They said that I had blessed them, but I certainly didn't know how. Would that I did. Had I not merely gone about my daily tasks, barely keeping myself going at times? If only they knew. That I should have been a blessing in the midst of my floundering could be by the grace of God alone. *How Mattie would laugh at the irony.*

Chapter 28

JULY 4, 1881

My Dear Mr. Wellman,

I have not heard from you in some time, so I trust all is well in Tarapacá. I have thought much about those thermal mud springs in Mamiña you so fetchingly described and wish I could visit them for myself, though I must admit, the idea of slathering mud all over myself holds little appeal. The restorative powers of those springs must be quite astounding for people to flock to them as they do. Is the experience truly as regenerative as they say? If it is, it is a wonder more people do not find their way to your little village.

All is well here at home. Though I confess a certain unrest regarding my future now that my school days have come to an end, I am endeavouring to entrust it to our Lord and rest in His plans for me. I have, therefore, returned to Ebor House to seek that calling of which we have spoken so much. At this year's Prize Giving ceremony, I found myself both overwhelmed and humbled by the undeserved praise of others, and yet I was touched.

Have you ever considered what it means to be a blessing to someone? Several very important people in my life declared to me that day that I have been a blessing to them. I suppose part of me understands, yet the idea of me being a blessing to anyone these past two or three years seems ludicrous to me. I have barely kept myself from drowning in the river of sorrows flooding my soul. However could I have been a blessing to others in the midst of such overwhelming grief? I am tempted to think their words trite, save that I know their hearts to be true. Is it possible that we can be labouring for our Lord apart from our conscious awareness? And if that be so, imagine the blessing we could be if only we applied ourselves more consciously to that quest.

Well, dear Mattie, the night grows dark and my lamp has begun to sputter. I must retire if I am to give my best to my boys at Sunday school come morning. The rector has asked me to take over the class from Mrs. Barrett now that I am home. It does my heart good to see the growth in these young men as they forge their way into manhood, though I still wonder if I am truly the one to guide them. Mother says that a big sister may be just the thing these boys need to become men. It could be she is right, though I confess I feel far from certain myself.

Whatever the case, God appears to have placed this ministry in my lap and given me a heart to embrace it, so I shall do precisely that. Tomorrow's lesson is on humility—an especially difficult topic for our young men of today, it seems. Alas, all the more reason for it to be addressed. It is something with which we all struggle, I fear. Would not the world be a better place if man would but welcome that one most godly attribute?

Well, I really must go. Be well, my dear Mattie. May God's hand rest upon you and grant you the power and strength to endure as you labour each day in His vineyard. Peace be with you, my love.

Affectionately,
Your Dora-girl

August 26, 1881

Dearest Miss Farncomb,

What great joy your letters bring me! My father tells me that you finished your schooling with great honour, receiving the First Religious Studies prize, no less. You did not tell me that, though you did allude to the fact that you were the recipient of much undue praise. Perhaps that praise was not as unwarranted as you led me to believe. I am so proud of you, Dora, and wish I could have been there to congratulate you in person.

What an exciting time this must be for you with so many opportunities opening up before you. I see so many ways that God might use you for His glory, though it seems to me that He has already given you a mission right where you are, in the lives of the young men He has called you to shepherd. My father tells me that the people of the village have even taken to calling them "Dora's Boys". Did you know that? Now that is a mission if I ever heard one! For the record, be it known that I, Matthew Wellman, am myself, the first of "Dora's Boys", unless, of course, you count Charlie. We must not forget him. It may, indeed, be that you have been engaged in this mission for longer than you might imagine. I shall be praying for you and your boys as you lead them in the way of our Lord. Do not be afraid, my love. God will equip you with all you need to accomplish His purposes.

As for the hot springs, would that I could share them with you. You would most certainly be surprised by their powers of rejuvenation. I, myself, was skeptical at first, but am no longer. Even some of the Peruvian soldiers have been known to visit now and again for a dip in the springs—not that they are exactly welcomed. The men charge them exorbitant fees to make use of the baths and render substandard service in return, but the veneer of civility has saved us from the bane of open hostility.

Each week, the number of folk attending services at the little church I have worked so hard to build seems to grow; there is a hunger here among the people that God alone can satisfy. I cannot help but acknowledge His great goodness in sending me here. Sadly, however, the opium industry grows daily at the expense of many hard working men whose lives—not to mention the lives of their families—are being destroyed by the ill effects of the drug they produce. So little is understood of such things in the more civilized nations from which the demand is greatest. It is my hope to begin talks with delegates from the Prime Minister's office, as well as from the office of the President of the United States, in an attempt to find ways to protect these people from the harm the burgeoning opiate market is incurring.

Other than that, there is little news from this end. I received word the other day that the archbishop is considering sending a new priest to the area to aid me in my work. If one can be spared, he will be stationed at Iquique, our nearest port city. It would be an ideal spot to establish a parish, although the city is currently being occupied by Peruvian troops. A co-worker would be a great encouragement and help to me, but we must wait to see what God ordains in the matter.

Alas, the dinner hour has come to an end and I hear the men returning to their work, so I must join them. I miss you, my Dora-girl, and pray God's blessings upon you as you shepherd those boys of yours. I do hope they realize how very blessed they are.

Love,
Mattie

Chapter 29

NEWCASTLE
OCTOBER 22, 1883

An icy breeze riffled through the trees, scattering a handful of brittle leaves across the lawn. With a shudder, I tightened my wrap around my shoulders and pulled the door closed behind me. Winter would be upon us before we knew it. Turning, I peered out the window at the cloudbank hovering over the millpond. *Oh, that autumn could simply melt into spring.* I fumbled with my wrap, loathe to surrender it to its hook, but a lone figure at the end of the driveway arrested me in my tracks. *Whoever could that be?* Shoulders stooped, a worn man plodded toward the house with the collar of his overcoat drawn up around his ears. *Father?*

I strained to see through the glass. *It couldn't be him.* Yet, to be certain, I rubbed my handkerchief against the grimy pane and looked again. I would have to speak to Betsy about her neglect. The weariness in the man's steps bothered me. Were it not for that—and the fact that it was mid-afternoon—I would have sworn it was Father. I glanced at the clock. Two o'clock. Father would not be home until half past six. Unless...

Throwing open the door, I leapt down the stairs two at a time. It *was* him. "Father?" I threw my arm around the man's shoulders and hurried him toward the house. "What happened? You look terrible."

His answering laugh, though no doubt meant to reassure me, ended in a rattling cough just as we crossed the threshold. Something was definitely wrong. Despite his protestations, I managed to manoeuver him into the conservatory—Mother's hurried footsteps close on our heels—before he collapsed.

"Frederick Farncomb, what is wrong with you?" she demanded. Alarm tinged her voice as I groped for something—anything—that I might say to make sense of Father's condition. After much urging, he finally slumped onto the divan and braced his head against its cushioned frame.

"Dora, have Betsy bring some blankets and warm water and send for the doctor—"

Father doubled over as another coughing spell wracked his body. He looked so helpless, like a bedraggled kitten abandoned by its mother. When at last his coughing subsided, he gasped for air and reached for mother's arm. "Ja-any,

Janey…" He coughed again, then waited for his breath to establish a more natural rhythm. "Do… calm down." Another deep breath. "I'm fine." He rested his head once more upon the back of the divan and closed his eyes. "It's naught but a touch of a cold." Another coughing fit brought his words to a sudden halt.

"Oh yes," she responded, her glare enough to freeze a cheetah in its tracks. "I understand. You trudge home in the middle of the afternoon—something you have never done in your life before—looking like death warmed over and hot as the coals on the hearth, with a cough that could wake the dead, but you are fine. Just fine. It's naught but a touch of a cold."

"Ja-ney…"

"Hush!" Mother scolded. "Dora, get the doctor and have Betsy boil the kettle and fetch an eiderdown or two." I glanced from Father to Mother and back, my mind reeling, my feet refusing to respond. "Dora!"

The sharpness of Mother's command propelled me forward. "Betsy…"

• • •

He's going to be all right. He's going to be all right. Almighty God, Eternal Father— Quiet murmuring arose on the other side of the door. *Breathe, Dora. Breathe.* I leaned against the doorframe, desperate to hear the quiet exchange, but to no avail. The whispered words trailed into silence before I could make them out. A deep, barking cough preceded a low moan and a few more whispered words. What was taking so long? I glanced at the heavy drapes covering the windows at the end of the hall. It had been dark for nigh unto two hours. Would the doctor never come out? *It's just a cold. An ordinary, everyday cold. Father said so himself. A day or two of bed rest and a few bowls of Anna's famous chicken soup and all will be well. It will be. It* has *to be.* My breath caught as the doorknob turned slowly to the left and I stumbled backward, my head spinning like a maple key caught on a breath of the wind. I reached out a hand to steady myself.

"Give him two drops of laudanum in a spoonful of tea every six hours to control the cough and apply a mustard plaster to his chest morning and night." The doctor closed the door quietly behind them and laid a reassuring hand upon Mother's shoulder. "Remember, bed rest is imperative, and go easy on the food. We need to do whatever we can to starve out that fever before it climbs any higher." Mother nodded, her face drawn as she led the doctor to the top of the stairs. "Your husband's life is in God's hands, Mrs. Farncomb," he assured her. "All we can do now is pray." He placed a restraining hand on her arm as she reached for the banister then tipped his head in my direction. "I think it best that

I see myself out. Call for me if his condition worsens." Their eyes met once more before she turned her attention my way.

"It's bad, isn't it?" I whispered. I pressed my lips together hard. Now would not be the time to submit to the dominion of unruly emotions. "He's going to die, isn't he?"

"We do not know that, Dora, and it would be foolish to fritter away our time in baseless assumptions. His prognosis is not good, but there is hope. People do recover from pneumonia."

Pneumonia? The word alone sent shivers up my spine.

"You heard what the doctor said, dear. All we can do is pray, so that is exactly what we shall do."

Chapter 30

OCTOBER 26, 1883

My Dear Mr. Wellman,

How are things in your part of the world? Things are not going particularly well here. Father has pneumonia. He swears it is nothing—naught but a touch of a cold—but his breathing becomes more laboured with each passing day and his fever shows no sign of abating, though we've done everything in our power to starve it out of him. Even Mother's meadowsweet tea does little to calm the fire that rages within his bones, and delirium frequents his dreams. Worse still, Alfred has cautioned us from afar to prepare for the worst. Pneumonia is a disease from which few recover, even in this age of unparalleled medical discovery.

A door opened and shut down the hall. Pen poised above the paper, I froze as footsteps sounded outside my door then retreated. Had Father taken a turn for the worst? An image of him tossing and turning on the bed, his sweat-dampened hair clinging to his brow, danced in my head. *Oh God...* I laid my pen across the letter and pushed myself away from the desk. *Don't let us lose him now. Please, please... do not let him succumb to this fearsome pestilence.* I gulped back the emotion welling in my breast and cinched my robe around my waist. I had to know.

The footsteps returned—rapid, though muted—each one reverberating through my soul, a dreaded harbinger of doom. Squelching a cry, I dove for the door and stumbled into the hall, barely in time to see the door to my parents' chamber swing shut.

With a strengthening breath, I stepped into the corridor. Light flickered from beneath the door of my parents' room as I tiptoed down the hall. I closed my eyes and exhaled slowly, the mingled scents of mustard and camphor knotting my gut. Pinching my lower lip between my teeth, I brushed a hand across my face and pressed my ear to the door. Ready or not, I had to know the cause of this sudden flurry of activity. I held my breath, straining to descry the whispered voices coming from within the chamber. Was that Mother singing? I stood motionless, concentrating on the warbled melody emanating from the other side of the door—thin, reedy, laden with emotion. "When peace like a river attendeth my soul; when sorrows like sea billows roll—"

No, God... please, please... I drew my fist to my mouth, choking back a sob as the waters of grief closed in around me. My ears roared, all but silencing my mother's quiet lament. *Not yet... Please not yet.* I gulped in air, my head spinning.

"I-it i-is well." A raspy tenor intruded upon my consciousness. I bent my head toward the door once again, straining to hear more.

"With my soul," came Mother's fragile voice.

"Wi-ith my-y soul." There it was again.

Father? I opened the door in one swift motion, flinging myself toward the bed. "You're ali-ali-al-l-l-ake! I-I mean... you're awake!"

"A-lake?" Father rasped. His eyes danced, despite his obvious weariness.

"Oh Dora..." Mother shook her head and patted my shoulder, her watery laugh saying more than her words ever could. "Though for many days we have feared the worst, it appears the Almighty has seen fit to spare him for us."

Father coughed weakly then cleared his throat. "Was I really that close to meeting my Maker?"

"Let us just say you are a-*lake* now, and leave it at that," Mother quipped. She angled her brow at him in mock rebuke.

"Oh, Janey..." He smiled and settled his head on the pillow. "I *am* glad. I know you would have been positively a-*sea* without me." Laughter descended upon us—warm, healing, heartening—until a fit of shuddering coughs reminded us of Father's precarious health.

"Come, Dora, it is time for us to go." Mother rose from her place on the side of the bed and motioned toward the door. "Your father may be a-*lake*, but he still needs his rest."

Giggling anew, I pressed my lips to Father's papery cheek and headed for my chamber. "Yes, Mother."

. . .

An ember popped in the grate. Could it really be morning already? Yawning, I snugged the counterpane around my ears and rolled over. Betsy bustled about the room, stoking the fire and drawing the heavy curtains as she did every morning, but this was no ordinary morning. *A-lake!* I smiled as the events of the night before paraded through my mind. Father's fever had finally broken; he would recover. My eyelids fluttered open and I rolled onto my back, the aroma of baking bread stirring me to wakefulness. *It must be later than it seems.* Folding my hands behind my head, I let my eyelids slide shut, relishing the unexpected reprieve. Breakfast could wait. *Jesus… thank You. I don't know what we would have done if You had taken him from us. I mean… I know that day will one day come, but… oh… just thank You. Thank You that day is not today.* I drew my arms beneath the counterpane once more and nestled into its warmth, revelling in the stillness of God's presence. So comforting, so real, so near. *Whatever my lot, Thou hast shown me the truth— It is well, it is well with my soul.*

Chapter 31

"Miss Dora. Miss Dora!" Awakening with a start, I flung the bed clothes aside and slid my feet into my slippers, jarred by the urgency in Betsy's whispered summons. Odd how one could go from utter peace to soul-numbing terror in the space of a heartbeat. The door cracked open before I made it across the room, and Betsy's head peeked in. "Betsy, what is it?" I rubbed my hands over the pebbled flesh of my upper arms. "Has Father taken a turn for the worst?"

"Goodness, no, Master Frederick is recovering well, Miss Dora. It's your mother."

"Mother?" Stepping backward, I fell against my writing desk, my lungs stubbornly refusing to fill.

"She wishes to know if you…" Betsy's face reddened and she averted her eyes, "… if you plan on staying in bed all day." She clasped her hands beseechingly. "She is going to the church to decorate for the harvest celebrations and hopes that you will see fit to join her."

Struggling to conceal my relief, I nodded. "Thank you, Betsy. Please tell her that I shall be down directly. It shan't take but a few moments for me to get ready." I lay my hand across my breast and sighed. Oh, the anguish I could save myself if only I would stop jumping to conclusions and simply trust.

Shedding my nightdress, I dashed my face with water and slid my best chemise over my head, wishing I hadn't been so quick to send Betsy away. I could have used a second set of hands to tie my corset laces and help me into that blasted petticoat.

•••

"My, my, ladies. What a marvellous job you are doing of decorating the church." I looked up from the arrangement of pumpkins and gourds I had clustered around the lectern to find the rector standing in the doorway to the vestry, surveying our work. "No one can decorate the church like the two of you. That young Mr. Wellman of yours always did say that you could turn a pigsty into a cathedral with naught but a handful of flowers."

My cheeks warmed at the mention of Mattie's name. What I wouldn't give to have him by my side. Swallowing hard, I turned my attention back to my work, hoping the rector wouldn't think me rude. We were, after all, here to beautify the church. My arrangement almost complete, I searched through the pile of unused produce beside me for the final touch that would bring it to life. Nothing. I shuffled to my feet and stepped back to get a better look. *Chinese Lanterns.* That was it. A smattering of their bright orange globes would do quite nicely, but to get them I would have to cross to the choir stalls beside the door to the vestry. I glanced around, looking for something I might use instead. Cornstalks, perhaps? They, too, were in the basket in front of the choir stall.

"You are most kind, Canon O'Conner," Mother responded. "We do our best."

I studied the floor, painfully aware of Mother's eyes boring into the back of my head. "Yes, Canon O'Conner…" My throat for some reason seemed incredibly dry. "It is our joy to serve." I swept toward the choir loft and secured a handful of Chinese lanterns then hurried back to complete the display.

The rector settled into his chair by the pulpit; it would seem that he planned to stay for a while. "The doctor tells me that Frederick's condition has improved markedly in the last few days."

"May God's name be praised," Mother breathed.

"I am so glad that he is doing better." The priest crossed his legs and propped his elbow on the edge of the chair. "It is such welcome news. Ol' Jenkins had a devil of a time figuring out when to ring the church bell last Sunday with Mr. Farncomb too ill to attend services." He chuckled appreciatively. "It seems that our janitor has taken to ringing the bell the moment he sees Frederick pass the Johnson house on Sundays." Mother shook her head, returning his smile as the rector continued. "It's a good thing your husband isn't sick more often."

"It is, indeed," Mother murmured.

Finished at the lectern, I busied myself tying yellow bows onto the ends of each pew. I yearned to ask Canon O'Conner if he had heard from Mattie lately, but thought better of it. Mother was sure to deem a query of that nature inappropriate. Yet, I couldn't help but wonder. Mattie's heart was forever entwined with mine, our souls hopelessly enmeshed. Though none but our Lord understood, we were a part of each other—wed in spirit, if not in law. Suddenly aware of a presence beside me, I stiffened, my fingers trembling as they sought to tighten the bow on the final pew. Did the rector know me so well that he could read my mind? Shuttering my thoughts, I dropped my hands to my sides. There would be no avoiding the topic now.

"Matthew misses you, too, Miss Farncomb." My eyes misted as I drew my chin to my chest. "He tells me that every time he writes." Shoulders trembling, I strove to hold back the tears. "He loves you very much."

By the time I had composed myself enough to look up, the rector was gone. Without a word, Mother gathered the empty baskets and carried them to the basement while I straightened the final bow and placed a handful of shiny apples on the table in the entrance way. *Mattie loves me, and Father will soon be well.* I took one last look around the church and breathed a silent prayer. Perhaps this would be our first truly happy Thanksgiving Day.

Chapter 32

NOVEMBER 15, 1883

"Welcome to Ebor House, gentlemen." Greeting the two young men at the door of the conservatory, I motioned them into the already crowded room. "Do find a seat and make yourselves comfortable."

"Thank you, Miss Farncomb," the tallest of the two intoned, the maturity of his response belying his fourteen years. The other boy smiled shyly and nodded his head as they passed, his eyes barely straying from the refreshment table by the window.

"Do help yourself to a glass of cider and a cookie or two before we begin," I said. Glancing around the room, I took inventory of the eager young men in attendance. Having donned their best manners, they sat in clusters around the fireplace, gulping hot cider and swapping stories. They were such fine young men—every one of them. A great guffaw erupted from the corner by the pianoforte, though it was quickly silenced. I would make gentlemen out of these boys yet.

"Good evening, Miss Farncomb."

At last. I smiled at the rumpled young man who appeared beside me. "Welcome, Byron. I'm so glad that you could join us." He, more than any other, reminded me of Charlie with his big, boyish grin and earnest eyes.

"I apologize for my tardiness, ma'am, but my ma needed me to run a few errands and… well… y'jist ain't say no to my ma, if y'know what I mean."

I nodded, hoping my amusement could not be seen in my eyes. The ire of Eliza Forbes was legendary. "Nor should you, Byron. I'm glad that you were able to make it." He looked pointedly at the refreshment table and I nodded again. "Help yourself."

"Hey, Byron," a tow-headed youth called, "what kept ya? Did y'ferget which way t'turn?" He elbowed the young man next to him as a gale of laughter swept through the room.

"Wouldn't you jist love that?" Byron shot back. A scowl darkened his face as he reached for a mug of cider. Someone had to put a stop to this nonsense before it got out of hand. He was, after all, his mother's son.

"That will be quite enough, gentlemen." My words, more clipped than I had intended, thundered through the room, bringing instant silence. "It's high time that we brought the first official meeting of St. George's young men's social club to order." Seeing that I had the undivided attention of all, I plunged forward. "Cecil, I hereby appoint you our scribe. The tow-headed boy blinked, his eyebrows almost disappearing into his hairline. "It will be your responsibility to keep a careful, written record of all we discuss." When he didn't move, I pointed to the side table next to his chair. "You will find everything you need to begin right on that table." He scrambled to pick up the hard-bound ledger and opened it to the front page, then raised his eyes beseechingly to mine. The poor boy. He knew how to read and write, that I knew, but he obviously had no idea of what to do next. "The first line should read 'November 16, 1883, Ebor House.'"

Dipping the pen into the ink, Cecil scratched it furiously across the page. "Got it."

I tried not to smile at the sense of triumph and relief mingled in his reply. "The next line should read as follows: 'Cecil Marek appointed secretary. Semicolon. Byron Forbes appointed treasurer.'"

"Treasurer?" Byron boomed.

"Order, gentlemen." The scratch of pen on paper filled the room. When it stopped, I continued. "Now the office of treasurer is very important. The treasurer's job is to collect the dues and take care of the purse, dispensing funds at the direction of the membership. You, Byron, are hereby appointed treasurer." My eyes shifted to include all fifteen boys. "See that your nickel is given to him before you leave this evening. There is a ledger on that table for you, also, Byron. The treasurer is responsible for keeping a complete and accurate record of all funds going into and out of the purse."

"Yes, Miss Farncomb." Byron stepped toward the table and picked up the remaining book. While his respect for me wouldn't allow him to defy the appointment, he couldn't quite hide his grimace as he reached for the second pot of ink and a pen. "Aw-right, men—who's first?"

I couldn't have been more proud of him had I been his own mother. "Ahem. Byron... I appreciate your eagerness to get started, but there are other things we must discuss. Let us attend to our agenda before collecting the dues." Byron nodded tersely and closed the book. He had spirit, that one.

"When our Lord Jesus Christ walked this earth, He told His followers that everyone would know that they were His disciples if they loved one another. In Matthew 22, verses 38 and 39, Jesus said that loving God is the 'first and greatest commandment and the second is like unto it.'"

"Thou shalt love thy neighbour as thyself." The reverent response of the boys spurred me on.

"We are the light of the world, gentlemen. It is up to us to be the hands and feet of our Lord in this world and in this community. How will our friends and neighbours understand God's love for them if we, His disciples, fail to show them that love both in word and in action?"

Byron's brows knit as he nodded thoughtfully, and Cecil's Adam's apple bobbed. At least two of my boys were taking this seriously. I glanced around the room, pleased to see others apparently contemplating what this could mean as well. Taking a deep breath, I plunged on. "That brings us to the purpose of our social club, gentlemen. It is the mission of this club to be the heart of Jesus to this community by serving each other in love."

"Serving each other in love?" Cecil repeated. His voice lacked its usual confidence.

"But how?" asked another.

"In *love*?" Cecil sputtered.

"In the love of our Lord," I affirmed. "Surely you boys know of people in our community who are in need. Perhaps they are lonely and need a friend, or maybe they are elderly or infirm and require assistance with daily chores. I'm certain you all know someone. To reach out to them in the name of Jesus is to serve them in love."

"Well..." All eyes turned to look at Mark Findlay. One of the younger boys, he spoke little, but when he did, the world stilled in anticipation. "There's Old Man Withers, if that's what you mean." The boys leaned forward, clearly eager for him to go on. "His wife passed away last year and his kids all went west to seek their fortunes, so since he fell and broke his leg a couple weeks ago, he's had a pretty hard time. He hasn't been able to return to work at the mill, and his place is a mess. He is, too." Mark stopped and shrugged.

"I would say that is exactly what I mean, Mark." I turned my attention to Cecil. "Let's keep a list in the minutes of people in need whom we can serve in the name of our Lord. Mr. Withers can be the first."

"But, Miss Farncomb..." Uncertainty edged Mark's voice. "Old Man Withers... well, he's a crotchety old codger, if you know what I mean."

Laughter rippled through the room. We all knew it to be true. "I have no doubt that he is, Mark," I responded, fighting to contain my amusement. "Most of us *are* in the face of hardship, but as Saint Paul reminds us, love is both patient and kind. Mr. Withers is a good man and he is going through a tough time. It is the mandate of our Lord to reach out to him in love."

"Yes, ma'am."

"After all, what reward is there for those who love only those who love them? Even the pagans do that. As followers of Jesus, we are called to love our enemies as well as our friends."

A noisy snort from Cecil elicited another bout of laughter. "Old Man Withers definitely qualifies as that!" He dropped the pen onto the side table and pushed the ledger aside. "Last time I saw him, he chased me down the sidewalk with a broom."

"A broom?" The boy beside him gave him a playful shove. "Were you stealing his walnuts again?"

"Would it matter if I was?"

"Ye-es." Byron rolled his eyes.

"Now who else should Cecil add to our list?" I picked up the ledger and perused the first page before handing it to the stony-faced scribe slouched on the divan, his arms crossed tightly across his chest. Somebody had to redirect this discussion before it descended into gossip. "Do you have a suggestion of someone we should include, Cecil?"

Scowling, he took the book and opened it. "No, Miss Farncomb, I do not, but I am certain that somebody else will."

Time flew as the boys offered their suggestions. Mr. Haines needed help repairing a fence and Mr. Thompson required an extra pair of strong arms at the general store while his partner recovered from a bout of rheumatism. Mrs. Sutherland was lonely and could use someone to sit with her on days when her daughter had to work late, and Miss Thurston would be thrilled to have a strapping young lad to chop wood and clear her walk. The list grew quickly.

I placed a hand on Cecil's shoulder. "Did you get all that, Cece?"

"Almost, Miss Farncomb." He dipped the pen into the ink once more and added a final word. "There. Got it."

"Wonderful." I stepped to the front of the room. "Let's set that discussion aside for the time being, then. We obviously have many needs in our community—needs that we can do something to alleviate. So how do you propose we proceed?"

"I could chop wood for Miss Thurston." Mark paused and shrugged. "I mean, I do enough of it at home, there's no reason why I can't chop a few more logs for her each day if you think that it will help."

"I'm sure that it would, Mark. Thank you."

"Well, I live right next door to her," another boy said. "I could take a few minutes to clear her walk when I do ours once the snow starts to fly."

"And I could help Mr. Thompson after school on Mondays and Wednesdays for a couple of hours—if it's okay with my da, that is. I'm sure he won't mind as long as I don't neglect my chores."

"Are you getting all this, Cece?" I glanced at the pen, still sitting on the table. "We will need to follow up on these offers at our next meeting. Love that shows itself merely in words is no love at all."

Cecil picked up the pen and dipped it into the ink. "Yes, Miss Farncomb."

When, at last, all the needs had been spoken for, Harvey Bains closed the meeting with prayer and the party began. While the boys produced games, Betsy replenished the dwindling food supply and I sat down at the pianoforte. The meeting had gone far more smoothly than I ever could have imagined. These were good boys—every one of them—with kind hearts and willing hands. Like Charlie. Would I never stop missing that boy?

A ruckus at the crokinole table drew my attention, and I turned to find Byron and Cecil standing nose-to-nose. Byron's hands clenched Cecil's shirt, drawing the bigger boy up onto his toes. Surely they wouldn't resort to fisticuffs here. I pondered whether to intervene, but thought better of it. They needed to learn how to handle situations like this on their own—like men—without the well-intentioned intervention of a meddling Sunday school teacher.

Obviously uncomfortable with the silence that had descended upon the room, Byron released his grip and shoved his opponent away. "Cheaters never prosper," he growled, his squint-eyed glare boring into Cecil. "Don't try that again."

A burst of activity filled the room with chatter as the boys resumed their games. Now would not be the time to be caught staring. I shifted on the bench and fingered the keys. My boys were growing up.

Chapter 33

APRIL 16, 1984

February 18, 1884

Dearest Miss Farncomb,

I have good news—at least, I think it is good news. I am still trying to make sense of it all. It seems that my time here in Tarapacá is coming to an end. With the war almost over, the archbishop has decided that my experience is required in a place closer to home—New York City, to be exact. Already, a replacement is on his way to continue the work I have begun in this wild and beautiful land. I am set to sail on the third day of April, provided the weather cooperates.

I glanced at the calendar. The third of April was nearly a fortnight past. *That would mean...* My heart fluttered as I snatched up the letter to read more.

Barring unforeseen difficulties, that should see me in port somewhere in late May or early June. How I wish that I could return to our dear little village for a visit before taking up my duties in my new parish, but the bishop is adamant that a furlough cannot be granted at this time. When I asked him when it might be considered, he refused to commit. It would seem that bishops are almost as impossible to pin down as a shipload of sailors! There are too many variables to accurately project timing, I suppose, but nevertheless, I find it terribly annoying. I had been looking forward to going home, if only for a time, and seeing you once more. Alas, God will provide us a way if we are ever to see each other again. It is difficult not to grow impatient, though.

So, how are you doing, Dora-girl? Has your father's health improved? How is that Sunday school class of yours going? The rector tells me that your boys have been very active in the community these past few months, abounding in every good work. He is impressed by the way this 'undisciplined brood of hooligans' has transformed before his eyes into a delegation of fine young gentlemen, eager to further God's kingdom on earth by serving their community. Your dedication to the mission God has entrusted to you shines in the lives of these young men, Dora. You are grooming the next generation of leaders by teaching them to serve and you are doing it well. It really is amazing to see how God equips us to do things we never could have imagined ourselves doing, is it not? May God continue to bless your ministry as you devote yourself to Him, my love. We serve a great and faithful God.

Love,
Mattie

My face warmed. Such high praise was unwarranted, perhaps even dangerous. It was true that my boys were turning into gentlemen, but to take credit for the work of the Holy Spirit within them was to blaspheme the One in whose service I laboured. He alone could turn them into men of the Kingdom. That He should see fit to use my efforts in the process inspired in me an awe no words could express. *Like King David, let them become men after Your own heart, O God.* I pressed a hand to my chest as image after image of my dear boys crowded my thoughts. *Draw their hearts to embrace the truth and love of our Saviour, Jesus Christ, and lead them in the way everlasting.*

Setting Mattie's letter aside, I fingered the orange cover of the latest *Advocate*. If only I had a few minutes to sit and read. I glanced at the clock on the mantel. I really ought to accompany Mother on her weekly visits to poor Mistress Forbes and the other dear souls she so faithfully supported. I breathed deeply. The aroma of baking bread filled the house as Anna worked to prepare baskets for delivery to each household.

Recalling our last visit to Mistress Forbes and the threadbare shawl she had worn to stave off the chill of her draughty abode, I retrieved the soft, woolen wrap I had stitched for Mother's birthday next month. Mother would understand. She didn't really need it and Mistress Forbes did. Besides, I could always make Mother another—if I could afford more of that lovely wool from which I knitted it. I raised the bulky bundle and rubbed it against my cheek. Perhaps one day I could even make one for myself. The thought made me smile. *'Twasn't likely.*

Grabbing the *Advocate*, I headed for the stairs. Father had indicated that he had seen a new column in the home portion of the weekly periodical which he thought might interest me. 'The Quiet Hour,' he had called it. Perhaps I would have a few minutes to check it out before Mother was ready to leave.

As I neared the bottom of the stairs, I spotted Betsy waxing the table in the dining room. "Betsy dear, please see that this wrap gets into the basket for Mistress Forbes. I shall be in the conservatory when Mother is ready to leave."

"Yes, Miss Dora." Betsy bobbed her head as she took the shawl and headed for the kitchen. How she and Anna would find room for it in the designated basket would remain to be seen, but it would not be fitting for it to look like a special gift.

A cozy fire blazed on the grate as I sank into the overstuffed chair nearest the hearth. Resting my head against the cushioned back, I closed my eyes, savouring the quietness of the moment. There were always so many things to do. So—many—things…

• • •

I opened my eyes but a few minutes later, or so it seemed to me. Yet the rainbows dancing on the wall puzzled me. I had only known rainbows to appear when the sun shone through the crystal droplets hanging from the lamp next to Mother's divan—the afternoon sun.

"Mother?" I rose quickly, surprised when *The Advocate* slid to the floor at my feet. I stooped to pick it up and laid it on the little table beside the chair.

"Miss Dora, you are awake."

"Yes—it seems it is a little later than I realized, Betsy. Has Mother left yet?"

"Goodness, yes. Mistress Jane left long ago. She has been home nigh unto an hour now. I understand that Mistress Forbes was quite touched by the thoughtful gift you included in her basket this week." Betsy smoothed the lacy coverlet draped across the back of the divan and straightened the cushions. "Your mother said the dear woman cried like a baby when she pulled it from the basket. Said she hasn't had a woolen wrap since she was but a child, poor wretch—though God Almighty knows she's had need of one."

"That is why He urged me to give her the shawl, I'm sure." I shuffled my toe on the floorboard, keenly aware that the gift had been meant for another. I still had to scrape up the funds to buy another skein of wool in time to make a new shawl for Mother. "It is no doubt a blessing that I wasn't there, lest her gratitude have been misplaced."

Betsy dipped her head and bent to empty the coal she carried into the bin. "I shall tell Mistress Jane that you have awakened."

"Thank you, Betsy." Returning to the haven of my chair, I scooped up *The Advocate* and began once more to leaf through its pages. *There it is.* I stopped at a page near the beginning of the Home section. "The Quiet hour," I read. Even the column's title encouraged the reader to stop and breathe. "By Augustus Hare, retired clergyman." *Sounds interesting.* Relaxing into the overstuffed chair, I lost myself in the article. *The road of life is not a turnpike road. It is a path which every one must find for himself, with the help of such directions as God has given us...* The godly wisdom and inspiration in this column was exactly what *The Advocate* had been missing. It took but a minute for me to devour the entire column. Short as it was, the Reverend Mr. Hare's article proved to be thought-provoking and sincere, but it was the note at its conclusion indicating that contributions were being welcomed that really caught my interest. I gazed out the window, my eyes coming to rest upon the swelling buds dotting the barren branches of the apple tree. *Maybe I should consider making a submission.* Miss Grier always told me that I had been gifted with the ability to write. Perhaps now was the time to see if she was right. *Is this a mission You wish for me to embrace, O Lord? I cannot deny the allure it holds for me, but is it a step that* You *wish for me to take?*

Silence. What was a person supposed to do with that? *I suppose I could make a submission and see what comes of it?*

An enthusiastic rap on the front door alerted me to the time. Father must be home, though why he should knock before entering perplexed me. I set the magazine upon the table once more and rose. *Who would come calling at this time of day?* Before I made it past the fireplace, an unexpected, though endearingly familiar voice, rang through the house. "Ho there! Anybody home?"

"Johnny?" I squealed, rushing toward the entryway. It had been months since I had seen my brother. *Whatever is he doing here unannounced?*

"Oh ho, so there *is* someone here after all," he boomed. "It's good to see you, little sister." Rounding the corner, Johnny swept me into an exuberant embrace, swinging me around like a little girl.

"You put me down right now," I scolded, mimicking Mother's sternest voice. I gave him the most searing glare I could manufacture, but nothing could stem the tide of giggles rising within me.

"And why should I do that, oh sister of mine?"

It felt so good to hear his voice, to feel his laughter rumble through my chest, to bury myself in his bear-like embrace. "Because I am a lady now, not a little girl." I huffed, affecting a sternness I didn't feel.

"Oh, you are, are you? Well then…" He set me on my feet and winked. He might as well have been Charlie!

"And Mother," he roared, rushing to embrace the woman who had appeared at the bottom of the stairs. "You're looking radiant, as usual."

"Did your father never teach you that flattery is the way of a fool?" Mother grinned, belying the reproach in her words. "For what occasion are we blessed with your presence?"

"Must there be a reason?"

"There always is." Mother and I glanced at each other in amused shock when we realized we had both spoken as one.

"Well then…" Johnny's eyes sparkled as he withdrew to the door and ushered a pretty redhead into the vestibule. "I would like to introduce you to Miss Jane Farncomb."

"Farncomb?" I clamped my jaw shut lest I be found gaping. *Jane Farncomb?* The only Jane Farncomb I knew was Mother. A blush crept over the young woman's features.

Aiming a disapproving look my way, Mother extended a hand to our guest. "Welcome, Miss Farncomb—Jane, you say?" The young lady nodded. "It is most lovely to meet you. You must be dear Thomas's daughter. I apologize for Dora's insufferable lapse in manners."

My face warmed. *Thomas? Uncle Thomas? From London?* I didn't know that he had children.

"Thank you, Auntie Jane. There is no need for apologies. My cousin is, no doubt, as astonished to learn she has cousins in London as I was to learn that I had cousins in Newcastle." The young woman inclined her head toward me and took a step closer. "Odd that Father never mentioned Uncle Frederick's family." She appeared to cast the thought away with the barest of shrugs and smiled, but the look on Mother's face troubled me. She obviously knew more than she was prepared to share.

Father almost never spoke of Uncle Thomas—or of any of his other siblings, come to think of it. That there were nine of them, I knew, all orphaned in their youth and left to fend for themselves. Their father's brother, the Lord Mayor of London, had taken an interest in them and dutifully seen to their welfare, even providing Father with his first job as he strove to hold the family together on his own. However, when Father married Mother and moved to the new world, they had lost touch with much of Father's family. His brother Thomas had accompanied them to the new land but had, for some unexplained reason, relocated not long thereafter and they, too, had lost touch. Seeing his daughter before me quickened my curiosity.

"Mother..." A stern glance from the older woman stilled my wagging tongue. I really did need to learn to exercise more self-control.

"Jane, darling..." Mother slid her arm around her new-found niece and guided her toward the parlour. "Do have a seat." When I moved to follow, Mother motioned me away with a tilt of her head. "Dora, dear, please arrange for Betsy to bring us some tea and perhaps you could whip up a plate of those award-winning butterscotch rolls of yours while you're about it. They are your father's favourite, you know."

"Yes, Mother." I lowered my chin submissively, though everything within me rebelled. It hadn't been a request; I had been dismissed—like a servant. Whatever she was about to tell Cousin Jane, she did not want me to hear. Johnny met my eyes, his brow furrowed with questions he, too, dared not voice.

"John—"

"Yes, Mother?" Was she going to send him away as well?

"Father has been rather busy lately and could use a hand with the wood. Anna's wood box has been empty for nigh unto two days now, and she and Betsy have more than enough to do without having to fetch the wood to fire the cook stove themselves. Would you be a darling and fill it for them, please?"

So, he was to be excluded as well. At least I wasn't the only one. "How did the two of you meet?" I whispered as we headed past the stairs to the kitchen.

He smiled ruefully. "She is beautiful, do you not think?"

"You didn't answer my question, dear brother."

He studied his feet, his words slowing. "Well, as you know, I was assigned the position of Assistant Curate at the Anglican church in the little village of St. Thomas some fifteen miles or so from London. One Sunday shortly after I arrived, two of my parishioners approached me with a lovely young lady in tow. They introduced her to me as their granddaughter, Miss Jane Farncomb, and marvelled over the unlikely fact that we should share such an unusual surname. I had to admit that it was definitely curious, but it is not as if we are the only Farncombs in this world."

Following him into the kitchen, I let the door swing shut behind me and instructed Betsy to prepare the tea.

"In the weeks that followed, I spent many hours at their home, getting to know our cousin, for we figured out the family connection almost immediately. It seems that as little as Father has spoken of Uncle Thomas over the years, Uncle Thomas had spoken of Father even less."

The kettle bubbled on the stove. Betsy poured the steaming water over the tea leaves while Anna arranged two china cups on a tray with a little jug of milk and a pot of sugar. I moved toward the sink and donned my favourite apron, anxious to start work on the rolls. The sooner they were made, the sooner I could join the conversation.

"Her time in St. Thomas passed far too quickly. Hence, when her grandparents suggested that I accompany them on their journey to London, I jumped at the opportunity. My first meeting with Uncle Thom was almost as awkward as Mother's first meeting with Jane, but by the time we left the next day, he had granted me permission to court his daughter. We're getting married, Dora. Married! Can you believe it?"

Johnny's eyes shone as he grabbed my hands and twirled me about the room. *Married. Our Johnny—imagine that.* And here I thought that Alfred would be the first to wed. *Or me.* I pushed the thought aside and threw my arms around his neck. "When is the big day?"

"As soon as it can be arranged. We shall celebrate the sacrament at Uncle Thom's church in London then will spend our wedding week here at Ebor House celebrating with friends and family from the village. After that, we shall head straight out to Stuartsville."

"Stuartsville?"

A boyish grin spread across his face. "Did I not tell you? I have been assigned my very first parish—a four pointer. As of August, I am the new rector of the Stuartsville parish. My induction will be held on July 20."

"Oh, Johnny…" I gave him an exuberant squeeze. "I'm so happy for you—and for Jane, too. So, so happy."

The kitchen door swung open, and Anna bustled in with Betsy close on her tail. "Your mother wishes to know how those rolls are coming along, Miss Dora." Betsy lowered her head apologetically.

"The rolls." Pushing my brother away, I grabbed a bowl from the pantry and plunked it onto the counter. "You'd better get that wood before Mother catches you, too, Johnny. It wouldn't be wise to risk her annoyance before delivering your news."

With a wink, he snagged the empty box by the stove and headed toward the door. "Mother annoyed at me? Never!" His merry laugh echoed in my ears long after the door had closed. He was becoming more and more like Charlie every day.

"Brothers," I muttered.

"What was that, Miss Dora?"

"Oh, nothing." I poured a cupful of milk into the bowl and squeezed the dough into a soft ball before dropping it onto the floured countertop. "I was only thinking about how dull my life would be without brothers."

A bell tinkled down the hall and Betsy jumped to respond while I spread a generous layer of brown sugar butter atop the flattened dough and rolled it into a log. Johnny entered with a boxful of wood and dumped it into the bin in the corner before heading out for more. *Curious that Mother didn't want us around while she spoke to Cousin Jane. What kind of skeleton was hidden in our family's closet?*

Chapter 34

The lamp gradually dimmed; had I really been writing that long? Replacing my pen in its holder, I hurried to cap the ink before the waning flame sputtered out completely. Why did inspiration always seem to wait until the middle of the night to reveal itself? I slid my toes out of my slippers and between the cold sheets, my mind enumerating the deluge of ideas I had failed to record. Eyes wide, I stared into the dark, rehearsing them so I wouldn't forget, but ended up toying with the idea of refilling the lamp instead. *It would be less troublesome than trying to remember all these ideas.* Teeth chattering, I ducked my head beneath the counterpane and squeezed my eyes shut. Perhaps I should try counting sheep. One, two, three... Now would that *not be a grand idea for an article—our tendency to count obedient little sheep that never stray from the flock as a means to induce sleep while our Good Shepherd busily counts His own as they wander wherever they please? Endowed with the precious gift of free will, Your sheep aren't nearly so cooperative as the ones I design to count each night, are they, Lord? Prone to wander... what an understatement. Are You not always on the chase? No wonder You neither slumber nor sleep.* I rolled onto my side and yawned. *Counting sheep must be the bane of every shepherd's labour... it certainly wasn't about to lull me to sleep.*

* * *

Light streamed across the room, illuminating a host of dancing dust motes. I squeezed my eyes shut and drew my hands up to shield myself from the sudden brilliance.

"Morning, Miss Dora. Did you sleep well?" Betsy laid a towel next to the basin on the dry sink. "You'd best be getting up before the church bells start to ring."

Groaning, I swung my legs over the side of the bed and felt for my slippers. Surely a whole night hadn't passed since I had finally succumbed to slumber. The mental list I had made as I drifted off to sleep began to surface and I rushed to my desk, eager to record it before the items on it were thrust from my mind by the obligations of the day.

"Miss Dora?"

"What is it, Betsy?" I paused, my hand in mid-air, and glanced her way.

"I wouldn't dream of telling you what to do, but ought you not to be getting ready for church?"

Smiling reassuringly, I turned my attention to the paper before me. "In a moment, Betsy. This won't take long."

With a final flourish, I set the pen down and capped the ink, wishing I could start writing immediately. Betsy's gentle admonition could not be ignored, though. I had to get ready, and fast. Father's heavy footsteps sounded on the staircase. I had about fifteen minutes. I splashed my face with water from the basin and patted it dry. If I hadn't been awake earlier, I certainly was now. Running a brush through my tangled hair, I quickly plaited it and surveyed the result in the mirror. Mother was right; I needed to adopt a more suitable hair style for my age. *Perhaps I should start wearing it in a bun like she wears hers.* I wound the braid into a tight ball at the nape of my neck and scowled. *Too severe.* Letting it drop down my back once more, I shrugged. It would do for today.

A gentle knock at the door reminded me of the hour. "Do come in, Betsy." I stepped out of my nightdress and slipped my corset over my head. "You're just in time."

Chapter 35

"Did you hear the good news, Dora?" The rector's eyes danced as he pumped my hand. "Our Matthew is coming home."

"Home?" I shifted uncomfortably. Mattie hadn't told *me* he was coming home.

"Well, closer *to* home, I suppose I should say." He tipped his head and gave me a lopsided grin. "Within visiting distance."

"New York City is still a long way from home, Canon O'Conner." *Would that it were closer.*

"Not when you compare it to Tarapacá." He winked before greeting the next parishioner. "Good morning, Mrs. James. And how are you today?"

"What was all that about, Dora?" Mother snagged my elbow and steered me out the door to where Father waited with Johnny and Jane. "Did I hear correctly that Matthew is home?"

"Oh—"

"Odd that he wasn't at church."

Words tangled on my tongue. All he needed was for rumours like that to get around. "No, Mother." I shook my head wearily. "Mattie is not home. He isn't even close to home." My shoulders sank as I blew out a long, slow breath. "The bishop has simply given him a new assignment."

"A new assignment?" Mother's eyebrows rose. "So soon?"

"It's been almost five years since he left, Mother. He's been relocated to New York City."

"New York City? Why that isn't so far from home, dear." She slipped her arm around my shoulders and gave me a reassuring squeeze. "The Grand Trunk Railway goes all the way to Maine these days. Why do you not plan a visit? Perhaps he could use another set of hands."

"And you and Father would send me there unattended to work hand-in-hand with the man to whom I was very nearly betrothed?"

The stunned look on Mother's face said it all. She tugged at her gloves as I climbed into the carriage and settled myself on the rear bench, awaiting her response. "Perhaps it is time your Father and I took a vacation."

Good recovery.

"The southern air would, after all, do your father good."

I welcomed the change in topic, not that New York City was appreciably south of us. "Is the doctor concerned about Father's lengthy convalescence?" Father's persistent cough and unwonted fatigue worried me. I watched him shuffle toward the carriage. He paused with one foot still on the ground as if summoning the strength to pull himself up, then hoisted himself into the driver's seat. Had it not been for his accompanying grunt, I might have convinced myself that his apparent weakness was naught but a product of my imagination, but the dark circles rimming his eyes when he turned to see that we were ready couldn't be ignored. It had been almost six months since his bout with pneumonia. While Alfred had assured Mother that these things took time—especially in one of Father's advanced age—my unease grew with each passing day. Part of me hoped that Father would be better by the time Alfred returned from his studies in England next month, but another part of me wanted Alfred to see him as he was now. Father had always bounced back so quickly when illness struck, though it was true he had never been in such dire straits as those he had traversed this fall. Besides, his strength *was* returning, slow though the process might be.

"I am certain your Father will approve."

Approve? Approve of what? "I apologize, Mother." I might as well confess before the conversation got out of hand. "My mind must have wandered. Of what are you certain Father will approve?" I folded my hands neatly upon my lap, chagrined by the knowing smile she shot my way.

"I shall speak to him immediately about planning a vacation in New York before the year is out. You and I could go ourselves if we only had a relative in the area, but alas, we do not and it would do your Father good to get away for a while."

I braced myself as the carriage turned into the drive. The thought of seeing Mattie again held great allure, but with it came a trepidation I could not explain. We had said our final goodbyes once; to do so again might rend both of our hearts beyond repair.

"We shall have to see what your Father says. It would be good for you and Mattie to see each other again." She raised a brow and grinned. "Perhaps now that he has moved closer to home, he will even ask you to marry him."

The carriage ground to a halt and Father appeared at the door, extending a hand to help us out. First Mother, then me. As soon as my feet touched the ground, I scurried up the porch steps and into the house, my cheeks blazing. The aroma of roasted fowl greeted me and my belly rumbled in response. Mother's plans could wait. I set my prayer book on the hall table and hung my shawl on the hook by the door, then headed for the dining room.

The door opened once more and Johnny's hearty voice boomed through the house. "Smells like Anna and Betsy have outdone themselves today."

"They surely have," I answered. He stepped into the room with Janey hanging on his arm. "I don't know about you, but I am most eager to sample their wares."

Betsy appeared at the entrance to the dining room, smoothing her apron. "Welcome home, Master John, Miss Dora." She nodded at Jane. "And you, also, Miss Farncomb. The mid-day meal is almost ready." She gestured toward the table. "If you will take your seats, we shall bring it out as soon as your parents arrive."

Father ushered Mother through the door just as the final words rolled from Betsy's lips. Lifting a finger to hush our response, he crept behind the oblivious young maid, his eyes dancing. "Thank you, Betsy." Like a startled kitten, Betsy leapt into the air, nearly falling into Father's arms. *Nothing like a good laugh to calm the galloping mind.*

Chapter 36

EBOR HOUSE
JULY 1884

"The clock is ticking, ladies. We're going to be late." Father stationed himself at the bottom of the stairs, his toe beating the thickly piled rug beneath his feet.

"Frederick, we are moving as quickly as we possibly can." Mother breezed into the vestibule, stopping before the hall mirror to pin a final strand of greying hair into place. "Patience, my dear. Young Jane shall be down momentarily. It isn't every day that we host a reception in celebration of our son's nuptials."

All the more reason to be on time," Father growled.

"We will be, Frederick." She patted him on the arm and swept toward the door. "Are you ready, Dora?"

"Yes, Mother." I switched my parasol to my left hand and rested my right on the doorknob. "Shall I take my place on the verandah to welcome our guests?"

"By all means." Father paced across the hall, his hands clasped behind his back, his teeth clenched in a tight smile.

"I shall see if I can hurry our new daughter-in-law along." Mother brushed past Father, barely making it to the first stair before Cousin Jane's dainty foot appeared on the upper step.

I glanced at the clock. *Five to two.* We still had time. Perhaps we wouldn't ruin Father's reputation after all.

• • •

The excited chatter of well-wishers had long begun to annoy me. "Yes, Mrs. Marley, Cousin Jane does make a beautiful bride—the most beautiful bride I have ever seen." I ground my teeth with each pronouncement, all the while schooling my features into submission. "Yes, Miss Weston, my brother is a most dashing groom. Thank you, Mrs. Francis. Jane did choose a lovely colour for her wedding gown."

The muscles in my cheeks ached from the effort to keep a smile upon my face. "No, Mr. Douglas, I doubt that I shall ever marry. That is not the profession to which I have been called." I glanced at the endless array of people shuffling around the parlour and stifled a groan. Everywhere I looked, couples milled about the room, their arms entwined as they made their way across the hall to the dance floor we had set up in the conservatory. Their quiet whispers taunted me; their tender smiles tore at my heart. "Why yes, Mr. Stevenson, it most certainly is a grand day for Johnny's wedding reception. A grand day, indeed." I dabbed my brow with my handkerchief, wishing I could sit down. "Of course, Mrs. Stevenson, I'm sure they will be blessed with many, many children."

A familiar hand slid into mine as I prattled on, and I swallowed hard. Mother knew me far too well. With a sheepish grin, I squeezed her fingers and gave a little laugh.

"You are a good sister, Dora," she whispered. "You do your brother proud."

• • •

July 24, 1884

My Dear Mr. Wellman,

How quickly time flies when busyness rules. Johnny and his bride moved into the rectory in Stuartsville less than a week after their reception at Ebor House. The parish was most grateful for their arrival, having been without a priest for almost a month. We are looking forward to attending his first service at his new church this Sunday. Meanwhile, Father labours night and day to direct the completion of Alfred's home and office before my brother's homecoming in August while Mother and her sister—my dear Aunt Mary—scheme and dream as they plan Cousin Hannah's upcoming marriage to Alfred. Nothing but the best will do, it seems. After all, Alfred is to be the esteemed village doctor. Long ago, old Doc Phelps vowed that the day Alfred returned from his studies overseas would be the day he retired his shingle for good, and as you well know, our good doctor never makes promises he cannot keep. "It is time for me to pass the torch, my friends," he is oft quoted as saying. "Young Alfred is a fine doctor and will keep us all hale and hearty for many years to come." My, but my brother has big boots to fill!

I tucked my pen into its holder and set the letter aside. While I would rather sit and write, Mother and Aunt Mary were no doubt waiting for me. Their catalogue of preparations for the big day was surpassed only by the list of errands they had set aside for me to complete, or so it seemed to me.

Chapter 37

The day of Alfred's arrival brought the worst storm of the season. White-capped waves swamped the pier as driving rain lashed the few of us determined enough to brave the elements in hopes of greeting the great ship at the harbour. A jagged streak of light rent the sky directly in front of us, and an odd tingling trembled through me. *Perhaps we ought to take shelter.* I clapped my hands to my ears at the sharp crack that followed. The storm was close. *Too close.* "Mother, come!" I shouted above the melee. Grabbing her arm, I pushed her toward the safety of the custom's warehouse, hoping Father would still be in his office. Unless the storm abated, there would be no ship today.

As soon as we stepped through the door, I fell against the wall, panting. "That has to be the worst storm I've ever seen!" I drew a hand to my chest. "It was right on top of our—"

"Dora? Janey?"

"Father!" I rushed into Father's arms with Mother but a step behind.

"Whatever were the two of you doing out in *that*?" He enveloped us both in a welcome embrace and steered us toward the fireplace in the corner. "I told you that I would see Alfred home as soon as his ship weighed anchor. Come and sit by the fire before you catch your death of pneumonia." He reached for our wraps and slung them over his arm. "I'll hang these by the door to dry."

"Has there been any word on Alfred's ship?" Mother asked.

"Not yet, but I imagine its arrival will be delayed." Father ran a hand through his hair. *When had it gotten so grey?* "No seasoned seaman would captain his ship through a storm like this just to make it to harbour on time." He set a chair by the hearth and went to fetch another. "How be the two of you sit here a spell and warm yourselves while I see what I can find out."

An hour passed before the wire came through announcing that the ship would be delayed. "It may come in tomorrow, but it is likely to be another day yet," Father stated as he studied the telegram. Mother's face fell, and he slipped his arm around her shoulders. "Come now, Janey." He bent a coaxing smile her way. "I know it is disappointing, but at least we know he is safely in port and not out on the open water in the midst of this storm."

Mother nodded and straightened, easing out of his embrace. "Then we shall return to the house and see to our daily chores." She rose and peered out the window at the sheeting rain then lifted her sodden wrap from the hook by the door. "Come, Dora. I suppose you shall be staying here, Frederick?"

"Yes." Father surveyed the stack of ledgers and stray papers littering his desk. "There may not be any ships to process, but there is never a dearth of paperwork to catch up on."

"We shall see you for supper, then." Mother held the door firmly as she eased it open lest the wind whip it from her hands. "And do stay out of the rain, Frederick. We wouldn't want you to fall ill again."

"Yes, Mother." He winked at me as he leaned in to brush his lips across her forehead. "Whatever you say, dearest. Whatever you say."

• • •

August 21, 1884

My Dear Mr. Wellman,

Alfred finally arrived home today after a four day delay due to a nasty storm. You should see the mess of downed trees and broken shingles we shall have to clean up in its wake. We even lost one of the shutters from the window at the end of the upstairs hall. Alfred made it home safely, though, and that is all that truly matters. It was so good to finally see him again.

I never did ask you how your voyage went. I trust it was less eventful than Alfred's. Canon O'Conner tells me that you are quickly settling into your new parish and starting to get to know your parishioners. Is it truly as impoverished an area as he makes it out to be? By the way he speaks, the people of Tarapacá are positively rich in comparison. It must be quite different from what you expected to find in that grand city.

Mother and Father speak of the possibility of us coming to visit sometime in early autumn, although whether or not that will actually occur remains to be seen. Mother says it will be good for Father to get away—which is no doubt true—but I fear she has ulterior motives in suggesting we holiday in New York. Even so, I must admit that it would be wonderful to see you again. I think of you every day and never fail to include you and the people you shepherd in my prayers.

Things continue to go well here. As I told you before, Johnny's wedding celebration was a grand success and Cousin Jane made a beautiful bride. Johnny's smile shone as brightly as the mid-day sun all day long. It has been three weeks now since they moved to their new home in Stuartsville—just enough time to prepare for Alfred's homecoming and finalize the plans for his upcoming marriage to Cousin Hannah. I do not know what it is with my brothers. With all the young women in this grand dominion of ours to choose from, they have both promised themselves to our cousins. Imagine that! It is not as if either of them is particularly shy! Alas, I suppose there is nothing wrong with wedding your cousin, but it does seem a trifle odd, do you not think? Not that it is not done. You never considered marrying your cousin, though, did you, Mattie? "Cousins make good soup," Alfred always says. Good soup, indeed! Still, they are truly lovely young women, and I hold them both most dear. I am glad for my brothers that they have found such gems and most eagerly look forward to the moment that they shall make me an aunt.

You must write soon and let me know how you are faring, my love. Now that we are on the same continent again, it should be much easier for us to keep up-to-date on the latest news. My boys continue to keep me busy, and I will soon have my first article ready to submit to the Quiet Hour column in The Farmer's Advocate and Home Magazine. It scares me to think of putting my writing out there for all to see, but I believe it is what God has called me to do. I cannot say exactly how I know that He has called me to this ministry, yet nor can I shake the assurance that He has.

Curiously, I feel compelled to submit not just one article, but a whole series of them, though I blush at my audacity in admitting it. It is almost as if my pen propels itself across the page whenever I sit down to write. When I read the words that appear on the paper, I am awed by the message they contain and wonder from whence it came, for of one thing I am certain: it did not come from the mind of this writer. Is that what the apostle Paul meant when he referred to the inspiration of God? It seems presumptuous to even ponder such a thing, but I know no other way to explain it. Perhaps it is as Jesus promised His disciples when they were called to testify before the courts. Did He not tell them not to concern themselves with what to say for the Holy Spirit would give them the words to speak?

Could it be that the Almighty has called me to testify, not before the courts, but before our countrymen, and is giving me the words to speak through my writing? It is a lofty thought. Each day, I grow more convinced that He desires I use these words to reach out to others. Even so, I confess, they are a treasure I am tempted to bury deep within my soul lest others fail to see their worth. One day I am all set to send the articles I have written to the London office, the next, I quake at the thought, horrified by my presumption.

Please pray for me, Mattie, that I would know God's will on this matter. I feel as if I am being summoned and my heart cannot rest until I respond. If only God would open His mouth to speak in a way that I could interpret with absolute certainty. I desire more than all else to do His bidding, but it is so hard sometimes to know what it is He bids me do. He spoke so clearly to you, Mattie. Why does He not speak that way to me? Why must I always be left guessing?

My, my, that reveals a demanding and complaining heart, does it not? I need to take a lesson from the apostle and learn to be content with whatsoever I have been given. God help me, Mattie! I am a fearful and complaining wretch. It is a wonder that our Father can stand to look upon me, let alone number me among His beloved. May He forgive my discontent and absolve me of all my sins, for His name's sake.

Alas, the supper hour approaches and I have yet to dress. With Alfred home for the first time in over four years, Anna and Betsy have prepared a feast to rival Christmas dinner at the palace. Janey and Johnny are *even planning to come from Stuartsville to celebrate the occasion. The only one missing will be Charlie—and you, of course—but I am certain you will both be present with us in spirit. You know, Samson still waits patiently beneath Charlie's empty chair every mealtime, even after all these years. I think he still misses his master as much as the rest of us do. He is quite a dog. When it is time for him to leave us, I fear it will be like losing Charlie all over again. May God grant us strength!*

Do take care of yourself, Mattie. I shall let you know if and when Father and Mother finalize plans for a visit. Until then, may God go with you and prosper you in your work.

*Affectionately,
Your Dora-girl*

Pushing myself from the desk, I reached for the tortoise shell combs on the dresser, the words of my letter tumbling about in my mind. How dare I demand the Almighty reveal Himself to me on my terms? What was I thinking? I jabbed the combs into my unruly hair and pinched my cheeks. Impertinence did not become a child of the Most High. *Father, forgive me for playing the part of the spoiled child. Reveal Yourself to me in* Your *time and in* Your *way and give me ears to hear Your whispers.*

The chiming of the dinner bell intruded upon my prayer and I scurried to the top of the stairs, suddenly aware of the din of happy voices crowding the hallway below. Janey and Johnny must have arrived. Purposely slowing my steps, I descended the staircase, not wishing to appear over-eager. We had plenty of time; the entire evening was ours. Pausing on the bottom step, I surveyed the happy throng before me. Somewhere along the line, laughter had returned to the halls of our home, though I couldn't quite pinpoint when or how. I glanced around the foyer, almost expecting to see Charlie. Weeping may endure for a night, but joy cometh in the morning, Father always said. Could the morning have finally arrived?

I descended the final step and cupped my hand around the free arm Father held out to me. "Nice of you to join us, Dora. Shall we?" He raised an eyebrow in my direction and I nodded, a burst of warmth blooming on my cheeks. "Mother?" He inclined his head toward his other side where Mother stood, her hand firmly clasped around his elbow. A slow, single blink signalled her assent. "Then, let us proceed." Immediately, the others fell into line behind us—first Alfred and Cousin Hannah, then her parents, Uncle William and Aunt Mary, and finally Johnny and his dear wife, Jane.

The table, glistening in the lamplight, was laden with a feast beyond compare. Roasted potatoes, green beans, corn, roast beef, Yorkshire pudding—the offerings seemed endless. Anna and Betsy stood by the buffet as we took our places around the table, their eyes alight with pride. Never in the history of Ebor House had this table seen such a sumptuous spread. It had hosted many fine meals over the years, but none as glorious as the one that graced it this night. The glassware sparkled, the polished silver shone; none but the bridal feast of the Lamb could surpass its splendor. I breathed deeply of the tantalizing aromas and my stomach rumbled in response.

"Hungry, Dora?" Alfred's lips twitched and he winked. "Father, I do believe we had better eat. Dora's stomach is giving her a piece of its mind again."

Big brothers! Restraining a snort, I gave his arm a playful shove. "You'd best behave yourself, big brother. We did without you for this long—"

Alfred's jaw dropped as he glanced from one amused face to the next, finally appealing to Mother. "Mother, did you hear what your daughter just said?" His feigned affront sent a ripple of laughter around the table.

"I did, indeed, my son, and I thought her comment most fitting."

With that, the whole table erupted. "Oh, Alfred," Johnny managed between guffaws, "you have been missed." He grinned and shook his head. "It's good to have you home."

Alfred squared his chin, but nothing could still the tell-tale trembling of his whiskers as he tried not to laugh. "Thank you, brother. At least *some*body around here loves me."

I swiped a tear from my cheek and gave his arm a playful shove as his resonant laughter joined the melee. Samson rose from his spot beneath Charlie's empty chair and made his rounds of the table, his tail beating against my leg as he passed. *Thank You, God, for restoring our joy. And please, please tell Charlie we love him.*

Part II

Chapter 38

EBOR HOUSE
THREE AND A HALF YEARS LATER
NOVEMBER 9, 1888

"Well, would you look at that! He's a beauty, Janey." Alfred gazed at the wailing infant wriggling in his hands as Jane sank into the pillows. "Johnny finally got his boy." He wrapped a flannel cloth tightly around the tiny body and grinned. "Just wait until that husband of yours lays eyes upon this little redhead."

"Excuse me... Alfred?" Hardly daring to breathe, I clutched my brother's arm and drew him to the base of the bed. "Look."

With an amused snort, he caught my eye and winked. "Our Johnny sure knows how to do things right, Dora."

Jane pushed up a little on her elbows. "Dora? Alfred? What's—"

Taking the precious bundle from Alfred's arms, I rushed to Jane's side and settled myself on the chair beside the bed. She reached for her son and blinked away a tear before lifting pleading eyes to mine. I couldn't help but smile. "You never told me there were going to be two of them."

• • •

Cradling baby Charles in the crook of my arm, I reached for my niece's hand. "Come, Winnie." I fluttered my fingers, hoping she would come without a fuss. "Grandmother will take care of little Marjorie and baby Jack while we go see your mama." I didn't have the heart to leave Mother alone with two active toddlers and a hungry infant to corral. The elder of Johnny's two girls, Winnie was the spitting image of her father with fiery auburn curls and sparkling blue eyes. Even at the tender age of three, her winsome smile could melt my heart. Responsible, yet sensitive, she had taken to the role of big sister like old Samson had taken to Charlie. For a moment, I feared she might resist the call to accompany me, but with a final glance at her two-year-old sister happily banging a block on the rug, she snagged the ragdoll I had made for her and took my hand.

"Mama going to feed baby Charles. Baby Charles hungry." She tugged on his blanket and I stooped for her to see the squalling babe more clearly. With the gentlest of hands, she patted the top of his head. "Dere, dere, Charlie. It be awright. Mama make your tummy feel better. Mama feed you." She gave his head another gentle pat and stared into his wrinkled face. "Auntie Dora gonna take us to Mama."

Sharing a smile with Mother, I rose and slipped my fingers around Winnie's. "You are a good big sister, Winnie-girl."

As soon as we reached the corridor, she pulled her hand from mine and scrambled up the stairs before I could do a thing to stop her. I shifted Charles to my other arm and grasped the banister as I began my own ascent. "Slow down, Winnie. Remember to stay close to the wall where the stairs are nice and wide." She paused but a moment, peering at the step beneath her feet, then scrambled on, heedless of the narrowing stairs. "Move over, Winnie." I closed the space between us and grasped her shoulder, steering her toward the wall side of the stairs. "That's it." Jane certainly had her hands full.

Obviously pleased with herself, the little girl tipped her head backward and beamed. "Go see Mama!"

"Yes, Winnie." She teetered on the edge of the step and I grabbed her arm to steady her lest she fall and knock all three of us down. *Just a few more steps.* It had been almost three months since the boys had been born. It could only be hoped that Janey would regain her strength soon. I loved being an auntie and spending time with Johnny's little brood, but they sure could wear a person out.

Gaining the final step, I snagged Winnie's hand once more. All we needed was for her to go barrelling into Janey's room unannounced. A lusty wail broke from the babe in my arms and I raised him to my shoulder.

"Charlie hungry," Winnie confided.

"Yes, Winnie, Charlie is hungry. Do you think you could take us to your Mama?"

As soon as the words left my mouth, she was gone. "Mama! Mama!" she cried as she disappeared into the room at the end of the hall. Exactly what I had been trying to avoid.

I blew a stream of cooling air across my face and patted Charles on the back. Perhaps it was time to start the wee one on a daily dose of cod liver oil. Mother swore by the good a drop or two three times each day did us as babes. Following Winnie into her mother's room, I deposited baby Charles into Jane's outstretched arms.

"There, there," she crooned, brushing her lips across his puckered brow. She fumbled with her blouse as his cries intensified. "Really, Charlie…"

Like the snuffing of a candle's flame, the room fell silent. Winnie crawled onto the bed and tucked herself beneath her mother's free arm, gently patting her brother's foot. "See, Charlie? I told you it be awright."

Janey snugged the little girl closer. "I love the way you take care of your little brothers, Winnie. You will make a wonderful mama one day."

A wonderful mama. An involuntary shudder shivered through me. That was what people always told me when I was young, but motherhood was not in God's plan for all of us, no matter how much we might desire it. I steeled myself against the tears gathering behind my eyes and backed out of the room unnoticed. Maybe Winnie would one day be a good mother, and then again, maybe she would not, but one thing was sure: the predictions pronounced over me when I was her age would never be realized. Swallowing the lump in my throat, I headed for the stairs. "You've got plenty of time yet, oh daughter of mine," Father would be quick to assure me, but he didn't understand. Some things were simply not meant to be. With each passing day, I grew more certain of God's call on my life to remain single. I didn't have to understand, nor did He require my approval. I simply had to accept this cross He called me to bear.

I stopped with one foot on the top stair and listened. When all I heard were happy chortles from below, I turned and slipped into my chamber. *Holy Father— You promise in Your Word that You will be a father to the fatherless and a husband to the widow. Be Thou a husband to me also.* I choked back a sob as I sank into the chair next to the fire. *And let not this sacrifice be made in vain.*

Chapter 39

SEPTEMBER 14, 1892

"Miss Dora?"

I lifted my eyes from the paper before me, my hand arrested in mid-air. "Yes, Betsy?" At this rate, I would never complete the new article I was working on. Lowering my pen, I set it aside. "Is Mother ready to leave?"

"No, mem. Harvey Bains just dropped by with a telegram—"

"A telegram?" I thrust my chair from the desk and jerked to my feet, my heart racing. "For me?" Betsy nodded. Alfred and Hannah lived uptown—it couldn't be from them—but Johnny and Janey were back in Stuartsville, and Mattie... I pressed a hand to my chest. Heaven forbid it was from him.

Fighting to maintain a degree of decorum, I extended a trembling hand and closed my fingers over the fragile paper. Shutting my eyes, I fumbled with the fold. *Jesus, let it not be bad news.* How much more could this beleaguered soul of mine take? I sucked in a ragged breath and blew it out through my mouth, my thumb catching on the edge of the paper.

> Miss Dora Farncomb, Ebor House, Newcastle
> Come to London at earliest convenience STOP Business proposal for your consideration
> Mr. William S. Weld
> Wm Weld Publishing, London, Ontario

"Oh." I fell onto my chair, my legs suddenly shaky.

"Be it bad news, Miss Dora?" The young maid blushed, training her eyes on the floor before my feet.

I shook my head. "It isn't bad news at all, thankfully. It seems that Mr. William Weld of the William Weld Publishing Company in London—the one that publishes *The Farmer's Advocate and Home Magazine*—has a business proposal for me." I shrugged, puzzled by the curious missive. I had been submitting articles to *The Advocate* on and off for several years now under the pen name Hope. While all of them had made their way into his publication, I had never been contacted by the editor-in-chief. Until now. "I wonder what manner of proposal he has in mind."

Betsy inhaled sharply, her face aglow. "Oh my! Congratulations, Miss Dora. Would you like me to book you a ticket on the next train?"

Dear, dear Betsy. Always looking ahead. "Not quite yet, Betsy. I must talk to Mother and Father first." The young maid bobbed her head and headed down the hall. Today was Tuesday. If I sent a letter to Uncle Thomas in today's mail, he would likely get it by Thursday, or Friday at the latest. I snatched a piece of paper from my writing desk and dipped my pen in the ink.

September 14, 1892

Dear Uncle Thomas,

I trust all is well with you and Aunt Catharine. I write to you because Mr. William Weld, editor of The Farmer's Advocate and Home Magazine, has bid me come to London for a few days to discuss a business proposal. Although it is dreadfully short notice, I was wondering if you would be so kind as to let me stay with you and Aunt Catharine while I am in town. I plan to arrive early next week. If this would be too great an imposition, please send word immediately so that I can make other arrangements. I would be glad to reimburse you for any costs incurred. Either way, I shall look forward to seeing you when I am in town.

Your loving niece,
Dora Farncomb

I glanced at the clock. The mail would go out in less than an hour. Scrawling my uncle's name and address on an envelope, I stuffed the letter inside and snagged a few pennies from my pocketbook. As I neared the bottom of the stairs, Betsy emerged from the conservatory with a dusting rag in her hand. "Tell Mother I have gone to the post office, please," I told her. "I may not return before she leaves on her rounds, but I shall do my best to catch up with her as soon as possible."

The sun rode high in the sky as I rushed along the road. About twenty minutes remained before the mail left the office for the station; would it not have caused a spectacle, I would have run. Hurrying forward, I clutched the letter tightly in my hand. If need be, I would intercept the mail cart on its way to the station. Surely the postmaster would see my letter made it onto the train with the rest of the mail.

I stopped at the tracks and peered right, then left. Certain no train approached, I picked my way across the iron rails and resumed my trek toward town, my arms pumping. As soon as I turned onto King Street, I noticed the mail cart outside the mercantile. Young Harvey Baines heaved a large canvas bag onto the cart bed and climbed into the driver's seat. "Harvey, wait!" I sprinted the final block, waving the letter in my hand.

"Do ye 'ave another letter fer me, Miss Dora?"

I drew my hand to my chest and nodded. I didn't run often. "I-need it-to go out-in today's-post."

Harvey took the letter and examined it. "I cin do that fer ye, Miss Dora." He reached into his pocket and pulled out a stamp, then licked it soundly and applied it with great care to the corner of the envelope before tucking the letter into the nearest mail bag. "That not be a problem at all."

I handed him three coppers and stepped away from the cart. "Thank you, Harvey. God bless you for your kindness. It is imperative that my uncle receive that letter before the week ends."

"The kinfolk be alright, ain't they, Miss Dora?" Concern wrinkled his brow and I nodded. Harvey had been the bearer of the telegram.

"Everyone is fine, thank you, Harv."

"I'm glad to hear that, Miss Dora. Glad indeed, what with the telegram an' all." He jerked his head in my direction and slapped the horse's rump with the reins. "Gee-up, girl. We 'ave a train t'catch."

• • •

"A business proposal, you say?" Father folded his hands across his belly and leaned back into his chair. "I must admit, it sounds intriguing. Do you plan to make the trip?"

"Yes. I sent a letter to Uncle Thomas in today's post, asking if he would take me in for a few days next week."

"Will you have your father accompany you?" Mother peered meaningfully at me, as if willing me to understand, her lips pursed in a disapproving moue.

Always thinking of my virtue. I inhaled slowly, choosing my words with care. "No, Mother, I don't believe that will be necessary. This is, after all, a *business* proposal, and I am no longer a young woman."

Mother drew in her chin as if offended. "It is not proper for a woman—young, or otherwise—to partake in a business transaction with a man."

There it was. Mother, while progressive in so many ways, simply could not let go of the social mores that governed her womanhood. "I understand your concern, Mother. Of course, it is up to the man to conduct the business affairs of the home—if there *is* a man to conduct them." I averted my eyes, knowing this, too, rankled the woman who gave me birth. Neither Mother nor Father understood my refusal to entertain a marriage proposal. I clasped my hands on my lap and pressed my shoes into the floor as the silence lengthened. Each tick of the hall clock ricocheted between my ears until I wanted to cover them both and scream. Unable to bear the tension, I pushed myself to my feet. "Mother, Father…" Why was this so hard? "I–I know you don't understand, but this is something I need to do for myself. Alone." I shifted my gaze from one to the other. "I know it concerns you that I do not have a man to care for me in this life, but I must follow the pathway God has ordained for me."

Mother's steely gaze softened as she rose to embrace me. "We only want the best for you, dear. Are you certain this is what God is calling you to do?" I melted into her arms, my whole body trembling. "You know, there is a convent in Toronto, dear—the sisters of St. John the Divine, I believe. If God has truly called you to the single life as you claim, perhaps—"

"Mother, please." I stepped from her embrace and settled my hands upon her shoulders. "The sisters do a wonderful work, but the fact that God has called me to remain single doesn't necessarily mean that He has called me to the sisterhood."

Father stood, extending a hand to each of his girls. "Oh, how you womenfolk do take on." He pulled Mother close to his heart and brushed a kiss across her brow. "Our little Dora is no longer a child, Janey. She is a woman grown." Mother laid her head upon his chest, and he stroked her greying curls. "We gave her to God before she was even born. Do you not remember?" His eyes grew distant, as if witnessing an event long past. "Who are we to try and wrestle her out of His hands now?"

Father motioned toward the door with his head, suggesting it might be better if I left them. Relieved, I started for the hallway. His soft voice drifted on the air behind me. "There, there, Janey," he crooned. "Her Maker is her husband—she will not go alone. Could there be any better catch?"

Chapter 40

LONDON, ONTARIO
SEPTEMBER 20, 1892

Steam hissed from the engine as the train wheels squealed to a halt. Shouldering my bag, I picked my way down the iron stairs and onto the platform. I'd have to wait for them to unload Father's portmanteau. I had hoped to travel lightly, but not knowing exactly what this business proposal entailed, I had ended up bringing far more than any sensible woman required for a few days in the city. A smattering of raindrops dotted the platform as I made my way to the baggage car. There it was—at the very bottom of the laden cart. The worn leather valise must have been one of the first to be offloaded.

I stepped into the building and found a seat in the waiting area while a brawny young lad trundled the cart to the claims area. Full as it was, I hoped he would make it. He stopped to brush a sodden lock of hair from his brow with his forearm and scowled at the darkening sky. The rain fell in sheets now, drenching the poor boy as he resumed his trek. At least the tarpaulin over the baggage area would help to keep the luggage somewhat dry—once he got it there. If water soaked through Father's valise, I would have nothing suitable to wear for my meeting with Mr. Weld.

I turned from the window, hoping to distract myself from the morass of anxious thoughts that had plagued me from the moment I left the village. *Oh Father—I am following Your call, am I not? Part of me is certain that Mother's misgivings are worth heeding, yet there is another part of me—a more trustworthy part—that knows, without a doubt, that this is an opportunity I cannot ignore.*

The bustling station grew quiet as one by one the patrons claimed their bags and headed for the row of hansom cabs lining the street. Father's portmanteau peeked from beneath a single valise now. Gathering my bag, I headed to the claims area. The sooner I got to Uncle Thomas's, the better.

"This be yers, ma'am?" The young man lifted the heavy bag from the cart and set it on the gravel. I smiled at the astonishment in his voice. "I'll get Pete there to give ye a hand."

Before I could say a word, he dashed across the platform, only to return a moment later with a man in a crisp, blue uniform.

"May I carry your bags for you, madam?"

"I would appreciate your service," I responded. I handed him my shoulder bag and pointed to the heavy valise. "I shall need to enlist a cab to take me to fifty-five Wellington Street."

"Consider it done, madam." The cheery porter hefted the bag as if it weighed nothing at all and motioned for me to follow. "It is too bad that you have the misfortune of visiting our fine city on such a dismal day."

"I am sure the rain will soon end," I assured him. I fished around in my pocket, hoping to find a penny or two to offer the kind gentleman. *How much, exactly, did a person tip a bluecap?* I hoped a penny would be enough. I would not have enough for the cab if I parted with much more.

"Here we are, madam." The man in the blue uniform stopped beside a worn, black carriage and hoisted my bags onto the baggage rack behind the seat. "Stevens here will see that you get to your destination."

I took his proffered hand and climbed into the carriage before handing him the green-edged coin. "Thank you, sir. May you have a blessed day."

He nodded his thanks. "And the same to you, madam." Turning to the driver, he lowered his voice. "Fifty-five Wellington Street, Stevens." He gave the nag a slap on the rump and it stumbled into motion.

"Gee-up, girl," the cabby clucked. "So, what brings a fine young woman like y'erself to Lond'ntown?"

• • •

Wherever had the time gone? Tugging at my peplum, I scanned the room for my gloves, hoping I was not overdressed. Uncle Thom had graciously offered to drop me off at the editor's office on his way to the woolen mill, but though that allayed my anxiety over how I was to get across town, it did little to calm my roiling belly. Mother was right. The business world was never meant for women. Who did I think I was? *A business proposal.* What was I thinking?

I closed my eyes and concentrated on breathing. *In. Out. In. Out. Jesus? Am I doing the right thing—what You want me to do? I was so sure You had called me to this a few days ago, but now—now I'm not so—*

"Dora?" Aunt Catharine appeared at the door of my chamber looking more than a little harried. "Your Uncle Thom is… my, my, but you look lovely, dear." I smiled at the sudden change of topic, praying my nervousness wouldn't show. "You are a courageous young woman to step forth like this into the business world." She laid a wrinkled hand on my cheek and gave it a gentle pat. "But God is with you; I can see Him in Your eyes."

I fumbled for a response, my mind whirling. "Thank you, Auntie. I—"

"You had best be getting on your way." She leaned forward, her lips brushing my cheek. "I shall be praying for you, dear. God's way for us is not always easy, but it is always worth it. Lean on Him, Dora. He who has called you is faithful." My eyes brimmed with unshed tears. How had she known? "Now go." She pushed me insistently toward the door. "Your uncle is waiting... but do hurry back. I'm as anxious as a mouse in a barn full of cats to see what God has in store for you this day."

Throwing my arms around her, I whispered my thanks and hurried down the stairs. Uncle Thomas leaned against the door jamb, chatting idly with his eldest son, but he straightened as soon as he saw me and gave a little bow. "Good morning, my lady."

I stifled a giggle at his formality and his son grinned.

"Shall we be on our way?" He swung his hat onto his head and opened the door, motioning for me to pass through. Alas, for the real business of the day. There could be no turning back now.

Chapter 41

"William Weld Publishing." I read the words emblazoned in gold on the sign above the door of the great stone edifice. "Home of The Farmer's Advocate and Home Magazine." Taking a deep breath, I reached for the heavy wooden door. *Jesus, help me.*

As soon as I crossed the threshold, the imposing façade of the great building fell away. A quiet hum emanated from a room to my left, masking the whisper of my shoes on the marble floor as I stepped into the foyer. A row of empty hooks on the wall to my right testified to the warmth of the day, despite the early hour. Ahead, a matronly woman sat at a desk riffling through a stack of papers. She looked up as I approached and removed her glasses. "Good morning, madam. Welcome to William Weld Publishing. May I be of assistance?"

I wrung my gloves in my hands and forced myself to make eye contact. "Good morning. My name is Dora Farncomb. I have an appointment to see Mr. William Weld at nine-fifteen."

The woman glanced at the wall clock adjacent to her desk and rose. "Why, of course." A welcoming smile spread across her face. "It is a pleasure to meet you, Miss Farncomb. My name is Florence Simms. Come." She stepped from behind her desk and motioned for me to join her. "Mr. Weld is expecting you."

We walked past the entrance to the bustling room on my left and I peeked in to see a handful of men—and women—bent over typewriters. "This is our newsroom," Miss Simms whispered, stopping before the open door, "and these are the people who comprise our journalistic team." Without waiting for a response, she moved down the hall. "They, together with regular contributors such as yourself, and our dedicated columnists, labour daily to make *The Advocate* the inspiring and relevant periodical it has become."

She stopped in front of a glass-paned door and knocked lightly. "Here we are." The door opened to reveal a balding man in his early fifties. His rumpled black suit and smudged shirt suggested a man more comfortable in the print shop than the office, but his authoritative demeanor left no doubt as to his position. "Mr. Weld, Miss Farncomb has arrived."

"Thank you, Miss Simms." He extended an open palm, gesturing toward a worn leather seat, and closed the door behind me. "So. Miss Farncomb." He settled himself on the corner of his desk with one foot still on the ground and sighed as if his labour had finally ceased. While I had met Emily's father on occasion when we were at school, he had always seemed rather stiff and aloof to me, quite unlike the genial man sitting across from me now. Perhaps that was the toll decorum took on a person. "I am so glad that you could make it," he said. "How was your trip?"

His conversational tone did much to calm the tremors in my belly, and the tightness in my chest gave way. "It was a lovely trip, sir—uneventful and crowned with the most glorious vistas."

"What was the best part?"

The unanticipated question rattled me. *What* was *the best part?* I leaned my elbow on the armrest and crooked a finger around my chin. "I believe the best part, sir, was the time alone to think and pray."

"And what was it you were thinking and praying about?"

"Oh, my family and my friends, of course. But mostly, I confess, about my appointment with you."

A great guffaw met my ears as he bounced to his feet and paced across the room. "I like you, Miss Farncomb!" His eyes danced as he returned to the desk. "Your candor is delightful. No wonder my office is inundated with letters from eager readers who desire to read more of your work." My eyes leapt open at his words. "I have a proposition for you." He continued as if this was the most normal conversation in the world. Circling his desk, he thumbed through a handful of papers. "Here it is." Pulling a crisp, white sheet from the pile, he hitched himself once more onto the corner of his desk and pinned me with his eyes. "I would like to make you a regular columnist here at *The Advocate*. I propose that we change our current column, "The Quiet Hour," to "*Hope's* Quiet Hour" and make you, dear Hope, its sole contributor."

I opened my mouth to speak, but before I could form any words, he blustered on. "I do not know what possessed you to write under the pen name *Hope*, Miss Farncomb, but you could not have chosen better. You, my dear, are a ray of hope to our readers—and, doubtless, to all you meet." He shrugged lightly and splayed his hands. "What do you say? Will you do it?"

His words hung in the air, demanding an answer. "My own column?"

His amused chortle caught me off guard. "Surprised you, didn't I?"

Heat rose to my cheeks, but I couldn't keep a smile from twitching at the corners of my mouth. "You certainly did, Mr. Weld; you certainly did." I licked my lips, searching for the best way to respond. "Do you suppose I might take the day to pray about your proposal, sir? I would not want to enter into an arrangement like this without seeking the Lord's will on the matter."

"Of course you may. I would expect nothing less." He rose from the desk and reached for my hand. "How be we meet again tomorrow? Would nine o'clock work for you?"

I nodded as I stood to shake his hand. "One thing, sir—would taking this position mean that I would need to move to London?" He lifted a finger to his chin. "I-I mean, my parents are getting older now and require my assistance more than they used to. I would not want to abandon them."

He rested a hand on my shoulder as we moved toward the door. "Your devotion to your parents is admirable, Miss Farncomb. I am sure that we can work things out so that you need not move to London."

"Thank you, sir." I dipped my head and stepped into the hall.

"I shall see you tomorrow, then," he responded.

•••

Filled with restless energy, I considered the distance to Uncle Thom's house and decided to walk. After all, it was a lovely day and a perfect time to explore the city. Besides, I needed time to process Mr. Weld's proposal. What I had been expecting, I could not say, but it certainly hadn't been a column of my own. *Hope's Quiet Hour.* I turned the words over in my mind. They did have a ring to them.

The business section of the city, which had seemed so quiet when I had arrived, teemed with people. A tall man in a black suit-coat doffed his hat as I passed, making me feel like a little girl again, forever playing grown up. *What am I doing, Lord?* I passed a sign on my left advertising a women's emporium and turned aside to check it out. A selection of ladies' fashions was displayed in the window alongside a bureau topped with an array of perfumes and lotions. *Frivolous accoutrements—but still...* Curious, I glanced around to be sure no one was looking then slipped through the door. My fine damask outfit seemed coarse beside the satins and brocades hanging from the walls of the little shop. Fingering a set of silky pantaloons, I wondered how they would ever stand up to daily wear and shook my head.

"Good morning, madam. May I help you find something?"

Startled, I dropped the offending lingerie as a trim young woman approached. "No, thank you. I am afraid we do not have stores like this back home and my curiosity got the better of me." The saleswoman, impeccably dressed in a lovely floral gown with a broad, lacy collar, smiled and nodded graciously, obviously accustomed to such encounters. "I am afraid your fine garments would be a trifle... impractical for my needs," I stammered. My cheeks warmed as I hurried toward the exit. "Thank you for allowing me the pleasure of dreaming."

A bell tinkled as I opened the door and stepped into the street. I definitely would not be doing that again. The musky perfume that had permeated the little shop clung to my clothes as I continued toward Wellington Street. Hopefully it would dissipate before I reached Uncle Thom's.

• • •

"So, how did your meeting go with Mr. Weld?" Uncle Thomas folded his napkin and tucked it beneath the edge of his plate.

"Very well, thank you, Uncle." Scooping the last morsel of brown sugar pie onto my fork, I paused before taking the final bite. "He has offered me my own column in *The Advocate*."

"Your own column?" Aunt Catharine sputtered. Her fork clattered from her hand.

"Every week," I responded with an apologetic shrug, struggling to keep my excitement from overflowing.

"Imagine, Thomas." Aunt Catharine clapped her hands to her chest, her eyes dancing. "Our very own niece, a columnist at *The Advocate*."

Uncle Thomas shared a subdued smile with his wife and reached for her hand. "And have you accepted the offer, Dora?" He raised a brow expectantly.

Such a wise and discerning man. "I asked him for a day to think on his proposal and seek God's guidance before I gave him an answer." Laying my fork across my plate, I covered it with my napkin. "We meet again tomorrow morning."

Aunt Catharine's jaw dropped before she remembered herself. "You didn't accept right away? Goodness, child! What will that man think? Indecisiveness does not become a woman, Dora."

"I believe, Catharine dear, *that man*, as you say, will think our dear Dora a very prudent young woman." Aunt Catharine's answering glare made me shiver, though it was not directed at me. "Taking the time to consider an offer is not a sign of indecisiveness, my dear. Many a man would do well to follow Dora's fine example." He looked pointedly at his eldest son.

I lowered my eyes, wishing I could escape. *Poor Cousin James.* I hoped conversations like this didn't often grace this table, but his slumped shoulders and mumbled response made me wonder.

Uncle Thom shifted his focus back to me. "Have you made a decision yet, Dora?"

"I believe so," I answered cautiously.

"And?" The annoyance in Aunt Catharine's voice could not be missed.

Honestly! Of all the meddling, presumptuous... "I shall let you know after my meeting with Mr. Weld tomorrow." I pushed myself from the table and stood. "May I please be excused, Uncle? It has been a long day."

"That it has." He slid his own chair back and stood to help Aunt Catharine from her seat. "Rest well, Dora. May God grant you the wisdom you seek."

"Thank you, Uncle Thomas. I just pray He will affirm His will in this matter before my response is due."

"He will, child. He will show you what to do. He may not reveal His will to you in advance, but when the time comes, you will know what to say. If I have learned anything about discerning the will of our Lord, it is that." I stepped into his embrace and kissed his weathered cheek, relieved when he offered me a gentle smile. "Would you like a ride to the office in the morning?"

"That would be such a blessing, Uncle Thom. I need to be there for nine."

"I shall be ready by eight-thirty sharp."

I nodded and bussed Aunt Catharine's cheek before heading for the stairs. "Thank you, Uncle. Goodnight."

Aunt Catharine's indignant whispers faded as I climbed the steep staircase to the slanted room above the kitchen. Whatever she had to say, I didn't want to hear it. *This is between You and me, Lord. Auntie's objections to the way I conduct myself are immaterial, right?* I stared at the ceiling imperiously, daring the Almighty to contradict my brazen declaration.

When the heavens failed to part and God remained silent, I fell to my bed and buried my face in my arms. *Am I making the right choice, Jesus? Is this contract truly what You desire for me, or am I merely choosing what I want for myself?* I rolled onto my back. *I want to do what You want me to do in this matter, but You are going to have to tell me what that is.* I closed my eyes and drew my hands to my belly. *Please make Your will clear, O Lord. I need to give Mr. Weld an answer tomorrow.*

I rose to change into my nightdress, surprised by the sudden sense of peace that blanketed my soul. *Is this Your answer, Jesus?* I pulled back the bedclothes and sat on the side of the bed. *I am to go ahead and accept Mr. Weld's proposal, aren't I?* Slipping my feet beneath the covers, I yawned, my body relaxing into the feather tick. Reveling in the quietness that enveloped me, I rolled onto my side, my eyes sliding shut of their own accord. *I am. I know I am.*" The ghost of a smile flitted across my face. *Could you not have simply told me that from the start?*

Chapter 42

SEPTEMBER 28, 1892

My Dear Mr. Wellman,

How are things going in New York? Your description of that stickball game you initiated with the youth left father howling as if he had been there to witness your humiliation himself. It has been several years since we have spoken of a visit, but if we ever do make it to New York, you shall have to arrange for another game of old timers versus youth. Perhaps you and Father together could beat those young rascals!

A lot has happened around here since I last wrote. The week before last, I received a telegram from the editor-in-chief of The Farmer's Advocate and Home Magazine requesting I make a trip to London to discuss a business proposal. To make a long story short, I screwed up my courage to make the trip last week and am now a weekly columnist for the Home portion of the magazine. My column is to be called "Hope's Quiet Hour" and will be launched the week after next. It is a scary step to enter the business world of men, but I am convinced it is a journey upon which our Lord has called me to embark. I am currently working to polish my first two articles so I can send them out in Friday's post. How I pray that God would add His blessing to each word and let his voice be paramount in every article I submit. I am thinking this *just might be the call for which I have waited so long, dear Mattie, although I must confess I have wondered that more than once before. Do you suppose God calls us to more than one mission in our lives or that His mission for us changes over time? I have wondered much about that lately. First there was my family, then the young men's group, now this column. Perhaps it is like having babies. One does not stop mothering one child simply because another comes along. Perhaps the mission He has given me has not so much changed as it has been expanded—as though I have birthed another baby, so to speak. What a thought that is!*

Well, Mattie, I must bid you adieu for now. Our young men's social club will descend upon me in naught but a few hours and I have yet to instruct Anna on the refreshments. She is sure to have my hide if I do not speak with her soon. I do hope your parishioners are taking good care of you. Write soon.

Affectionately,
Your Dora-girl

Folding the paper with care, I spritzed it with lavender water and slipped it into an envelope. Mattie's faithful correspondence warmed my heart, but it was no substitute for the ardent conversations of our youth. Affixing a stamp to the corner of the envelope, I set out to find Anna. I checked the side kitchen first, expecting to find her peeling potatoes—or some such thing—by the fire, but the kitchen was as deserted as a church at midnight, so I wandered into the back kitchen, surprised to find it, too, empty. "Anna?" I stepped across the hall to check the dining room and ran headlong into Betsy.

"Miss Dora…" She drew a hand to her chest, puffing as if she had run all the way home from town. "Can I help you with something?"

My heart lurched. Betsy could be high-strung at times, but it was unlike her to display such nervousness. "Is everything all right, Betsy?" She averted her gaze, her eyes pooling. "Yes, mem."

I slipped my fingers beneath her chin and lifted it until our eyes met. "Shall we try that again?" I gave her a sympathetic smile, willing my galloping heart to still. "Is everything really all right?"

In a burst of tears, she threw her hands over her face and shook her head. Alarm coursed through me. What had happened? Schooling my features, I gathered her into my arms and stroked her hair, rocking back and forth until she finally relaxed into my embrace. "Can you tell me?"

"It's–it's... Anna." Her sobs intensified with each word.

I swallowed hard. *Anna. Dear, sweet Anna. Always there, ever ready to serve...* "What about her, Betsy?" I clamped my lips shut lest I reveal my own panic.

"She's sick, Miss Dora." Raising her head, she stared at me, her eyes pleading. "Real sick." She paused to draw a shuddering breath. "I think she's going to die."

"Have you sent for Alfred?"

"Yes, mem. Mistress Jane had me send the stable hand to fetch him almost an hour ago. He should be here soon."

She swayed and I grasped her elbows to steady her. "Come, sit down, Betsy. You're not looking so well yourself." I led her to a chair, alarmed by the heat emanating from her body. Perhaps her quaking was attributable to something other than nervousness or strain. I laid my hand across her brow. "On second thought, dear, perhaps you should retire to your room. I think our good doctor should take a look at you, too."

"Oh no, Miss Dora." Betsy struggled to her feet, shaking her head, her breath coming in shallow puffs. "I'm fine. Really, I am." She rocked to the side and reached for the chair. "I just need to make Anna a cup of tea and fetch some cool water to—"

"What you need to do, Betsy, is go and lie down. I shall make the tea and fetch the water. Here, let me help you." Hooking my arm around her waist, I guided her through the back kitchen and up the rear stairs to the quarters she shared with Anna. I pulled down the sheets and helped her into bed, then unlaced her shoes and tugged the blankets over her shivering form. "Now, you rest here while I brew the two of you a pot of tea."

Mother, who had been busy tending to Anna when Betsy and I came in, stood by the door, her face grave. She waited for me to step into the hall and followed me out, her voice hushed. "You had best cancel your meeting for this evening, Dora." I raised an eyebrow, about to object, but thought better of it. She was probably right. "It looks like the influenza to me. I understand there has been a bit of an epidemic down Newtonville way in recent weeks, but I had not heard of any in Newcastle yet. I suppose it was only a matter of time."

Influenza. My mind whirled at the thought. *Again?* Of course, there were instances of it every year, but memories of the serious outbreaks the last couple of winters still haunted me. The death toll had been staggering, even among the youth. For every twenty who contracted the dreaded illness, one had succumbed to its ruthless grasp and died. The priest had barely been able to keep up with the demand for his services.

"…as soon as he arrives, be sure to send him up."

My eyes darted to Mother's. *As soon as he arrives…* "I apologize, Mother. As soon as who arrives? Are we expecting someone?"

"Never mind, dear." She patted my arm absently, her eyes curiously fixed upon the space behind my head. "Alfred, thank you for coming so promptly." I snapped my head around to see my brother mounting the final stair, his black bag in one hand, his top hat in the other. "You made good time." She took his hat and pushed him toward the chamber door. "They are in there."

"They?" He stopped mid-step, his eyes widening. "Stanley only told me that Anna had taken ill."

"Yes, we didn't realize when we sent for you that Betsy wasn't well, either." Mother leaned in close, her voice but a breath. "I think it might be the influenza." She clasped her hands at her waist, a tell-tale sign that she was on edge.

In one, swift motion, Alfred turned away from the sick room, nearly scooping us both off our feet as he ushered us to the top of the stairs. "Wait for me in the kitchen while I see to Anna and Betsy. I'm certain it is nothing so serious as the influenza, but if it is, it would not do for you to be exposed any more than you have been already." Mother hesitated on the top step, opening her mouth as if to speak. "Go on with you now." Alfred gave her shoulder a reassuring squeeze. "I shall join you shortly."

Halfway down the stairs, I looked back. Worry lines furrowed Alfred's brow. He knew Mother every bit as well as I did. She had seen influenza before; her best friend growing up had died of it, and she had treated nearly as many cases of it over the last two years alone as Alfred had himself. If she thought Anna and Betsy suffered from influenza, they no doubt did. Alfred pressed his hand against the wall and met my gaze with a measured blink.

"Come, Mother." I slid my hand into the crook of her arm as we descended the final few steps. "Why don't you put the kettle on and brew us some tea while I find Stanley. He can see that word gets to my boys about tonight's meeting. Perhaps they can meet in the church basement instead. Surely Cecil and Byron could run things without me for once." I fed an extra log into the wood stove and replaced the cover while Mother filled the kettle with water. "I shall be but a moment."

• • •

Mother handed Alfred a gold-rimmed china cup and a biscuit left over from breakfast. "It didn't take long for you to examine them."

He lifted the cup to his lips and sipped his tea then shook his head slowly as he set the cup on its saucer. "As you well know, Mother, when once one has witnessed influenza, it is not difficult to recognize. I have seen five cases of it already this week. Anna and Betsy make seven."

"I had been hoping that I was wrong." Mother set her cup on the table beside her and folded her hands on her lap. "What must we do to nurse them back to health?"

"You know the ropes, Mother." He took another sip from his cup and set it on the table beside hers. "Starve out the fever and give them both plenty of meadowsweet tea. See that they stay in bed and be sure to keep them well hydrated."

Mother closed her eyes, visibly composing herself. She was, without a doubt, the strongest woman I had ever known, perhaps the strongest woman I ever would know. When she opened her eyes, her face bore a calmness I yearned to emulate. "Is there nothing else that will help?"

"Perhaps an onion or two at their bedsides would do some good, but I cannot say for sure. I know Old Dr. Phelps used to swear by them." He tipped his head toward me, suppressing a chuckle. "Remember when we all got the measles? Mother had our sick room so full of onions that we could still smell them a month after we recovered." He winked at Mother and grinned. "The smell of onions still makes me itch!" Alfred smoothed his moustache with his thumb and forefinger as his merriment dissipated. "Seriously, though, influenza spreads quickly and you have both been exposed." He gazed meaningfully into my eyes then turned his focus to Mother. "You must eat well and get plenty of sleep, avoid chills and wash your hands whenever you leave the sick room. Perhaps a few onions at your besides might be helpful as well." He pressed his hands against the table and pushed himself up. "And, until further notice, this house is under strict quarantine along with anyone who has had any contact with Anna or Betsy in the past forty-eight hours."

"Alfred…" Mother trailed him to the kitchen door. "Be reasonable." She gave him that stern, no-nonsense grimace she had perfected when we were children. "Surely a quarantine is taking things a little bit far."

"Not if you don't want a full-scale epidemic on our hands, Mother," he responded, "which I, for one, do not." He lifted his bag from a hook in the hall and set his hat firmly atop his head. "I shall be in to check on you this evening. Remember, no one is to enter or leave this house without my permission, save me."

I slipped my arm around Mother's shoulders and drew her close. "Yes, Alfred. But what about Father?"

"I shall send him home immediately. He, too, has been exposed."

Discussion over, Alfred climbed into his carriage and headed down the drive. With a final wave, I drew Mother inside and closed the door. "I had better go find Stanley. Betsy spoke to him earlier when she sent him to fetch Alfred."

• • •

Monday morning a heavy drizzle painted the sky beneath dark, ominous clouds. I pushed aside the drapes next to Anna's bed and rested my hand against the windowpane. For the first time in days, Betsy slept soundly on the bed across the room, her fever finally broken, but Anna continued in restless delirium, her raspy breaths slow and laboured.

I dipped a cloth in the basin under the window and dabbed her face and neck with the cool rag, gratified by her involuntary sigh. I couldn't do much, but the knowledge that this one small act brought her even a breath of relief comforted me. A series of deep, choking coughs wracked her body and I sank to her side, lifting her into a sitting position. When her coughing finally subsided, I edged her limp body back onto the pillow, my heart racing. Blood spattered my apron and dotted the bedclothes. Wiping a scarlet drop from Anna's lip, I examined it in the dimness of the chamber. Not a good sign. Alfred was sure to drop by after lunch, but perhaps it would be wise to call for him now.

I plunged my hands into the bowl and scrubbed them together. Mother would know what to do. She always did. No sooner had the thought crossed my mind than familiar footsteps echoed on the stairs. "How went the night, dear?"

"Good morning, Mother." I wiped my hands on the skirt of my apron and strode across the room. "Betsy's fever broke several hours ago and she has slept soundly since, but Anna—"

A rattling gasp turned both of our heads and Mother rushed to Anna's side. "Send for Alfred, Dora." She replaced the damp cloth I had draped over Anna's forehead with another. "And be sure to change your apron."

Chapter 43

OCTOBER 17, 1892

Anna's sudden passing jarred us all. Were it not for Betsy's robust recovery, I'm certain the whole house would have come to a standstill. I fished four large potatoes from the box in the corner of the basement and snagged a handful of carrots from the rafters before heading up the rickety stairs to the kitchen. Depositing the vegetables on the floor by the stove, I grabbed a knife and sank onto Anna's chair. Before long, a pile of twisted peelings lay in my lap. How often had I walked into the kitchen and found Anna in this very spot, potato peelings curling from her knife as they now did from mine? Many happy hours I had spent in this room learning to prepare a meal from that woman. Just being here made me feel closer to her. *You must not hold the potato like it might escape, dear.* A smile tugged at my lips as Anna's voice replayed in my memory. "A bruised potato is never nice." *A bruised potato.* Who but Anna could conceive of such a thing?

And be sure to keep the peelings thin. It would not do to waste good food. A picture of an earnest little girl wielding a knife far too big for her little hands leapt into my mind. Her teeth gripped the tip of her tongue as she pared huge chunks of potato away with the skin. *Like this.* An older woman relieved her of both potato and knife and deftly peeled away the remaining skin. *See how the peels curl when you cut them thinly enough?* The little girl picked up a long peel and stretched it in front of her then reached for another potato, her brows drawn close in concentration. "Oh Anna—I miss you so."

"I miss her, too."

Startled, I fumbled the half-peeled potato and gouged it with the knife. "Betsy, I didn't see you come in." A mere shadow of her former self, Betsy bore the weight of Anna's passing more deeply than any of us. More like mother and daughter than fellow servants, the two had served together since the day Anna had begged Father to allow her to care for her dying sister's five-year-old daughter. Anna had taught the little girl everything she knew and had loved her as if she had been her own. The feeling was mutual. "Did Alfred give you a clean bill of health?"

"Yes, Miss Dora." Donning her apron, she strode across the room, pausing briefly to stir the glowing ashes that powered the woodstove and add a new log.

"He asked that I send you up for an examination also. He is with your mother and father right now. If all three of you are symptom free, he promises to lift the quarantine."

"It's about time," I muttered. The lengthy confinement had frayed my patience more than I wanted to admit. Sliding the last potato into a basin of water, I scrubbed away the final vestiges of dirt clinging to its surface.

"I can take it from here, Miss Dora. Thank you for filling in for me."

I wiped my hands on my apron and draped it over the back of the chair. "It has been my pleasure, Betsy. I shall check in on you later to see if you need a hand." I stepped into the hall before she had time to protest. We'd have to consider hiring another kitchen maid soon.

Mother met me on the stairs. "There you are. We were starting to wonder if Betsy had gotten lost." She waited for me to pass then turned to follow. "Your brother has given the rest of us a clean bill of health."

I mounted the final steps and headed toward Alfred's old room at the end of the hall. It had become a hospital room of sorts since Alfred had returned, mostly housing new mothers during their time of travail as the need arose.

Alfred greeted me with a beaming smile. "So, most favoured sister-of-mine, at last you decide to grace me with your presence." He motioned for me to sit in a chair by the fire. "How are you feeling today?"

Inexplicably annoyed by his playful greeting, I forced an answering smile. *Has he forgotten so quickly that we are a house in mourning?* "Fine, thank you."

"Fine, thank you?" He arched his brows.

"Yes. Fine. Thank you." Irritation clipped each word, followed immediately by a wave of remorse. A heavy sigh escaped my lips, and I raised a hand to massage my temple. To his credit, Alfred didn't try to rush me. Perhaps he remembered our sorrows after all. "Look, Alfred…" I straightened in my chair and rearranged my skirt. "I'm sorry. You didn't deserve that. I really am fine. I am weary and sad and burdened for our dear Betsy, but apart from that, I am well."

In one, smooth step, Alfred closed the space between us, pulled me to my feet, and wrapping me in his arms. Tears sprang to my eyes, but I refused to let them fall. If once I let them go, I might never be able to contain them.

"Relax, Dora." Alfred pressed my head to his shoulder, rocking me gently in his arms. "I've got you," he whispered, "and I'm not going to let you go." He brushed a strand of hair from my face and tucked it behind my ear. "Let the tears come. It isn't good to keep them bottled up inside."

How long I wept in his arms, I cannot say. When at last my tears were spent, Alfred eased me into the chair and handed me a handkerchief. He laughed when I gave a delicate little blow. "Oh, Dora, the unfair expectations we impose upon our womenfolk. Blow, girl, blow—like you mean it." I blew lightly into the cloth once more and gathered the sodden rag into my fist with a quiet sniff. "Come on, Dora, you can do better than that." I lifted a second handkerchief to my face and, looking him defiantly in the eye, gave the longest, noisiest blow I could muster. "Now that's a good one." He clapped his hand on his knee and chortled. "Father himself would have trouble beating that one." A watery laugh hiccupped past my lips. Father was known to be the most hearty nose-blower in the county—unrivalled, if truth be told. A ship without a foghorn would have no need to fear so long as Father was aboard. "And how do you feel now, oh sister of mine?"

"I feel much better, thank you." I caught my lower lip between my teeth and drew my chin down as if I were a mischievous child caught in a harmless prank.

He pressed his stethoscope to my chest, instructing me to breathe deeply, and held a hand to my forehead. "No chills? Aches and pains? Unexplained exhaustion?" I shook my head in response to each question. "Well then—it looks as though we can lift the quarantine."

"Finally."

Alfred chuckled at my heart-felt response. "Feeling a wee bit house-bound, are we?"

I stood, my eyes level with his, my hands digging into my hips. "Feeling a wee bit brave, are we?"

"I suppose that means yes." He grinned, obviously amused. Lifting my hands to his chest, I gave him a playful shove and turned to leave.

With an affected yelp and a grand thump, he landed in the chair behind him, laughing. "You're welcome!"

Chapter 44

OCTOBER 29, 1892

October 15, 1892

Dearest Miss Farncomb,

I trust this letter finds you well. Father told me about the trial you have been through this fall with the influenza and the passing of dear old Anna. You must miss her terribly and feel quite lost without her. I am so sorry for your loss.

Things are going exceedingly well here. As you might guess, I find myself pouring increasing amounts of time and energy into corralling our youth—putting them to work, engaging them in leisure pursuits and, of course, encouraging them to choose the path of Light and Love. I have worked hard to raise up a league of women like yourself to visit the poorest families in the parish and see that their needs are met, but volunteers are few and the needs are great. Keep praying for more willing to serve.

I am so excited to hear of the new ministry God has placed into your hands, Dora. Father sent me your first column segment and I have taken great joy in reading it over and over again. I have even submitted the funds for my own yearly subscription. There is no doubt in my mind that this is yet another "baby" God has called you to nurture. I like that analogy, by the way. I think it quite fitting.

It would be most lovely if you and your parents could find the opportunity to visit. You are welcome to come at any time; there is plenty of room at the rectory for all three of you. Perhaps it would even be good for Betsy to come along, since you are, as you well know, the only family she has left. However, I shall leave that up to you. Know that we can accommodate her also should you wish to bring her with you.

My goodness, time has gotten away from me. Saturday Evensong is generally well attended and I would not want to be late—have to set a good example and all, you know—so I must close now. God be with you, my Dora-girl.

Love,
Mattie

Setting the open letter on the bedside table, I turned down the lamp and yawned as the final glow gave way to darkness. A visit to Mattie would be more wonderful than I could imagine, and he was so right about Betsy. I would have to mention that to Mother and let her know that we could stay at the rectory. Perhaps it was finally the right time. Heaven knew I had waited long enough.

Pictures danced in my head of majestic waves crashing at the foot of the Statue of Liberty and elegant women in fancy dresses prancing along busy streets amid the clatter of horse-drawn carriages. The viewing machine Father had bought us two Christmases ago had included several scenes like that from New York City, but the reality of the images Mattie shared were the ones that tugged most at my heart. Dirty children being dragged by the ear into disheveled houses; unruly young men shouting expletives at frightened shopkeepers while stealing armloads of their goods; famished old women pawing through garbage heaps in search of a crust of bread. I pulled the covers over my head, desperate to dispel the horrifying images. The need, indeed, was great.

It suddenly felt tremendously important that we visit as soon as possible. *Maybe I could even stay for a while and help him form that women's league of which he so earnestly spoke.* The thought of working side by side with Mattie sent tingles up my spine. Could it be that God's call on both of our lives would only separate us for a season? I stretched out my legs and wiggled my toes against the sheets. *I could still keep up with my writing and I am certain that Mattie could use my services in the church. But my boys—what about my boys?* A sleepy yawn overtook me and I rolled onto my side. *Mmmm—they'll be fine... They are, after all... almost... grown...*

• • •

With dreams of squalid dwellings and sickly children vivid in my mind, I awoke, eager to share my latest plan. "But Father, do you not think it an important mission to minister to the poor and needy among us?"

"By all means, Dora. My question is not whether it is a worthwhile mission, but whether it is the mission to which God has appointed *you*. There are plenty of poor and needy here in our own little village. Are they not equally worthy of your compassion and care?"

"But Father—" This was not going at all as I had planned. Why could he not see the wonder of God's hand in this new opportunity?

"Your father is right, dear." Mother patted my knee and rose, as if the conversation had come to an end. "Your place is here—with your family, your boys, with the poor and needy of our own parish. New York is an awfully long way away."

"We know your love for Matthew is great, Dora," Father added, "but does it really surpass your devotion to all else?"

I opened my mouth to speak, but snapped it shut before a word could cross my lips. *Honour thy father and mother. Honour thy father and mother.* The childhood admonition ricocheted through my mind. *Even when they are wrong?*

"I know that is not what you wanted to hear." Mother stroked a hand across my shoulder. "But you must know the truth."

The truth? I scraped my chair across the floor and stood. "May I please be excused?" Without waiting for an answer, I bolted from the room. *The truth, indeed. The truth was, they didn't want me to go. They wanted me here—with them—the dutiful daughter content to care for them no matter the cost.*

I waited until I was in the hall before expelling my frustration in an angry huff. My uncharitable thoughts were anything but fair. I knew Mother and Father better than that. They had supported me in some very unconventional choices, so why not in this? Could they not see the hand of God at work? *Holy Father, what do You...* The realization that I had yet to enquire of the Lord rocked me; the dread I felt at the thought of doing so drew my feet to a stop. This was not a call God had placed upon me. It was a call I longed to embrace, not for the welfare of the people I would serve, but for me—for Mattie—for the two of us together.

A wave of nausea gripped my belly. Hitching my skirt, I ran the rest of the way up the stairs and locked myself in my chamber. Tears scalded my face as I fell to the floor next to my bed. *Please, God! Please? I want to be with Mattie. I can help him. I can be Your hands, Your feet, Your heart to the needy people of New York. I can...* A fit of sobbing seized me, and I pounded my fist on the bed. *Why, God? Why? Why must You deny Mattie and me the pleasure of being together?* Silence bore down upon me, squeezing my heart until I could barely breathe. Chest heaving, I prostrated myself on the floor and wept. *I* love *him...*

I know you do. The unexpected response jarred me. *But do you love him more than you love Me?*

Renewed tears gushed from my eyes. *I love you both.*

I know that, beloved.

So why must I choose?

The choice is not whom you will love, dear one, but whom you will serve.

I dropped my head onto my hands. Why, oh why, had I even let myself entertain the idea of renewing a romantic relationship with Mattie? Mother and Father were right.

"I love You more," I whispered into the silence.

A blanket of peace descended upon my soul. *I know, beloved.*

Rolling onto my back, I pressed my fists to my eyes. *Can I at least go and visit him?* An answering lightness stirred within me. *I suppose I may take that as a yes?* I stood to brush the wrinkles from my skirt and dabbed at my red-rimmed eyes with a handkerchief. *Whatever would Mattie think if he knew the thoughts my heart had entertained?*

Chapter 45

The thought of facing Mother and Father after the scene I had made that morning sickened me. Humility is a virtue—one I fear I do not possess in abundance—and I would have to admit that I was wrong. I had presumed upon the will of God by claiming His blessing upon my own willful scheming and had to confess that my high and mighty concern for others was naught but a flimsy veil concealing an uncharitable regard for my own selfish desires. *Father God, forgive me.* I squeezed my eyes shut, repeating the well-worn words like a mantra. *How could I have been so deceived?*

My stomach roiled as I descended the staircase. The supper hour was nearly upon us. Although I had opted to skip the mid-day meal and remain in my chamber, the thought of eating turned my stomach. *Why does this have to be so hard? I really do have a problem with pride, Jesus, don't I?*

A hint of rumbled laughter rippled through my mind and I jerked my head up, eyes wide. *Did you just laugh at me?* I paused, waiting for a response, only to sense another ripple of quiet laughter. *This is not funny! It may be true, but it isn't funny.* I would have stamped my foot had I dared, but I could do nothing to keep my fists from clenching at my sides.

Oh, my child—my precious, precious child—I love you.

The welcome voice of my Lord reverberated through the clouded recesses of my mind and brushed away the gloom. *Does that mean I am forgiven?* My stomach settled almost immediately and I inhaled deeply.

Again, the sensation of laughter rippled through me. *Well done, my good and faithful servant.*

I shook my head. *After that fiasco?*

What you call a fiasco, beloved, I deem a victory.

A victory?

The trap was set, the temptation real. Yet, you chose to listen to My voice. You surrendered your pride and submitted to My call, though everything within you yearned to resist. I call that a victory.

I stepped into the dining room, glad to find it empty. I hadn't thought of that. *Does that mean I don't have to tell my parents?* Again, that wonderful laugh. *Well, I had to try...* The supper bell rang and my stomach growled.

"What brings such a beautiful smile to your face, Dora?"

I scrambled to my feet as Father entered the room, his arm tucked securely around Mother.

"Oh, I was just thinking." He held out a chair for Mother and I resumed my seat. "You and Mother were right. It is not God's will for me to abandon the ministries He has appointed me here in the village in favour of a ministry He has not given me near the man I love."

Mother nodded sadly. "I'm sorry, dear."

My smile flickered. Mother's sympathy was the last thing I needed. *Keep me strong, Jesus.* "A visit, however, is definitely in order."

"Oh, it is, is it?" Father unfolded his napkin and smoothed it over his knee. "So… when do we leave?" The pride in his eyes was unmistakable.

"Yesterday?" I quipped. A helpless shrug lifted my shoulder when both Mother and Father broke into laughter, and I couldn't help but join them.

"Well then, that's settled. I shall make the arrangements first thing in the morning," Father declared. "Suppose we wait until after Easter. May, perhaps."

May. It seemed so far away, but with winter approaching and the cold, snowy conditions it was sure to bring, May would certainly be a better choice. The city would no doubt be beautiful in May with the dregs of winter swept away by the first-fruits of spring.

Betsy appeared at the door with a steaming tureen and a basket of biscuits. "Mmmm—creamy tomato soup, my favourite." I straightened in my seat and reached for my spoon.

"I hope you are feeling better, Miss Dora." Betsy ladled the fragrant soup into Father's bowl then moved to fill Mother's cup.

"Much better, thank you, Betsy." My stomach rumbled its assent. "Much, much better."

Chapter 46

MAY 13, 1893

A bag in each hand, I stepped onto the porch, mentally reviewing the list of items packed into each valise—three practical, everyday outfits suitable for almost any occasion, two formal gowns for church or gallivanting on the town, a selection of undergarments and slippers, a cotton nightdress, a set of combs, a handful of ribbons, and a few other unmentionables. With nowhere else to go, my prayer book and journal poked out of the satchel I had slung across my shoulder, jostling with the woven wrap and parasol hanging loosely from my wrist.

Father scooped the two bags from the porch as if they weighed nothing at all and bundled them into the back of the carriage. "Is that the last of them?" he asked.

"Except for these." I joined him on the hard-packed roundabout and handed him my satchel and parasol.

He eyed them skeptically, his focus shifting to the overstuffed baggage compartment. "Ah, yes, you wouldn't want to leave anything behind."

"Fa-ther—" I caught the teasing glint in his eye and tried not to smile.

"Between you, your mother, and our dear Betsy, I would wager I have packed the whole house into this little carriage." He offered me a hand as I climbed into the back seat and arranged my skirt around my ankles. "So, what do you think? Should I go in and see what is keeping the others?" No sooner had the words left Father's mouth than Mother breezed through the door with Betsy firmly in tow, a basket swathed in kitchen cloths swinging precariously on her arm. "Ladies." Father doffed his hat, dipping his head as he slid the aromatic basket from Betsy's arm. "Dear Betsy, you do think of everything." He rearranged a bag or two to make room for the basket and secured a tarpaulin over the baggage compartment while Betsy helped Mother into the carriage and clambered in behind.

Removing a key from his pocket, Father mounted the stairs to the house and inserted the key into the lock. With a jaunty grin, he hoisted himself into the carriage and took the reins. "All aboard?" Seeing we were all firmly settled in our seats, he clicked his tongue and flicked the reins lightly across the horses' rumps. "Giddy up now," he urged as the wheels began to roll. He pulled the horses to a stop at the end of the drive. "Anyone need to visit the outhouse?"

"Frederick!"

The undercurrent of amusement colouring Mother's response matched the boyish bravado in Father's. "My good woman, I fear I hast offended thee. I prithee accept my most humble apology." Father swung his hat through the air and dipped his head regally in her direction.

With a roll of her eyes, Mother pushed his hat aside. "Thou, oh husband of mine, had best attend to the driving."

Betsy clapped her hands to her mouth, but not before a giggle escaped through her fingers. With a dashing smile, Father turned to her and winked. "Methinks we had best be on our way."

Laughter punctuated the drive to the train station. "Will Stanley come to pick up the rig once we are on the train?" I asked.

"He is, no doubt, already there," Father answered. "I sent him on ahead with a message to hold the train should we be late."

"Fa-ther, you know the train cannot delay its schedule at the whim of its patrons."

"Well, there is always a first." Father chuckled as he pulled into the station and brought the horses to a stop in front of a hitching post. "One can always ask." He hopped out of the carriage and looped the reins loosely around the post before helping us from the overloaded vehicle. Ready with a baggage cart, Stanley busily unloaded our bags and rolled the cart across the platform just as the great iron horse puffed into the station. The gigantic wheels screeched to a halt and a hiss of steam billowed from beneath the massive beast, sending a whoosh of air swirling across the platform. I clapped a hand to my head to secure my hat. *Right on time.*

"Afternoon, Miss Dora." Harvey Bains trundled by with the mail cart. "Mrs. Farncomb." He tipped his cap and gave a little bow. "Miss Betsy." Colour leapt to Betsy's cheeks as she murmured a quiet good afternoon. "You folks enjoy yer trip to the big city now." He stopped briefly at the baggage car to hand a canvas bag to the attendant then turned the cart toward the main building. I smiled at the way Betsy's eyes trailed his every move. Could it be the attraction was mutual? The two of them would make a great pair.

"Ready to board?" Father appeared at Mother's side and slipped his arm around her waist. The door to the first class carriage stood open with a uniformed attendant stationed on the platform below next to a portable staircase. Father handed our tickets to the attendant and helped Mother up the steps.

"Enjoy your trip, Mr. Farncomb," the attendant intoned as Father returned to escort Betsy and me into the lavish train car. My eyes widened as they swept the opulent interior. I had never before been afforded the luxury of first class passage. Stopping at the seat opposite Mother, I stroked its rich, velvety cover, my fingers delighting in the unexpected softness. Betsy had already taken the seat adjacent to the window, her mouth agape as her eyes leapt from one grand sight to the next. I tried to catch Mother's eye to see whether I should sit in the seat next to hers or in the one facing it, but her attention, firmly fixed upon Betsy, never wavered. The adoring smile playing in her eyes warmed my heart. How often I had caught that same look fastened upon me when she thought I wasn't looking.

Father stepped up behind me and gestured for me to take the seat by the window as the conductor boomed, "All aboard!"

I shared a smile with Father, and he winked. "Looks like we're off to a good start." The train chugged forward, gaining momentum with each turn of its massive wheels.

Mother took a deep breath. "When did you say we are scheduled to arrive, Frederick?"

"Twelve minutes past seven, I believe the ticket master said."

"Tonight?" Now that my reunion with Mattie was imminent, an inexplicable shyness gripped me. It had been so long.

"Heavens, no," Father responded. "Tomorrow morning." He grinned when I exhaled in relief.

"Are you nervous, dear?" Mother took my hand and patted it gently. "I do expect young Matthew is feeling likewise. It has been many years since the two of you have seen each other. You are no longer the school girl he left behind."

I lowered my eyes and nodded. *Fourteen years, almost to the day.* How grown up I had thought myself when last I saw him, yet I had been scarcely more than a child. I shifted my gaze to the kaleidoscope of greens and browns rushing past the carriage window. Things changed so quickly. I thought of my excitement that fateful day so long past as I waited for Mattie to arrive, and the devastating disappointment that had followed. Whatever was I thinking going to see him now? Not that I could turn back at this point. *Jesus, what have I done in arranging this visit?* The train whistle blew as we approached the Newtonville crossing. A single wagon drawn by two chestnut roans waited on the south side of the tracks as the train sped by. *I wonder where they are off to.* Without thinking, I waved to the driver, and was gratified when he smiled broadly, returning the gesture. Mattie was a friend. If a stranger like that driver could muster such joy in a simple greeting, would not Mattie's reception be even more welcoming? Trying to expel my jittery thoughts, I turned to Betsy. "So, what do you think?"

Her eyes danced as a torrent of words spilled from her lips. "Oh, Miss Dora, I have never, ever been on a ride more glorious! The train, why, it goes so fast! I can barely see the trees before they fly past the window." I smiled when she paused to take a breath then rushed on, her words tumbling over each other like pebbles on the beach. "And these seats…" She rubbed her hand across the plush, red fabric. "Why the queen herself would think them most extravagant." Mother and Father and I shared a smile at her enthusiasm while she prattled on. It was not like her to talk so much, though perhaps we had simply never given her the opportunity to speak her mind so freely.

The hours wore on. Betsy produced the basket she had stowed beneath her seat and handed each of us a thick ham and cheese sandwich on my favourite oatmeal bread with a butterscotch roll for dessert and a cupful of lemonade. Never had an evening repast tasted so sweet.

Gradually, the shadows lengthened as the train chugged on. My eyes fluttered and I yawned. "Excuse me," I gasped, snapping my hand to my lips. "That was most rude of me."

Father chuckled merrily. "We shall think about it, daughter." Folding his jacket into a neat, pillow-sized square, he handed it across the narrow aisle. "It's been a long day. You should try and get some sleep."

I wedged the bundled jacket between the window and my shoulder and rested my head against it with a sigh. Perhaps Father was right. It certainly had been a long day and tomorrow promised to be even longer. *Alas, tomorrow… Mattie, I sure hope we know what we're doing.*

Chapter 47

NEW YORK CITY

The train squealed to a halt amidst clouds of billowing steam. Despite the early hour, the platform swarmed with eager travellers and busy porters. As I awaited the call to disembark, I scanned the crowds, searching for Mattie's familiar face. Was that him back there? I squinted to see through the dusty windowpane, willing the figure to reappear.

The iron door at the end of the train car clattered open as a pimply-faced young man wheeled a set of steps into place, his forehead glistening in the early morning sun. It was going to be a warm one. Grabbing my parasol, I hurried down the aisle after Mother, glad to stretch my legs after so many hours of forced inactivity. Accepting the attendant's offer of assistance, I placed my hand in his and descended the steps to the platform, my eyes searching for a glimpse of those dark, chestnut curls I so adored. Where on earth was he? My heart plummeted as I perused the crowd. Surely he hadn't forgotten. Making my way through the throng of passengers, I plodded toward the edge of the loading area where Mother waited, surprised to find Betsy and Father close on my heels. "Any sign of Matthew?" Father asked.

I shook my head. "Not yet."

"Don't worry, Miss Dora, he'll come. I know he will." Betsy's boldness in speaking her mind had grown over the course of our train ride. It wouldn't take much for her to become the sister I had never had.

"Thank you, Betsy." I patted her on the arm, amused by the tell-tale blush rouging her cheeks. "I'm sure he will."

"How be we head into the station and wait for him there." Scanning the busy platform, Father pointed to an arched doorway. "I would think that would be the most sensible place for him to await our arrival."

A train whistle blew and a lusty voice cried, "All aboard!" as we made our way to the hub of the famed Grand Central Depot. Thankfully, the crowds grew thinner the closer we got to the building. I glanced sheepishly at Mother when I found myself searching the face of each passing man for the slightest sign of familiarity. *He had better show up soon.*

After dropping us off in the women's waiting area, Father disappeared to gather our luggage. My hands twitched in my lap as the minutes ticked by.

Mother and Betsy chatted quietly beside me, but I had long lost track of what they were saying. Where was Mattie and why had he not been there to greet us on the platform when we arrived? I brushed my hands along my skirt and folded them neatly on my lap. What if something had happened to him on the way? It wasn't like him to be late.

"Dora." I jerked my head around at the sound of my name. Betsy lowered her head toward mine, whispering, "There's a man—over there." She pressed her hand to her belly just below her bosom, her finger extended toward the marble archway on our left. "I think he's been watching you."

Raising my eyes as surreptitiously as possible, I looked toward the entryway. A middle-aged man with wire-rimmed spectacles and a receding hairline stood by the door, fumbling with his pocket watch. *Mattie?* My heart fluttered when his eyes locked upon mine. He had aged so much. Had it really been that long since we last saw each other? I lifted a hand to smooth my hair, suddenly cognizant of my own age. Fourteen years was a long time.

Betsy touched my arm. "Is it him?"

I rose, barely acknowledging her question. He looked so different. Mother reached for my hand and gave it a squeeze as I took my first, halting step forward. A smile tugged at the man's lips and he lowered his eyes, apparently feeling every bit as shy as I.

Courage renewed, I quickened my step, eager to see the awkwardness of our long-anticipated reunion behind us. My pace slowed as I drew near, my feet straining to propel me forward. We had both changed over the years. What if the changes in me were greater than he had anticipated? I pressed a hand to my gut, chiding myself for allowing such outlandish ideas to occupy my thoughts. This was Mattie—the man who knew my heart, the man with whom I had shared so many of my inmost struggles and triumphs, the man who loved me. Like I loved him. Inhaling courage, I strode the final two steps to the archway and fell into his open arms, my reticence evaporating in the warmth of his embrace. His arms tightened around me and I responded in kind, resting my head upon his shoulder and yearning to hold him closer still, yet fearing I might never be able to let go.

His breath whispered across my ear and I lifted my head, our eyes meeting as he bent to lay a kiss upon my forehead before pressing my head once more to his shoulder. How foolish of me to worry. A sudden flurry of activity drew us apart as Mother and Betsy arrived from one side and Father from the other. Mattie slipped his hand around mine and squeezed it hard as if willing strength to us both.

"Mr. and Mrs. Farncomb, Betsy." He shook Father's hand and cleared his throat. "Do forgive my manners. Welcome to New York City." Our eyes met once again and I rubbed my thumb across his knuckles, unwilling to break the connection. He inclined his head toward our luggage and extended his free hand. "I see you have already fetched the bags. I have a carriage waiting for us just around the corner." He gestured toward the bustling entrance, and with a rueful glance, loosed my hand. "Right this way."

Before Father could respond, Mattie stooped to lift the handles of the baggage cart and headed across the busy foyer. Father held out one arm for Mother and the other for me, leaving Betsy to scurry along behind as we hurried to catch up.

"He would make a fine husband, you know," Father murmured.

I lowered my eyes, refusing to give in to the flood of tears pricking the backs of my eyes. "It is not to be, Father." I paused, determined to master the tremor in my voice. "God has made His will plain. Mattie and I are wed already in heart and soul, and that bond strengthens us both to do the work God has called us to do, but we shall never be wed as this world defines it."

I shifted my gaze, allowing it to rest upon my beloved as Father drew his arm around me. "That makes you sad."

I nodded, swallowing the lump in my throat. "But what we do share is better still. I would not trade one for the other." *Maybe.* The great glass doors loomed before us. Father slid his hand to the small of my back and urged me through to where Mattie waited with the cart, his hair shimmering in the morning sun. No, I would not trade one for the other, but how sorely I wished I could have both.

Chapter 48

The breakfast table, though long abandoned by our host, was laden with offerings fit for a king by the time Betsy and I made an appearance the next morning. A platter of hot, buttered toast sat next to a jar of grape preserves, and a cup of steaming coffee accompanied each plate. "Glad you decided to join us." Father stood to pull out a chair—first for me, then for Betsy—returning to his own seat just as Mrs. Perkins, Mattie's part-time housekeeper, arrived with a platter of bacon and a porringer of scrambled eggs. "What a fine meal," Father pronounced. "I take it our host has long been about the business of his day."

Mrs. Perkins clasped her hands at her waist and nodded. "Ah yes. Our dear Father Wellman is a dedicated man and an extremely early riser. He suggested that you might wish to stop by the church before heading out to explore." She wiped the back of her hand across her glistening forehead. "That women's group he is working so hard to form is meeting at ten, and he wondered if you ladies might wish to join them."

I glanced at the clock on the mantel, relieved to see that it wasn't quite nine. Still plenty of time to finish up here and get to the church before the meeting began. I scooped a mound of eggs onto my plate and snagged a rasher or two of bacon as it passed, eager for the day to begin. If we could help mobilize these women, I could only imagine the impact it would have upon the vulnerable in this great city—upon the Everlasting Kingdom, itself. "Of course we would, Mrs. Perkins." I smiled at Mother and raised a questioning brow, hoping I had not spoken out of turn. "Perhaps if we were to share with them our experience with the ladies' group back home, it would inspire the women with ideas they, too, might wish to pursue."

I spread a dollop of jam over a piece of toast and chewed thoughtfully, not wishing to appear overly eager. Was this not the very reason we had come? I thought back to the last letter Mattie had written. How long ago that seemed, though in truth, it had been but a month. If we could only inspire these women and leave them with a mission and a plan, Mattie's job would be so much easier.

Finishing the last crumb of toast, I excused myself from the table. The sinking realization that my concern for Mattie was the primary motivation behind my eagerness to help troubled me. Were it not for him, would my desire to aid these women be so keen? Slipping into the chamber I shared with Betsy, I sank to my knees beside the bed in which we had slept so soundly the night before. The answer was obvious. *Is it so wrong that I want to help him, Jesus?* Silence permeated the room, threatening to undo me. *By helping him, am I not helping You?* Still no response—no gentle words of affirmation, no answering wave of peace—nothing. The silence within me intensified and I collapsed in a puddle on the floor. *Is it not enough that I want to help?* Frustrated by the conglomeration of motives driving my desire to lend a hand, I tried again. *Are we not supposed to go to this meeting?* I pushed myself into a sitting position and swiped a lock of hair from my face.

Go, beloved.

I angled my eyes skyward and sighed. *Go?*

Peace welled within me. *Go and listen.* I straightened to kneel once more beside the bed.

A rueful smile tugged at my lips as I rose from my knees and turned to survey my rumpled dress in the glass. *This isn't over yet, is it?* I raised my brows and stepped closer to the mirror to examine a smudge beneath my left eye.

Did you think it was?

● ● ●

"Good meeting, ladies." Mattie nodded at the final two women as they disappeared through the arched doors then turned his attention to Mother and Betsy and me, his face alight. "Did you see the way the women devoured the stories you told? You were such an encouragement to them. A true inspiration."

An inspiration? I dabbed the back of my neck with my handkerchief, wondering if Mattie and I had attended the same meeting.

"Never before have I seen those women as engaged as they were today," he added. "I can hardly wait to see what grows from the seeds you have planted."

"Engaged?" Try as I might, I couldn't conceal the incredulity that drove me to respond.

Mattie closed the space between us and held out his arm. "Come. Sit down." I slipped my hand into the crook of his elbow and allowed him to lead me to a nearby pew. He waited while Mother and Betsy arranged themselves on the bench beside me then slipped into the pew directly in front of us. When he paused to bow his head, I wondered if he wished us to pray, but almost immediately, he turned to face us. "I forget this is a very different world for you. A different world entirely. If those women seem to you to be sullen and morose, you must understand it is not for no reason." He brushed a hand across his face. "Unlike the poverty of the village where people yet care and are generally willing to lend a hand, the poverty here is different. Many of those women are immigrants, far from home and shunned by the greater community. They have little for their families to subsist upon and no hope for a better life—for themselves, or for their children. Worst of all, few New Yorkers care and fewer still are willing to lend a hand." He sighed heavily and his whole body sagged. "Those women, and countless others like them, are treated like refuse—used, discarded, trodden upon, despised. All they desire is a better life, yet they are afraid to hope. You offered them today a glimpse into how they might help to make their lives—and the lives of their neighbours—better, but they are afraid to embrace it."

My shoulders drooped and I closed my eyes, for the first time feeling an inkling of their pain.

"They are poor in spirit, as well as in resources, and cannot conceive of how they can minister to anyone, especially when they think they have nothing to share. And those are the rich of this parish." Betsy shuffled her feet on the floor and shifted, clearly uncomfortable. "Your words today inspired them with hope from others in situations like their own, though they have yet to see in it hope for themselves."

"We must build them up in spirit and give them hope in Christ." My words, though spoken quietly, reverberated through the room.

Mattie nodded, a smile crinkling his eyes. "It is as you say, Dora. Only when they are rich in spirit will they have the resources they need to minister to others like themselves, lost in the darkness of fear and shame."

"They believe it is physical resources they need," Mother added, "but those are immaterial." Leaning forward, she gripped the back of Mattie's pew, her words rushing out in a most uncharacteristic way. "Do you suppose there are some women in a parish situated in a richer part of the city to whom we might appeal for aid? Surely if they knew of the plight of these dear women—"

"What a splendid idea, Mrs. Farncomb!" Mattie jumped to his feet and began pacing in the aisle. "Why, perhaps the rector of our parent church, the Church of the Ascension, would be able to help us out. With you ladies pleading the case of these dear, down-trodden women, surely hearts would be moved to give practical aid."

"As surely as God wills it," I breathed. Mattie's pacing escalated, his feet fairly flying across the worn hardwood floor. Bracing myself on the back of the pew before me, I scooted forward in my seat. "Perhaps that is the way we are being called to help—not by mobilizing the women of this parish, but by freeing them from the bonds of hopelessness by mobilizing the women of another."

Mattie came to an abrupt stop at the end of our pew and laid his hand on its swinging door. "We must pray and ask the direction of our Lord."

As one, we slipped to our knees and bowed our heads. To step forth in our own strength, pursuing the path which seemed best to us, would prove vain if God willed that we go in a different direction. I closed my eyes, breathing in the serenity of the chapel as Mattie brought us before the throne of grace. "Yes, Lord," I whispered in response to his words, "show us what You want us to do."

• • •

"There you are." Father met Mother halfway to the carriage and offered her his arm. "I was beginning to wonder if you ladies had gone off gallivanting on your own." He affected a courtly bow as he helped us one by one into the carriage. "Was it a profitable meeting?"

"It certainly was," Mattie declared. "I shall let you ladies know the result of my conversation with Father Thames this evening. I am hopeful that we will be able to schedule a meeting with the women of his parish before the week is up."

Father secured the door to the passenger compartment and mounted the driver's bench before responding. "Who is this Father Thames of whom you speak with such confidence?"

Mattie ran his hand along the horse's rump and gave it a gentle pat. "Father Thames is the rector of the Church of the Ascension on the other side of the city. It is a wealthier parish than mine and is situated in a far more prosperous area of the city." He gestured toward the carriage. "Thanks to these dear ladies, we may have found the key to restoring the hope of the defeated souls I minister to each week by appealing to our sisters at the Church of the Ascension." He shrugged. "I wonder that I never have thought of appealing to the women of another parish to lend aid to the sheep of my own."

"God gave us our womenfolk for a purpose, Matthew, my boy." Father winked as he gathered the reins in his hands and clicked his tongue. "We shall see you at the rectory in a few hours."

• • •

"...and the Brooklyn Bridge..." Betsy babbled on, awed by the majestic sights we beheld on our afternoon excursion. "It has to be the biggest, most beautiful thing I have ever seen. However did the architect conceive of such a massive structure? I actually heard someone say it is over one mile long!"

Mattie dabbed his mouth with a napkin, hiding his smile. "New York certainly does not lack for enthralling sights. If you can imagine it, you can probably find it in the Empire City."

"So we saw." Father set his napkin on his empty plate and pushed his chair away from the table. "I must say, I think the thing that impressed me the most was the navy yard with its grand warships."

Mother patted his arm indulgently. "That was most definitely impressive, dear, but I did prefer the Ladies' Mile with all of its splendid shops."

Father captured her hand in his and cradled it on his knee. "Yes, darling." She nudged him playfully with her shoulder and everyone laughed.

"And what was your favourite part, Dora-girl?"

I fumbled for a response. The afternoon had held such wonders; I could hardly conceive of one being more remarkable than another. "I suppose I especially enjoyed our trip to Central Park. It was such a delight to watch as people of all ages and from all walks of life took a break from their busy schedules to refresh themselves in the beauty of God's creation."

"Rich fodder for a writer's active imagination, I expect." Mattie stood to offer us each a cup of tea. "Shall we retire to the parlour?" He held the chairs for Betsy and myself as Father escorted Mother to the next room, then followed us out the door. "It sounds like you had quite the day."

"Indeed," I responded, taking a seat next to Mother on a threadbare settee. "But I am anxious to hear about yours. Did your meeting with Father Thames go well?"

Mattie set his teacup on the mantel and drew up a chair. "As a matter of fact, it did." He retrieved his cup before sitting and taking a sip of the fragrant brew. "Better than I expected, actually." He gazed around the room, his eyes meeting each of us in turn. "He has invited the three of you ladies to present a plan of action at his church's ladies' Bible study on Thursday evening while we men address ways we might minister to some of the housing issues with which these folk must deal." He paused to offer another round of tea. "Imagine having to raise your children in some of these tenements where rotting doors and broken stairs put your family at risk every day and unsanitary conditions eat away at their health. I'm afraid the city's sanitation reforms that began a few years back have yet to reach the tenements." Mother tsked softly and shook her head. "We may not be able to fix them all," Mattie added, "but for every tenement we undertake to repair, think of the lives that will be changed—touched by the love of God through the practical care of His people."

"Is there a particular tenement on which our initial efforts should focus?" I set my cup on the tea table and folded my hands on my lap.

"I suggest we begin with the one right down the street. Thirteen of the twenty apartments in that building house families who regularly attend my church." Mattie set his own cup down and nodded thoughtfully. "Yes, I do believe that would be the place to begin." He stood and walked to the fireplace. "I'm certain the owners of the building will not allow us to make any structural changes, but surely they wouldn't deny us the right of repair."

"Do you think we can awaken the compassion of the men of this other parish and spur them on to help?" Father had a point. All the scheming and dreaming in the world would prove useless if it fell upon deaf ears.

Mattie paced to the window and stared into the street. A field of electric lights flooded the infamous Longacre Square in the next block, and a wave of raucous laughter rolled through the open window. With a heavy sigh, he drew the shutters and snapped the window shut. "If God is in this, we need not concern ourselves with the results." He ran a hand through his hair and returned to his seat. "Only He can move the hearts of His people, Mr. Farncomb. We can merely provide the opportunity."

"Well stated, Matthew." Mother pursed her lips as if she wished to say more.

Hmmm. It is ours to obey, but His to accomplish the task. It sounded like a good theme for a new article. I scanned the room for a pen and paper. The words were flowing and I had to get them down before they disappeared from my mind. Without a word, I rose and left the room, only dimly aware of the confused stares that followed me. I'd have to explain later. Right now, I needed a quiet spot to pen the flow of words that gushed from my soul.

Returning to my borrowed chamber, I rooted through my bags in search of my journal. Suddenly missing my well-stocked writing desk at home, I sat on the edge of the bed and smoothed the worn book open on my lap. This would have to do. I uncorked the little bottle of ink and set it securely on the bedside table next to my pen. *This could be tricky.*

"Miss Dora?"

"Yes, Betsy?" I slid the tip of the pen into the ink pot, carefully schooling my features lest they betray my annoyance at the interruption.

"Is everything all right?"

I nodded absently as I retrieved my pen and tapped it gently on the side of the bottle. "When inspiration strikes, one must act, I'm afraid." I scratched the date onto the page. *May 16, 1893.* "Please convey my humblest apologies for my sudden departure and assure everyone that I shall join them again as soon as possible."

"Yes, Miss Dora." Betsy dipped her head in the distinctive half curtsey our beloved Anna had taught her so well. I couldn't help but smile; she really was a dear girl. "Do hurry back."

I nodded, my hand poised above the page. Now, what had I been about to write?

Chapter 49

"Ladies and gentlemen..." Father Thames scanned the room, making eye contact with each parishioner. There was a good turnout—more than I had anticipated. "The faithfulness of your parents—and their parents before them—in stepping forth to establish the mission church down in Longacre Square is known by all. It was with great sadness then, that earlier this week I received a visitor from that very church who shared with me the sorry plight in which so many of its congregation find themselves." He gripped the lectern in both hands and lowered his eyes. "As I listened to the stories of those dear men and women, my heart became increasingly distressed. How could this be in our fair city? Recalling the faithfulness of our forebears, I floundered in unanticipated guilt. How dared we forget the less fortunate among us for whom our Lord so clearly bid us care?" He paused, clearing his throat. "My dear brothers and sisters, the time has come for us to shoulder the mantle our ancestors left behind and reach out to the dear souls of that parish that we might lend our aid in the midst of their suffering."

Silence permeated the room, and I shifted in my seat. Would the people of this church, privileged as they were, embrace the opportunity to serve our Lord with the time and resources He had entrusted to them? *Open their hearts, O Lord, and fill them with compassion.*

"Ladies, I have invited here this morning three dear women who happen to be visiting from the Dominion of Canada. They have seen firsthand the neediness of our brothers and sisters in our own mission church and wish to do something to help. These are women who desire to restore hope to the poor folk of Longacre Square and see them thrive in their faith; women who, being active in a mission group designed to aid the poor and needy of their own parish, would beg you in the name of Jesus to consider the plight of 'the least of these, His brethren' and unite in Christ to put your faith into action.

"Meanwhile, we gentlemen will meet with Mr. Frederick Farncomb, Esquire, in the basement room. He, too, would like to speak to us of the situation in which these people find themselves and how we, together with our womenfolk, might be the hands and feet of our Lord to them." Father Thames stepped from behind the pulpit and raised his hands, palms up. "Gentlemen—" Rustling filled the nave as the men departed.

Inhaling deeply, I stood, following Mother to the single stair at the front of the room. "Well, that was quite an introduction, was it not?" Clearly uncomfortable, Mother took a step or two closer to the pews. "It is lovely to be with you today, ladies." She gestured for them to move forward. "Come, gather around and let us talk." Content to let Mother take the lead, I slid into the first pew and patted the seat for Betsy to join me. "Do I understand there are chairs in the church hall?"

A murmur of assent rippled through the room, though no one rose to move. They didn't seem particularly happy to have us here. "Help us, Jesus," I whispered beneath my breath. "Open their hearts to see and respond."

"Supposing we move ourselves into the hall then." Mother swept an arm toward the door. "Shall we? I am certain we could speak more freely without the barrier of pews between us."

I caught Mother's eye as the ladies filed from the room. It wasn't often I sensed a spirit of intimidation buffet my Mother, but I knew no other word to describe the emotion lurking in her eyes. Grasping her hands, I squeezed hard. "Be strong and of good courage," I whispered into her ear. "God is in this and He can soften the hardest heart. He *is* with us."

She nodded and returned my squeeze before trailing the ladies out the door.

By the time we arrived in the hall, the ladies had formed a circle of chairs with three set apart by themselves along the side closest to the windows. "I suppose those are for us?" Betsy pointed to the solitary trio of chairs not far from where we stood, and I nodded for her to take a seat. "Do you suppose we could pull them a little bit closer to the others?"

With a quick blink, I signalled my assent. The emotionless response of these women to our visit troubled me. In our quest for decorum, was this what we all had become? Contrasted with the emotion-laden dismay of the ladies we had met on Tuesday, the chilly reception of these women smacked of condemnation and disdain. Suddenly inspired, I snagged Mother's arm and hurried her to her seat. "God has given me words," I whispered. "I must speak."

I sucked in a breath and breathed a silent prayer. "Ladies, my mother and I have been in New York for little more than two days now, but I have learned something—something important. Do forgive me, Mother..." I turned to glance at the woman who had taught me so much, my eyes imploring her to understand. "I grew up never questioning the idea of decorum. The need to retain composure in all settings and in all circumstances was drummed into me at a very young age, as likewise, I am certain, it was drummed into you. Yet, today, God has revealed to me the folly of that path."

In one collective gasp, the air whooshed from the room and my courage faltered. *God, if this is truly what you wish me to share, You're going to have to give me the words—and the courage to speak them.*

"Ladies, I realize how scandalous those words must sound. I find them rather shocking myself, but I implore you not to close your minds to them." I glanced at Mother. She and Betsy sat perched on the edges of their chairs, their heads bowed, their lips moving in silent prayer. "Perhaps we should begin our time together with prayer," I murmured. As one, the ladies lowered their heads and closed their eyes. "Heavenly Father…" Formality forgotten, I plunged ahead. "The message You bring to us today is shocking to us all and runs counter to every rule we have ever been taught. Reveal Yourself to us, we pray, and help us to understand that we might truly be Your church in this world. As it was in the beginning, is now, and ever shall be, world without end. Amen."

"Amen," a few voices echoed.

A surge of boldness seized me and I stepped forward, opening my arms to the women. "From the time we were very young, our mothers taught us many things. They taught us how to bake and how to mend, how to clean a house and order a household, how to plant a garden and embroider a pillow, but above all else, they taught us the rules of proper behaviour. Now my mother here…" I set my hand upon her shoulder, "… despite how it may seem at this particular moment, did an exceptional job in this area." A quiet titter brought a smile to the ladies' faces, relieving some of the tension. "You see, as proper women, for generations we have been taught to cherish the rigid rules of decorum. To stand religiously by them as if they came straight from the mouth of God. They are the glue that holds our society together—or so we have been led to believe—the cornerstone of respect. But what if they're not?"

I paused, stunned by the rapt attention of these women who had, to this point, seemed so hostile. "On Tuesday, ladies, I was witness to something I had never seen before. When we met with the ladies of your mission church, I saw for the first time a depth of hopelessness in their eyes I had never dreamed possible. These were women who did not even attempt to conform to our so called rules of decorum." I gazed around the circle as the words flowed from my lips, vaguely unsettled by the fact that I knew not where they were taking me. "They said little in response to what we had to say, but their body language spoke volumes. That they doubted their ability to make a difference was clear in their pointed looks and sardonic smiles." Eyes widened around the circle before the masks of decorum I had so suddenly come to despise snapped back into place.

"You know..." I pulled the empty chair forward and sat, smoothing my skirt beneath me, "... like you, I imagine, at first I was taken aback by their patronizing and unmannerly display. That their brows should furrow in disbelief, their heads shake in denial, their eyes meet in unspoken agreement—that they should deign to expose the undercurrent of emotions that drive us all—bothered me. But then, a series of pictures scrolled across my mind."

I stared at my hands folded so primly on my knees and leaned forward, overwhelmed by the flow of words flooding my soul. "A man stood by a sealed tomb, surrounded by grieving people and curious onlookers. The man wept, his tears bathing his face, his grief apparent to all. Then the scene changed. Tears gone, the man stood in the midst of a marketplace, his face etched with anger, overturning tables and wielding a whip fashioned of rope as a throng of priests looked on aghast. The scene changed again. The man was in a garden, crying out with a loud voice, begging his father to let this cup pass, to grant him a less difficult path."

A quiet sniffle punctuated the silence as I strove to still the quivering of my own chin. "You see, ladies..." I waited for them to raise their heads. "Our Lord was not one to stand on decorum." Murmurs of assent filled the room and I closed my eyes. *Thank You, Jesus, for giving me words and for moving the hearts of these women.*

"The Pharisees of the day to whom Jesus spoke with such harshness... they were the ones obsessed with decorum. Oh, may we not be guilty of the same." More murmuring. *Oh Lord, I can hardly believe what You are doing in this room.* "We have seen people in need," I continued, "people whom God has equipped us to help. If Jesus was, as we are told, moved by compassion when He saw the neediness of the people of His day, should our hearts not also be moved by the plight of His people in our own?"

The portly woman sitting in the seat opposite me raised a handkerchief to her mouth and coughed lightly. Her eyes glistened as she peered around the circle. "But what can we do, Miss Farncomb?" Heads bobbed at her simple plea. "We already give as much money as our husbands will allow. Do these people not need to learn to provide for themselves?"

As the conversation turned to the more practical matters of how the ladies could help, I let Mother take the lead. *You really aren't One to stand on decorum, Lord, are You?*

Did you think that I was?

I stifled the chuckle that threatened to escape as the conversation around me intruded upon my stolen moment of prayer. *Maybe it is time I concentrated a little less on it myself.*

Yes.

Yes? Is that all you have to say on the matter—yes?

A ripple of laughter rumbled deep within my soul. *Yes.*

• • •

"Well, ladies…" Mattie squatted by the fireplace, scattering the glowing embers. "I wonder what our dear Mrs. Perkins was thinking lighting a fire in the grate at this time of year." He rocked to his feet and pulled a chair up to the hearth. "In any case, as I was saying, I do not know what you said or how you did it, but the ladies of the Church of the Ascension have been rattling the doors of our little church all week long bearing gifts of food and clothing and seeking ways that they can help. Some have even taken it upon themselves to shadow a woman from Longacre for a day to see what life is really like for these dear souls." I leaned forward, eager to hear more.

"As is to be expected, the women of my parish are cautious of the intentions of these 'fancy dames' and are overwhelmed by the unaccustomed attention being lavished upon them, but they are most thankful for the practical aid."

"Is it not amazing to see God at work in His people?" I jumped to my feet and crossed to the window, peering down the busy avenue. For better or for worse, we certainly were at the hub of activity in this grand metropolis. "Imagine how the world would change if all of God's people would open their hearts, as these women have, to hear the voice of our Lord and act upon His bidding." I raised my hands to the heavens and twirled in a circle, as if I were, once more, a child.

Mattie rose from his seat. "There's no telling where it would stop." Taking my hands in his, he twirled me across the room. "What say you, we go dancing tonight?"

"Dancing?" A giggle from Betsy reminded me that we were not alone. "Tonight?"

Mattie laughed as he spun me onto the settee. "Of course!" He waved his arm to include Mother and Father and Betsy. "All of us. What do you say?"

Mother looked to Father, her lips parted, as if she was recalling something beautiful. "Why not?" Father boomed. "It has been many moons since we have enjoyed a night on the town."

"Fine!" Mattie clapped his hands and glanced at the clock. "I shall arrange for young Mr. Perkins to accompany us." He winked at Betsy and she lowered her eyes. "You do know that his frequent visits to help his mother out at the rectory have only begun since your arrival in New York, do you not? I am certain he would be most delighted to be your partner for the evening."

"But, I-I don't have anything fitting to wear," she stammered. Her hand fluttered to her chest as a rosy blush crept up her neck.

"Oh, but I do." I sprang to my feet, pulling Betsy along with me. "I have a gown that would look splendid on you."

"But—"

"Come on, Betsy." I dragged her toward the door. "This is going to be a night you shall remember for a very long time."

• • •

A heavy knock sounded on the front door, followed by the click of a latch and a murmuring of happy voices. "Are you almost ready, ladies?" Mother nudged our chamber door open and peered within.

"Almost." Fastening a strand of pearls around Betsy's neck, I stood back to admire my handiwork. "You look positively magnificent, Betsy."

A sheen of maternal pride misted Mother's eyes as she took in the scene before her. "You both look lovely. Now, let's go. The gentlemen await us in the parlour."

Snatching one of the wraps strewn across the bed, I followed her from the room, my dress swishing pleasantly with every step. This might be a night Betsy would recall for a very long time, but it would be one that I would remember forever.

Chapter 50

JUNE 4, 1893

"I *am* going to miss you, my Dora-girl."

Averting my eyes, I tried not to squirm, determined to maintain my composure beneath the weight of sorrow crushing us both. *Miss* didn't come close to describing it. "And I, you, Mattie," I managed. *Why, oh why can we not remain together, Lord? Is it really so much to ask?* The sun sparkled on the Hudson River, dancing on its rippling swells. The day of our departure—the day I had been dreading since the moment we first arrived—loomed but a day away. It could no longer be ignored. *Why, God? Why must we part so soon?* I turned my gaze toward the grassy sward where Mother and Betsy had spread out a blanket. As they laid out our lunch, Father snoozed beneath a tree. *Why must we part at all?*

Mattie wrapped his arms around my waist and pulled me backward to rest against his chest. "I cannot bear the thought of parting, either," he whispered. He brushed his lips against the nape of my neck as I snugged his arms tighter around me. It would have been easier if I had never come.

A gentle breeze riffled my hair, enfolding us both in its tender embrace, and I sighed. "At least we will not be alone."

"You feel His presence, too?" Mattie's chest filled, then rapidly deflated. "Father God, we know You are with us, but as our parting grows near, we cannot help but be sad."

He fell silent as we swayed in the breeze. *It is as he says, Oh God.*

"The love You have given us for each other is great—greater than we know how to handle—but our love for You is greater still."

Again he fell silent. *That, too, is as he says, Jesus. I don't want to leave him—not now, not ever—nevertheless, not...* I pinched my lips together. I needed to say the words, though everything within me rebelled. "...not my... will—"

"But Thine." I didn't realize that I had spoken aloud until Mattie's ragged voice joined me on the final two words. Twisting toward him, I threw my arms around his neck and sobbed. However would we manage to bid each other goodbye?

• • •

Tears streamed from my eyes as I pressed my hand to the grubby windowpane, my heart reliving each tender moment of the past three weeks. The train swayed as it switched tracks and my stomach plummeted. *Different tracks.* I dabbed my eyes with my handkerchief. Mattie and I had always been on different tracks. While those tracks periodically shared a station, and most certainly were headed for the same destination, they could not be merged. It simply was not meant to be.

The final blocks of the Empire City gave way to rolling countryside as the train gained momentum. Leaning my head against the back of the seat, I closed my eyes and let the rhythmic motion of the great iron horse lull me into the nether land between wakefulness and sleep. I imagined for a moment that I felt Mattie's arms surrounding me as they had yesterday on the banks of the Hudson River, and I fancied I felt his breath tickling my ear as he whispered my name. *I love you, my Dora-girl. You must not forget that. Forever and always, I will love you.*

I shook myself from the oblivion threatening to engulf me. It was useless to dwell on things that could not be. If it pleased our Lord to place us upon different tracks, who were we to bemoan our lot? He alone knew why it should be so, and He alone needed to know. I opened my eyes to gaze out the window. Heavy clouds obscured the sun, plunging the world into unexpected darkness, yet behind those clouds the sun still shone as brightly as ever, even if my eyes perceived it not. This I knew, though my every sense dared me to deny it. Rain spattered against the window and a great clap of thunder split the air, making Betsy jump. She never had liked thunderstorms. I moved to take her hand, but before I could, the heavens opened and a torrent of driving rain descended upon us. Betsy squealed and threw her hands to her mouth, her eyes fixed on the curtain of water sluicing the sides of the train.

"There's no need to fret, dear." Mother leaned across the narrow aisle and patted Betsy's knee. "It's naught but another storm. It shall pass."

Naught but another storm... That was exactly what this parting was—naught but another storm. We had weathered many over the years, my Mattie and I, and we would weather this one as well. A ray of sunlight glinted through the clouds and the rain began to abate, though thunder yet rumbled in the distance. Yes, we would brave this storm, and doubtless many more to come, because God was with us both. I fingered the sealed envelope Mattie had slipped into my hand as I boarded the train, yearning to open it and devour his parting words yet recalling his admonition to wait until I was alone. My eyes fluttered closed. *Grant me strength for the journey, O Lord. Grant us both strength. And let us learn to be content with whatsoever Thou hast given us.* I yawned. *Let us be true to the call You have placed upon our hearts, Jesus, and may we... bring... glo...ry... to... You...*

Part III

Chapter 51

EBOR HOUSE
TEN YEARS LATER
JULY 1, 1903

"When did you say Johnny and the family will arrive, Mother?" I poked my head into the parlour, my arms laden with gingham tablecloths for our picnic at the harbour. Mother paused in her attempt to arrange Father's chessmen on the checkered stand by the piano. "What was that, dear?" Deep circles framed her eyes. I had never thought of Mother as being old before, but lately, her age had begun to show. The six months since Father's passing had been hard on her—even harder than they had been on me. She had handled his death as matter-of-factly as any woman who truly loved her husband could, but the toll it had taken upon her health could not be ignored. Tucking a trembling hand beneath her apron, she lowered herself to the piano stool.

"Mother..." I darted across the room. "You don't look well today. Why do you not lie down and let me take care of the final preparations?" I moved to retrieve the marble chessman she clenched in her fist, but thought better of it. *The black knight. Father's favourite liegeman.* "I miss him, too," I whispered. Helping Mother to her feet, I slipped my arm around her waist and led her to the couch Betsy had set up in the solarium.

"This was always his favourite holiday, you know."

"His and Alfred's both." I drew a brocade blanket over her legs and tucked a pillow beneath her head. "Imagine them declaring Alfred's birthday Dominion Day. As if our Alfred needed any more fanfare to herald the anniversary of his birth." Mother tsked playfully and we both broke into laughter. Every year, the whole town turned out for Alfred's birthday. As dusk crept in, young and old alike would stand at attention to sing "God Save our Gracious King" followed by a rousing chorus of "Happy Birthday" to Doctor Alfred before the skies would erupt with the most delightful light show this side of the Atlantic—or so I was led to believe. No wonder Alfred loved this holiday above all others; he claimed all the hoopla was for him.

"Now, you stay put, Mother. Betsy and I have everything under control. Betsy has ordered Edith to take care of the cleaning while she herself sees to the food preparations and I pack the picnic basket." Mother nodded, her eyes slipping shut. A good rest would do her good. "You just take some time to relax."

She patted my hand absently and handed me the chessman. "Whatever you say, dear." The warmth of the solarium, combined with the pungent aroma of Betsy's herbs, begged me to join Mother in repose and let the duties of the day fend for themselves, but my conscience left no room for dalliance. Fetching the abandoned tablecloths, I hurried from the room and headed to the kitchen. Perhaps Betsy or Edie would know when the boys were expected to arrive.

The aroma of baking cookies greeted me as I pushed through the door of the side kitchen. Oatmeal raisin—Alfred's favourite. Betsy would do anything for that boy; Anna had taught her well. I set the tablecloths on the board beside a basket of cooling scones and snagged a strawberry from the bucket at Betsy's feet. "It looks like we're almost ready, Betsy." I stashed the tablecloths in one of the baskets by the door and plucked another strawberry from the bucket. "Do you know when those brothers of mine plan to arrive?"

Popping the final strawberry into her own mouth, Betsy handed me the bowl of sliced berries she cradled on her lap and pushed herself to her feet. "I reckon they ought to arrive sooner rather than later, Miss Dora." Relieving me of the bowl, she sprinkled a liberal scoopful of sugar over the luscious fruit and gave it a hearty stir. "The festivities begin at the eleventh hour, and I'm certain our Johnny's two boys would rather die than miss even a moment of the fun."

I chuckled at her apt assessment. "You know them well, Betsy."

"That I do, Miss." Pulling a towel from a rack by the stove, she swung open the door and retrieved the cookies. "Remind me of their dear Uncle Charlie, they do—always horsin' around and lookin' for fun."

"Do you suppose we'll ever stop missing that lad?" I leaned against the board as Betsy loosened the cookies from the baking sheet and transferred them to a cooling rack, the rapid blinking of her eyes the only acknowledgement of my question. "Do you remember the time he told Cousin Bertha that the skunk behind Grandfather's barn was a poor, little lost kitty?"

"I expect everyone within ten miles of the barn remembers that, Miss Dora." She set the rack of cookies on the sideboard and brushed her hands on her apron as she surveyed her domain. "He got into a tidy bit of trouble over that one, though it seems to me I caught your father and uncle sharing a good chuckle over it long after the little rascal was abed."

"I would have thought it was terribly funny myself, had I not had to share a bed with Cousin Bertha that night," I replied. A great guffaw sounded from the doorway, startling us both, and I whirled around. "Johnny! Whenever did you arrive? We didn't hear you come in. Are Janey and the children with you? Did you remember to bring the lemonade?"

"Whoa, girl!" He held up his hands in mock surrender. "I'm glad to see you, too, sis." I nudged him playfully as I pushed past in search of dear cousin Jane. How I rejoiced at the firm friendship that had grown between us since Johnny succeeded Canon O'Conner as rector of St. George's last year.

Strains of Mozart drew me to the conservatory. Winnie, Johnny's eldest, sat at the pianoforte, her back straight as a rod, her fingers dancing across the keys like a troupe of skilled contortionists. Jane stood by the chess stand, absently completing the job Mother had begun. "Janey!" I rushed to her side and enveloped her in a welcoming embrace.

"I was wondering where you had gotten to."

"I was just in the kitchen giving Betsy a hand." Releasing myself from Janey's grasp, I patted Winnie's shoulder as I passed, pleased to see she didn't skip a beat. "It's nice to see you, too, Winifred." At nineteen, she had grown into quite the beauty. "And where, pray tell, are you hiding Marjorie and the boys?" I looked pointedly around the room.

"Nothing could keep them from the call of the beach, I'm afraid." Janey smiled. Hooking her arm into mine, she led me to the settee. "They were off to the lake as soon as the carriage wheels hit the drive."

"Wouldn't want to miss a moment of the fun." I chuckled at the thought. Just like their Uncle Charlie... and Alfred and Johnny, for that matter. "So..." I crossed my ankles and relaxed against the back of the settee. "With Winifred getting married next week and those two young rascals of yours set to graduate from Trinity in less than a year, have you and Johnny given any thought to whether you will settle here in Newcastle permanently?"

Janey propped her elbow on the back of the couch. "That is the plan." Cocking her head, she grinned. "Some days when I look at our life together, I very nearly need to pinch myself to make sure I'm not dreaming." I nodded encouragingly. "I mean, with Jack planning to follow in his father's footsteps by entering the priesthood, young Charles hoping to become a barrister, and Winnie fixed to wed the finest young man a mother could pray for, what more could I ask?" Her shoulder lifted in the tiniest of shrugs. "But to settle here in the village with you and have our dear young Margie to light up our days—could anything be more wonderful?" She shot out a hand and gripped mine. "To think I could actually become a grandma in the next year or so ..." Her voice faded as the song Winifred played came to an end.

A sudden pang constricted my chest. *Grandma…* The word struck my heart like a lash, and I felt as if my feet had been swept out from under me. "Grandma Jane," I managed, though I know not how. "It has a nice ring to it."

She tilted her head, her eyebrow raised. "It does, indeed." Grabbing my other hand, she pulled me to my feet. "Why don't we start walking to the lake and let the others follow when they are ready. You can tell me about the source of that sudden gloom that clouds your countenance."

"Was it that obvious?"

"Only to me, dearest." Her skirt swished as she tugged me into the foyer. "Johnny," she called. "Dora and I are on our way."

Johnny appeared with crumbs in his beard and a half-eaten cookie in his hand. "Wha–? Without me?" His feigned affront made us both laugh.

"Yes, without you, Canon John." Jane inclined her head imperiously. "You and Winnie may join us later with Mother."

"Your wish is my command, my queen." Johnny's eyebrows waggled as he affected a courtly bow.

"Ack, men!" Jane blustered, grabbing my arm and spinning me toward the door. "I swear they're all naught but little boys trapped in the bodies of adults." Johnny's hearty chuckle followed us out the door. There could be no doubt that the two of them were made for each other. No doubt at all. I blinked away a tear as memories of Father's playful jibes began to surface. "He learned it from Father, I'm afraid." I kicked a stone to the side of the drive as we headed toward the road. "They both did."

"They?"

"Yes." I rolled my eyes. "Johnny *and* Alfred. They had a good teacher."

• • •

Despite the early hour, fiddle music issued from the makeshift stage beneath the maple tree and several couples danced on the surrounding grass. Oh, to be young and in love. Janey cocked her head toward the dancers. "I shall have to see if I can convince Johnny to take me for a whirl later on." She stifled a snort as we headed for the tables. "It's been simply ages since the two of us have danced."

"I'm certain he will be most happy to oblige—if you can pull him away from the games, that is." The clang of metal on metal was followed by a triumphant shout from the horseshoe pit.

"Looks like Mr. Hodgeson got another ringer," Janey observed. "I'd wager he's the one to beat again this year."

"He always is." I turned toward the pier, hoping to catch a glimpse of my nephews amongst the group of young men horsing around in the water. A flash of white in the rushes near the shore caught my eye, and I smiled at the sight of my dear Marjorie crouched in the midst of them, feeding a few crumbs to the resident swans.

"You know, she's named every one of those birds, I think." Janey, too, peered at the diminutive seventeen-year-old quietly coaxing the drake to partake of her offerings.

I laughed aloud. "So she told me. Wherever did she come up with such names? I mean, Hector I've heard before, but Heloise?" I know an Auntie is not supposed to have favourites, but there was something so endearing about that girl. She and I had always shared a special bond. Somehow, we had understood each other right from the very start.

"There they are." Janey's voice broke through my reverie. Her arm nearly bumped my nose as she pointed to the harbour, and I drew back. "Over there."

Training my eyes upon the cluster of young men splashing about in the water, I searched for the boys' familiar silhouettes. "Ought they to be bathing so close to the docks?" I squinted my eyes, drawing my hand up to shield them as I searched the sparkling waters.

"Honestly, Dora…" Frown lines formed on Janey's brow. Obviously I had hit a nerve. "Charlie's death was a tragedy, to be sure, but it was a fluke, an unfortunate accident, a horrifying mishap. It's not as if it's going to happen again. I will not permit their uncle's death to steal from my boys the glory of their youth. You and Johnny need to let it go."

Stricken by the vehemence in her tone, I blinked rapidly. "I apologize for my careless words, Janey. My intent was not to tell you how to care for your children."

Janey's shoulders drooped. "No, Dora…" She shook her head and exhaled sharply. "I'm the one who should be apologizing; the fault is mine alone." She raised her eyes. "I know you weren't trying to interfere. I just get so tired of Johnny harping on the dangers of the boys swimming in the harbour." I slipped my arm around her shoulder and drew her close. "I didn't intend to dismiss Charlie's death as insignificant," she whispered.

"I know, Janey—and you're right. Fear is a monster we all must battle in our lives—some of us more than others, it would seem." A comfortable silence stretched between us as we walked across the pebbly beach.

"Ho, Aunt Dora!"

I waved at the tow-headed youth bouncing in the water. "Now which one, pray tell, is that?"

"Jack," Janey responded.

"You would think I'd be able to tell them apart by now."

Janey stooped to pick up a rock and tossed it into the shallow water. "Oh, you can, dear. You have had them straight for years." She flapped her hand dismissively. "It's even difficult for me to keep them straight from a distance, especially when they're in their bathing trunks." She bent to pick up another stone and rubbed her thumb across its worn surface. "They're such good boys, always full of life and ready to lend a helping hand. A mother couldn't ask for better."

"You certainly have been blessed." I waved again as a second head emerged from the water, blinking in the morning sun. There was no question that the two were twins. I adjusted the brim of my hat to better shade me from the sun. "Are they ever one without the other?"

"Not if they can help it, I'm afraid." Janey pointed to the lighthouse and I nodded. It was a good day to wander about at its base. "I do wonder how things will go next year when they part ways for school," she continued.

"I can see how that would be a concern." I stole another glance at the two brawny lads racing toward the buoy at the entrance to the harbour. Jack—or maybe it was Charles—swam a mere stroke behind his brother. "So, how is that mama's heart of yours faring with the thought of letting them go?"

Silence met my words. Had my question offended her in some way? I couldn't imagine how. Her voice, when it came, wobbled with emotion. "Can a mother ever be ready to let her babies go?"

"Especially, I suspect, her sons?"

Sniffling into her handkerchief, she gave a lopsided smile and sighed. "Is that bad, do you think?"

"Is what bad?"

"That it's more difficult for me to let go of my boys than it is for me to let go of my girls?"

"The boys are your babies." I directed her to a bench at the foot of the lighthouse where we could sit and enjoy the view. "Besides, you've always known that one day the time would come to give your girls away in marriage and have been preparing your heart accordingly. I think it's different with boys. It doesn't mean you love your daughters any less."

A triumphant crow split the air, drawing our eyes to the harbour. Young Charles clung to the buoy, his right arm pumping the air as his brother yanked on his leg. "Race you back," he yelled. In a flash, the two were off, their powerful limbs churning the water.

"They're quite the swimmers." I shielded my eyes as I followed their progress to the pier. "I'm betting Jack will be the winner this time."

Janey stood, picking her way across the rocks, and I followed. "There are none better. You do know they tied for the athletics award at school this spring, do you not?"

I nodded. Strength, speed, agility—they had it all in abundance. A companionable silence fell between us once more. A beautiful day, a good friend, a family to cherish, a reason to celebrate... I sighed. "You're right about us being blessed, Janey. So, so right."

She nudged a stone with her toe and raised her eyes to the heavens. "I know."

• • •

"Now that's what I call a good meal." Alfred pushed his plate toward the centre of the table and patted his belly.

"Honestly, Alfred." Shaking her head, Hannah reached for his empty plate. "You call *every* meal a good meal."

I smiled. He'd been doing that for as long as I could remember.

"That's because it is." He winked at his blustering wife then turned to bounce his eyebrows at his two young sons. "No one on the face of the earth can make a meal like your mother."

"And no one in the entire universe can consume one like you, oh husband of mine." She gazed down her nose at the man sitting across from her, her lips twitching despite her obvious attempt to appear stern.

Alfred's great guffaws joined the answering laughter of their neighbours until the whole bench shook. "Would you like a second piece of cake, Doctor?" Mrs. Babcock asked, moving to dole out another hefty slab. "After all, your birthday comes but once a year."

"Pshaw!" Hannah waved her offer away. "Don't you offer him that!" More giggles erupted around the table. "He'll take it and then he'll be up all night long wondering why that iron gut of his won't settle." She grabbed his fork before he dared accept the tempting treat.

"There you have it," Alfred announced. "My wife has spoken." He grinned, first at Mrs. Babcock, then at Hannah. "She's a wise woman, my friends."

Clatter resumed around the table as the womenfolk cleared the dishes and the children returned to their games. What a day! If only Father could have been here with us. And Charlie. The sun neared the western horizon, its final rays gilding the water. Settling Mother near the shore on the wicker chair Johnny had brought from home, I busied myself among the women, packing up baskets and loading them into the waiting carriages.

The warmth of the day began to fade as the first stars appeared. We had certainly been blessed with a beautiful, clear night for the fireworks. A blanket over one arm and Mother's best woolen wrap over the other, I headed to her place on the pebbly beach. The highlight of the day would soon be upon us—and the most difficult. If only we could go home now, not that it would do much good. The day's levity forgotten, I hesitated, the heaviness in my heart slowing my steps. Had there ever before been a Dominion Day where Father had not himself released the first cracker to burst above the harbour? I closed my eyes, fighting the onslaught of emotion. That Alfred should take Father's place in lighting the first firecracker in memory of the man whose love for us had never faltered warmed my heart, yet it also enflamed my grief.

Taking a steadying breath, I braved the final steps to the beach and spread the blanket on the ground next to Mother's chair.

"The fireworks will begin soon." Not a twitch betrayed the emotion behind Mother's words, yet the pain lacing each syllable cut like a lash. I closed my eyes. *Breathe in. Breathe out. Breathe in. Breathe out.* This was not the time to give in to hysteria.

A hand settled on my back, and I looked up to find Janey by my side, her eyes overflowing with compassion. She pressed her lips to my ear. "Are you all right, Dora?" I blinked rapidly and nodded. "It's not unseemly to grieve, you know." I nodded again, my lower lip clenched tightly between my teeth. Silence blanketed us as the darkness of the evening deepened. Johnny came over and wedged himself between us, drawing us both into his arms, and before long, we were surrounded—by Hannah, by Johnny and Janey's rambunctious crew, by Alfred and Hannah's growing brood—by everyone but Alfred... and Father. I leaned against Mother's leg as the mayor stood to bid us all a happy Dominion Day. *Happy Dominion Day, indeed.* I almost snorted, but Mother's calming hand cradling my head reminded me of where we were.

"And now, without further ado," the mayor intoned, "let the fireworks commence!"

A roar of approval ripped through the crowd as the first rocket burst above the water. Red and yellow streams of fire erupted like a fountain followed by a colossal boom and trails of wispy smoke.

"All hail to the harbour master!" somebody yelled, and a chorus of voices cheered.

"Hear! Hear!" came a quiet voice at my side, husky with emotion and laden with grief.

I slid a hand onto Johnny's knee, echoing his whispered, "Hear. Hear." A shower of blue fire illuminated his face, revealing the trail of tears flowing shamelessly down it. *Jesus...* A series of rockets burst above us in a shower of radiant sparks. *How does one live without the ones she holds so dear?*

In incomparable pain. I gasped beneath the weight of the words, wondering if they came from within or without. *I could not bear an eternity without my beloved ones.*

Sudden clarity loosed the voice of my heart. *That's why you sacrificed Yourself on our behalf.* Why had I never seen the significance of His sacrifice before? If, through a sacrifice of my own, I could return Father and Charlie to my arms, there would be no question as to what I would do. Yet, what sacrifice could be made save that which had already been offered? For through our Lord's sacrifice, we, though parted for a time, would be reunited once more. We would not be apart forever. Our temporary separation was but a taste of the pain our Lord bore that drove Him to the cross.

"Are you coming, Dora?" I jerked my head up at the sound of Mother's voice, only to find myself the only one still sitting. Jack, already halfway to the carriage, carried Mother's chair. I scrambled to my feet and bent to collect the blanket, but before I could do so, Johnny swept it from my grasp.

"I'll get that." He folded the corners together and flipped it over his arm. "You go ahead with Alfred and Mother." Looping my hand around Alfred's elbow, I shuffled toward the waiting carriage, still trying to orient myself. Had I really missed the whole fireworks display?

"You were awfully deep in thought." Alfred tipped his head close to mine.

"It's been a difficult evening." Sticks crunched beneath our feet as we crossed the pile of bracken edging the beach. "A lot of memories."

Tugging his elbow gently from my grasp, he wrapped one arm tightly around my shoulders and the other around Mother's. "Are you ladies going to be all right?"

A long-forgotten toad peeked from the recesses of my mind and hopped its way across my memory. "We'll be fine, Alfred. Really," I added when he raised a questioning brow. "Father may no longer be with us, but we are not alone."

He nodded and opened the door to the carriage. "I leave you in good hands, then."

"There are none better, big brother." I paused as the truth of my words took root in my heart. "There are definitely none better."

Chapter 52

AUGUST 24, 1903

My fingers clung to the back of my mother's settee, knuckles white as the fur of the mighty polar bear I'd read about in my brother's *National Geographic* magazine. Why I should have noticed such a thing when the billows of life crashed around me threatening to sweep me off my feet, I cannot say, yet I could not pull my eyes away. White and waxy and unnatural they looked, standing in such stark contrast to the rose-patterned tapestry beneath them. Who could have guessed that a person's knuckles could turn so white?

I tightened my grip, a curtain of black hovering at the edge of my consciousness, and my body swayed. I had to be strong; my family needed me. "Please God..." The whispered words rushed past my lips before I could stop them. My mouth felt like it was coated in sawdust and I swallowed hard. "...not again."

Surveying the room, I choked back a sob. Johnny sat at the far end of the settee, rocking Janey as she wailed in his arms, her face buried in her hands. "Charles... Jackie... No-o-o-o-o-o." Her keening wails ripped at my heart, slashing at the edges of an old wound.

Oh Lord, not the twins, too. With a pain so intense I thought I would die, the dungeons of my heart broke open and searing memories gushed forth—memories I would just as soon forget; memories I had spent years trying to suppress—and I fell to the floor in a heap.

When I came to, I was surrounded by a knot of anxious faces staring into my own. As usual, Mother was the first to respond. Her hand trembled as she ran a wrinkled knuckle down my cheek, her watery eyes gazing into mine. "Dora..." She stopped, her face contorted in pain, her voice strangled by grief. Thrusting her arms around my quivering shoulders, she pressed me to her bosom, enveloping me in a fierce embrace. Her heart beat against my chest, drumming in time to my own, and a precarious peace descended upon me. We were going to be all right.

With an unladylike sniff, I loosed my death grip on Mother's neck and rocked back to look her in the eyes, a quiet knowing passing between us. We had been here before and survived. All of us. With the slightest dip of her head, she accepted Alfred's hand, and he helped us both to our feet. If only Father were here to guide us as he had that day so long ago. In his absence, I looked to Alfred and laid my head upon his shoulder.

"Weeping may endure for a night," he rasped, quoting the scriptures of which Father had been so fond, "but joy cometh in the morning, Dora. This, too, shall pass." His voice faded with each word. Patting my shoulder, he led me to the overstuffed chair by the fireplace. I tried to be strong, tried to resurrect a smile, but the pressure building behind my eyes would not be ignored, and the tears I fought so hard to restrain burst forth. The nights were getting longer; morning would be a long way off.

In the silence that followed, the new harbour master quietly showed himself out. Alfred pulled nervously at his beard. "Shall I see to the arrangements, Johnny?" A muffled wail. A strangled sob. Alfred glanced my way, no doubt recalling, as I, that horrible moment so long ago when we had tiptoed into the parlour to find Mother sitting awash in grief while Father spoke to the man who had directed the search for our little brother. "Dora, would you be able to accompany me?"

Our eyes met and I nodded, pushing aside the emotion of the moment. There were things that needed to be done. "We should speak to the Reverend Mr. Gilson in Bowmanville to see if he can conduct the service," I said. Johnny buried his face in Janey's neck, his shoulders trembling.

"That sounds like a good idea, dear." Mother rose and began issuing orders. "Marjorie, you go help Betsy in the kitchen. Alfred, you and Dora talk to the minister and see that Winifred gets the news. She needs to know immediately." She glanced at the couple huddled together on the couch and closed her eyes.

That history should so cruelly repeat itself disturbed me. *Why, God?* I railed. *Was it not enough that Mother had to lose her son? Did you really have to steal her grandsons from her as well?* Alfred rested a hand on my shoulder, bringing me back to the moment. What was I thinking? The Lord giveth and the Lord taketh away. Who was I to question His purposes?

Mother closed the space between us and patted my arm. "Dora, you can help Alfred word the telegram as gently as possible?" She gazed beseechingly into my eyes, and I blinked my assent.

"Don't worry, Mother," Alfred assured her. "We will take care of it." He slid his hand down my back and pushed me toward the door. "We shall be sure Winifred gets the message and that it is delivered as kindly as it was once delivered to us."

A tight smile. A heavy sigh. The barest of nods. "Do you think Mother will be able to help?" I whispered as we stepped into the foyer.

Retrieving his hat from its hook, Alfred prodded me through the door. "She understands what they are going through; if anyone can help, she can. And we..." He inhaled deeply. "We understand what our dear Winnie is about to face. We had best start thinking about how to break the news to her."

I wracked my brain, searching for words that didn't exist as Alfred helped me into the carriage and guided the horse onto the road. Poor, poor Winnie. She would be devastated when she heard the news. "Why do we not send word to her husband instead?" I vividly recalled the evening Alfred had come to the school to tell me about Charlie. His face held the same stoic expression now as it had then. "He will be able to break the news to her more gently than a telegram ever could, no matter how carefully it is worded."

"You're a wise woman, Dora." Alfred slowed the horse to a stop at the railway crossing as a rail cart clattered down the track. "So, how should we word the telegram to our young Mr. Fitz?"

I slumped against the back of the seat, the rhythmic clopping of the horse's hooves enumerating each passing second. Why could I not think? *Clip, clop. Clip, clop.* "I fear there is no gentle way to convey such news, Alfred." I trained my eyes upon the road ahead. "You're a doctor—surely you know better than I the right words to say." *Clip, clop. Clip, clop.* Was he not going to respond? As if ignorant of the exchange, Alfred stared into the distance, barely flicking the reins when the horses approached the hill at the edge of town. *Clip, clop. Clip, clop.* The sun beat down upon us. How had I managed to leave the house with neither parasol nor hat?

"I just cannot believe they are gone," he whispered. He shook his head and grimaced. "A boating accident? Seriously?" He darted a glance my way. "Those two could swim like fish."

Willing myself to be strong, I brushed away a tear, hoping that Alfred wouldn't notice. "I can't believe it either. How can this be happening all over again?" I lowered my head, pressing my fingertips to my temples. "I wonder if we'll ever truly know what happened out there."

Air hissed from my brother's mouth in an angry huff. "It just doesn't make sense!"

Recalling the boys' spirited races on Dominion Day, I swallowed hard. Two strong, young swimmers in the prime of their lives wiped out in the blink of an eye? It didn't make sense at all. Still... "I suppose the fact that they died as heroes, striving to save the Bailey boys' uncle, should bring some measure of comfort to us, though I confess my heart takes little solace in the knowledge." Silence lapsed between us, and I reached for his hand. "Whoever said that time heals all wounds never lost a brother... or a nephew."

"Or a son," Alfred added, his voice flat. "Heaven forbid that I should live to grieve the death of my young George or Alfie." I squeezed his hand, knowing it would do little to console, yet hoping it might remind him that he was not alone in his grief. With a heavy sigh, he continued. "I can't imagine the pain rending Johnny's heart at this moment—or Janey's either, for that matter. Their sons—not one, but both—have been torn from their arms at the height of their youth, and there was nothing—not one thing—they could do to stop it." Alfred smacked the mare's flanks with the reins and she lunged forward, quickening her pace. "Not one–blasted–thing."

"You're angry." It was an observation, not an accusation, though Alfred obviously perceived it otherwise.

"Yes, I'm angry. Of course I'm angry." He spat the words from his mouth, his eyes blazing. "Are you not also?"

I gripped the bench beneath me and took a deep breath, praying for the wisdom of God to respond. Choosing to ignore Alfred's question, I posed one of my own. "With whom are you angry, Alfred?" His mouth clamped shut as I forced myself to continue. "The boys? Their friends? The man they tried to save from drowning?" He stared straight ahead, his eyes glazing. "Who, Alfred?" I pressed. "Johnny and Janey? The harbour master? The townsfolk who spent hours searching for them?" I let my voice trail off, certain I knew the answer, but knowing he had to come to it himself. "With whom are you really angry?"

The horse slowed as we neared the outskirts of Bowmanville. Alfred still hadn't spoken. Words burned within me, but I dared not let them free until he had admitted the truth.

Even so, when he finally spoke, the venom in his words startled me. "I'm angry at God, all right?" He tossed a glance heavenward then pierced me with a glare as sharp as any arrow. "There. I said it. Are you happy now?" He reined the horse to a halt outside the church. "I am angry at God."

I lay my hand on his forearm and waited for him to look at me. Such feelings could not be allowed to fester. "Why, Alfred? Why would you be angry at God?"

His mouth dropped open. "Why?" With a shake of his head, he pushed himself from the carriage and jerked the reins around a hitching post. His back toward me, he stopped. Stiff. Rigid. Unyielding. And then his head drooped, though the tension in his posture remained. Turning, he helped me from the carriage.

"God did not kill Johnny's boys, Alfred." I let the whispered words drift away on a prayer. Tears stabbed the backs of my eyes, demanding release, but I pressed my lips together, determined to stem their flow.

"Well, He certainly didn't do anything to stop them from dying now, did He?"

I swallowed hard as he grasped my elbow and headed for the arched doors of the church. I practically had to run to keep up with him, taking two steps for every one of his and fighting the tangling of my skirts around my ankles. What could I say? His words bore a truth I did not wish to acknowledge. *He's right, God. You could have stopped this from happening. You could have let them live.*

Yes.

Yes? Is that all…

Yes, I could have saved them from drowning.

So why—why would you let them die? It was a plea more than a demand. *I don't understand.*

Do you have to?

A vision of a frightened toad hopping into a thorn bush reeled across my mind, and I drew my hand to my chest, transfixed by the memories it elicited.

"Dora, are you all right?" Alfred's fingers tightened around my arm as he opened the heavy, oaken door. I nodded, not trusting myself to speak. "I'm sorry I upset you with my careless words," he mumbled.

"Please do not apologize for sharing your heart, Alfred." I paused as a wave of grief rolled over me. "I don't understand why Jack and Charles were taken from us any more than I understand why Charlie was, but it's not always given to us to understand the ways of our Father."

"May I be of some assistance?" Straightening, I pulled my arm from Alfred's grasp as a priest approached, extending his hand to my brother. "I am Father Gilson. You look distressed." His eyes flickered toward me then back to my brother.

Alfred cleared his throat. "Yes, I suppose we are. I am Doctor Alfred Farncomb, brother of Canon John Farncomb, rector of St. George's in Newcastle. This is our sister, Dora."

"Ah yes—Johnny. How is the old chap doing?"

"I'm afraid he is not doing particularly well right now." I cringed at the irritation in Alfred's reply.

"I'm sorry to hear that." Father Gilson motioned toward a narrow doorway off the nave. Perhaps we should step into my office where we can talk."

∙ ∙ ∙

An hour later, Alfred reined the horse to a halt outside the telegraph office.

```
Andrew Fitz, Esquire, Toronto
Accident at harbour STOP Jack and Charles drowned STOP Funeral
tomorrow at two
Aunt Dora
```

"I don't know, Alfred." I gazed beseechingly at my brother. "How can one deliver a message like that gently at all, let alone in a telegram?"

Alfred nodded to the telegraph operator and handed him three tarnished dimes. "You said what had to be said, Dora." He shrugged, motioning toward the building across the street. "There is no easy way to convey such things, especially when you are limited by the number of words you can use. Sometimes the kindest thing is to get straight to the point."

I squared my shoulders, suppressing a sigh.

Looping his arm around my waist, Alfred drew me into a long, strong embrace. "All will be well, dear sister of mine—isn't that what you always tell me?" The warmth of his breath whispered past my ear. "I may be angry at God, but He is still in control."

I nodded my head against his sleeve, struggling to draw breath. "And He is good, Alfie... no matter how it might seem to us at this moment."

Tightening his arms, he expelled a measured breath. "I know, Dora-girl. I know. But you're going to have to keep reminding me."

Chapter 53

OCTOBER 3, 1903

The days wore on, each more difficult than the one before. With a deadline looming, I scrambled for words to put on the page as I watched my brother's family flounder in the aftermath of the tragic accident that had ripped from them their boys. Johnny immersed himself in his work, leaving Janey to wander the house like a wraith or sit by the hearth like she did now, staring into the flames. Gazing across the room, I shuddered at the emptiness in her eyes. Were it not for the barest rise of her chest when she breathed, I might have thought her dead. If only there was something I could do to comfort her.

Unable to watch any longer, I turned toward my desk and thrust my pen into the inkwell. Poor, dear Janey. She hadn't spoken to anyone since the funeral. If she didn't snap out of it soon…

With a heavy sigh, I set pen to paper and wrote the first words that came to mind.

Difficult times are a part of life.

The familiar skritch of pen against paper calmed me, and I let loose the fountain of words that bubbled up from within.

'In this world you will have trouble,' our Lord assures us.

I glanced toward the settee and rose reluctantly.

"Can I get you some tea, Janey?" I asked, silently willing her to respond. Her face looked pale, even in the light of the flickering fireplace. Had she, too, left us? I rested a comforting hand upon her shoulder and felt her stiffen. She had certainly had more than her fair share of trouble in this world. Far more. Would she ever be able to break out of the melancholia that held her so firmly in its grip?

I squeezed my eyes shut and stifled a groan as the haggard face of my brother filled my mind. What was to become of them? They had loved those boys so much. Whatever were they going to do without them? Laying a gentle kiss upon her head, I shuffled back to my desk. I had a column to write, and it wasn't going to write itself.

'In this world you will have trouble,' our Lord assures us...

I read the words aloud and paused before picking up my pen to continue.

'But be of good cheer, for I have overcome the world—weeping may endure for a night, but joy cometh in the morning.'

My eyes darted toward my sister-in-law. *Let it be so, O Lord. Let it be so.* I dipped my pen once more into the ink and blotted it on the desk pad. The hope was real, but how…

The question is, how does one keep hope in the darkness of night? When tragedy strikes and sorrow engulfs, how does one cope? We know God is good, and we know He is in control, but what happens when the realities of life conspire to shout, "It is not so!"

"In this world, you will have trouble…" The words of Jesus pound against our hearts. He did not want His disciples to expect a life of ease, for He knew that would cripple their faith. Jesus' disciples of old lived in the same fallen world in which we find ourselves today. Our Lord is a mighty Lord, in control of all things. His purpose is not to grant His children a life free of suffering, but to draw our hearts—and the hearts of all mankind—to Himself. To fill us with love and with joy and with peace in spite of our pain. Though we beg with all our hearts, in His goodness He does not remove from us the very trials that

will draw us closer to our Father. Instead, He gives us the strength to persevere when they strike.

Yet, what happens when the clouds of sorrow so obscure one's vision that he loses sight of the Son?

Lifting a hand, I massaged my temple. *Oh, that I knew the answer.* I glanced at my sister-in-law's motionless form. *What then, Lord?* I waited, hoping for a ready answer, fearing no answer under heaven would suffice. Replacing my pen in its holder, I rose to attend the fire. Sparks flew as I tossed another log onto the grate, and I scrambled to extinguish an errant ember. "Would you like me to get you some tea, Janey?" I asked again. Not waiting for an answer this time, I poured two cups of the amber brew from the silver tea service Betsy had brought in earlier. I added a splash of milk to hers, along with a smidgen of sugar, then stirred it with her favourite teaspoon. "Here we go." I handed her the saucer and wrapped her fingers around the cup until I was certain she wouldn't let it drop. "There is nothing quite like a spot of tea to calm the frazzled soul."

Taking my own tri-legged cup from the tray, I settled on the settee beside her. "It's a beautiful day out there, Janey. Have you noticed the fiery-red foliage of the maple tree at the end of the driveway?" I paused, debating if I should continue. Avoiding all mention of the boys was making me crazy. The pain of their absence could not be relieved by silence. It wasn't as if they were ever far from any of our minds. "I seem to recall those two young rascals of yours spending a great deal of time in its branches over the years." I gazed deeply into Janey's eyes. Was that a flicker of remembrance I saw in their depths? "I could swear there was nowhere on earth either of them would rather be than up in that tree." I watched her expectantly, certain I had seen the ghost of a smile playing at the corners of her lips.

Lost in a treasure trove of memories, I lapsed into silence. Charlie used to love that tree, too. He would spend hours swinging from its branches with Samson gazing up at him from the ground. How I missed that old dog. The day he died, we finally buried Charlie for good, leaving naught but his memory to comfort us.

Blinking tears from my eyes, I set my teacup on the table. "Are you finished with your tea, Janey?" I reached for her empty cup, surprised to see tears dripping from her chin. Prying the cup from her hands, I set it on the table and drew her into my arms. "I loved them, too, Janey. They were such beautiful boys." A sob escaped her and I tightened my embrace, rocking her like a child. "Take heart, my dear sister, they *are* well. Even now, they are with their uncle and their grandfather, safe in the arms of God. Though we miss them with all of our hearts, we *will* see them again one day. And when we do, we shall never fear parting again. Never."

The keening that erupted from the crumpled form beside me nearly tore my heart in two. This was the first I had seen her cry. "They have not been taken from us, dear Janey—they have merely gone on before us."

A low moan. A quiet whimper. My heart soared at the first signs of her awakening from the deadly stupor that had claimed her. And then it was gone, replaced by a palpable silence as heavy as lead. Easing her back to lean against the settee, I folded her hands on her lap, my new-found hope evaporating like dew on a summer's morn. *Why, God? Why can we not reach her? Nothing any of us does seems to do any good. Even Alfred, with all of his fancy degrees in women's medicine, seems at wit's end. He and Johnny have even started talking about committing her to the insane asylum. Show us, I pray You, how to break through this debilitating melancholia that has gripped her... and bring her back to us soon.*

Replacing our cups on the tea tray, I covered Janey's legs with a blanket and returned to my writing. *What* does *happen when the clouds of sorrow so obscure one's vision that she loses sight of the Son?* I knew the answer, though I hardly dared to acknowledge it. *Insanity—complete and utter insanity—like Janey's.* Once more my thoughts turned to prayer. *What can I do to help her out of this cesspool of despair, Jesus? What can I do to help her?*

Hold forth the light that she can no longer hold for herself.

I stilled at the quiet response. I had grown so accustomed to God's silence in the past month that I had stopped expecting an answer. *Hold forth the light?* I drew my thumbnail to my lips. How was I supposed to do that?

You must keep reminding her, beloved. Remind her that she is Mine—as are her sons—and that my love for them surpasses all earthly understanding. Remind her that I have not abandoned her, that I am with her no matter where this life takes her, that death is not the end.

I picked up my pen, eager to capture His words before they drifted from my mind.

We hold forth the light of our Lord and cling to His promises for those who can no longer see it for themselves. Yea, we raise it high for all to see, that the love of God might break through the clouds of sorrow and heal the despairing soul. But how exactly do we hold forth that light? We...

Warmed by the revelation, I relaxed as my pen wrote on, almost as if it had a life of its own. I may not be able to banish the melancholia that held my sister so firmly in its sway, but at least I knew now what I could do to help. I could hold forth the light in these days when she was too weak to hold it for herself, praying that her eyes would be opened to see it and her heart awakened to claim it as her own. But how? Knowing *what* to do always seemed so much easier than knowing *how* to do it.

I plunged the nib of my pen into the pot and waited for the ink to fill its hidden recesses. *How am I supposed to hold the light for her when I'm not even certain that I know how to hold it for myself?*

I tapped my pen lightly on the edge of the ink well and dabbed the nib on the blotter.

Yet, how exactly does one hold the light for another?

I scratched the words onto the paper.

Simply put, we be to them the hands and feet of Jesus. We walk with them through the valley, sharing in their grief and reminding them of the truth. We are not alone. We have not been abandoned. God really does care for us and can be trusted unconditionally, even when the unfathomable threatens to devour us whole. We are now, and ever will be, His precious children. Our Lord has overcome. Read to them, sing to them, and pray for them when they are too weak to do these things for themselves. Laugh with them. Cry with them. Be for them a picture of our Lord Jesus Christ, who warned us that in this world we will have trouble, yet bid us take heart regardless, for He has overcome the world.

I removed my spectacles and rubbed my eyes. *Now that is an answer if I ever heard one.* My thoughts drifted to Janey. She hadn't moved since I had left her. *What would You do for her right now, Jesus, if You were me?* A picture of her hands, so colourless and frail, flitted through my mind. It seemed as good a thing as any. Rising, I joined her on the settee and took her icy hand in mine. Without saying a word, I caressed it in my own. *Is this what You meant, Jesus?* Silence. *I mean… is this how I hold forth Your light?* A slight relaxation of the claw-like digits. An almost imperceptible slowing of the pulse in her wrist. Was I imagining things? I studied her, my brow furrowed. Was this the way to break through the crushing melancholia and bring her back to herself?

That is not up to you.

What? I jerked my head upward, ignoring the rudeness of my response.

That is something only I can do, beloved. It is a burden too great for you to carry.

Tightening my grip on her hand, I closed my eyes as the breath I had been holding bled from my lungs.

It is not up to you to bring her out of the wretched state in which she finds herself, beloved, but to walk with her through it.

To walk with her through it. To walk with her through it. I opened my eyes, surprised to see that Janey had mimicked me in relaxing against the settee.

The shuffling of feet drew my eyes to the doorway where young Marjorie stood, her mouth agape. Smiling, I beckoned her forward. As seamlessly as possible, I wriggled from my spot beside her mother and slid to the side so that she could take my place. Janey stiffened for a moment, then relaxed even more, the minutest of smiles replacing the expressionless façade masking her face. "She's glad to have you with her," I whispered, not wishing to upset the fragile balance of the moment.

"She is?"

The skepticism in Marjorie's voice tore at my soul. Nodding, I pointed to Janey's face. "Do you see that smile?" Marjorie glanced from her mother to me, her eyebrows quirked. "It wasn't there a few minutes ago."

"It wasn't?"

For the first time, I heard the tiniest spark of hope in her voice. "Just sit with her, dear. Your presence will speak the words her ears are no longer able to hear. She will know, if only for a minute, that she is not alone."

Retreating to my writing desk in the corner, I weighed my pen in my hand and glanced at my final line.

Be for them a picture of our Lord Jesus Christ, who warned us that in this world we will have trouble, yet bid us take heart, for He has overcome the world.

Where to from there?

Alas.

The word fell from my pen like a sigh.

How prone we are to forget. Our minds cling to the truth that He has overcome, but when the realities of life seem to contradict that truth, our hearts cannot help but quake.

Once again, I rose from the table, unable to continue. This wasn't getting me anywhere. I needed to bring this article to a conclusion, yet all I had to offer were questions. Hard questions. The kind of questions that could cause the most faithful soul to tremble.

"I'm going out for a while, Marjorie." Questions flared in the young woman's eyes as she cradled her mother in her arms. "I won't be long," I assured her. "I just need to get some fresh air. Your grandmother is upstairs resting should you need anything, and Betsy is in the kitchen."

"Are you well, Aunt Dora?" She bent forward as if to get up.

"I'm fine, dear. There's no need to fret." I sagged against the door frame and tried to smile. "I just have one of those questions that God alone can answer, and I'm awaiting His response."

Averting her eyes, she tightened her hold on her mother. "Do you really think He will answer?"

I bowed my head, moved by her candour. *Did* I think He would answer? He always had, though not necessarily at the time I saw fit or in the way I expected, let alone desired. I cast a glance heavenward, praying for the right words. "The question is not so much whether I think He will answer, dear, as whether I will recognize the answer when it comes, and whether I will appreciate the answer He provides." I straightened to leave. "Difficult questions, I'm afraid, too often elicit answers I do not wish to hear. Pray for me, dear. Just pray."

Tears seeped from beneath the young woman's lashes—tears no words could assuage. Slipping from the room, I donned my woolen cape and stepped into the fading sunlight. A gentle breeze riffled through the branches above me, sending the Hallelujah trees a-trembling. *Hallelujah trees.* I smiled at the unexpected emergence of my childhood name for larches. *When did I start calling them that?* Perhaps it was the summer Aunt Caroline came to visit. Fanciful as she was, I had adored her and spent many hours beneath the tutelage of her vivid imagination. Though I knew not when I had renamed the graceful trees, I could never forget why I had adopted the fanciful nomenclature.

I contemplated the trees. Poplar leaves trembled at the slightest stirring of the air around them. Poplars, birches… larches of all kinds. They all did it. Dancing on their boughs, the leaves would rustle about in excited abandon, their voices rising in a cacophony of praise as if calling to each other, "He's coming! He's coming! Get ready for the King!" The slightest hint of a breeze would set them a-flailing, but the greater the stirring of the air, the more urgently they proclaimed their message until even the trunk would begin to sway, shouting, "He is here! He is here! He is here! Hallelujah!"

Yes, in the midst of the greatest storms, my ears could hear their eager voices shouting forth their message. "He is here! He is here! Hallelujah!" Oh, why could I not be more like those ever-faithful trees? When the storms of life intensified, my hands were far more apt to be found grasping a shield and sword than raised in open praise, my eyes more focussed on my pain than upon the presence of my Lord. *Jesus, make me like those Hallelujah trees—my attention fixed upon You despite the pain writhing in my heart—my soul overflowing with unrestrained delight.*

A soothing breeze wrapped its arms around me as if in answer to my plea as the cry of the trees shook the heavens. "Hallelujah! Hallelujah! Hallelujah!" *Hallelujah, Jesus! You, O Lord, are greater than all imagining, more beautiful than the finest sight my eyes could behold, more steadfast than the mightiest mountain.*

I wrapped my arms around my body, not realizing where my feet were taking me until I fell to the leaf-littered grass beneath the thinking tree. How long it had been since I had dared to rest beneath its sheltering arms! A handful of yellow-brown leaves yet clung to the barren fronds cascading around me, maintaining a semblance of the illusion of privacy I had always felt beneath its tent-like boughs.

From the heights of the storm, I cry to You, O Lord—to You who bid the waves be still and calmed the raging winds. Give me Your strength to endure the force of the gale when the world around me is swept away. Grabbing a fistful of fallen leaves, I let them filter through my fingers and flutter to the ground from whence they had come. *I so want to be like those Hallelujah Trees: the greater the winds that buffet, the more insistent my praise.* I threw myself onto the ground and raised my arms above my head, drawing them down through the leaves as I had so often done as a child to make angels in the snow. *If only I knew how, Jesus. In the midst of great trial, I'm afraid that praise is not my most natural response. Would that it were.*

With a heavy sigh, I pushed myself into a sitting position, glad that nobody was around to witness my lack of decorum. *He gave me beauty for ashes, the oil of joy for mourning, the garment of praise for the spirit of heaviness…* The words of the prophet seemed to come out of nowhere, repeating themselves over and over in my mind. *He gave. He gave. He gave.* The joy, the praise… it was not something a person did; it was a gift he was given in the midst of great trial. A gift—unmerited and unearned—not the product of one's own accomplishment or will.

Rolling to my feet, I ducked from beneath the great willow and wandered toward the pond. If there was something I coveted, it was that. *Grant me the oil of joy, Jesus, for my heart surely mourns—and the garment of praise, for my soul bears a heaviness greater than it has ever before known. My spirit withers within me, parched for that Living Water You promise to supply, and I stumble through each day overwhelmed by the task of remaining strong.*

Your own strength will fail you, beloved; it is not enough. I squeezed my eyes shut. That I already knew. *But My strength is sufficient, no matter what disaster befalls. It will never fail you.*

"I know. I *know*." I wanted to shout. If only I knew the psalmist's secret of how to live in the strength of my Redeemer. Even more agitated than before, I kicked a pebble into the pond and turned toward home. I dared not leave Marjorie and Janey alone for long.

A flock of geese flew southward as I trudged across the meadow, their incessant honking urging each other onward.

Take courage, beloved, and be at peace. I am with you. Always.

The autumn breeze caressed my face—the sacred touch of my Creator's hand—and suddenly the day seemed brighter. The fiery red of the maple tree across the way glowed like I had never seen it glow before, and the brilliant yellow of the oak shone with a radiance I never could have imagined. Even the sound of the crickets hidden in the grass seemed sweet. It was as if the whole world had been made new.

"Then sings my soul, my Saviour, God, to Thee—How great Thou art. How great Thou art…" I broke off, astounded by the song that spilled from my lips.

I couldn't recall the last time I had burst into spontaneous song, though I used to do so all the time. Since when had the trials of this life stolen the song of my heart?

My steps quickened as I neared the house, and I bounded up the stairs as if I were a little girl again. "I'm back!" I called as the door latched shut behind me.

Marjorie appeared at the top of the stairs, a worried frown wrinkling her face. "Aunt Dora—you're here. You need to come right away. I've already sent for Uncle Alfred. Something is wrong with Grandma."

Chapter 54

OCTOBER 25, 1903

My Dear Mr. Wellman,

How are things in New York? I am so glad to hear that your congregation is growing, albeit rather slowly. Is the pairing between your church and the church downtown still producing fruit? I pray often for you and the people of both churches.

 As for me, sometimes I wonder how much more I can take with one catastrophe following another. I know that God is in control of all things, but somehow, in the midst of my trials, it is so very difficult to hang on to the reality of that truth. Mother is now bed-ridden following a fit of apoplexy, and Alfred sees little hope of a full recovery for her. She is, however, still herself in other ways and is doing an admirable job of ordering household affairs from her bedchamber.

 With great heaviness of heart, Alfred and Johnny finally took the step to commit Janey to the Asylum for the Insane at the beginning of this week. Johnny has made arrangements to switch parishes with Father Duncombe of St. Matthew's in Toronto as soon as possible as he wants to be closer to his dear wife. I so wish that I could go with him, but Mother needs me here. I suppose there is little I can do to help him through this deep valley, though, regardless of where I am. Nor do I seem to have the words to help Alfred. He has felt the loss of Johnny's boys nearly as keenly as Johnny himself and is struggling with the fact that, specialist though he be in women's health, he has been woefully unable to treat the hysteria which has led to Janey's acute melancholia. We are all hoping that the doctors at the asylum will have greater success with their moral therapy treatments, but I am afraid I am more than a little skeptical. How I dread the things our dear Janey may have to endure at their hands.

Young Marjorie, too, is suffering. She has opted not to move to Toronto with her father next week, instead deciding to stay here with Mother and me, taking on the role of companion to us both in our aging years. Alfred will employ her two or three days a week at the pharmacy he recently opened in the village, and I will keep her busy the rest of the time waiting on Mother and expanding our ministry to the poor and needy of the community. She is a good girl and I shall welcome her company, not to mention the additional set of hands.

Pray for her, Mattie, will you not? She has effectively lost her whole family in one fell swoop. Her sister, Winnie, is taken up with her own family now, and our dear Margie not only suffers from the loss of her brothers but from the abandonment of her parents as well.

Her mother—as she knew her, anyway—has completely disappeared inside herself, and her father, overwhelmed by his own sorrow, has buried himself so completely in the work of the church that it seems he has all but forgotten that he has a daughter who needs him. How my heart weeps for them all. I do not see God's goodness in this, Mattie, nor do I see His footsteps in the depths, yet I will not let my blindness blot out what I know to be true. He is good, I keep reminding myself, and He is here. Why, oh why does life have to be so harsh? Why must such suffering seize us in its grip? Why can it not simply be easier? Why, Mattie? Why?

I know. You do not have the answers any more than I do. I keep telling myself that I do not need to know the whys and wherefores of my every grief, but that does not stop my heart from trying to make sense of it all. Are we being punished for some unknown sin? Why, oh why would God allow this?

And then I am reminded of the Hallelujah trees. You remember when I told you about those, do you not? God has been impressing it upon my heart that I need to be more like them. The fiercest gale does naught but intensify their praise. It does not threaten to undo them or tear their leaves from their branches, but sets the whole tree to trembling, its leaves shouting forth the wonder of His presence. "He is here! He is here! He is here! He is here!" The stronger the wind, the louder and bolder their insistence, "He is HERE!"

How I yearn to be like them—a pillar of strength and truth in the midst of the storm—even when I do not understand. Does the sturdy birch understand the storm that assails it? Does the stately aspen comprehend the gale? Alas, Mattie, I need your prayers more than ever before. I am weak, but He is strong, and His strength *is sufficient. Is that not what you told me once? I only wish I was better at surrendering my weakness that His strength might prevail.*

Well, the time grows late and I hear Mother calling, so I must, once more, bid you adieu. Write soon, dear Mattie. I miss you.

Affectionately,
Your Dora-girl

I sniffed as I put the final flourish on my name and blew gently across the page. *Your Dora-girl*... How long it seemed since that summer of bliss before the reality of life in this fallen world ripped from me the innocence of my girlhood. Was that even me back then? I touched a fingertip to my name and checked to be certain the ink was dry, then folded the flimsy paper and spritzed it with lavender water before committing it to the envelope. "Coming, Mother," I called. "I shall be there in a moment."

Donning my robe, I fetched the lamp from my writing desk and slipped into the corridor, pulling my chamber door closed behind me. It would not do to let what little heat there was on these cool autumn nights escape. Light from the lamp spilled across the Persian runner as I made my way down the hall, my slippers shushing lightly with each step. The reality of life, indeed, was harsh, but it was not without its joys. "Did you need something, Mother?" I stuck my head into Mother's chamber, pleased to see her resting comfortably.

A sad sort of smile emanated from her eyes as she stretched forth her hand. "Just a little company, dear... if you wouldn't mind." I set my lamp upon the table by the door and crawled into bed beside her as I had so many times since this wasting illness had struck. Pressing my shoulder against hers, I cradled her hand in both of mine, waiting for her to continue. Long moments ticked by. A comfortable silence enveloped us as I moved to wrap my arm around her shoulders and she rested her head upon my heart, her lashes rimmed with dew. "Oh, Dora—I do so miss your father."

Tightening my arm around her, I touched my head to hers. Her hair wasn't as soft and full as it used to be, but the fragrance of rosemary yet clung to its tresses. "I miss him, too, Mother." I tugged a handkerchief from my sleeve and dabbed her cheeks.

"I only wish I could hold him one last time," she murmured. "Just once."

I nodded. "Me, too. But I hardly think that would satisfy us." A giggled snort was followed by a noisy blow into the handkerchief balled in Mother's hands. Of course it wouldn't satisfy us. It would only mean another painful goodbye. "But the day will come, Mother, when we shall see him once more—him and Charlie and Jack and young Charles…"

"If only that made our separation less difficult to bear."

I cringed at the raw pain lacing Mother's words. The promise of a glorious future with the ones we love did much to buoy the grieving soul but little to salve the gaping wounds of separation left by their absence. "I know," I whispered into her hair. A vision of Mattie flashed through my mind. His eyes bore into mine, liquid pools of love reserved for me alone, yet laced with a dread mirroring my own as he leaned in to whisper his final goodbye. Willing away the image, I shifted Mother's head to a stack of pillows and tucked the counterpane around her chin. "Rest now, Mother. I shall stay with you until you fall asleep."

"Mmmmm," she responded. I stroked a finger through the grey hair curling across her forehead and relaxed into the pillows myself. Yes, knowing we would all be together one day surely helped, but it did nothing to ease the pain of today. I pressed a knuckle to my mouth, choking back a sob. *And in this I am somehow to lift my arms in praise?* I hurled the accusation heavenward, forgetting to Whom I spoke.

No one renders praise for the pain, dear one. I saw immediately a picture of Jesus in Gethsemane pouring out His heart to God in tears and sweat and blood. *Instead, rejoice that I am with you in your pain. You do not suffer alone.*

Forgive me, Jesus.

For sharing in the pain of separation I, too, feel?

For believing I ought to be spared.

Chapter 55

HOSPITAL FOR THE INSANE, TORONTO
ONE AND A HALF YEARS LATER
APRIL 19, 1905

Stark, white-washed walls. The click of wooden heels on polished tile. The deceptive charm of Toronto's most notable architectural edifice.

"Miss Farncomb, how nice to see you." Nurse Bennett strode across the foyer, handing a stack of folded sheets to an attendant. "I am told that your sister-in-law is alert and in good spirits today. I hope you enjoy your visit."

Enjoy my visit? As if any visit to the lunatic asylum could actually be enjoyed. I nodded as cordially as I could and made for the great oaken staircase. The putrid stench of burning sulphur accosted me as soon as I reached the upper hallway. Burning sulphur and human waste. I swallowed hard, fighting the gorge burning in my throat, and stepped into the sterile corridor. Agonized cries ripped at my heart as I passed a room full of terrified patients undergoing the most inhumane treatments imaginable at the hands of doctors sworn to help yet lacking the knowledge to cure the mind gone awry. My heart went out to them all.

"Get in that tub and stay there," an angry voice bellowed. A hefty splash was followed by the wailing scream of a woman. I shuddered when it came to a sputtering stop and hurried down the hall. It could have been Janey in there being plunged into a vat of icy water and forced to stay until her mind had once more cleared or hypothermia threatened her heart—whichever came first. I struggled to see how such treatments could do anything but harm, yet Alfred vowed that the doctors knew what they were doing and would not unnecessarily cause distress. I could only hope he was right.

I had to admit, in the year and a half since Janey had been admitted, there had been evidence of at least some improvement. She spoke now—sometimes—and there were moments, few though they were, when she appeared to recognize me. Even so, I wondered if she wouldn't be better off at home, cared for by the hands of those who loved her rather than by frazzled nurses and attendants to whom she was naught but a wretched woman in need of care and doctors whose macabre treatments might make a lunatic out of anyone.

As my steps drew me closer to the ward Janey shared with thirty-nine other women, I strove to clear my mind. Who could have imagined the devastation the new millennium would wreak on our family? Odd how we had all looked forward to it with such anticipation. *How much more can this weary heart bear, O Lord?* I wished that Marjorie had come with me this morning, yet understood why she had opted to visit her father instead. Visiting Janey was a burden none of us felt equipped to handle.

I shuddered to think of the last time our dear Marjorie had dared to visit. For the first time since that fateful day so long ago, her mother had seemed to recognize her, yet all she could do was ask about Jack and Charles, berating her daughter for keeping them from her and accusing the poor child of always envying her mother's special relationship with her sons. It had been so, so unlike our Janey. *Will she ever return to herself, Lord?* It had been all I could do not to walk out on her that day, but lost in the darkness of her own pain, she knew not the torment she inflicted upon others. I considered for a moment turning around. These bimonthly trips to the asylum were starting to wear me down. Between Mother's deteriorating condition and Janey's... *Does she even know when I am here, Jesus?*

I peeked through the door before entering. The room, stark but clean, held two rows of beds, several of which had yet to be abandoned by their inhabitants. Janey sat in a chair by the window at the far end of the room, rocking a child-sized doll on her lap. *Lord, give me strength.* I blew a stream of air across my sweating brow and stepped into the room.

"Janey, dear, how are you today?" The figure at the window turned, her eyes locking onto mine. *She heard me... and responded.* I stepped closer and drew her into a light embrace.

"I was hoping you would get here soon, Dora. We have been waiting for you."

I smiled, hardly daring to breathe. *She knows me.* Could she really be back after all this time?

She thrust the half-dressed doll into my arms. "Here. You take Jackie for me and finish getting him dressed while I see to wee Charles. They have both been fussing all morning long. You would think the world was about to end with the way they have been carrying on." She stepped toward her bed and retrieved an identical doll as hope bled from my soul. "You came just in time, Dora." She swept toward the door. "You know how Johnny despises it when we are late for church."

I raised my brows, desperate to know how to respond. The doctors had implored us to simply go along with whatever she said at this point, but was that truly the right thing to do? I had never seen her quite so entrenched in this fantasy world of hers as she was today. What was I supposed to do when she demanded I take her to the church?

"Honestly, Dora! Why are you just standing there?" She snatched the doll from my arms and shoved the other toward me. "There, there, Jackie-boy. Mama's got you," she cooed. With a practiced hand, she slid a pair of baby bloomers over the doll's legs and boosted it into her arms. "Done. Now don't be too hard on your dear Aunt Dora, Jackie. She tries. She has never been a mother, you know."

Hardening myself to the jibe, I motioned toward the door. "Shall we go for a little walk this morning?"

A shadow crossed Janey's face. "Whyever would we do that, Dora? We must get to the church before the bells toll the beginning of the service. What is wrong with you this morning?"

What is wrong with me? I fell in behind as Janey hurried from the room. *Should I send for Johnny?*

"By the way, have you seen that little scamp, Marjorie?" She shot a cursory glance down the hall before resuming her stride. "I hardly see that girl these days." She raised a knowing brow and tsked disapprovingly. "A more jealous little girl I have never seen."

I bristled at Janey's brazen pronouncement. *Jealous?* I opened my mouth to speak, then snapped it shut before I said something I would regret. Yet I could not keep silent. Not on this. "*Our* Marjorie?"

"You sound so incredulous, Dora. Of course *our* Marjorie. The child has been jealous of her brothers since the day they were born. You would see that if she didn't have you wrapped so tightly around her baby finger, as they say."

Suppressing my ire, I stared down the hall. "Had we not best be on our way?"

"I suppose we must." Janey reached for the doll in my arms. "Here. Give me Charles. We shall have to leave that young hooligan of mine behind. Come, Dora." Turning on her heel, she strode down the corridor, her leather slippers slapping steadily on the tiles. I followed, grating my teeth, a dutiful servant cowed into obedience. Even her silence was preferable to this.

"Here we are," Janey announced, throwing open the door of the asylum's little-used chapel. "Good. The service hasn't started yet." She slipped into the third pew and settled the dolls on the bench beside her, one on either side.

Moving into the seat next to the doll she called Charles, I slid to my knees. I yearned to pray—I needed to pray—but no words would form. How long could this nonsense last? Had she truly convinced herself that these two lifeless dolls were the lively little tots she had nursed at her breast? And the things she said about Marjorie! I couldn't blame the girl for not wanting to visit her mother. *Father God, why can't Janey simply snap out of it? I know the loss of her boys was great—greater than I can possibly imagine—but there comes a time when a person must accept the trials of life and move on. It's been almost three years.*

Remember that she is but dust, child... just like you.

My self-righteous rant died on my lips. *I feel so helpless, Lord. I don't know how to help her and sometimes...* My chin bumped against my chest. *I'm not even sure that I want to anymore.* Tears sprang to my eyes at the horrifying confession. I understood why many of the patients never saw a single visitor, why the attendants got so irate with their charges, why the world outside these walls pretended the inhabitants of the asylum didn't even exist.

Janey rustled in the pew beside me, gathering the two dolls gently into her arms. "My, but that was a good sermon today, was it not?"

I stared at her, my mind frantically trying to follow.

"If there's one thing Johnny knows how to do, it's deliver a good sermon." She stood, quirking a brow in my direction. "You look confused, Dora. Come on, get up. Let's take the boys for that walk you suggested earlier." When I failed to move, she beat her toe against the floor. "Well? Are you going to kneel there all day?" I moved to rise. "Let's go before these two squirmy-wormies start to get antsy." She gazed fondly at the straw-haired dolls and bounced them in her arms.

My knees creaked as I straightened them. "Here, let me take Jackie." I reached for the nearest doll.

"Honestly, Dora. Can you not tell your two nephews apart by now?" She released the doll into my arms. "That one is Charles. Char-les. Got it?" She repeated the words slowly, as if speaking to a child.

Lord, grant me patience. I bit my tongue, fearing the damage I would do should I give it free rein. This visit could not end soon enough.

• • •

"So how was Mother today?" The familiar plodding of the horse did little to still my racing thoughts.

"She's not at all herself these days, I'm afraid, Marjorie." I slid my hand over hers and gave it a gentle squeeze. "It's probably good that you went to see your father instead." Marjorie grimaced, her eyes fixed on the horse's bobbing tail. "Was he in good spirits?"

"As good as he gets, I guess." She shrugged and adjusted her skirt. "He didn't really have time for a visitor today." Eyes flickering from place to place, she firmly avoided my gaze as her voice trailed off. "Several of his parishioners dropped by for a chat, but once they left, he could think of little other than tomorrow's services."

"That must have hurt." Another shrug. A suppressed sob. "I know it doesn't seem like it these days, but your parents really do love you, Marjorie."

"Do they?" Her melancholic response worried me. The protective walls she had built around her heart seemed to rise with each visit. "They love my brothers, Aunt Dora, dead though they be. They don't love me." What could I say? Had I been her, I no doubt would have come to the same conclusion. "Sometimes I wonder if they ever really loved me at all."

"You know that's not true, dear." I leaned forward, searching for something—anything—that might bring a vestige of comfort.

"Do I?"

Stiff-backed, she reminded me of a china doll—beautiful, yet aloof. Hard, brittle, fragile. "Well, *I* love you," I whispered. I folded my other hand around hers, relieved to feel some of the tension in her grip bleed away.

"I know." Her voice broke. "I'm sorry for allowing my hopelessness to colour our homeward journey."

For the first time since that morning, our eyes met. "You are allowed to hurt, Marjorie. There is no greater pain than the pain of abandonment and rejection." Tears rimmed both of our eyes. "And I know naught that can salve the wounds they leave behind but the fellowship of Him who suffered the greatest rejection of all." A tear dripped down Marjorie's nose, then another and another. Framing her face in my hands, I thumbed them away. "Jesus, help us bear this cross, knowing that You have gone before us. That You understand. That You know."

Marjorie fell into my arms and sobbed. She may have been abandoned by the ones she held most dear, but she was not alone. Neither of us were.

Chapter 56

EBOR HOUSE

Weary though I was, I knew as soon as I stepped through the door of the house that something was wrong. How I knew, I could not say—it looked the same, it smelled the same. The days of incessant noise and ceaseless activity long gone, it even sounded the same. Yet somehow I knew that something was wrong. Very wrong. Hanging my wrap on a hook, I peeked into the kitchen. "Betsy?" The empty room stared back at me. I drew my hand to my belly and braced my shoulder against the wall. Why an empty room should portend such ill escaped me. "I'm going up to check on Mother, Marjorie. Would you mind making us a pot of tea?"

Marjorie's brow knit. "Of course, Aunt Dora. Is something wrong?"

"I'm not certain." Slipping past her, I took to the stairs, purposely slowing my pace lest I needlessly alarm the poor girl, but three steps from the top, I froze. Betsy leaned against the wall opposite Mother's room, a limp handkerchief pressed to her mouth while Edith patted her shoulder awkwardly, her stony expression impossible to read. Mother's door stood ajar, a wan light illuminating its opening. *Not now, Jesus. Please not now.*

Sucking in a breath, I placed my foot on the next step and pushed myself forward, ignoring the distraught women in the hall. Tiptoeing to the door, I edged it open enough to peek into Mother's bedchamber and swallowed hard. My eyes lit upon Alfred first. Doubled over in the straight-backed chair drawn up to the bed, he swayed back and forth, his face buried in his hands. His shoulders trembled and a soulful whimper broke from the deep places of his heart. Hardly daring to breathe, I forced my eyes to focus on the bed. My legs wobbled beneath me, and my breath caught in my throat. How much sorrow could one family bear? White and waxy, yet serenely beautiful, the body that once housed my mother lay beneath a quilted coverlet. Had it not been for her pallor and the unnatural stiffness of her form, I might have thought she slept, so peaceful was her countenance. Yet it was obvious that her soul had flown, escaping at last the mortal confines of its earthly shell.

I gasped and rocked sideways, catching myself on the doorframe. *It cannot be. It can't. No, God. Please, please don't let her be gone.* A hand caught my elbow and I glanced up to find Alfred at my side, his red-rimmed eyes swollen with grief. "She has left us," he whispered, helping me to the chair he had occupied but moments before.

"But... but, she was fine this morning when I left." I floundered, trying to make sense of her sudden passing. "I never would have left her if I had thought her unwell."

"I know, Dora." Alfred brushed his hand across my shoulder and let it come to rest upon the edge of the chair. "It all happened so quickly." Moving to the window, he pulled the heavy drapes closed. "Betsy noticed a sudden, unexplained weakness in her this afternoon and sent for me immediately." He raised his hands helplessly. "By the time I arrived less than an hour later, she was gone." Again, that soulful whimper, the comfortless cry of a little boy trying to be brave. "Betsy was with her when her final breath was spent; she did not die alone."

His words, doubtless meant to comfort, did little to salve the searing pain in my heart. That I should be happy for our mother, I knew—she had, after all, finally escaped the crumbling ruins of her aging body—but all I felt was sorrow.

"You can see she was at peace." Alfred touched his lips to the lifeless forehead and stepped back. "I'll leave you to say goodbye while I send word to Johnny and summon the carpenter."

Say goodbye? I stared at the ashen body. How did one say goodbye to someone who was clearly already gone? I reached to take her hand in mine one last time, but drew back, stung by the cold, hard flesh my fingers encountered.

With a strangled cry, I fled the room. *Oh God, did You have to take her now?* I pressed my handkerchief to my mouth as I flew down the stairs and out the door I had so recently entered. *Everyone is leaving me. Everyone!* Barely able to see, and scarcely stopping to look, I ran across the road, not stopping until the familiar fronds of the thinking tree enveloped me. *I'm losing everyone, Jesus. The very people You called me to support slip from my grasp like sand from the hands of a child, like salt from a broken cellar, like water in a cracked bucket.* My chest heaved. *What will I do without Mother?* I drew my hand to my chest once more, gulping for air. *Was it not enough to take the others?*

A gust of wind came out of nowhere, rustling the willow leaves around me and making me wish I had remembered my wrap. And yet, it was somehow comforting. My irrational ranting subsided as the breeze swirled around me and a familiar peace settled upon me. *You're here, aren't You?* The wind grew more gentle, caressing my face with its breath, and I lifted my arms in welcome. *I am not alone.* A fresh flood of tears bathed my face, but these were different.

Cleansing... healing... comforting, they rushed from my eyes, warming my spirit and restoring my vision. "I am not alone," I repeated aloud. Wonder stole over me. "Though the whole world desert me, I shall never be alone." With each statement, my galloping heart slowed and my voice rose. "Never."

"Miss Dora?"

I spun, my hands dropping awkwardly to my sides. "Edie, you startled me."

"I'm so sorry, Miss Dora." Edith clasped her hands at her chest and dipped her head, her eyes flickering upward to meet mine. "I didn't mean to intrude, Mistress."

Mistress. I schooled my features lest I reveal my revulsion. Mother was the mistress of Ebor House, not me. She always had been. How dare she be dismissed so easily? Swallowing the bitter response rising within me, I nodded as cordially as I could. "What is it, Edie?"

"Master Alfred has returned with the carpenter, and he asked me to fetch you."

"Already?" I glanced at the darkening skies. When had the sun started to go down? With a weary groan, I stepped from beneath the gnarled tree, thankful for the cape the young maid wrapped around my shoulders. "I suppose we should be readying ourselves for visitors," I stated flatly. "News of Mother's passing is sure to travel fast, and many will wish to pay their final respects."

"She was most certainly well-loved," Edith responded.

I nodded again, holding back a sigh. "She was that." We plodded across the road, the hardened earth jarring my aging bones with every step. Was it possible that I was truly naught but forty? On days like this, I could swear I was double that and more. "She was a good woman, Edie. She helped a lot of people."

"She certainly did," Edith answered. She patted my forearm as she helped me up the stairs to the house. It must have seemed to her that I had aged as well. *Father God, get me through this day... and give a hug to Mother for me. Tell her that I miss her already.*

Chapter 57

APRIL 23, 1905

My Dear Mr. Wellman,

When I look back over the past few days, I scarcely know where they have gone. If word has not reached you already, I am certain it will do so before my letter finds its way into your hands. My dear mother was gathered into the arms of our Lord three days ago. Alfred speculates that her passing was the result of apoplexy or some sort of malady of the heart, but says that he cannot be certain.

Whatever the cause, she went peacefully into the arms of her Lord. Sadly, I was visiting Janey at the time of Mother's passing, so was not by her side when she took her final breath, but she was not alone. Betsy, the dear girl, never left Mother's side. As good as a second daughter she was to Mother. Since it was not ordained that I should be at Mother's bedside, I am grateful that Betsy was with her to the very end. It is a comfort to know that Mother did not walk those final steps alone. If only there had been some warning, I never would have left her side, yet there was none—no indicator of distress, no sign of illness, no hint of decline. There was nothing at all to suggest her earthly sojourn neared its end. Even Alfred, prompt though he was in responding to the call, did not arrive in time. People have been pouring into Ebor House ever since, all wishing to pay their final respects and offer comfort to the "poor dear souls" Mother left behind. I cannot count the number of people who have told me how very much I remind them of Mother. How dearly I wish I favoured her more. It is a fight every day, I am afraid, to counter the lie that I have been orphaned and left to fend for myself. I find myself wondering how I shall ever be able to live bereft of Father and Mother, and at times, even begrudging them their hard-earned rest. The loss is staggering, but the weight of shame my selfishness piles upon my heart can hardly be borne. I envy them, Mattie. Can you believe that? I envy them. Ungrateful wretch that I am, I envy their release from the pressures and sorrows of this fallen world, their reunion with loved ones long gone, their ceaseless communion with our Lord. Now, when my joy for them should be most full, my heart is filled with sorrow—not for them, but for me. The shame of the struggle is almost more than I dare confess, but I cannot keep it inside.

Do you ever wish that God would just take you, too? That He would sweep you away from the never-ending hardships of this life to welcome you into His glory forever? Do you ever simply get tired of the constant outpouring of your very being in His service?

Tossing my pen on the table, I pushed myself from the desk and paced across the room. *Jesus... Jesus...* I wanted to pray—I needed to pray—but I had no words. A groan escaped me as I slid to my knees beside my bed. When was the last time I had actually prayed? "Jesus," I whispered. Burying my head in my hands, I sobbed, releasing the grief I had suppressed since the moment I realized Mother was gone. What was wrong with me? "Jesus?" I tried again. Why was it suddenly so hard to pray? "Have You left me, too?"

I shifted on my knees. The room had grown dark, the fire reduced to naught but embers on the cooling hearth. "I feel so alone." The clock chimed the hour. *Five, six, seven, eight, nine. Nine o'clock.* I hugged my arms across my chest and squeezed my eyes shut. Was this a taste of the emptiness that had crushed Janey's spirit and driven her to insanity? I choked back another sob. "Jesus, no—please..." I shook my head wildly from side to side. "Do not give me over to insanity. Do not let lunacy o'ertake me. I am not alone. I am not alone. I am not alone." Gasping for breath, I clamped a hand to my mouth, desperate to still the quivering of my chin. "I. Am. Not. Alone." My teeth ground together with each fractured word. "Why can I not feel You here with me?" The moments ticked by in silence, each one expanding to fill an eternity. "It isn't fair." A quiet knock sounded at the door, but I ignored it. "You promised You would never leave me!"

In one swift movement, I jumped to my feet and tore the counterpane from the bed then threw myself onto the mattress. "I thought that You loved me." Grasping the downy quilt, I drew it up to cover my ringing ears. "I know You're here," I railed.

I shuddered at the image of an unruly child caught in the throes of a horrifying temper tantrum, her eyes scrunched shut as she flailed her arms in the air. I tried with all my might to banish the image, but the harder I tried, the more fiercely it exerted itself until I couldn't help but laugh. "Really?" I rolled my eyes. "That. Is. Not. Me."

Oh?

A wave of joy overwhelmed me at the sound of His voice. *Why wouldn't You answer me when I cried out to You?* I sat up in bed, my eyes searching the darkness, and a shiver ran up my spine. His presence seemed almost palpable.

Were you ready to listen?

"I am now," I whispered. Lying back on the bed, I let out a long, slow breath, my eyelids suddenly so heavy I couldn't keep them open.

Sleep, my beloved. Let go of your pain and rest. I will never—not ever—abandon you.

Ne-ver—not ev...

Chapter 58

MAY 25, 1905

"Are you almost ready, Aunt Dora?" I ran my fingers one last time across the yellowed keys of Mother's pianoforte, recalling the hours of companionship spent around it in times of celebration and in seasons of deepest grief. Heart-rending strains of *Für Elise* echoed along the corridors of my memory to the accompaniment of a dog's haunting howl. Some of the most significant moments of my life had been played out in this very room around this most beloved piece of furniture.

"Aunt Dora?" Marjorie appeared at the door, her hair sticking out in all directions from beneath her hat.

"Yes, dear?"

"Uncle Alfred has sent the luggage on ahead to the station. "Are you almost ready?"

I gazed about the beloved room. Alfred's family would be moving into Ebor House within the week. His youngest daughter, Helen, showed quite an affinity for her grandmother's pianoforte and would see that it didn't remain silent for long. Still, I felt as though I was abandoning an old friend. Tearing my gaze from the keys, I nodded. "I shall be out directly, Marjorie." The soul-stirring strains filling my mind faded, leaving behind an emptiness it would be hard to fill. The pathway ahead was shadowed and dim, filled with all manner of spectres and uncertainties. Why did change have to be so frightening? *One step at a time, Dora-girl.* Father's admonition lingered in my mind. *Just one step at a time.*

Determination sped my feet out the door and into the carriage; a new life lay before me. I smiled at the thought of the quaint little bungalow that awaited me in the heart of Johnny's parish where Marjorie and I would make our new home. There would be children's plays to direct and choirs to lead, women's Bible studies to teach and needy people to aid. And I would be close to Janey—Janey *and* Johnny. Who knew what adventures God had in store for me there? Perhaps I could even start on that book my readers were begging me to write. Mr. Weld had certainly made it clear that he would support me in the endeavor, even going so far as to claim the publishing rights himself. Imagine that! As if I would know the first thing to write about.

The carriage swayed as we rounded the curve north of the house. "We seem to be going a little fast, do we not?" The stern look I cast upon my brother was met by a teasing grin.

"We would not want to be late now, would we?" he countered. He urged the horse to increase its speed yet more. "However are you going to keep our dear Dora here on time for her appointments once the two of you are on your own, Marjorie?" The seriousness of his tone might have offended had the smile lines crinkling the corners of his eyes not given him away.

"The two of us shall do just fine, oh brother of mine," I announced. I tried to keep my face straight, but my lips twitched despite my best efforts.

"Besides, Uncle Alfred, my father is sure to keep her in line." Eyes wide, I gaped at Marjorie. Clearly amused, she rewarded me with a mischievous grin and winked. "After all, Grandfather did teach him well."

Alfred's great guffaw rattled the whole carriage as all three of us dissolved into laughter. Of all of Father's children, Johnny alone had gained notoriety for his incessant tardiness. How he had failed to internalize the value of promptness beneath Father's able tutelage, no one knew, but fail he had. Abundantly.

Alfred reined the horse to a halt outside the station then rounded the carriage to help us out. "I shall surely miss you, dear sister—and you also, sweet Margie." He slipped an arm around each of our shoulders and directed us toward the track. The train had already pulled into the station, and a pair of young men busily loaded our belongings into the baggage car. "Do remember that you will always have a home at Ebor House." He looked pointedly at Marjorie. "Both of you."

His beard tickled my face as he leaned in to brush his lips across my brow. "I'll miss you, too, big brother," I whispered, not daring to meet his gaze. My vision swam as I stepped toward the conductor and handed him our tickets. Only when we were securely seated on the great iron horse and its hulking wheels had begun to inch forward did I chance a look at the solitary figure waving to us from the platform. Offering a wobbly smile, I raised my hand to return his wave, only to see that he was not alone. On either side of him stood Mother and Father, and just a few feet in front, my dear Charlie with Johnny's boys, all waving and shouting their goodbyes. I jolted forward and rubbed my eyes. To my dismay, Alfred stood alone on the platform, looking incredibly old, his left hand stuffed in his pocket beneath his long-tailed jacket like always`. Had it been my imagination, or had God parted the curtain between this world and the next that I might see the great cloud of witnesses surrounding me and know I was not alone?

"Are you well, Aunt Dora?"

I sat back in my seat and tried to blink away the confusion. "Did you see anyone waving to us from the platform with your uncle?"

Her brows knit. "No, did you?"

"Not exactly."

"Not exactly?"

I directed my gaze out the window. "I thought for a moment that I saw your grandmother and grandfather together with your Uncle Charlie and your little brothers all waving to us and cheering us along." I cocked my head in a child-like shrug and shifted in my seat. "It may have been my imagination, but I'm thinking that perhaps it was a vision sent from beyond the veil. We are not alone, Margie—no matter how sorely it feels to us as if we are." I picked a pill ball from my shawl and rolled it between my thumb and forefinger. "The ones we love may no longer be within our grasp, but they have not ceased to exist."

A lone tear slid from Margie's eye and trickled down her face. Reaching for her hand, I brought it to my cheek and sighed. "We shall survive this new adventure, my dear... and thrive." I inhaled deeply, an unexpected assurance throbbing within me. "God has a job for us that He has ordained for us to do since before the foundations of the earth." Smiling at Marjorie's wide-eyed stare, I glanced toward the heavens, awed by the truths infusing my soul. "We have been commissioned, Margie. There is no telling what God has in store for us." I sat forward in my seat, suddenly unable to sit still. My niece's brow lifted, but she said nothing. "You shall see, dear. God has a plan, and His plans never fail."

She nodded dully, twining her fingers through the tassels on her shawl. The poor girl had endured more loss at her tender age than I could even imagine. Difficult as it was to suffer through the death of my parents at the ripe old age of forty-two, I could hardly imagine the devastation of losing them in my youth to something more akin to abandonment than actual death. The weight of rejection that poor young woman couldn't help but harbour must surely be almost more than she could bear.

Lapsing into silence, I gazed at the passing trees, awed by the celestial send-off we had been given. What it foreboded, I knew not, yet it brought assurance to my wavering heart nonetheless. We were doing the right thing, headed in the right direction, walking the pathway our Lord had pre-ordained for us to trod—and all of heaven had gathered to see us off. I stilled, recalling the vision. There had been others there as well—Mattie's father, Bishop Thomas Wellman, and old man Fraser. Mrs. Toddman and her infant daughter, Glenda. My childhood friend Susannah and a host of others—familiar and not—their faces alight with anticipation, their arms waving wildly in the air. Whatever did God have in store for us with a send-off like that?

Pulling a pencil and a well-worn notepad from my bag, I closed my eyes in prayer. *Help me, Jesus. Give me the strength and the courage to accomplish the work You set before me, no matter how difficult it might be.*

I studied Marjorie, wishing that God had opened her eyes to see the vision He had given me. Red-eyed and sombre, she gazed out the window, heedless of the tears that rained from her eyes. Yearning to comfort her yet knowing no words of mine could salve the wounds she bore, I once more turned to prayer. *Help her, Jesus. Open her eyes to see that she has not been abandoned and that Your love for her is far beyond any she could ever imagine. Cradle her heart in Your hands, O Lord, and show her in ways she cannot deny that she is not alone.*

Turning to the paper before me, I tapped my pencil against my lower lip. How to begin…how to be—

Surrounded by so great a cloud of witnesses," Paul admonishes us, "let us run the race not only for the prize—" Dear Christian, have you ever stopped to wonder to what the beloved apostle was referring? A great cloud of witnesses? Who exactly are these witnesses with whom we are surrounded and to what are they witness? Has it ever crossed your mind to consider such things?

I believe the apostle gives us a hint as to their identity when he goes on to speak of "those who have gone before us"—our loved ones, our acquaintances, the people who have impacted our lives and whose lives have been impacted by our own; our cheerleaders, our brothers and sisters in Christ now resting in the arms of our Lord. These, it would seem, comprise that great cloud of witnesses that surrounds us.

My mother was recently added to their number.

A tear splatted onto the page and I swiped it away. Reviewing what I had written, I paused, my brows furrowing as I scrutinized each word. That final sentence didn't seem to fit. Scratching it from the page, I puzzled over what to write in its stead.

I was recently reminded of that in the passing of my dear mother.

Yes. That sounds better, but where to now? When nothing more impressed itself upon my heart, I returned the notebook and pencil to my bag and shifted my attention to Marjorie. How lonely the poor dear looked—like an abandoned waif lost in the wastelands with nowhere to go and no one to care. *Oh, but you do have someone who cares, Margie, dear. More people than you know.* Loathe to disturb her private ruminations, I averted my gaze. *Jesus, reach forth Your hand to pull our dear Margie from the pit of despair in which she now abides. Let me be to her Your hands, Your voice, Your comfort—Your heart—in the midst of her pain, and let her find rest in You.*

The train clattered along the tracks, swaying from side to side whenever it rounded a curve. It had stopped twice now to load and unload passengers, leaving few seats unoccupied. As I peered from face to face, a heaviness gripped my heart. The elderly man across from us stroked his heavy white beard. His eyes drooped beneath deep, dark folds of skin. *Jesus, help him,* my heart cried. *He looks so sad. You alone know the weight he carries.*

A little girl next to him tugged on his sleeve, "Grandfather, where are we going?" My heart skipped a beat. "Why will you not tell me?" Her curls bounced around her face, but the loss in her eyes could not be missed.

The old man stared straight ahead, barely acknowledging the child's presence. "To a place where they will look after you better than I ever could."

"But I want to stay with you, Grandfather."

He blinked twice and cleared his throat. "The decision is already made, Marta."

"Will I ever see you again?"

Lord Jesus, help them both! We weren't the only ones suffering. What had brought the two of them to this place, I could only imagine, but the tragedy of their plight tore at my heart. *Give them courage and strength for all that lies ahead. Let this dear child not be destined for a broth—* I couldn't even say the word, especially not in prayer. Surely her grandfather wouldn't sell her into a life of perversion; it was obvious that he loved her. *And let them see each other again, Jesus—for both of their sakes.*

On the other side of the aisle, two young women chattered excitedly. "And when we get there, the first place I wish to go is Hanlan's Point." The eyes of the woman who was speaking grew wide. "I hear they have a diving horse act right there on the island."

"They don't! A real diving horse act?"

"They certainly do. Why, their horses jump from forty feet up right into Lake Ontario," a man's voice interrupted. It held more than a trace of amusement. "Their names are King and Queen."

"I wonder if the horses neigh as they make the dive." The first young woman drew a hand to her mouth, her eyes alight.

Her seat mate giggled and gave her a playful shove. "Imagine such elegant creatures diving into the harbour. Cousin Elspeth went to a Carver show once down in Atlantic City. Said it was the most astounding thing she'd ever witnessed. Only those horses actually dove with riders on their backs!"

Their happy banter reminded me of the carefree days of my youth when nothing worse than a scolding troubled my soul. How quickly things could change. *Let these young women escape the weight of grief that I, and my family, have been called to bear, save that it be requisite for the well-being of their souls.* I bowed my head, my fingers tensing. *Has the pain we have borne over the years been somehow requisite for the well-being of our souls, O Lord?*

Yours, and others.

Now, that was something I had never considered. Could it be that the trials we'd been called to bear were not for us alone? After all, didn't Jesus Himself suffer on behalf of His beloved brothers and sisters and bid us follow His example? Though God was no doubt working His good will in us through our every trial, could it be that some of those difficult times were also suffered for the welfare of others? Could I even accept the seeming injustice of that thought? The very idea of a God who would allow—even ordain—one to suffer that he might bring blessing upon another...

I inhaled deeply, smoothing my furrowed brow. Jesus accepted it... even embraced it. Did He not so love the world that He sacrificed Himself for it? He did not deem the cross—horrifying as it was—too great a cost to pay; the redemption it would bring was to Him worth the suffering He would endure. And to think that He commanded us to love each other even as He loved us—with that same self-sacrificial love that drove Him to accept the torture visited upon Him on our behalf. If but one person, by my suffering, was drawn into the fold or encouraged in his or her walk to keep striving, was it not worth it?

Surrendering to the rhythmic chugging of the train, I closed my eyes. Did it really matter for whom I suffered so long as the Almighty remained at the helm, using it to work His will in this world and in my life? "Wake me when we get to Union Station, won't you, Margie dear?" I mumbled.

"Of course, Auntie." How very far away her sweet voice sounded. "Rest well."

Chapter 59

TORONTO
THREE YEARS LATER
DECEMBER 23, 1908

"Come, come, children!" *Whose brilliant idea was it for me to direct this Christmas pageant?* I threw back my head, casting my eyes heavenward. If it weren't for the angelic smiles of the children and the proud faces of their parents...

I clapped my hands sharply together and was rewarded by a semblance of attention. "Now, Amelia, you must stop unwrapping the baby Jesus. Nobody wants to see that he is just a doll made of straw."

The boy beside her made a face and pushed her off the three-legged stool. "See? I told ya so."

"Hey!" she yelled.

"And Henry—" I levelled my gaze on the bigger boy. "Joseph would never treat Mary as roughly as you just treated Amelia." He hung his head, his attention apparently arrested by the toe he rubbed against the wooden floorboard. "Now lay down your shepherd's staff and add a little fresh hay to the manger so she will have somewhere to lay the baby."

"Yes, Miss Dora." Henry bent to obey, but Amelia made a face behind his back and stuck out her tongue.

Lord, help me. The shepherds and wisemen giggled in the wings. He really did deserve that the way he had been needling her all practice long. "Now, Amelia, do you suppose Mary would have done that to Joseph?"

Her face reddened when a little voice from the choir added, "I gonna tell Mama on you."

Amelia grimaced. "No, ma'am. I apologize for sticking my tongue out at you, Henry," she added saucily.

"What?" Henry cried. "You stuck your tongue out at me? You little beast!"

Gales of laughter rang through the church as Henry lunged toward his sister. Amelia dropped the baby head first into the manger and scooted toward the choir loft.

This is ridiculous. I thumped the hymnal I held onto the pew beside me. Instant silence. "Children! Children! I would have you remember that this is the house of God."

"The house of God?" It took but a moment for me to locate the source of the awe-filled voice. Our youngest angel, Livy Peterson, was barely four years old. "Is this really where God lives?" she lisped.

Several of the bigger angels tried to hide their giggles in their sleeves, though our dear old Joseph wasn't nearly so kind. "Ha!" he chortled. "Widdle Wivvy thinks God actually lives here!"

A smattering of snickers followed. That boy would be the death of me yet. *However am I supposed to reestablish control now?*

Both fists clenched at her sides, Livy stamped her foot on the ground with all the force of an angry bull. "I am *not* Widdle Wivvy," she shouted. I looked on in wonder, impressed by her courage. Even Henry stopped as if stunned, the smile dropping from his face. "I am Little Livy," she finished calmly.

Laughter filled the room as her tiny brows drew together. Swallowing my amusement, I ran a hand through my hair. "That you are, Little Livy. That you are." The room hushed at the sound of my voice. "And you asked a very good question." A smile stretched across her face, and she brought her chin down in a firm nod. "God lives in Heaven, but long, long ago, He told His people to build a special house for Him here on earth where His presence could abide with them." Glancing uneasily at the collection of wrinkled noses and puzzled frowns staring at me, I decided I had said enough. "Now, let's—"

"What do you mean by His presence?" an older girl demanded.

"Yeah! Is there one for me?"

One for you? I cocked my head at the shy young shepherd beaming up at me, his gap-toothed grin filling his whole face. "One what, Tommy?"

"A present!"

"O-oh." I stifled another chuckle lest I embarrass the dear soul. "His *presence*—not *presents*." He gawked at me as if I had gone mad. "I guess, well—I guess you could say that His presence is the Holy Ghost."

"The Holy Ghost?" A chorus of voices repeated.

Livy clamped her arms across her chest and tapped her toe. "So, is this the house of God or isn't it?"

I sighed, massaging my temples. However was I to explain to a four-year-old the sacred mysteries I had yet to grasp myself? "It is," I announced hurriedly, reaching for my hymnal. "Now take your places for the final scene. Your parents will be expecting you home before dark."

• • •

Far down the street, the gas lights flickered to life as I stepped into the night, carting a basket laden with fresh bread and fruit for the widow on the corner. Still reeling from the unexpected death of her husband the day before Thanksgiving, she struggled to keep food on her table from one day to the next and needed someone to look in on her to be sure her needs were met. Thankfulness warmed my heart as I thought of the generous donations afforded by my Quiet Hour readers for situations like this. I lugged the heavy basket down the walk, my feet crunching in the snow. Thanks to them, there was even a spot of coffee and a tin of ham hidden away in the basket for her Christmas dinner.

My heart quickened at the sound of rapid footfalls on the walk behind me. Mother would turn over in her grave if she knew I walked the streets of Toronto alone after dark, but some things couldn't be helped. *Jesus, protect me from evil.* I tensed as the footsteps drew nearer.

"Dora? Is that you?"

Spinning toward the familiar voice, I nearly upset the contents of the basket. "John Farncomb! What were you thinking, sneaking up on me like that?" I scowled at his half-hearted attempt to conceal a smile. "You scared me half to death."

"And what exactly do you think you're doing walking the streets of this city alone after dark?"

"Exactly what needs to be done." I snapped my mouth shut and reeled around, hardly missing a beat as I marched toward the little house on the corner.

"Come on, Dora." Johnny jogged forward, hooking his arm around my elbow. "That wasn't an accusation."

"You could have fooled me." The words ground from between my teeth. Odd how the unspent energy of fear can so quickly find an outlet in anger. Hastening my steps, I marched through the darkening night, wishing I could go home instead.

"Look." Johnny pulled me around to face him. "I saw the lights go out in the church and realized that rehearsal must have gone longer than you anticipated. Knowing you didn't have access to a buggy, I decided to see my little sister safely home myself." He rolled his eyes at my stoic response. "Is it such a crime that I worry about the only woman left in my life who hasn't abandoned me?"

The raw pain in those words dashed against my heart like a pail of ice water in the middle of winter. *My poor, poor Johnny.* Irritation forgotten, I lowered my head. "I'm sorry, Johnny. I knew I should come and get you, but I was loathe to disturb you, knowing the extra duties that consume your time during this most holy season." I slid into his arms, aggrieved by my childishness. "I am afraid I'm far too independent for my own good, big brother."

"Such is the curse we all must endure, it seems," he murmured.

Independence, the curse we all must endure. My mind whirled with the implications. That would be a great topic for my next Quiet Hour article. Did we not all kick against the goads of dependence in our determination to rule our own lives? If not for our infernal self-reliance, would we not find it easier to entrust ourselves to the Almighty in seasons of sorrow and despair? Independence and surrender could not coexist. Neither could independence and union—and was not union with our Lord at the crux of all we professed to believe?

"So where exactly are we headed?"

I turned my head sharply, my brows knit. "Where are we head…" Realizing we were about to turn the corner onto Simpson Avenue, I paused to orient myself. A candle lit the front window of Widow Robson's clapboard bungalow to our right. "Here we are." I pointed to the dilapidated house, noting the rotting boards edging the ground. I'd have to see if I could round up some men from the church to take care of that. After a quick knock, I cracked the door open and stuck my head inside. "Mrs. Robson?" No answer. "Mrs. Robson? It's me—Dora."

Shuffling feet. A raspy breath. I opened the door a little wider and stepped inside in time to see an old woman enter the foyer, the stump of a candle flickering dully in her shaky hands. "I hope you don't mind, but I brought my brother John with me today since it was getting dark." Hefting the basket into Johnny's outstretched arms, I took the candle from the old woman with one hand and wrapped my other around her shoulder, guiding her to a well-worn rocker by the fire in the parlour. Waving Johnny in to join us, I seated myself on the low stool across from her. "You know, dear, you really ought to keep your door locked after dark."

She nodded, averting her eyes. "I was waiting for you."

The childlike vulnerability in her admission reminded me somehow of Janey. "Shall I fix you something to eat?" Again she nodded. "John, why do you not add a wee bit of coal to that fire and see if you can warm things up a smidge."

"Oh, no dear—please, do na' do that!" I stopped, basket in hand, my feet rooted to the floor. *Another thing to add to the list.* "I will na' have enough coal to make it through the winter if I squander it needlessly." She snugged her threadbare wrap around her shoulders. "I'm quite warm enough." Nodding convulsively, she straightened in her chair as if trying to convince us. *Whyever were her children not here to take care of her?*

Shaking off the uncharitable question, I carted the heavy basket into the kitchen and set it on the lone table. Where her children were or were not was no business of mine. Slicing off a piece of bread, I spread it with a wee bit of bacon fat I found by the stove and cut up an apple to go with it. Before long, the kettle was singing on the stove and the aroma of simmering tea filled the little room.

Laughter emanated from the parlour as I entered with a tray and placed it on the hearth. "Ah, but you remind me of my own, dear Tommy boy," Mrs. Robson was saying, her face lit with a beatific smile. Chatting away as if she hadn't seen company in months, she sipped her tea and nibbled at the plate I had prepared.

"Well, you know, Mrs. Robson," I said, lifting the tray from the hearth, "it is time we headed off. My dear Marjorie will be wondering what has become of me." *She's probably worried sick.* "I'll wash up these few dishes, then I think we had better be going."

"Of course, Dora. I'm so glad you came by. You do an old woman's heart good."

Mentally composing a list of items to bring by on my way to church in the morning, I wiped the dishes and stacked them on the shelf. *Candles, a warmer wrap, a bar of cheese, a handful of tea leaves, a scuttle of coal...* If I couldn't convince Mrs. Robson to spend Christmas with us, at least I could see that she was warm and well-fed.

With a final goodbye, we slipped into the night, locking the door behind us. "She is quite the woman," Johnny said, taking my hand and hooking it around his elbow once more. "We shall have to visit again."

"Indeed we shall," I answered. "Tomorrow." I stopped to look him in the eye. "You bring the coal."

"Yes, Mother." Tenderness burned in his eyes, belying his teasing words. Though spent from years of sorrow and fractured by loss, he was still, and ever would be, my Johnny.

"Merry Christmas, big brother," I whispered, pressing my head against his shoulder.

He untangled his arm from mine and wrapped it around my waist, drawing me close as we rounded the corner to Simpson Avenue. "Merry Christmas to you, too, Dora-girl."

Pricked by memories of our many happy Christmastides of years long past, I nestled further into his embrace. "Do you ever wonder that Jesus chose to come to us, knowing the grief and pain He would be called to bear on our behalf?"

"We don't know the half of it, do we?" Johnny whispered. "It's far too easy to forget when we gaze upon the face of that babe in the manger that the scope of our sorrows is as nothing compared to the burdens He bore for us."

"Isn't that the truth," I breathed. "The birth of our Lord was miraculous on more than one level." We stepped onto the walkway in front of the bungalow Margie and I shared. The windows, alive with candles, called me to take refuge within, reminding me of the blessings that I so easily took for granted.

Johnny lowered his head, falling silent once more. "Miraculous doesn't even begin to describe it."

"Will you join us for a bite to eat before you head home?" I asked.

He shook his head, giving me a lop-sided grin. "Not this time, sis. Sermons do not write themselves, I'm afraid—though this one seems to be giving it a pretty good try." He bent to lay a kiss upon my cheek. "See you tomorrow."

Chapter 60

TORONTO HOSPITAL FOR THE INSANE
DECEMBER 25, 1908

My feet slowed as I crossed the hospital's sterile foyer. *Business as usual.* Did nothing ever change? Progressive as this hospital was in word, it was still naught but an asylum—a place to hide people away who didn't fit the norms society had embraced, a prison to isolate those dear, troubled souls lest they sully the ideals the world around them held so dear. Though someone had attempted to bring a little Christmas cheer by erecting a sparsely decorated spruce in Janey's ward, life went on as it did every other day in the asylum, a wearying cycle of toil and grief, labour and decay. If anything, the world within its walls seemed even drearier than usual, given the festivities of the world without. While two of the women who shared Janey's room had been granted weekend passes to share Christmas with their families, sadly, our Janey had not been one of them.

"Give me back my boys!" a lone voice shrieked. *Oh, Janey, will you never recover?* Discouragement slowed my steps as Janey's piercing wail penetrated the corridor. "You cannot have them!" Her cries intensified, ending in a chorus of screams when a scowling attendant stomped out the door trailing a partially clad doll in each hand.

"Is that really necessary?" I demanded. Eyes narrowed, the attendant glared at me, pushing past with nary a word. I steadied myself against the wall as I stared after her, appalled by how keenly I could relate to her irritation. I never wanted to see those dolls again in my life.

Janey's screams escalated, but instead of rushing to her side, I found myself pressing yet harder into the wall, fighting the urge to cover my ears and run. What was wrong with me? *I cannot do this, Jesus.* I blinked away a tear, wishing I could turn back time. *I don't know how to help her.*

Just go to her; sit with her, a still, small voice instructed. Breathing deeply, I stepped from the wall and faced the ward. I had to do this. It was what Jesus would do. Janey's screaming continued, unabated.

Tell her that I have not forgotten her, that my love for her cannot be extinguished.

I straightened, concentrating on the rhythmic intake of each breath, preparing myself for the battle ahead. One foot in front of the other, I made my way to the door, the heartbeat pounding in my ears almost drowning out my sister-in-law's screams.

Swaddled in a wet sheet, Janey writhed against the bondage, her back arching as she pushed her heels into the bed. The taut sheet rippled when she flexed her arms in protest, but didn't give way. Irritation forgotten, I ran to her side. "Janey–Janey—listen to me." I slid a hand down the side of her head, but she flicked it away with a jerk, her screams growing sharper. "Janey—it's me. Dora." No response. "You've got to listen to me," I pleaded. Tears rained from my eyes as I leaned over her, doing my best to gather her squirming body into an embrace while ignoring the frigid wetness soaking through my bodice. "You have to stop struggling. You're going to hurt yourself." I licked a salty drop from my lip and lowered my head to her ear, relieved to find her screams begin to give way to a low-toned wail. "God has not forgotten you, Janey…" I whispered, "or your boys." Startled by the sharp rap of her head against my ear, I drew back.

"Get away from me!" she shrieked. "I want my babies back. Give them back. Give them back right now!"

I pressed my hand to my ear and waited for the throbbing to subside. *I did what You said, Jesus.* I glanced heavenward. *I told her that you haven't forgotten her, and it didn't help one bit. Look at her! Is there nothing else I can do?*

You only gave her half of the message.

Blocking out her rabid screams, I leaned close once more and clamped my hands around her head, drawing it to my shoulder lest she butt my ear again. "Nothing can extinguish God's love for you, Janey."

"Lie!" she shrieked. She pulled her head away and threw herself back onto the bed. "Lie, lie, lie!" Thrashing her body from side to side, she struggled to free herself from my grip. "He hates me. I know it!" Her voice broke as her shrieks turning into a heart-rending wail. "He took my ba-a-a-a-ab-ie-e-e-s…"

Hastening to free her from the sheet binding her upper body, I drew her into my arms once more, relieved to feel her arms tighten around my shoulders. "He-e to-oo-oo-ok my ba-a-bie-e-es." She repeated the words over and over, her voice growing more bewildered and childlike with each repetition.

"I know." Cradling her face in my hands, I thumbed away her tears. Was this the first time she had truly cried? It was certainly the first time I had witnessed it.

"How can He love me and rip my boys out of my arms at the same time?" Brushing me aside, she pushed at the sheet restraining her feet and kicked it off the bed. "I hate Him!"

"Do you really?" *How am I supposed to respond to that, Jesus? She doesn't hate You—I know she doesn't. Please, please—let not her sorrow turn to hate.*

"Yes—noooooooo!" She threw herself against the thin mattress, clapping her hands to her face. "I hate that He took my boys from me."

Tossing the wet sheet beneath the bed, I pulled a dry blanket over her naked body and stroked her hair, longing for just the right words to say—a word of comfort, a tidbit of wisdom, a thought to inspire—yet my mind was as blank as a cloudy sky at midnight.

"If God really loves me, why, oh why did He take my babies from me? Why is He punishing me?" She stared intently into my eyes for the first time in years, her fingers squeezing my wrist, demanding an answer.

"I don't know, Janey." I freed my wrist from her grip and placed her hands gently beneath the cover. "Some things are simply not given to us to understand." I smoothed her hair across her brow. "I don't believe He is punishing you, though. Why do we not talk to Him about it?"

She turned her head toward the wall, but said nothing. I'd take that as consent.

"Jesus..." I blinked my eyes rapidly, my heart overflowing with compassion for the broken woman before me. "Father, we simply do not understand. We trust Your purposes for we know that You know all things and love Your children more fiercely than we ever could, yet it doesn't feel much like love right now. It feels more like You have abandoned us. You have the power to restore our joy, yet..." Quiet sniffles emanated from the bed. "O Lord, the horror of losing a child pains the heart in ways no words can describe."

I know.

My eyes flew open. "Janey—did you hear that?"

Her eyes met mine, tears gushing down her cheeks. "It isn't the same, Dora, and you know it."

"Isn't it?"

"He's God, Dora. He didn't carry His baby around in His arms... hold His little boy's hands when he took his first steps... guide his decisions as he grew... devote Himself to His Son's care every moment of every day."

"Did He not? Perhaps he was not physically there to hold His Son's hand through the ups and downs of life, but did He not hold Jesus every bit as securely in His heart as you held your own babes?"

She shook her head, turning away once more.

Jesus, I see it so clearly, but I cannot make her understand.

You do not have to, dear one. Don't burden yourself with things I alone can do. Keep praying.

My shoulders sank as I pressed my eyes closed once more. "Loving Father, reveal to Your servant Janey the depth of Your love for her and comfort her with Your presence. You know the pain of surrendering a son—Your only Son—and the grief only a parent can know. Grant her Your grace to yield to Your sovereignty in this, though everything within her would rebel. Restore to her the gift of a sane mind and give her the strength to let go of the resentment that holds her in its grip." I glanced up to see the nurse I had spoken to earlier hovering at the foot of the bed. "And may Your peace baptize us all. Amen." I finished hurriedly, knowing this nurse to be more impatient than most of the attendants assigned to Janey's ward, and certain I was in for an earful. One did not remove the cold, wet shroud believed to calm a mad woman without leave, despite the misery it begat.

"I see you are more yourself, Jane." I scowled at the forced smile she aimed at my sister. "It seems you are no longer in need of this." She made a production of bending to pick up the pile of wet fabric from beneath the bed. I glared at the woman, trying to decide whether to confront her rudeness or pretend I hadn't noticed.

"Yes, Nurse Benson," Janey answered contritely. "I'm so sorry for having vexed you yet again. I don't understand what comes over me." The nurse huffed dismissively as she turned her back on us and headed to the door. "I didn't harm you in my madness, did I?" Janey squeaked.

Nurse Benson, hard-hearted though she appeared, stopped mid-step, her shoulders visibly relaxing. Slowly, she turned toward my sister-in-law, sporting the first genuine smile I had ever seen upon her face. "No, Janey dear, you did not harm me, and it is to my shame that I was vexed. I know you cannot help yourself." Casting a glance my way, her eyes lowered yet further. "And I apologize to you also, Miss Farncomb, for my atrocious behavior. You did the right thing in removing her restraints. It's obvious that they had done their job."

I nodded, biting my tongue lest I tell her what I really thought of her blasted cures. Sometimes I wondered why we had ever committed our Janey to this asylum in the first place, but there had seemed to be such little choice at the time.

"Perhaps you could take Jane down to the sewing room for a while."

"The sewing room?" The words escaped before I could stop them. "But it's Christmas Day. Surely you aren't suggesting that she be required to work on a holy day."

The nurse stiffened. "Meaningful labour is the best cure for the afflicted, Miss Farncomb. Insanity does not take a break because it's a holy day."

"No, I don't suppose it does," I stated flatly. How could I argue a statement like that?

"It's all right, Dora." I glanced toward the bed, surprised that Janey hadn't tuned out as was her wont. "Nurse Benson is right. A little light work would do me good. Why do you not help me dress, then perhaps you could walk me to the sewing room."

To her credit, Nurse Benson had left the ward by the time Janey finished speaking. I'm not sure what I would have done had I seen the self-satisfied smirk she was sure to have worn had she stayed.

"Are you certain, Janey?" I extended a hand to help her sit. "You're under no obligation to work on Christmas Day. I will speak directly to Superintendent Clarke if need be."

"Yes, Dora. I am certain." She said the words slowly, as if speaking to a child. "I may be insane, my dear sister, but I am not an imbecile." My jaw dropped. Could it be she was coming back to herself? "Now help me dress. Those wet wraps will be the death of me yet."

•••

"How was Mother today?" Marjorie pushed a forkful of roast beef dully around her plate.

"Actually, she seemed surprisingly like her old self—once she settled from the distress of having her *babies* forcibly removed from her for cleaning." I waited until Marjorie lifted her head. "She very much enjoyed the lovely Christmas dinner you sent, as did Nurse Benson with whom she shared it. Your mother asked after you."

Marjorie scooped a morsel of potato onto her fork and dabbed it into a puddle of gravy left on her plate. "I ought to have been there to see her."

"She would have liked that, dear, but she does understand. She, too, despises the distressing estate to which she has descended."

"Did you get to see her, Father?" Marjorie set her fork, still laden with potato, on the side of her plate.

A far off look came into his eyes. "It's hard to leave her on days like this, I'm afraid." I patted his hand, giving him time to collect himself. "Yes, I saw her," he continued, "and yes, she did seem very much herself—for the first time since..." He cleared his throat once more, his eyes dancing. "I visited the woman I fell in love with today, Marjorie. Your mother was back. She even asked where I hid the Christmas mouse this year."

A smile flitted across Marjorie's face at the mention of the Christmas mouse. Until the year Charlie died, every Christmas Eve, Father had hidden a little woolen mouse about the house for us to find on the morrow. Apparently that had been a tradition at the orphanage he grew up in, a tradition he decided to continue with his own family. Many happy Christmas morns had been spent searching for that mouse until, at last, we had to abandon the quest in order to attend services. The happy child who finally found it received a special gold-trimmed cone filled with treats all his own, though he was, of course, expected to share at least a few of them with his fellow searchers. That Johnny had kept the tradition alive with his own family didn't surprise me, since he was almost always the first to find the mouse when we were young.

"She wondered if you would be the one to find it again this year, Margie." Johnny quirked a brow in her direction, a long-missed grin lighting his face. "Said you always were the one to find it on Christmas morning." He paused, a mischievous twinkle in his eyes as he glanced from Marjorie to me and back again.

"You didn't!" Margie squealed.

Johnny nodded smugly, clearly pleased with himself. "'Now you go right home and hide that Christmas mouse,' your mother told me. 'I don't want my dear Marjorie to be disappointed.'"

Bittersweet though the words were, nothing could dampen the excitement of a long-lost tradition brought back to life. "Come on, Aunt Dora. We have to find the mouse!"

Scrambling from my seat as fast as my aging joints would allow, I followed Marjorie into the parlour where she was already at work pulling cushions from the divan, shaking the folds of the heavy drapes, bending to peek beneath the overstuffed chair. "Maybe it's in the kitchen," she panted, darting past her father who stood, arms crossed, in the doorway. "That's where Father came in, isn't it, Aunt Dora?"

Johnny winked at me, and my heart swelled with joy. "I do believe he did, Margie." But she was long gone. Wishing to prolong the game as long as possible, I jogged past my brother in pursuit, hoping she wouldn't find the mouse before I arrived.

By the time I reached the archway into the kitchen, Marjorie swayed precariously on the kitchen counter, peering into the empty jars on the board above the window. "Not up here," she declared. She jumped to the floor, scanning the room for another hiding place. "Where would you hide the mouse if it was up to you, Aunt Dora?"

I gazed around the room thoughtfully. "Well, not in the dust bin and not in the stove…"

"Aunt Dora, be serious!" Margie exclaimed. "I'm sure I already know where you would *not* have hidden it. Where *would* you have hidden it?"

"Under the stairs?" I may have been granted the imagination to write, but the imagination of the young to hide and seek eluded me.

Before I could say another word, Marjorie shot past me. "Wait." She stopped dead a few feet from the door. "What stairs?"

I cocked my head.

"There are no stairs in a bungalow, Aunt Dora."

"Oh dear," I responded, chuckling. "I suppose I was thinking of by-gone days. Your grandfather hid it in the cupboard beneath the stairs in Ebor House more than once, you know."

A great guffaw came from the corridor. "That he did, oh sister of mine. And I believe you were the first to think of searching in that dark and dreary cupboard amidst the bottles of preserves."

"The pantry!" Margie darted past me once more and threw open the slatted wooden door of the cupboard nearest the stove. After a moment of frantic scrambling, she rocked onto her heels, affecting an exaggerated pout. "It isn't here."

"No, Marjorie dear, it is not," John pronounced proudly. He stuffed his hands into his trouser pockets, knocking the flap of his dress coat back in the process.

"There it is!" Marjorie cried. She lunged toward her father, plucking the tattered mouse from the inside pocket of his coat. "That was hardly fair, Father."

"No?" He quirked a brow in my direction. "Didn't Father do the same to us one year?"

Joining hands with Marjorie, I took a menacing step toward my brother. "He did indeed, oh brother of mine—and it seems to me he got the very same response."

Johnny took a step backward, raising his hands in playful resignation.

"Now where's my prize?" As soon as the sassy words crossed Marjorie's lips, we all collapsed in gales of laughter.

"I do believe there is a Christmas tree awaiting our company," Johnny said as our laughter began to subside.

Marjorie cleared her throat expectantly. "You didn't answer my question, Father." Her eyes sparkled with merriment.

Clamping an arm around each of our shoulders, Johnny paraded us down the hall to the parlour. "You get to keep the mouse."

Chapter 61

TORONTO HOSPITAL FOR THE INSANE
MARCH 29, 1909

"Have you noticed how well my sister-in-law has been doing lately, Dr. Clarke? Do you suppose she might be released soon?" Tired of the bureaucratic hedging, I thought it best to go straight to the superintendent. "She seems so much more herself these days—almost back to normal, in fact."

The superintendent steepled his fingers and nodded sagely. "Indeed, Miss Farncomb. You are most observant." I shuffled my feet, sensing a *but* coming on. "However..." Inhaling deeply, he studied his hands. "...the operative word here is *almost*. I am certain you will agree that we would not want to release our dear Mrs. Farncomb before she is fully recovered." I fumbled for a reply, my heart plummeting. "We wouldn't want to see her regress when she has been doing so well."

He rose as if the interview had come to an end, but my questions were far from answered. "And how, exactly, will we know when the time has come for her discharge?"

He stepped nearer and I rose, in no wise comforted by the hand he laid upon my shoulder. "I will let you know, Miss Farncomb." He glanced at the wall clock next to the door. "The decision to discharge a patient is an important one with many considerations. Rest at ease, knowing that we all have the best interests of your sister-in-law at heart." Opening the door, he gestured for me to pass through. "Do give my regards to Canon Farncomb."

Scarcely realizing how it had happened, I found myself in the foyer as a tearful woman and her husband followed the doctor into his office. I'd heard that, once admitted to the asylum, a person rarely saw the outside world again, but I'd always assumed that the reason lay in the fact that cures for insanity were faulty and unreliable. I never dreamt that a person, having been restored so nearly to normalcy, would be denied discharge. *Perhaps she has made herself too valuable to them as an expert seamstress.* Dismissing the preposterous thought before it could take root, I sidled toward the stairs.

"Morning, Miss Farncomb." A young nurse bobbed a curtsy as I passed. "Do you have a publication date yet for that book you are writing?"

Book... book... It took a moment for me to switch gears. "Oh yes, good morning, Nurse Prins. My publisher assures me that my book will be ready for distribution by November if I get the amended manuscript to him before the end of March."

"I'm so looking forward to reading it," the girl effused. "You will be sure to keep a signed copy for me, will you not? I take such comfort from reading your column in *The Advocate* each week."

"That is most kind of you to say, my dear. I'm glad that God has blessed you through my words." I proceeded to the stairs, my mind consumed with pulling Janey from her toil, if only for a few minutes.

• • •

"Good morning, Dora." Janey's cheery voice greeted me. "I was hoping you would drop by for a visit today." She patted the empty chair next to her. "Come sew with me. The boys are upstairs in the nur…" Confusion clouded her eyes, and she shook her head. "Oh dear, I'm afraid I still struggle at times with the delusions that have held me for so long. Do forgive me, Dora."

I shoved my basket beneath the empty chair and unfolded the half-sewn apron the matron thrust into my hands. "Of course I forgive you, Janey. It must be very difficult for you, but the progress you've made astounds me." Her needle never skipped a beat as it wound its way through the coarse linen fabric of the short coat she assembled. She truly was an expert seamstress. "Dr. Clarke and I were just speaking about the possibility of your discharge." Janey's needle stopped in mid-air. "Although he doesn't feel you are ready for release just yet," I added quickly.

A flicker of relief sighed across her face as her needle resumed its rhythmic tattoo. Did she not wish to be released? Despite the boredom and cantankerous conditions of life within the asylum, did the possibility of living beyond its protective walls frighten her? Had the Hospital for the Insane actually become her home? I threaded the needle the matron handed me and slid it through the fabric. Janey hummed softly as her needle worked the fabric—in, out, in, out. The short coat she worked would be done before tea.

"Do you like living here, Janey?"

Her humming stopped, though her fingers continued their elegant dance. "Sometimes." Finishing the final buttonhole, she knotted the thread and bit off the tail. "Truth be told, I can hardly remember what life was like before I entered these walls." She approached the matron for buttons and settled back into her chair to sew them into place. I had hardly completed my first seam. Had I been an inmate in the asylum, the matron would certainly have punished my incompetence. Visiting as I was, though, she had not the authority to harass me, provided Janey's work was not affected. Besides, despite my slow pace, my contribution to her day's quota was incontestable.

Janey sewed in silence for a time, her head bowed in concentration, until I was certain she had forgotten me. "Tell me about life on the outside, Dora."

The whispered plea pierced me to the core. Laying the half-finished apron on my lap, I leaned toward Janey. Story after story poured from my heart as Janey sewed on, her expression bouncing between confusion and awe, joy and painful reminiscence.

"And how is Mother faring these days?" Janey asked. A tremor ran up my spine and I drew back. Johnny and I, together with the superintendent, had decided it was best to keep her ignorant of Mother's passing, especially should she one day begin to regain her sanity. A blow of that magnitude could have devastating repercussions for the recovering psyche.

"She's better than ever," I replied. "Indeed, she's filled with peace and overflowing with joy." I squirmed in my seat. Though my words held not a whit of dishonesty, the intent to deceive could not be denied. Should Janey find herself privy to the truth one day, would she ever trust me again? "Now, did I tell you about young George—Alfred's oldest son?" Janey raised her brows, though whether in eagerness to hear more or in confusion over the sudden change of topic, I couldn't say. "He's asked Constance Dalrymple to marry him."

"At last," Janey breathed, a smile dimpling her cheeks. "He always was sweet on that curly-headed princess."

Odd the things she remembered. "Yes, he was," I affirmed. "And a better match no one could imagine."

"Ahem. Ladies—" I looked up, startled to find we were alone in the great chair-lined room with the matron. "I appreciate your devotion to your work, but it is time for Mrs. Farncomb to return to the ward. Tea is about to be served."

I glanced at the handsome pocket-watch tucked into my bodice. "Oh my! We apologize for keeping you, Mrs. Hill. It was good of you to let the two of us catch up like this."

She dipped her head. "I'm just glad to see our Janey doing so much better." Retrieving our needles, she deftly speared them into the numbered holes of the needle holder. Should one be unaccounted for, she was sure to pay dearly for the loss. "Now off wi' ye, ladies. Do enjoy your tea."

With a hearty hug, I bid my sister-in-law goodnight at the door to the tenth ward dining hall and headed down the spiral staircase. The building itself was a magnificent edifice. Had there been more dollars available for upkeep, it would surely have been the most beautiful building in Toronto.

Dr. Clarke stepped from his office as I reached the final step. "How did you find our Mrs. Farncomb today?"

"Very well, thank you," I responded. I met him halfway across the lobby. "You're right, though. While she seems very much herself these days, there are still minor lapses and she seems quite anxious about the thought of leaving the asylum."

Dr. Clarke patted my shoulder, a compassionate smile lifting the corners of his lips. "It is to be expected, I am afraid. Her last recollection of life outside these walls was a traumatic one."

I hadn't thought of that. To leave the asylum would require Janey to return to the moment of her greatest pain, which could take her right back to the state for which she was committed. This place, though it may not always have seemed it, had been a refuge for her. "You're right, Doctor. I hadn't considered that."

With a cordial nod, he hurried toward the stairs. "Give my regards to your brother." Darkness wrapped itself around me as I stepped into the night, uncertain of how I was to get home since Johnny apparently hadn't arrived as arranged.

"Dora."

"Johnny, you're here." Relieved, I turned to see the silhouette of my brother leaning against one of the pillars framing the entrance way.

"Yes. I'd hoped to see Janey, but they'd already gone to tea by the time I got here." Stepping out of the shadows, he offered me his arm. He moved slowly, as if he bore a great weight, and his voice lacked its usual lustre.

I hesitated before taking his elbow. "You seem upset."

Leading me to the rickety carriage, he helped me into the seat without saying a word. My feet grew cold in the short time it took for him to climb into the driver's seat, and I wiggled my toes in my boots. Something was definitely wrong. The harness jangled as the horse set the creaking wheels into motion, and a chill ran down my back. Had something happened to Marjorie? To Alfred? Engrossed in my musings, I almost missed his quiet admission.

"I got a telegram this afternoon."

A telegram? My heart pounded in my chest. "From whom?"

"Alfred." He stared straight ahead, the reins hanging limply in his hands.

It wasn't Alfred then, nor Marjorie. "It's bad news, isn't it?" I pulled a blanket from the floor of the carriage and smoothed it over my knees. The barest jerk of his head confirmed my fears. "Who is it this time?"

"Young Alfie—Alfred's son."

"No." I shook my head vehemently. "Not Alfie. He's naught but eleven years old. You must be mistaken." I blinked rapidly, willing myself to be strong. Of all my nieces and nephews, Alfie reminded me most of our dear Charlie. They even looked uncannily alike. Had not our family suffered enough? Back stiff, Johnny remained silent as the horse made its way down the broad street. A heavy sigh ripped from deep within me. "What happened?"

"Pneumonia."

The word alone struck fear to my heart. *Pneumonia?* I squeezed my eyes shut. "Is he all right?" The grimace on Johnny's face clearly said that the boy was not. Oh, that this brother of mine would be more forthcoming. "Alfred *can* do something for him, though, can't he?" I pressed. Johnny's lips tightened into a straight line, yet still, he did not speak. "How is poor Alfred handling it all? Hannah?" My voice broke.

He looked at me for the first time, his eyes narrowing. "It was a telegram, Dora, not a personal letter. The boy is dead. That's all I know." His stinging response smarted, though I recognized the grief from which it sprang.

"Dead?"

Johnny exhaled sharply. "Yes. Look, I'm sorry. You didn't deserve that. I don't know how Alfred and Hannah are faring, I only know the pain they must be enduring at this moment."

I directed my gaze toward the buildings lining the busy street. "It brings back a host of unhappy memories."

Johnny grunted, plainly agreeing. "Memories I'd just as soon forget." His Adam's apple bobbed. "We can only pray that Hannah fares better in this than my Janey did." He fell silent, obviously deep in thought. "How was she today?"

Stunned by the sudden change of topic, I scoured my brain for something to report. "She was good—very good, actually. We chatted all afternoon." Johnny glanced my way, his eyes wide. Gulping to clear the mass of emotion clogging my throat, I stifled the urge to turn the conversation back to young Alfie. "She wanted to hear stories of life on the outside."

"What did Dr. Clarke say about the possibility of her discharge?"

I paused, weighing my words. "He didn't dismiss it entirely, but in the end, we both agreed that she isn't quite ready to take that step." Johnny peered at me, questions flickering in his eyes. "She's afraid, Johnny." I picked a ball of lint off the blanket on my lap. "The only thing she clearly remembers about her life before she was committed is the trauma of the boys' deaths."

His eyes filled. "That's all there is to remember."

His statement jolted me. "Johnny, the joy of living wasn't eradicated when Charlie died, though for a time it was greatly dampened. Will you really allow young Jack's and Charles' deaths to steal that joy from you now? Wouldn't the boys be horrified to think that they had stolen from you all that made life worth living?"

Johnny's eyes hardened. "How dare you speak of things of which you know not a whit. Losing a brother is nothing compared to losing a son." He drew his lips into a hard line and reined the horse to a stop outside the rectory. "Wait here while I pack a bag."

I stared at his retreating figure. His stiff-legged steps beat soundlessly on the snowy ground, his rigid back belying his usual calmness. *What just happened, Jesus?* I drew a knuckle to my mouth. *Why can I not keep my blasted tongue from wagging?*

You said the words he needed to hear.

Did I? I pulled the blanket higher to cover my shoulders and tucked it clumsily behind my back.

Often the words a person needs to hear are not the ones he wants to hear.

A parade of painful images flashed through my mind—tearful moments of disappointment and surrender punctuating season's of heartbreak and renewal. Often the words we needed to hear really weren't the ones we wanted to hear, but knowing that did little to make them easier to bear. *Is there anything I can do to ease his pain?*

Johnny appeared with a sloppily filled carpet bag and tossed it at my feet before climbing into the driver's seat. He slapped the reins against the old mare's rump and clucked his tongue, his eyes fixed upon the road. "See that you and Marjorie pack quickly—and lightly," he said, his words clipped. "The train leaves at nine eleven and I want to be there early."

"You're angry." I kept my voice level, lest he hear in it even a hint of accusation.

"You don't know what it's like, Dora." He ran his fingers through his hair.

"No, I don't," I confessed.

"What if Hannah loses herself in her grief like Janey did?" Pain laced his voice. "We all share the same blood."

I studied the overstuffed bag at my feet. That insanity ran in families could not be denied, yet neither could I accept heredity as the only factor in Janey's lengthy illness. After all, Mother had lost a son in his youth and she remained sane. "You cannot dwell on things like that, Johnny." I blinked my eyes slowly, desperate to think of something else to say.

Turning onto Simpson Avenue, the carriage slowed to a stop at the end of our walk. "Remember, pack lightly and be fast," Johnny ordered. He jumped from the carriage and helped me down. "I apologize for being such a bear."

I slid my arms around his neck and pressed a kiss to his cheek. "Nonsense, brother." I gave him a saucy grin. "I love bears." Before he could respond, I jogged up the walk and threw open the door. "Margie dear, you need to come quickly…"

• • •

A house exudes an aura of grief when its inhabitants mourn. Though I fail to understand the mysteries of this phenomenon, over and over I have found it to be so. Barely had our carriage turned into the drive of my childhood home when the oppression hit, nearly sucking the air from my lungs. "You go ahead, Johnny," I announced as soon as the wheels slid to a stop. "Marjorie and I will see that the bags are brought in." Johnny gave a curt nod as he stepped onto the icy ground and I clasped his arm briefly. "May God grant you courage and imbue you with words of comfort."

Carson, Alfred's man servant, slid from the driver's board and offered Marjorie a hand. "Watch the ice now, Miss Marjorie." After seeing her safely to the steps, he returned to help me down. "You, too, Miss Dora. It's awfully slippery out here today."

"Thank you, Carson." I hooked my hand around his elbow, allowing him to lead me all the way up the stairs to the door. "Might I impose upon you to see that our bags are brought in?"

The big man stopped on the verandah to offer his other arm to Marjorie before ushering us both into the foyer. "It is no imposition whatsoever, ma'am." He bowed regally, as if the queen herself had come to call. "I wouldn't have it any other way."

"Miss Dora!" I turned at the sound of the familiar voice, warmed by the sight of my dear Betsy rushing down the hall toward me. Though a brave smile trembled on her lips, her eyes pooled when I held out my arms to welcome her.

Swaying in her embrace, I marvelled at the growing assurance I felt that all would be well. "You know, of all the treasures I left behind in my move to the city, you, dear Betsy, are the one I miss most."

"I've missed you, too, Dora."

My heart swelled at her lapse in formality. "Tell me what happened." I slid my hand through the crook of her elbow, inclining my head toward the conservatory.

At her nod, I led her to the cozy nook by the fire with Marjorie trailing behind, her face as white as the snow atop Mount Everest.

Betsy bent to stoke the fire while Marjorie and I seated ourselves on Mother's old divan. Swallowing hard, I tried to clear the lump in my throat. Mother had sat on this very divan the day we received the devastating news about John's two boys. It was on this divan that Janey had pined away her final days at Ebor House in the weeks following my nephew's deaths. However would she respond to the news that young Alfie had died? *Another secret we'd have to keep from our beloved Janey. Yet, could not a surprise like that—should she ever be released—be enough to send her back to the asylum for good?*

"Auntie Dora?" A child's hand came to rest upon my shoulder as a pair of soft, warm lips fluttered against my weathered cheek.

"Helen, darling." I drew the petite young lady to my side, kissing her bouncy curls. At eight years old, Alfred's youngest ought to have been abed long ago.

"Alfie's gone."

"Gone?"

She nodded, her brow furrowed. "He's gone to be with Jesus."

I took both of her hands in mine, caressing them with my thumbs. "You must miss him terribly." Again she nodded. "I remember when your Uncle Charlie went to be with Jesus. He was *my* brother."

"Were you sad?"

I blinked rapidly. How could the pain of his passing still be so intense? "Very, very sad. I missed him so much." I squeezed her trembling hands in mine. "I still do. What about you? Are you sad?"

Helen scrunched her nose and nodded. "Mother cries all day long and Mary and Georgie won't play with me."

"What does your father do?"

With a heavy sigh, Helen flopped onto the divan next to me. "I don't know. He's never here." I studied her troubled eyes, willing her to explain. "He has patients who need him—lots of them."

I nodded. Of course he had patients who needed him—he would always have patients who needed him—but that was only part of the story. "I'm so sorry, Helen." I curled a lock of her hair around my finger and slipped it behind her ear. "They are sad. Very, very sad. But their sadness will eventually lessen; their smiles will return."

"When Alfie comes back from visiting Jesus, I'm going to tell him never to go away again."

A choking sob issued from the seat beside me, and I restrained an answering sigh. Stroking the young girl's cheek with one finger, I tried to resurrect a smile. "Alfie can't come back, honey. He's going to live with Jesus from now on—with Uncle Charlie and Cousin Jack and Cousin Charles and your grandfather and grandmother."

Her little brow wrinkled. "But I want him to live here with me."

I brushed a hand across my eyes lest she see the moisture clinging to my lashes. "That's how I felt when your Uncle Charlie passed on."

"Me, too," Marjorie whispered. "When my brothers passed, I prayed every day that Jesus would send them back." Marjorie never spoke much about that dreadful time in her life. Perhaps this was exactly what she needed to begin the healing process.

"Did He?" Helen asked.

"Did He what, dear?" I ran a hand down her bare arm. Whatever happened to her robe?

"Send Cousin Margie's brothers back?"

Marjorie pressed her lips shut, her chin quivering. Only a child could ask such a thing. I slid a hand over to squeeze Marjorie's knee. "No, Helen, I'm afraid not. Their work on earth was complete, just like Alfie's is. Besides, they wouldn't have wanted to return. They're happier now than ever before. Nothing can hurt them or make them sad ever again."

"Helen…" Hannah beckoned her daughter from the door and directed her to go to her chamber. How long she had been at the door, I knew not. "Betsy told me that my talkative young daughter had accosted you." In a trice, I was on my feet, my arms extended in invitation.

Hannah's mouth contorted as I approached, and I drew her into a tight embrace. "I'm so sorry, Hannah." I led her to the divan, nodding my thanks to Marjorie when she moved into the overstuffed chair next to the fire. "Is there anything we can do to help?"

Hannah shook her head. What a foolish question. Of course there was nothing we could do when the only thing that could truly help at this moment was the return of her son. Chiding myself for my insensitivity, I tried again. "Do you need help getting the children ready for the wake?" Hannah's brow furrowed, but she didn't respond. "How be Marjorie asks Edith if she needs help with anything while we just sit here and rest."

Responding immediately to my unspoken request, Marjorie left the room, leaving us alone. Though my tongue seemed determined to wag with meaningless questions, I corralled it into silence as I waited for Hannah to speak.

An ember popped on the grate, sending a shower of sparks onto the hearth as the clock chimed eleven. "It all happened so quickly," Hannah whispered, staring straight into the flames. "We barely had the chance to say goodbye." I forced myself to remain silent lest my words bring more harm than help. "One day he was a strong, healthy eleven-year-old with naught but a little cough…" Her voice trailed off as she dabbed her handkerchief to her nose. "A week later…" She splayed her hands.

"Pneumonia is like that." I rested my forehead against hers, letting my tears convey what my words could not. "Alfred has grieved sorely over the many patients he's lost to that dreaded disease over the years, but to lose his own son—" A whispering of footsteps at the door brought my thoughtless words to a halt. "Alfred…" I sprang from my seat to embrace my brother. Deep, dark bags sagged beneath his eyes. "I'm so sorry. So, so sorry," I murmured.

His chest heaved as he tightened his arms around me. "I know," he whispered. I lifted watery eyes to his, knowing words alone could never bring relief from the pain searing his heart. I couldn't help but recall the anger he had aimed at God when Johnny's boys had died. *Oh God, do not let him harden himself to Your comfort and sovereignty in this. I know he doesn't understand—none of us do—but grant him, and our dear Hannah, the grace to accept this tragedy as from Your hand in spite of the pain it brings with it.*

Releasing a long, slow breath, he took a step backward and leaned his head down to my ear. "Pray for me, Dora." He raised his head and I nodded, my lips pressed into a tight smile lest the tears begin anew. "Come, everyone. It is time we got some sleep. Johnny, you take the extra bed in George's room, and you, little sis, can bunk with Marjorie in the hospital room. It's empty at present and has been well scrubbed." Hannah hurried to her husband's side as he turned toward the stairs.

"May the peace of God which passeth all understanding keep us through this night and grant us rest," Johnny intoned.

A feeble chorus of amens followed as we dispersed. If rest could be had, it would come from Him alone.

Chapter 62

APRIL 12, 1909

My Dear Mr. Wellman,

My best wishes to you on your fifty-second birthday. I hope you were well celebrated by your congregation on your special day. Did Mrs. Perkins make a hummingbird cake for you like she did last year? You never did send me a piece, you realize. Perhaps this year?

My, my, it feels good to laugh. As I am sure you have already heard, tragedy has once more struck our family in the passing of Alfred's youngest son, Alfie. Poor Alfred! The sweet child died of pneumonia and, skilled though his dear father is, he could do absolutely nothing to prevent it. Johnny is in almost more turmoil about it than Alfred, though, reliving, as you can imagine, the deaths of his own two sons and the rending of all he held dear.

I am afraid to tell Janey. She is doing so much better these days. In fact, she is almost back to her old self and may even be headed toward release, but news like this is sure to reawaken in her a deep melancholia and reverse the miraculous changes we have seen in her of late. I would not even consider telling her except for the possibility of her release. I wish I knew what to do. I have to give Janey some explanation for my absence last week, and Johnny has closed himself to all but the work of his parish right now as, once again, our family struggles to right itself. I worry about young Helen, too. She is Alfred's youngest daughter, if you recall. She is so little and does not understand at all the tragedy that has struck her family. The fear in her eyes when she bid Marjorie and me goodbye at the train station smote my heart.

I must confess that I do not understand why God allows so much suffering to buffet my family. My head knows that it is a result of living in this fallen world, but my heart fails to comprehend how our loving God, the Supreme Ruler of all things, can allow it. And then I think of the suffering of our Lord Jesus and feel such shame. I do not even know how to pray these days, Mattie. Next month's articles are due at The Advocate before week's end, and I do not know what to write about. I had started composing a series on hope last week, but the glorious hope flooding my soul as I wrote has popped like a bubble on a pin and is no more. Perhaps that is the point, though. What kind of hope is it we cherish if we only embrace it when there is evidence of joyful tidings afoot? True hope is rooted in the presence of unseen victory. Perhaps the only place true hope is revealed is in the midst of our darkest storms where the presence of God is veiled from our sight.

Well, it would seem I do have something to write about after all. I so wish you were nearer, Mattie; you have a way of helping me to see things so much more clearly. I miss our conversations more than I can say *and yearn for the warmth of your embrace—if but for a moment. Keep well, my love, and write soon. My prayers are with you.*

Affectionately,
Your Dora-girl

Rummaging through my desk for an envelope, I happened upon the old silver locket my grandmother had given me on my sixteenth birthday. Gently prying the hinge open, I smiled at the age-worn photos within. Had Mattie really been but a boy when we first began to court? He had seemed so much more mature to those sixteen-year-old eyes of mine. And Charlie—why he looked positively infantile—or pretty nearly so. How could it be that we had all thought ourselves so grown up? I snapped the locket shut and clipped it around my neck. Odd how wearing it close to my heart made them both feel somehow nearer. With one hand wrapped firmly around the precious necklace, I pulled out a clean sheet of paper and pressed the nib of my pen to the blotter. It was time I got those articles written.

Chapter 63

APRIL 14, 1909

"Well, Margie, I told your mother about Alfie today." I folded my napkin and tucked it under the edge of my plate.

Marjorie's hand stopped mid-way to her mouth. "Do you think that was wise?"

"That I cannot say, I'm afraid." I lowered my eyes, recalling Janey's noticeable withdrawal after I shared the news. "I only know that, if she is ever to come home as we hope, she must not be met with a host of painful surprises. She asked where I had been and I told her."

"How did she take the news?"

Pushing my plate aside, I reached for the teapot. "There was, by the time I left, a noticeable withdrawal in her demeanor, but she didn't immediately revert to her former distress. We can only pray that the news will not lead to serious regression." I poured the tea into two china cups and offered one to my niece. "She kept asking why God always takes the best."

Marjorie winced. It was no secret that she believed her mother had always favoured her sons above her daughters, whether or not it was true. "I tried to explain that God doesn't take His children—that rather than take them, He welcomes them home when their work on earth is complete—but she, like all of us, has difficulty seeing through anything but the lens of her own loss." I reached for a butterscotch roll. Marjorie sure knew her way around the kitchen. "I wish I knew how to help her understand."

Collecting the dirty dishes, Marjorie set them in the sink and turned on the faucet. "Will you go and see her again tomorrow?"

"Yes, I suppose I had better." I didn't usually visit the asylum more than three times a week, and my Wednesdays were generally taken up with the women's Bible study I led at the church and visits to the widows of the parish who were in need of assistance, but with Janey's fragility of mind, a visit to the asylum needed to take priority. "Do you suppose you could visit the widows on your own tomorrow afternoon so that I could slip over to see her?"

Marjorie nodded as she immersed her hands in the sudsy water. What a blessing it was to have indoor plumbing. There were certainly perks to living in the big city. "I shall tell them that you had an important visit to make to your ailing cousin." She plunged a cloth into the water and swished it through the suds. "You will tell Mother that I miss her, won't you?"

"Of course, dear." I snagged a towel from a peg and started wiping the plates. "She speaks of you often, you know." Dishes clanked in the sink. "She would enjoy a visit from you sometime." Drying the final cup, I hung the towel on its peg and stacked the dishes on the shelf while Marjorie wiped the crumbs from the table.

"Maybe next week," she mumbled. I could hardly blame her. The poor girl had been so hurt by her mother's apparent abandonment. Her love and care for her mother was clearly evident in word and deed, but should Janey ever actually come home from the hospital, I had to wonder if her daughter would truly be able to welcome her. The two hardly knew each other.

"If you don't mind, auntie, I think I shall turn in for the night." Marjorie folded the dish rag over the faucet and gave it a little pat.

"Of course," I responded. I flipped the switch on the wall, still awed by the wonders of gas lighting. "She loves you more than you know, dear," I whispered into her ear when she leaned in to buss my cheek.

"Sleep well, Aunt Dora." She ran her finger beneath her nose, barely concealing a sniff.

Jesus, let Janey retain her sanity through this latest tragedy, and let Marjorie see how greatly her mother loves her. Closing the door to my own chamber, I creaked to my knees at the side of the bed. I might as well retire also. It would do me good. *May Your will alone be done when it comes to Janey's release, O Lord. I so desire her homecoming, yet somehow I find myself wondering if it is the best thing—for her, or for Marjorie, or even for Johnny.* The powers that be thought it best that his parishioners believed Janey to be convalescing due to chronic illness rather than know of her confinement since many would question his competence in shepherding their little flock if they knew the truth. If she were suddenly to appear out of nowhere… I cradled my face in my hands, shaking my head. *I don't know how much more of this I can take, Lord.* I sniffed back a tear. *What if I made the wrong decision in telling her about Alfie? What if tomorrow I find her once again caught in the grip of insanity? What if—*

What if you leave her in my hands?

My breath came in short, shaky bursts. *I–I'm afraid.*

Do I not love her even more than you do?

But what if Your will for her includes the horrors of increased insanity?

I know the plans I have for her, beloved—for her and for you—plans for peace and not for evil.

I folded my hands beneath my chin, recognizing the words God spoke to Israel through the prophet Jeremiah.

My grace is sufficient no matter where My will might lead.

Why was it so infernally difficult to rest in that knowledge when my whole life was a testimony to its veracity? *Give me peace, Holy Father, and grant me a heart of acceptance for I am weak and fearful and riddled by grief.* A great weariness engulfed me, and I crawled into bed, yawning. I had yet to undress, but that could wait a few minutes more. Another great yawn stretched my lungs as I drew a corner of Mother's old quilt across my legs. *For so God giveth His beloved sleep...*

Chapter 64

"Good morning, Dr. Clarke." Sighting the hospital superintendent as he set foot on the bottom stair, I heralded him from across the foyer. "Might you have a moment to talk?"

He glanced at his pocket watch, waiting for me to approach. "I must not tarry long, Miss Farncomb. Perhaps you would like to accompany me." He motioned for me to precede him up the wide, spiral staircase. "As it happens, I am on my way to visit your sister-in-law's ward right now."

"How was she last night?" The words burst from my lips without preface. "I mean, did you see any signs of regression?"

"You told her about her nephew, I take it," he responded.

"We all agreed that she needed to know, sir." Why did I feel as though blame was being laid upon my shoulders?

"Yes, yes. Of course we did." He pushed his spectacles into place as if trying to buy time.

"She has regressed, then," I stated flatly.

"Well, not necessarily, Miss Farncomb." We stepped into a long hallway, the amiable Dr. Clarke greeting patients and attendants alike as we moved toward Janey's ward near the end of the corridor. "She was somewhat withdrawn yesterday evening and I'm told that she passed a restless night, but that does not mean she has regressed." He paused to exchange hushed words with a nurse outside the ward. "It is, I should say, a most sane reaction to the news." He resumed our conversation as if it had never been interrupted. Nodding, he pushed his spectacles once more into place. "After all, did you not withdraw somewhat yourself when you heard the news? Surely you passed a few restless nights of your own."

My rigid stance relaxed but a hair. "You are a wise man, Doctor."

"Wise?" He cocked his head. "Perhaps; perhaps not. Merely experienced as a student of human nature." He opened the door to the ward and held it for me to enter. "Let's see how she is doing today, shall we?" The nurse on duty greeted us as soon as we walked through the door. "Good morning, Nurse Bennett. And how are our patients this morning?"

"Dr. Clarke. Miss Farncomb." The nurse nodded at each of us in turn. My eyes darted around the near-empty room. Most of the beds, including Janey's, were neatly made, their inhabitants notably absent, while a handful yet lay rumpled and in need of fresh sheets. One woman, still abed, lay thrashing her legs in the tangled sheets, clearly in need of attention.

"Flora, dear." Dr. Clarke went immediately to her side. Deftly untangling her sheets, he smoothed them over her feet and laid a hand upon her brow. "You seem upset. Is there something I can do to help?"

A series of unintelligible grunts issued from the woman as her legs came to rest.

Moving to join the doctor, the nurse rested her hand on Flora's knee, ignoring the woman's obvious flinch. "She has been like this for hours, I'm afraid." The nurse met the doctor's eyes and lifted a shoulder dismissively. "I have no idea of what ails her."

"Well, something certainly does." The doctor ran his hand along the woman's body, his brow furrowed in concentration. "This certainly isn't normal behavior for our Flora May, now is it?" He smiled, crooning the final three words at his patient as if she were a much-adored child. That the good Dr. Clarke truly cared for his patients could not be questioned. A sudden yelp from the woman brought his hands to a stop over her left side. "It seems we have found the source of the trouble," he said. "Now, let's take a peek to see what seems to be causing the pain."

With a start, the poor woman drew away from his touch, her eyes firmly fixed upon Nurse Bennett. Shaking her head wildly from side to side, she clasped her hands protectively over her midriff and responded with a spate of gibberish.

The doctor drew his eyebrows into a tight vee and peered at the nurse. *Why wouldn't the poor woman want the doctor to examine her?* Nurse Bennett grunted in response and tipped her eyes heavenward. "Surely you don't expect me to interpret, Doctor," she spat. "The woman is an imbecile."

"Insane, yes," Dr. Clarke corrected, "but an imbecile, I think not." I stepped away from the bed, allowing both doctor and patient a modicum of privacy. Ignoring his patient's protestations, the doctor gently peeled back her night dress to reveal an angry red and black bruise over her left ribcage. "What happened here, Flora?" Concern etched his words as he lightly probed the area around the bruise. The woman jerked her head to the side, her lips clamped in a hard, white line. "Nurse Bennett?" the doctor asked, his tone demanding an explanation.

Moving closer to peer at the bruise, the nurse folded her arms tightly across her chest. "Oh my," she responded, her voice strained. "However did you do that, love?"

"As if you didn't know."

Startled, all three of us turned at once to see a frail old woman shuffling from bed to bed with a feather duster.

"Good morning, Ethel. You're doing a fine job of dusting this morning," the doctor said. I so appreciated the way Dr. Clarke greeted every one of his patients as if she were important. "Do you know what happened to Flora's side?"

"Why don't you ask Nurse Bennett?" Ethel jutted her boney chin at the nurse. "She knows." She opened her mouth in a gap-toothed grin. "She did it." The nurse's face paled, and she shook her head at the doctor as Ethel continued her tirade. "She thumped her 'cause she wouldn't stop babbling."

"Honestly, Doctor," Nurse Bennett gasped. "I did no such thing. The dear girl had a hard time settling last night and thrashed around something fierce whenever I approached, but I certainly did not *thump* her as my delusional friend here claims." She gestured toward her accuser, punctuating her words with a laugh. "I think it more likely that Ethel here is the one who did the thumping, sir—if indeed, any thumping was done. You know her history of violent outbursts toward her fellow inmates." She blew a strand of hair from her face. "Seriously, Doctor, these women are in here for a reason. What kind of nurse would I be if I went around *thumping* my patients?"

Ignoring Nurse Bennett's plea, Dr. Clarke returned his attention to his patient and completed his examination. "Well, Flora, it seems that you have yourself a broken rib." He dug about in his bag for a long bandage. After helping her into a sitting position, he proceeded to bind it tightly around her midriff. "Did Nurse Bennett do this to you, Flora?" he asked amiably.

"No-o-o-o-o-o," she wailed, her eyes wide as she jiggled her head from side to side.

"Did Ethel?"

"No-o-o-o-o-o."

"Did you do it yourself?" Again her head jiggled, first from side to side, then decidedly up and down. The poor woman looked terrified. Janey had told me how rough the nurses could be with their charges when the doctors weren't around, but I hadn't really entertained the possibility that the nurses might be abusing some of their patients. I had heard whispers of such things, but only from Janey's most seriously disturbed ward mates, and who would take the word of a lunatic over that of a person whose sanity had not been compromised? Surely the nurses were driven to madness themselves at times, but the thought that Nurse Bennett—or any other nurse, for that matter—might take out her frustrations on such a helpless wretch as Flora was beyond imagining. Surely it couldn't be true.

"Well, Flora, I think it best that you stay a-bed for a day or two until that rib heals up." Dr. Clarke patted Flora's shoulder gently. "Nurse Bennett, please see to it that Flora's breakfast is brought to her here and that word is sent to the laundry that she will not be attending her regular chores until further notice." Nurse Bennett nodded, her face hard as flint. Moving away from the bed, the doctor surveyed the room. "Now, how is our dear Janey doing today?"

The nurse pointed to the door of the breakfast room. "Perhaps you should see for yourself, Doctor Clarke. She hasn't come back from breakfast, yet."

Preparing myself for the worst, I followed the doctor into the dining room. While most of the residents sat silently at their tables sipping coffee, a handful of kitchen helpers bustled from table to table collecting dirty dishes and uneaten food. Janey sat by herself in the corner nearest the verandah, staring into her coffee. Her lips moved as if she spoke, but nary a sound broke the unnatural silence permeating the room.

"She's struggling," I stated dully.

"Are you not also?" the doctor responded. "Were she not, I would have reason to be concerned about her growing sanity." He motioned for me to precede him. "The question is whether or not she has receded into the world of fantasy she so recently abandoned."

Janey looked up as we approached and blinked twice, cocking her head as if confused. "May we join you, Janey?" Dr. Clarke asked. At her nod, he pulled out the chair adjacent to my sister-in-law and waited for me to get settled before seating himself in the empty chair on her other side.

"Good morning, Janey." My voice, though barely above a whisper, sounded startlingly loud in the quiet room. A hundred vacant eyes turned to stare at me from every corner of the room. "How are you today?" I whispered more softly still.

Janey's nose wrinkled. "Do I know you?"

Of all the responses I had expected, the possibility of her not recognizing me had never crossed my mind. While that had been the norm for her first year or so at the asylum, the relentless heartache of that time seemed far removed from the cogent conversations we had enjoyed even yesterday. *Can she truly not know who I am?* A calming hand stole over my own, and I looked up to meet Dr. Clarke's understanding gaze. Pressing my lips together, I straightened in my chair, determined to hide my shock.

"Janey," the doctor began. He looked approvingly at me and patted my hand. "This is Dora. I know that it is difficult for you to remember right now, but she is your sister-in-law and cousin. She visits you often."

Janey's eyes narrowed. "She does?"

Dr. Clarke nodded. "How are you feeling today, Janey?"

Abruptly pushing herself from the table, Janey stood, the conversation obviously over. "I am just fine, thank you, Mr.—forgive me. I seem to have forgotten your name—presuming I ever knew it in the first place," she muttered. "Good day." The leather soles of her shoes slapped the floor as she flounced across the dining room.

"Well, I suppose that answers our question." The doctor rose, leading me back through the ward and into the main corridor. "Give her time, Miss Farncomb. She came back to us once; she will do so again."

Part IV

Chapter 65

TORONTO
FIVE YEARS LATER
APRIL 15, 1914

"Excuse me, Dora, but when you are finished with your ladies, might I see you in my office, please?" Johnny dug his hands into his pockets, his face a mask. I stiffened at the seriousness in his voice. Clearly something was wrong. Again.

Who could it be this time? It had been a difficult winter. First Mary Stevenson and her lovely daughter, Sadie, had fallen prey to the influenza, then Robert Jarlsburg had succumbed to a heart attack. The Belmont twins had been next, followed by Mrs. Bradford's stillborn son. Death was certainly no respecter of age. Soon after, Enid Hough had passed, then Johnson Mathers, Henry Gilson and Harvey McRobbie. The list seemed endless. How so many people in one parish could pass in a mere three months was beyond comprehension. "Certainly, Father John," I responded. "We are almost through." Johnny nodded and melted into the shadows beyond the door as I returned my attention to the ladies in my weekly Bible study class. "So, Martha, does the story make more sense to you now that you understand how astoundingly rude it was for the master of the house to neglect his duty like that? It would have been a shocking breech of decorum."

"I suppose so, Miss Dora, but her courage, nonetheless, confounds me. From whence came her boldness to enter that room full of men and throw herself at the feet of Jesus?"

"I, too, am challenged by that," I confessed. "Such boldness can come from love alone." I closed my Bible and set it on the chair next to me. "I wonder sometimes if I have that kind of love—the kind of love that would propel me to go beyond the bounds of propriety to honour my Lord like she did, regardless of the social repercussions." A chorus of mumbled assents rippled through the gathering. "Come, my friends, let us pray."

• • •

"Pneumonia?" I sank into the cracked leather chair next to Johnny's desk. "I thought she was doing better after her bout with influenza earlier this month."

I drew my handkerchief from my sleeve and dabbed my forehead. "She seemed fine yesterday." Johnny leaned forward, his hands clasped on the desk before him. His head was bowed, his face strained. I twisted the handle of the purse I held in my lap. "I mean, she had a bit of a residual cough, but it didn't seem to be anything serious."

Slapping his hands on the mahogany table, he stood and rounded the desk, perching himself on the corner. "Well, apparently it was more serious than it appeared, Dora. She was moved to the infirmary this morning."

"Is she allowed visitors?" I asked.

"Not at this point, I'm afraid." Johnny gripped the edge of the desk, his knuckles white as snow.

"What are you trying to tell me?"

Johnny squeezed his eyes shut then opened them once more to stare across the room. "They do not believe she is going to make it."

"But she was fine yesterday." I jumped to my feet, jamming my fists into my hips.

"Perhaps so, but this morning her chest was so full she could barely breathe."

"How can that be?" I grabbed Johnny's arms, shaking him, determined to snap him out of his stoicism.

"I don't know, Dora. Pneumonia can stalk a person without her even knowing it... or so I've been told." He pressed my head to his chest and drew me close, his voice catching. "I've seen it before. I just never thought it would happen to my Janey." With a heavy groan, he dropped his chin to rest upon my hair. "Has the dear woman not suffered enough?"

Pushing myself from his arms, I fingered the locket hidden beneath my blouse. *Not another one, Jesus. Please, not another one.* "We have to see her."

Tipping his face heavenward, Johnny grimaced and exhaled sharply. "They will not allow it, Dora. They do not wish for the infection to spread to others."

"But what if she..." I couldn't bring myself to say the word.

"She won't." The words exploded from Johnny's mouth. "She can't." His glassy eyes glared into mine, daring me to contradict his words.

"You dare not shut your mind to the possibility," I murmured.

Turning abruptly, Johnny seated himself at his desk and straightened the stack of papers awaiting his attention. "If you don't mind, Dora, I have a sermon to write. I shall summon you if something changes."

Like a beleaguered servant, I backed from the room, biting my tongue to keep from saying more. *We live in a fallen world, buffeted by one sorrow after* another, where death is the final curse. O Lord, don't take our Janey from us; we... I mean she... I mean... O Jesus, what do I mean? Would she not be far better off with You than she is here with us? How dare I deny her that joy simply because I don't want to let her go? Yes, we may live in a fallen world, buffeted by one sorrow after another, where death is the final curse, but thanks be to God, the curse has been broken and we have been set free.* I swallowed the lump wedged in my throat. *Set her free, O Lord, and help me to let her go with dignity and grace.* I paused in the nave to pull a notebook and pen from my purse. That would make the perfect topic for my next article.

Resisting the urge to stay and write more, I slipped from the pew and pushed through the heavy door. Somebody had to tell Marjorie, and it might as well be me. Then, regardless of Johnny's assertion, I would head to the asylum. Surely they wouldn't be so heartless as to deny a dying woman her final goodbye.

• • •

"I'm sorry, Miss Farncomb. Your sister-in-law is not entertaining visitors today."

I tried not to scowl at the young attendant. Of course Janey was not *entertaining* visitors. "It is not my intent to visit with her today, Nurse Mavis," I answered. "I merely want to sit by her side and hold her hand. I do not wish for her to walk this road alone."

The nurse's brow furrowed and she glanced over her shoulder. "I shall see what the doctor says, Miss Farncomb, but you mustn't get your hopes up." She looked down, wringing her hands. "Mrs. Farncomb is a very sick woman. We wouldn't want you to be exposed to the contagion unnecessarily."

"She is dying, Nurse Mavis." I rubbed my fingers across my forehead. "We both know that."

The nurse's eyes shifted, avoiding my gaze. "No, we do not know that."

I placed my hand upon her shoulder and waited until her eyes met mine, emboldened by the certainty building within me. "You may not, but I do." I paused, breathing deeply, awed by the peace flooding my soul. "My dear sister's trials will soon be over." The nurse fidgeted beneath my gaze as I pressed on. "Why do you not summon one of the doctors?"

With a curt nod, she entered the infirmary, leaving me to pace away my restless energy. *I don't want to let her go, Lord, yet for the love I bear her, I commit her spirit into Your hands. The trials she has borne in this world are great. Comfort her, precious Jesus, and encompass her with Your peace as her sojourn on this side of the veil comes to an—*

"Miss Farncomb?"

With a start, I glanced up to see Dr. Clarke striding down the hall.

"Good afternoon, Dr. Clarke. It was kind of you to come. I expected the nurse to summon one of the lesser doctors." He stared at me blankly. Summoning what little energy I had left, I tried again. "You mean Nurse Mavis didn't summon you?"

The door of the infirmary opened and a short, round-faced doctor emerged, mopping his brow with a wrinkled handkerchief.

"Good afternoon, Dr. Haynes." Dr. Clarke greeted the flustered man as if he had been expecting him. "I was just going to make my rounds of the infirmary. How is Mrs. Farncomb doing this afternoon?" Dr. Haynes looked cautiously from his superior to me and back. "You may speak freely, doctor," the superintendent said. "Miss Farncomb understands the seriousness of her sister-in-law's condition."

I nodded, relieved to have an ally in my quest. "I know our dear Janey is dying." I lowered my head, my chin quivering. "I just don't want her to die alone." I glanced from one man to the other. "Please allow me to sit with her and hold her hand."

"Your sister-in-law has, I am sorry to say, passed the point of being comforted." The doctor pushed his spectacles into place then buried his hand in his pocket. "She has been unresponsive for the last two hours."

"But, she would know that I was there," I countered. "She may not be able to respond, but she would know that she is not alone." Dr. Haynes directed a meaningful look at Dr. Clarke, his lips pursed. "Please." I blinked away the tears stabbing the backs of my eyes.

"Could it hurt for her to be there?" Dr. Clarke asked.

Dr. Haynes shook his head and scowled. "Pneumonia like this can be quite contagious."

"I'm certain that Miss Farncomb would take every precaution to protect herself, Doctor." His eyes met mine and I nodded, knowing he understood. "She's a sensible and dedicated woman whose heart for her sister has never wavered. It wouldn't be right for us to deny her this final farewell."

Chin quivering, I stared at the tiled floor. *Let him say yes, Jesus. Let him say yes. I need to say goodbye.*

"Come." Dr. Haynes' voice, though pinched, exuded kindness. "There are some simple rules you must observe in order to limit the threat of contagion." Nodding eagerly, I followed him through the door with Dr. Clarke close behind. "First…"

Chapter 66

"That was a beautiful service, Johnny, "I whispered. He nodded, his eyes fixed upon the Tiffany window at the front of the church. Following his eyes, my gaze came to rest upon the window we had presented to the church in memory of our parents. "Janey would have loved the hymns you chose."

"Father John." A middle-aged man approached, his hand extended. "I'm so sorry for your loss. It saddens me that I never had the opportunity to meet your dear wife. It sounds like she was quite the woman."

I cringed at his words, knowing that he, like most of the people milling about the crowded church, knew nothing of her confinement. Johnny shook the man's hand, humbly accepting his condolences. "She was a good woman, Seymour. Though her convalescence separated us more than I would have liked, I will miss her."

There it was—her convalescence. While some openly wondered about it, few beyond the family actually knew of Janey's life in the asylum, and none but a fool would reveal it now. Difficult as it was to avoid deception in keeping the reality of her situation from our friends and acquaintances, it could not be denied that caution was warranted. I glanced around the room. *Would her funeral have been this well attended had these people known the truth?*

Marjorie beckoned from across the room, her eyes pleading for me to rescue her. Surrounded by a gaggle of chattering women, she looked like a little lost waif about to be devoured by a pack of wild dogs. I blinked slowly, surreptitiously bobbing my head. "I shall return in a moment, John."

Johnny's gaze followed mine as I took my first steps toward his daughter. "By all means," he responded, snagging my arm. "Did any of those women even know Janey?" His voice held a harshness foreign to the young man I once knew.

Leaning in close, I lowered my voice. "They did not come for Janey, brother." He lowered his chin, his lips drawn. "They came for you and Marjorie." With a solemn nod, he closed his eyes and lowered his chin. "They love you, Johnny, and do not wish for you to be alone in your sorrow."

Obviously chastised, he swallowed hard and peered across the room. "Nonetheless, my daughter looks as if she needs a knight in shining armour to rescue her from the dragons." Resolve shone in his eyes as he stepped toward the centre aisle. "May I accompany you, my lady?" He held out his arm expectantly. "I believe it is time this gathering came to an end."

Chapter 67

APRIL 25, 1914

My Dear Mr. Wellman,

I trust this letter finds you well. By now, I am certain that you have heard of our dear Janey's passing. It is difficult to put into words the maelstrom of emotion I am experiencing right now. I miss her more than I ever would have imagined I could, given the state of her mental faculties these past eleven years. Yet, while everything within me mourns for my dear sister-in-law, I cannot help but rejoice. Her travail has come to an end, Mattie; her sorrows have been wiped away. She is with our Lord—and with her sons—her infirmities made whole. She is truly sane, perhaps for the first time ever. How can I not give thanks?

Strangely, I have taken great comfort in returning to the asylum these past few weeks to visit with her friends and aid the attendants wherever I am able. I have, in fact, dedicated a full day each week to this endeavour, though prior to Janey's passing I typically dedicated three. I find such peace in helping these, the least of our Lord's brethren, for in doing so I sense His presence engulfing me.

Johnny is, as you can imagine, having an especially difficult time with Janey's passing. He has informed the general Synod of his decision to take immediate retirement and is barely making it from Sunday to Sunday until his replacement is appointed by the bishop. He will move home to Newcastle to live with Alfred and Hannah as soon as the transition is made, while Marjorie and I stay here.

I do not believe that God's purposes for me in this fair city are complete. There are still so many who need the touch of our Lord, both within the asylum and without, and He has yet to free my heart to leave them. When you told me so long ago that God had bestowed upon me a calling, I supposed that you spoke of a single, static entity that would somehow transform the world. Never did I imagine it would entail such a series of shifting, work-a-day missions which, to these earthen eyes of mine, hardly connect and far too often appear to bear little fruit. Yet, that is what it has turned out to be—or so it would seem to me. I wonder sometimes if I have missed something and if I shall ever truly discover the calling He has placed upon my life. I certainly worry that I am not fulfilling it well when after all these years I am still so uncertain as to what it actually entails.

But enough about that; we cannot rush the hand of God. How go things in the Longacre parish? I suppose I should refer to it as the Times Square parish now, but old habits die hard. It strikes me that now might be a good time for me to hop a train and come for a visit. It hardly seems possible that over twenty years have passed since that glorious summer when Mother and Father and Betsy and I visited New York. Somehow it seems like just yesterday that you and I stood on the banks of the Hudson River, bidding each other adieu. Do you remember how the sun sparkled on the rippling waves? I thought my heart would never recover from the pain of our parting, yet God, in His grace, has enabled us both to press on. Perhaps a visit now would be a mistake, for I am not sure that my heart could withstand yet another goodbye, but oh, how I long to see you!

Well, I have a column to write and a trolley to catch if I am to get to the asylum today as planned, so I must close. I pray for you every day, dear Mattie; you are never far from my thoughts. Do keep Johnny in your prayers as he adjusts to life without Janey. How he yearns to join his beloved and the boys they lost so long ago. Every day is a struggle for him. I worry about the melancholia I see creeping over his soul and fear where it might lead, for I cannot abide the thought of Johnny ending up in the asylum like our dear Janey. It scares me sometimes that I might end up there myself, sharing as I do the Farncomb blood. God help me, Mattie—there are things worse than death.

On that morbid note, I shall bring this letter to a close. I apologize for my less than sanguine remarks. I am truly blessed to have a friend like you for whom I never need mask my deepest self. God bless you, Mattie, my love.

Affectionately,
Your Dora-girl

Returning my pen to its holder, I bowed my head, overwhelmed by the turmoil engulfing my soul. *Oh God, Holy Father—give us not over to the insanity of our loss. That either of us should succumb to lunacy terrifies me. Gift us, I pray, with the ability to see as You see and accept the trials we receive from Your hand as willingly as we accept the joys.* I pulled Father's watch from my pocket and flipped open its case. Nine-thirty. There would still be time to catch the next trolley, if I hurried.

"Marjorie," I called.

Emerging from the kitchen, Marjorie wiped her floury hands on her apron. "Yes, Aunt Dora?" Deep circles rimmed her eyes; it looked as if she hadn't slept in weeks. How I hated to burden her with yet another errand, but it couldn't be helped.

"Could you please see that this letter makes it into today's post?" I sat on the chair by the door to don a pair of worn, leather shoes. "I'm headed to the asylum and do not wish to miss the next streetcar."

"Of course," she responded. She turned the letter over in her hands. Mattie's name, scrawled across the manila envelope, could not be missed. "Do you ever regret not marrying the esteemed Canon Wellman?"

"Regret?" I straightened on the chair, lowering my foot to the ground. "No…" I studied my feet. "It has saddened me at times, for I miss him greatly, but I cannot say I have regretted our decision to remain single." I stood to wrap my shawl around my shoulders. "God made His will for us in that matter undeniably clear. It may not have been the road either one of us would have chosen to travel, but I cannot regret doing so, for I know that it was, and is still, the will of our Lord." Marjorie sniffed, averting her gaze. "Why do you ask?" I probed. Do you regret your decision to remain single?"

"No—yes—I don't know." Marjorie flopped into the chair I had just vacated. "It isn't the same for me as it is for you." She propped her elbows on her knees and leaned forward to rest her chin on her fists. "I've never been in love."

I paused, gauging my response. "You know, there was a time when I might have considered that a blessing, Margie, but I can see that it weighs heavily upon you." I rested a hand upon her shoulder, trying to imagine the weight of rejection she bore from the simple fact of not being chosen. "A burden every bit as heavy as the one Mattie and I share because of our separation." I paused. *The one Mattie and I share.* "Perhaps a burden even greater for the fact that there is none to help you bear its weight."

"Greater?" A puzzled frown creased her brow. "I think not, Aunt Dora." Rising, she reached out a hand to straighten my hat. "Only different. We all have our crosses that we are called to bear." She opened the door for me to pass through. "I just think I need to grow some more muscle."

I chuckled at her attempt to lighten the mood. *Grow some more muscle. What a girl!*

Marjorie glanced at her watch and gestured toward the road. "You had better run if you plan to catch that streetcar. I'll be sure your letter is posted before noon." She leaned close to plant a kiss upon my cheek.

"If only you could see the treasure you are, child," I whispered against her cheek. I stepped off the verandah, my hand atop my hat. "And as for muscle, my dear—I do believe you have far more of it than I."

Chapter 68

MARCH 22, 1915

"Listen to this, Marjorie: 'British By Desperate Charges Against Series of Barricades Drove Germans From St. Eloi. Fighting in Village Was of Bloodiest Character and Streets Were Cleared of Enemy at Severe Cost—British Officers Heroically Sacrifice Lives in Reconnoitring'."[1] I paused for a moment to skim the rest of the page. "And as if that isn't enough, it says that the Princess Pat's Regiment Commander, Col. F. D. Farquhar—you recall him, do you not?—was killed in action while leading the Pats into battle near St. Eloi. 'The message from the war office read: Col. Farquhar, Princess Patricia's, dead. Lieut. Mason, of the same regiment, dead. Three killed, twenty wounded.'"[2]

Marjorie scraped her chair across the floor and jumped to her feet. "Somebody has to stop this war before it destroys the entire world." She shoved the chair into place and shook her head.

Setting my empty coffee mug on the table, I swept the paper aside. "I only wish I knew how to help."

Marjorie lifted her head. "Maybe you could write an article about it in your column."

"Perhaps." Could she truly not see that the time for words was past? "The question is, does the world really need another article on the atrocities of war? There has to be something else we can do to aid the war effort."

With a sigh, she yanked the chair out again and resumed her seat. "I suppose you're right, but what else can we do?" She fidgeted with the spoon lying on the table before setting it in her mug. "The boys are off on the frontlines doing something tangible for the war effort, but what of us?" Lifting a stack of dishes in each hand, she carried them to the sink. "So I got a part time job working in the airplane factory and I wrap bandages once a week with the ladies' auxiliary—it hardly seems like much. There's got to be more I can be doing."

I ran a hand through my greying hair. "I know it doesn't seem like much, but suppose no one back home was supporting our boys like that? What would

---

[1] The Toronto Sunday World Volume XXXV, Sunday March 22, 1915, page 1 (source: BGSU University Libraries Historical Canadian Newspapers Online: Ontario)
[2] The Toronto Sunday World Volume XXXV Sunday, March 22, 1915, page 1 (source: BGSU University Libraries Historical Canadian Newspapers Online: Ontario)

become of them in their fight against the enemy without ammunition and first aid supplies, not to mention warm clothes to wear and those lovingly prepared care packages we work so hard to create?" I pushed myself away from the table. "You know, it seems to me that the most important thing we can do for our troops is to encourage the loved ones they have left behind." I pursed my lips, recalling the countless letters I had written to fearful mothers and grieving widows over the past two years. "In the heat of the battle, our soldiers should not have to worry about the welfare of their loved ones back home."

Marjorie opened the ice box to replace the precious crock of butter we scrimped to afford each month. "Speaking of which, has anyone heard from Cousin George lately?"

One of the first from the village to be conscripted, Alfred's oldest son, George, had been on the frontlines since August 1914 when the Ontario Regiment had first been deployed. "Letter writing has never been his strong suit, I'm afraid, even when he was a child. We must hope he communicates more frequently with his dear wife than he does with us."

Marjorie chuckled. "Probably not."

"Well, the fact that he is about to become a father just might change that." I winked. I had work to do. My second book was due at the publisher's in less than a week and a number of edits still needed attention. Rising from the table, I discarded my napkin in a basket by the door. "Thank you for the lovely repast, Marjorie. You surely know how to make this old gal feel like a queen."

• • •

Finished at last, I hit the carriage return and released the paper, adding it to the growing stack beside the typewriter. Though once I had sworn I would never get one for myself, I could not deny the increasing need for a writer to have access to a typewriter. Yet, as useful and necessary as it was, I still favoured the good old-fashioned pen and paper approach to recording my thoughts. The typewriter did a fine job of creating a final copy, but any creative flair I possessed fled as soon as I set fingers to its keys. *Modern technology!* If it hadn't been for the insistence of my publisher, I no doubt would never have acquiesced, but I suppose one cannot halt progress, or so the saying goes.

Picking up the newly-revised manuscript, I turned it over and tapped it on the desk to straighten its pages. Done—and with no time to spare. I glanced at the clock, calculating how long it would take to get to the train station. "Marjorie, have you seen my satchel?" I set the papers on the hall table and perused the cluttered entry way. "I was certain that I set it with my carpet bag by the door."

"I have it right here, Aunt Dora." Marjorie appeared with a worn leather satchel dangling from her shoulder. "I thought you might need a bite to sustain you on your trip." She patted the bulging bag.

"Thank you, dear. That was most thoughtful of you." I took the proffered bag, wondering how I was supposed to find room in it for my manuscript. "Perhaps it would be best if I only took a few cookies, though." I pulled two large apples, a ham sandwich, a sizeable packet of cookies, and three freshly baked butterscotch rolls from the bag, marveling at how she had gotten them all to fit. "I only have so much room." I slid the manuscript into the satchel then began replacing the carefully-wrapped food packets. "Let's see…" After a few false starts, I managed to cram all but the apples into the little bag. "And you," I said, "tossing one of the apples into the air and catching it again, "can go in my pocket."

Marjorie laughed as I stuffed the apple between the folds of my dress. "Maybe it would be best if I only took a few cookies," she parroted. "Cookies, shmookies! I know you better than that, Aunt Dora."

I slung the satchel over my shoulder and reached for my wrap. "And it's a good thing you do."

"Here, don't forget this." She handed me my favourite hat ringed with delicate pink cherry blossoms along with a pair of matching hat pins. "You'd cause quite a sensation if you left the house bare-headed."

With an affected gasp, I set the hat on my head and pinned it into place. "And we wouldn't want to do that now, would we?"

Marjorie giggled. It relieved my heart to see a window of lightness peeping through her grief-ridden soul. "We most certainly would not, Auntie."

"Goodbye, dear." I drew her close and kissed her cheek. "I shall be back on Friday, God willing." Grasping my carpet bag, I headed out the door and down the walk.

"Godspeed, Aunt Dora," Marjorie called after me.

I nodded and winked. "Don't do anything I wouldn't do."

Chapter 69

LONDON, ONTARIO

"You have outdone yourself once more, Miss Farncomb." Mr. Weld laid the manuscript on his desk and puffed thoughtfully on his cigar. "Your readers will be most thrilled to add yet another Dora Farncomb book to their collections." He rose from his perch on the edge of the desk and paced across the room. "There are few more dedicated readers around here than those who read your column." Dragging a bulging bag from behind his desk, he deposited it at my feet. "Or communicative."

"More mail?" My eyes widened, though I strove to appear nonchalant. The corner of an age-stained envelope protruded from the top of the over-stuffed bag. "Those are all for me?"

Mr. Weld nodded slowly, amusement crinkling the corners of his eyes, and my heart sank. It would take days to respond to every one of the letters in that bag. I rubbed a hand across my face. While most of my readers' correspondence came directly to my house, some still insisted upon sending it to the office. It had been a long time since I had seen a bag this big from them, though.

"People are eager for the curious blend of encouragement and admonition our dear Hope nourishes them with each week, especially now that the war has hit so close to home." Mr. Weld rested a hip on the corner of his desk and laced his fingers over his ample belly. "If ever the world needed a message of hope, it is now, and if ever a person was called to write that message, it is you."

Called to write. Of course! That was the calling I had been waiting for since my youth. I drew a hand to my heart. "It is as you say, Mr. Weld, but it is only by God's grace that my words resonate so deeply within the hearts of my readers."

He inclined his head toward me, his eyes twinkling. "Whatever you say, Miss Farncomb. Whatever you say." Moving around his desk, he seated himself in the cracked leather desk chair. "Now, let's see here. If all goes as planned, these new books of yours should roll off the press in about four weeks." He tabulated the time on his fingers. "Then another four weeks for binding and two for distribution…" He studied the ten fingers he held firmly in the air. "That should put them in hand about mid-June." With a curt nod, he returned his attention to me. "How does that sound?"

I barely managed an answering smile before he pressed on. "Now, I was thinking that we should make the cover of this one green—green with gold print on a lightly embossed floral brocade rather than the ordinary weave we used on the cover of your first book. Perhaps something with a bit of a sheen to it."

I leaned forward, awed by the extravagance of what he proposed. "How much would that add to the selling price of the book?"

"Not as much as adding a picture would." He tapped a stubby finger on a nearby chart. "Perhaps a few cents."

Drawing my legs back, I crossed my ankles beneath the chair. *A few cents. Surely my readers could afford that.* "That sounds lovely to me, Mr. Weld. I shall leave it up to you to do what you think is best."

"Very good. Now, to whom would you like to dedicate this book?"

• • •

The paradox of time has always baffled me. How some seasons of life can seem to pass by so quickly while others seem to crawl, I cannot fathom. "With God, a day is like a thousand years and a thousand years is like a day," Peter reminds us in his second epistle, and there are times when I wholeheartedly relate. We put a lot of stock in time—the amount we have, the amount we do not have, the way we invest it, or squander it away. Time is a most valuable commodity.

With an exaggerated huff, I tore the paper from the typewriter and tossed it onto the desk with the other discards from my morning's work. *So much for productivity. Why can I never seem to compose my thoughts to my satisfaction on a typewriter?* I picked up the shimmery green volume on my desk and traced my finger across the golden words stamped on the cover. *Dora Farncomb.* No matter how many times I saw my name on the cover of a book, it never felt real. *Dora Farncomb? An author? Preposterous!* I flipped through the pages, stopping as I had so many times before at the dedication page. "To those who have gone before, lighting the way that I might follow, and to our Lord God Almighty who calleth us to be His own. May the words of my pen and the meditations of all our hearts be ever pleasing in Your sight, O Lord, our God and our Redeemer."

Blinking away tears, I hugged the little volume to my chest. Father would have been so proud of me—and Mother, too, for that matter, though she probably would never have said so. And Janey—dear, dear Janey—even during the times when she had been most lost, she had always seemed to take comfort from my writing.

My writing. As if I could create such a piece myself. I stared at the name emblazoned upon the cover. I didn't write this book any more than St. John wrote the great Revelation—not that I had received the kind of inspiration he obviously had been given. True, the words had flowed from the nib of my pen and carried a voice uniquely my own, but the insights it contained were as far from my own as… as… well, as the earth is from the heavens.

Turning to the box of carefully ordered correspondence awaiting my response, I riffled through the nearest pile. An hour would not be enough. I slid my letter opener beneath the flap of the first envelope and extracted the letter.

March 7, 1915

Dear Hope,

I trust you do not mind me calling you that. I simply cannot bring myself to think of you as Miss Farncomb. Though you know me not, I feel as if you are a very close friend. I pore over your column each week and pray that the truths I find within would be mirrored in my life. I cannot wait to read your latest book. Would you be so kind as to send me two copies—one for my friend, Judith, and one for myself (Abigail). I have included $2 to cover the cost of the books and the postage. I trust that will be enough. If you could see fit to inscribe them, it would be most appreciated. May God continue to bless your ministry, dear Hope.

Sincerely,
Mrs. Gerald Taylor

I reached for a paper and penned a quick response before inscribing the requisite books and wrapping them in a square of brown paper. *One down, how many to go?* I slid the letter opener beneath the fold of the next envelope, chagrinned by the backlog of correspondence I had allowed to build.

March 9, 1915

Dear Hope,

My name be Lettie Dwyer. Your new book be wundaful. Even my husband read it and say so and he not read much. Please pray for us, dear Hope. Our youngest son just leave for the trenches and our oldest have not been heard from in over six week. I try to keep my eyes on

Jesus like you say, but my heart still fret for my boys. My husband be angry. With Austria, with Germany, with Italy, with ev'ryone. I know you not know me an' my husband, but you pray for us, please? I write you because I tink you understand. Your words bring such hope to us both. Our God be so good! I forget that sometimes wid my boys so far from home, but you help me remember. Tank you, dear Hope.

Mrs. Marcus Dwyer

My eyes swam as I reached for my pen. Whatever was I to say to that? *Jesus, what do You wish me to say to this woman?* I weighed the pen in my hand, my fingers poised above the page, awaiting inspiration.

March 27, 1915

My Dear Mrs. Dwyer,

I can only imagine the burden you and your husband must bear. War is a terrible thing. Of course I will pray for you and your husband and your two boys. The testimony of your faith inspires me, dear Lettie. May God grant you the grace to endure these difficult times. If there is anything more I can do, please do not hesitate to let me know. Our God, indeed, is good, even when the evils of this fallen world threaten to undo us. Do let me know when you hear from your boys.

With love and prayers,
Dora (Hope) Farncomb

The clock chimed the half hour and I jumped, my pen leaving a trail of ink across the page. *Lord Jesus, help this woman and her husband. Give them peace and strengthen them to trust You no matter what may befall. And watch over their boys. If You could see fit, preserve their lives, O God, and bring them home to their parents. Nevertheless, not our will, but Yours be done.* I licked a three cent stamp and stuck it on the corner of the envelope. Scanning the pile of unopened letters, I pulled another from the stack. "Mrs. Wilhelm Goertz…"

Chapter 70

TORONTO
JUNE 28, 1916

"What do you say, Margie?" I plunged my fist into the yeasty mass and felt it pop beneath the pressure. Covering it with a damp cloth, I returned it to the table to rise in the warmth of the afternoon sun. "Are you up to making the trip to Newcastle for the Dominion Day celebrations this year?"

Marjorie shrugged a lock of hair from her face and fetched a cloth to wipe her doughy fingers. "Would Uncle Alfred ever forgive us if we dared miss his birthday?" Her eyes held a mischievous glint, too long absent.

I laughed. "Of course he wouldn't." The playful banter did my heart good after the heaviness of the past few months. "Your father will be glad to see you."

A chill descended upon the room, despite the warmth of the afternoon sun. "Will he?"

"Of course he will," I answered, though I couldn't fault her for wondering. I had lost count of the number of times I had begged him to reach out to his dear girl, but Johnny had changed dramatically since the passing of his wife. Retiring from the priesthood, he had moved back to Newcastle and taken up residence in Ebor House with Alfred's family, but the struggles of life had aged him, belying his sixty-three years. By all reports, he spent his days rocking on the porch and leafing through old newspapers, silent unless spoken to—a corpse of a man neither living nor dead.

Marjorie pinched the dough and emptied it onto a floured board. "Have you decided when it would be best to leave?"

"Well..." I drew out the word, uncertain of how she would respond. "Supposing we make a holiday of it and stay for a full week?"

"A full week?" The large, wooden pin Marjorie rolled over the dough came to an immediate stop.

"Perhaps even two," I added, eying her hopefully. "Alfred assures me that we are most welcome to stay as long as we wish, provided we don't mind sharing a bed."

Marjorie set the rolling pin aside and spread the sugar mixture across the flattened dough. "Do you think we can spare the time away?"

"Jesus himself called his disciples—in the midst of their busyness—to come away to a quiet place for a time." I gathered the rolling pin and the empty sugar crock from the counter and deposited them in the sink.

"Yes…" Her response, though measured, held a grain of hope. "But that was Jesus speaking to His disciples—"

Aha! A chink in her logic. "Are you suggesting that the words He spoke to His disciples of old are not relevant for His disciples today?" I reached for the circle of dough falling from her knife and pressed it into the sugar mixture at the bottom of the nearest muffin cup.

"That's not what I meant and you know it." Harsh as her voice sounded, the glint of amusement in her eyes gave her away.

"We go tomorrow," I announced. "You'd best pack for a couple of weeks." I took the pan from her hands, enjoying her gape-mouthed response.

"But—"

"But nothing, dear." I closed the oven door and noted the time. It wouldn't do for our favourite treat to burn, especially when the rector was coming to visit. "The time away will do us both good." Reaching behind my back to undo my apron strings, I lifted the floury cover-up from my neck. "Now, off with you, girl. Canon James will be here in half an hour and you have flour from head to toe." I winked and gave her a playful shove. "Besides, methinks you have some packing to do."

Chapter 71

NEWCASTLE

"A motor car? Why Alfred—" The words had barely left my tongue when a pair of big, burly arms enveloped me.

"Welcome home, Dora-girl. It seems so long since your last visit."

"Goodness, Alfred." I waved my eldest brother away with an amused snort. "I know we missed being here for Christmas this year, but it isn't as if it's been years." Alfred shrugged, averting his eyes, and I grinned. "Besides, you know I always come for your birthday."

"I know… but is it a crime for a brother to miss his favourite sister?" he responded, a sheepish smile twitching his moustache. He tucked an arm around Marjorie's shoulder. "And how, pray tell, is my favourite niece?"

"You'd better not let Winnie hear you say that!" Marjorie smiled, nestling into her uncle's embrace.

"Pshaw! She's my favourite niece, too, and you know it. It is the prerogative of an uncle to have more than one favourite, n'est-ce pas?"

"Oh, you speak French now, Uncle?"

"Oui, mademoiselle," Alfred answered, feigning affront. "I did, after all, learn *something* from your aunt when we were growing up."

He winked at me as I inclined my chin, pleased to see them both laughing. Jovial as my brother seemed, I sensed a disquieting undertone belying his lighthearted exterior. The peculiar droop of his shoulders, the overly cheerful lilt in his voice, the teasing grin that didn't quite reach his eyes—while I couldn't quite put my finger on the incongruities, the signs were clear. An intense heaviness weighed upon my brother that I had not anticipated. I longed to press him for the source of his uncharacteristic gloom, but there would be time for that later.

"Well, ladies…" Alfred touched a hand to his hat and affected a jaunty bow. "Your chariot awaits." Offering an elbow to each of us, he led us toward the shiny new McLaughlin Model D-60 parked at the edge of the platform. "As you so aptly noticed when you arrived, oh sister of mine, I finally decided that the health of my patients requires more immediate availability on my part. Hence, the new motor car."

"And has it helped?" Marjorie ran a finger almost reverently across the painted metal.

"My patients, or me?" Alfred's eyebrows bobbed, his eyes dancing.

Stepping into the vehicle, Marjorie scooted into the back seat, leaving room for me in the front. "Oh, Uncle!" She gazed around in wonder. "I never thought I would actually sit in the seat of a motor car." She leaned forward. "Do you suppose the horse and buggy might truly become obsolete like Mr. McLaughlin claims?"

Alfred cranked the motor and slid into the driver's seat. "Possibly. The automobile certainly has its advantages."

The short drive to the house I had called home for so many years, though filled with jovial banter, felt somehow strained. I longed to ask how Johnny fared these days, but feared to hear the truth, especially with Marjorie present. That his condition was the source of Alfred's unspoken heaviness, I had little doubt.

"So, what did you think of your first car ride?" Alfred brought the vehicle to a stop at the base of the verandah stairs and cut the engine.

The sudden silence startled me. How we could have made it all the way home without me noticing the rattily hum of the engine baffled me. I took a deep breath, relishing the quietness. Odd that I had never experienced relief like this when the clopping of the horse's hooves stilled after a long journey.

"It was a lovely ride, Uncle Alfred." Marjorie nudged me toward the door. "Do you think we might get a motor car, Aunt Dora?"

I smiled at the youthful enthusiasm infusing her voice, curbing the urge to instruct her in the ways of decorum. "I suppose we might have to—one day." I grinned, standing aside as Alfred helped her from the car. "Why don't you see if you can find your cousin Helen, dear? Perhaps she can answer those endless questions you've been asking about MacDonald Institute."

"Oh, that she can," Alfred quipped. "She would be most delighted to bend your ear with all of her marvellous adventures."

Marjorie whisked past us both and flew up the stairs, barely avoiding a collision with her father when he appeared at the door with a rumpled newspaper tucked beneath his arm. "Father!" She fell back, immediately subdued.

"Marjorie Ellen, when will you learn a little decorum?" He glanced at me and scowled. "Not that you've had much of a teacher." Hardly seeming to notice his daughter's chagrin, he shuffled past her and lowered himself into the wicker chair nearest the door.

"Forgive me, Father," Marjorie mumbled, her eyes fixed upon her feet. "I should not have been in such a hurry." She blinked a few times and turned to face him. "I'm glad to see you."

I glared at the brother I once knew so well, appalled by his silence. *Answer her, Johnny. Come on!*

"How are you doing, Father?" My heart ached for the poor girl. She was trying so hard.

Johnny grunted, burying his face in his newspaper. "How do you think, daughter? If you came by a little more often, perhaps you would know."

I winced at his words, stung by his careless reply. "She has not been by, John Farncomb, because your move to Newcastle has rendered the casual visit impossible." I balled my fists on my hips in perfect imitation of our mother. "The least you could do is tell your daughter you've missed her and that you are glad to see her."

"I missed you, daughter," he parroted, his eyes never leaving his paper. "I am glad to see you." He straightened the newspaper on his lap, losing himself in the pages he had no doubt read a hundred times before.

Marjorie pressed a hand to her mouth and fled down the stairs, disappearing around the corner of the house. "Marjorie," I called after her, my voice fading on the wind. Storming up the steps, I snatched the paper from my brother's hands and cuffed him on the shoulder. "Now, you listen to me, John Farncomb." He stared up at me, his eyes empty of emotion—the eyes of a needy child, lost and alone, yet afraid to admit the vulnerability that clothed him in despair. My ire evaporated like dew on a sunny day. "Look…" Seating myself on the corner of the crate he used for a foot stool, I rested my hand upon his knee. "I know you are hurting. You've lost so, so much and I know it must feel like God has abandoned you."

My chest tightened when tears began streaming down his face. Once again, the Holy Spirit had used my words, halting and uncertain as they were, to reach the heart of one of our Lord's lost sheep. "Perhaps it even feels like nothing else matters anymore. But Johnny…" I leaned forward, my eyes drilling into his. "It does matter. Whether it feels like it or not, you are surrounded by people who love you and need you and cannot imagine life without you." I paused. *Where did that come from?* Johnny pulled his leg out from under my hand and fished a handkerchief from his pocket. "I know we are not the three people you desire most to have by your side, Johnny, but we *are* here, and no matter how hard you try to push us away, you will not succeed."

I stood, certain I had said more than enough, and turned to follow Marjorie, but before I had taken a single step, an image seared itself upon my mind. My heart plummeted. Harsh though it was, I knew that it was an image I needed to share. I swallowed hard, afraid to face my brother. "Imagine a little boy on Christmas morning," I said, "surrounded by a cache of exquisitely crafted toys any young lad would covet for his own. Now imagine that same boy sulking in a corner because he did not get the shiny new ball he desired." I turned to look my brother in the eye. "That's the picture I see when I think of you right now, Johnny." I shook my head slowly. "Don't discard the treasures that surround you for want of those that do not."

With that, I brushed past Alfred and headed after Marjorie. *Oh God, let him hear Your voice in my words and let him not be crushed by them... and give me the words to help Margie understand her father's distress. Let not his actions and responses colour her understanding of You.*

• • •

Johnny's empty seat at the supper table troubled me. "Don't concern yourself with his absence, Dora." Hannah patted my hand. "He often skips meals, and when he doesn't, the meal is a terribly sombre affair." She eyed her husband. No wonder my brother seemed so incredibly weary. Alfred's moustache twitched, but he said nothing. With an exasperated sigh, Hannah shook her head. "Betsy will fix a tray for him and see that he gets something to sustain his body, if not his spirit."

"I only hope I didn't go too far." I stirred my fork through the pile of mashed potatoes on my plate and laid it on the edge of the dish without taking a bite. "I never should have shared that image with him."

"Are you sure?" For the first time since the meal had begun, Alfred spoke. "Perhaps it was just the thing that our dear brother needed to hear." He folded his napkin and set it beside his plate. "He and I had a good chat after you left." His eyes locked on mine as if willing me to understand. "He wept, Dora... wept like I have never seen him weep before, even when the accident first occurred."

I searched my mind for something to say, but those two powerful words dominated my every thought. *He wept? Our Johnny wept?* I inclined my head. Had I heard correctly? "He wept?"

"Like an infant whose mother had passed beyond the veil." Alfred lowered his head. "This just might be the breaking point for him, Dora. With all that ensued, it strikes me that Johnny has never truly mourned the loss of his sons—nor that of the wife he lost long before her body departed this world." He leaned back in his chair, resting a hand upon his beard. "And without the mourning, the healing cannot begin."

Without the mourning, the healing cannot begin... Slowly, reverently, my mind caressed the words. Something lurked beneath their surface that I couldn't quite grasp. Something broader, deeper, more powerful. The Spirit stirred within me and I longed to pick up my pen and plumb the depths of this new revelation. *Without the mourning, the healing—*

"Dora?" A hand squeezed mine and I jumped. "Where were you?" Amusement lightened the heaviness in Alfred's eyes.

"Your words hold great meaning, Alfred, though I'm not yet certain I fully understand. The importance of mourning *is* integral to the healing process, but we, by nature, would rather skip directly to the healing and bypass the grieving entirely."

Alfred nodded. "I hadn't really considered that aspect of it, but it is true. We avoid our grief at all cost."

"But as Saint Matthew reminds us, Jesus said, 'Blessed are those who mourn, for they shall be comforted.'" I rushed on, my mind swarming with new insights. "The person who doesn't mourn cannot be comforted." Marjorie's gaze bounced from me to Alfred and back again, a puzzled frown creasing her brow.

"Do you not see?" I jumped to my feet. "If a person refuses to face his sorrows and allow himself to experience the pain of mourning, he, in essence, is refusing the offer of comfort our Lord extends to those who mourn." I paced along the side of the table, tapping my finger on my chin. "And is it not in the comforting embrace of our Lord that healing begins its restorative work?" My head snapped up to meet my brother's gaze. He, too, had risen, his eyes alight.

"Yes." A smile spread across his face. "Yes. Yes! But it must begin with mourning. True mourning."

I cocked my head. What was he trying to say? "Is that not what I just said?"

Alfred tapped the tip of his index finger on his upper lip. "Don't you see? No amount of self-pity can substitute for mourning. Jesus doesn't say that those who feel sorry for themselves will be comforted—only those who mourn."

"Yes! That is the missing piece." I pressed my palms against the table and leaned in, our eyes locking once more. Excitement stirred in the depths of his eyes, sparking a glimmer of hope. "Until we get past the unspoken belief that we are in some way to be pitied as the victim of our circumstances, it is impossible to mourn our actual loss. I mean, it grips us all in times of loss, but..." The words tumbled over each other in my haste to express the epiphany of truth flooding my heart. "If we are stuck lamenting our woes and the unfairness—or perceived unfairness—of our plight, we cannot actually mourn the loss behind the suffering we bear."

"Of course!" Alfred banged his fist on the table. "But masquerading as grief, our self-pity tricks us into holding a grudge against our Sovereign, and instead of being but the perceived recipient of the unfair treatment of our Lord, we become true victims of our own making." He drew his fist upward, stopping it halfway to his mouth where it bobbed with unrestrained energy. "But how? How can we help Johnny to understand without destroying his fragile psyche?"

I blew out a long, slow breath. "How can one even suggest that he has suffered more from self-pity over the years than from true grief?"

His fist dropping to his side, Alfred slouched onto his chair. "And have we truly any right to suppose that he has? We have walked this road beside him, but we have not shared his boots."

The silence that descended upon the room was broken by a series of quiet sobs. Hannah had moved into the seat I had vacated, her arms firmly wrapped around Marjorie, her hand gently patting the younger woman's hair.

"Oh, Margie..." I ran to her side. *Oh God, let not our words have harmed her.*

Marjorie lifted her head from Hannah's shoulder and opened her arms to my embrace. "All these years when I thought I was mourning—when I could not understand why our Lord refused me the comfort for which I yearned... Aunt Dora, I see now." She stopped to dab her handkerchief beneath her nose. "I have been caught in that web of self-pity you and Uncle Alfred have been talking about." She raised her head and contemplated her uncle. "I have not truly mourned the loss of my mother, or my brothers, or my father, for that matter. I have only really dabbled in grief—foregoing it for anger at God that He should so unjustly smite me, and pity for my sad state of affairs."

"Now, now, dear." Hannah patted her back, hushing her. "You ought not to be so hard on yourself."

Marjorie sprang from my arms, turning fiery eyes on my sister-in-law. "No, Aunt Hannah. You're wrong. I know you wish to spare me, but..." She shook her head, her tears now gone. "I must not deny the truth. If I do, I condemn myself to walk in misery forever." She swallowed hard, her brows drawn. "Like Father." Jumping to her feet, she pinned me with a look I couldn't quite interpret. "Perhaps I can be the one to help him see, Aunt Dora. Maybe he and I can let go of our self-pity and walk the road to healing together."

I stood to embrace her once more. "If anyone can help him, dear, it will be you."

∴

The hinges squealed their disapproval as the bedroom door edged open. Framed by the glow of a candle, Marjorie paused on the threshold as if steeling herself to enter. "Margie?" I shifted the bed clothes and swung my legs over the edge of the great, feather mattress. "How did your talk with your father go?"

She grimaced, setting the candle on the bedside table. "All right, I suppose. I don't know..." She unpinned her hair and combed her fingers through the auburn tresses. "He's such a stubborn man."

"Is that not the plight of every Farncomb?"

She eyed me reproachfully; we, too, were Farncombs. "I'm not stubborn, Aunt Dora—I'm *persistent*." She fluttered her eyes innocently. "And so are you."

"I see." I rubbed my finger along my chin. "So what you are saying is that we are a good kind of stubborn and he is—"

"Just plain old stubborn." She flopped onto the bed beside me, throwing us both onto our backs. "He wouldn't even listen to me."

I struggled to an upright position. "You were hoping that he would see the light as clearly as you saw it when Alfred and I were discussing it at dinner this evening."

She sat up as well. "He listened politely enough, then patted my shoulder and told me that he was glad I was feeling better."

"Glad you were feeling better?" I snorted, not knowing whether to laugh or to cry. "He actually said that?" Marjorie nodded, her mouth drawn in a grim line. That Johnny had not been ready to hear his daughter's plea didn't surprise me, but his inability to respond must not be allowed to infect her heart with doubt. "The soil of his heart may still be being tilled, dear." She trembled slightly as she rested her head upon my shoulder. "You've planted the seeds, Marjorie. It's up to Another to see that they grow." I unbuttoned her blouse and helped her slip her arms out of it. "Come. It's time we were both abed." I slid my feet beneath the feather counterpane and waited for her to join me. "Goodnight, Margie."

She sniffed, dabbing her nose with a handkerchief. "Goodnight, Aunt Dora."

∙ ∙ ∙

The early morning light peeked through the heavy curtains long before my body signalled that it was time to get up. Rolling over, I drew a pillow around my ears to block out the incessant singing of the birds. Beautiful as their song was, a deaf man couldn't have slept through their rising symphony.

"Are you awake, Aunt Dora?"

I opened my eyes. Margie sat propped against the bedpost, her arms folded behind her head. "Mm-mmm. You?"

Marjorie giggled. "Can anyone sleep through that musical medley?"

I propped myself up on my elbow and yawned. "Is it just me, or was that an awfully short night?"

"Too many things to think about."

I stifled another yawn. "Like..."

"Like how much I miss Mother." Marjorie stretched her arms above her head and lowered them again, tossing the bedclothes aside. "Like how I regret not spending more time with her when she was in the asylum." She stood, her back to the bed. "If only I could be with her once more—to tell her I'm sorry for blaming her for her infirmity... to remind her of the wonderful mother she was to me... to assure her that I never stopped loving her despite how it may have seemed."

I swung my legs over the side of the bed. "There are so many things I wish I could tell her also, but I take comfort in knowing that she is with Jesus and that one day we will see her again."

Margie traced the curve of the bedpost with her finger. "I still wish I could sit down and talk with her." She raised her eyes to meet mine. "Right here. Right now." She pushed away from the bed and scrounged through the bureau drawer.

"Perhaps she is nearer than we suppose, Margie." I stood, shaking out my nightdress. "Remember that great cloud of witnesses the esteemed Apostle Paul refers to in his epistle to the Hebrews?" Marjorie held up a pair of bloomers and nodded. "Is it not logical to suspect that your dear mother is among that blessed throng listening to us speak even now?"

She hugged the bloomers to her chest, her tears flowing freely. "Mother, if you can hear me—I want you to know that I love you and... and I'm sorry. Sorry for blaming you for the misery and abandonment I allowed to fester within me for all these years." She swiped at the tears rolling down her cheeks. "I-miss-you, Mama."

I wrapped my arms around her, our tears mingling as we wept. "I miss you, too, Janey." My voice trailed off. "I miss you, too..."

Tap. Tap. Tap. My arms fell to my sides as I turned toward the door. Margie eyed me as the door crept open, revealing the face of my youngest niece. "Aunt Dora? Cousin Marjorie?" Her voice sounded tentative and uncertain, belying her sixteen years. "Are you awake?" I swung the door open and she fell forward, landing in my arms. "Oh!"

"Good morning, Helen." I pressed a kiss to her forehead and helped her right herself. "Heavens, child, it must be long past breakfast. Of course we are up." I patted the edge of the bed, inviting her to sit. "We're about to get dressed."

"Mother sent me up to get you. She's already hard at work preparing for tomorrow's celebrations." Helen walked to the bed and pulled up the sheets as we busied ourselves with our morning toilette. "Father has already come and gone and Uncle John with him," she prattled on. "I don't know what you said to him last night, Marjorie, but this is the first time I've seen him show his face before noon since I came home over a month ago." She placed the pillows at the head of the bed and patted them into place. "And Mother said that she can't remember the last time he left the house... even to go to church."

My fingers stilled mid-button. "He hasn't been going to church?" Helen shook her head, suddenly silent. Things had to be even worse with my poor brother than they seemed. *Johnny not go to church?*

Helen glanced at Marjorie, obviously weighing her words. "Mother thinks that he's angry at God for taking Auntie Jane and his boys from him."

Blinking rapidly, Marjorie took a steadying breath. "He is. He doesn't understand how God could rip from him all that was most precious to his heart when he has served Him so faithfully for so many years." She tucked a shawl around her shoulders and turned to the looking glass. "He can't quite bring himself to accept the loss of Mama and the boys as from the hand of God, meant for some great purpose beyond that which eye can see. Nor, I am afraid, can he accept their passing as the tragic curse of living in a fallen world." She clipped a loose strand of hair into place and turned to face us. "The pain is too much for him; it's clouding his vision."

I resumed the task of buttoning my blouse, wondering whose brilliant idea it was to fasten it with so many tiny buttons. "Pain does have a way of doing that." Finished the last button, I turned to find Marjorie holding my skirt, ready for me to slip my head through the opening. "Perhaps the talk you had with him last night had more of an impact than you realize, dear."

"Maybe," she responded. I turned so she could fasten the skirt around my waist. "I do hope so. He didn't appear to be too receptive to my words when we spoke."

Tucking Father's pocket watch into the fold at my waist, I draped a strand of Mother's pearls around my neck. "There's no accounting for the ways God can speak to a person in the darkest watches of the night." With a final glance in the looking glass, I headed for the door. "Alas, there may be nothing we can do to salve our Johnny's angry heart, but we can hold forth the light as he makes his way through the darkness."

"And we can pray."

I blinked as Helen rose from the edge of the bed; I'd nearly forgotten she was there. I reached an arm around my young niece's shoulders and leaned my head against hers. "Yes, we can pray. We *must* pray." I breathed deeply, overwhelmed by the warmth of God's presence. "For him *and* for us." Releasing her, I stepped into the hall, a lightness speeding my steps. "Now Helen, dear, you must tell us all about this women's institute you've been attending in Guelph. MacDonald Institute, isn't it?" Helen nodded. "If it's half the place we hear—"

"Oh, it is, Auntie!" Helen's eyes sparkled as she spoke, telling story after story of her exploits at the renowned women's institute of Ontario. Long after breakfast ended and the day's work had begun, she continued to regale us with her stories until, at last, her mother sent her out to work in the flower gardens.

"That girl will talk the ear off an eel," Hannah muttered, tossing her soiled apron into a bin by the door and unfolding another. "Dora, would you grace us with a batch or two of your famous butterscotch rolls for our picnic tomorrow?"

"Of course." I slid an apron over my head and reached for a bowl. "There hasn't been a Dominion Day in the history of this great land of ours without a platter of those delectable treats." Marjorie donned an apron and added two good-sized logs to the stove. "They are, after all, Alfred's favourite, and the first of July was his birthday long before our country claimed it for its own."

Hannah's eyes crinkled. "He reminds me of that every year—in case I should happen to forget." She disappeared into the back kitchen, only to return moments later with a bushel basket full of dried bean pods. "Marjorie, could you start shelling these beans for Edith, please? She and Betsy are run off their feet. I'm certain they would appreciate the assistance."

"Certainly, Aunt Hannah," Marjorie answered. She pulled a three-legged stool close to the hearth and grabbed a bowl to catch the red-brown beans. "I'll have them done in no time."

Hannah nodded her thanks and left the room, her skirt swishing with every step. Memorable and welcome as they were, holidays took a lot out of a person.

Chapter 72

TORONTO, AUGUST 16, 1916

Marjorie folded the newspaper on her lap and leaned back in her chair, fanning herself with the pearl-embellished fan her father had given her for her birthday. "I see the CNE is set to open at the end of next week," she noted. "Will you be accompanying the asylum folk on their annual outing to the exhibition this year?"

I bobbed my head, recalling the excitement of Janey and her friends as they bustled from display to display. "It's such a treasured opportunity for those poor, dear souls. If my assistance can enable even one more inmate to partake in the adventure, I can do nothing but." I peered at the portrait of Janey on the mantelpiece and knew she would agree. *As much as ye do for the least of these my brethren—*

"Do you suppose I might be of assistance as well?"

I peered at my niece, trying to conceal my surprise. "Now that marks a change of heart."

Marjorie shrugged. "I suppose. Perhaps if I had spent less time resenting my mother and her condition and more time doing what I could to improve it…"

"You know, Margie, regret is a cruel taskmaster, every bit as destructive as the resentment you carried for so long." She squeezed the paper in her hands, riffling the corners of the pages with her thumb, but she didn't look up. "This I know," I continued, "for I lived beneath its merciless command myself for longer than I would like to admit." She opened her mouth as if to speak, then closed it again. "But as for helping with the trip to the exhibition, I'm certain that the asylum staff would be most grateful to have an extra set of hands, and I would be thrilled to enjoy your company."

She looked up, her face a mask. "When you go to the asylum this afternoon, would you be sure to enquire about the possibility of my assistance?"

"I most certainly will." I examined the half-knitted shawl on my lap. *Knit, purl, knit, purl, knit, knit purl, knit, knit…* "Purl." Jabbing the needle into the next stitch, I imagined the sweet elderly woman who would wear the finished product. A long-time resident of the asylum, Audrey's family had abandoned her years ago to the mercy of the public's generosity. Whether it was because they couldn't afford the extra dollar or two a month to remove her from the squalor of the public ward and secure her a place in a ward with a higher standard of care, I could only imagine, but the poor woman never had any visitors and hadn't received a single letter in all the years I had known her.

Even before Janey left us, I had begun paying a limited fee each month to enable Audrey to live in the least expensive non-public ward in the hospital, not that it was much of an improvement over the public ward. Yet, it was something, and after Janey died, I was able to see the dear woman into one of the more expensive wards where her health and quality of life had improved immensely. I would have given her Janey's clothes as well had she not been too thin and wiry to wear them. I smiled at the thought of her wearing the colourful shawl that snaked across my lap. She would love it; it was so her. In fact, she might never take it off. How little it took to unearth that bright, toothy grin of hers. *If only I were as easy to please as she.* Laying my needles aside, I reached for my notebook.

> Have you ever known a person so easy to please that you would do almost anything to bring her joy? I know a woman like that. Her name is Audrey. Audrey is a simple woman, abounding in gratitude and overflowing with joy. The smallest of gestures can stir her soul, the most inconsequential comment make her face shine. While I have known her for many years, not once have I heard a complaint cross her lips, though if there is a woman with reason to complain, it is she. I have seen her weep and watched her hobble, but never have I heard her complain. She crowns the slightest kindness with gratitude and blesses the giver with her joy. Yet, I confess, she sometimes troubles me, for I am not nearly as easy to please as she is, though I should be. And I fear I am not alone, for is it not true that the more we have been given, the more deserving we deem ourselves of more and the less happy we become with the blessings bestowed upon us?

My pen stilled as my mind blazed with the impact a simple lack of gratitude could have on a person. Setting my notebook on the table, I resumed my knitting. Had this very thing not been a theme in my life? *I want, I want, I want. I want You to give me a mission, O Lord. I want it to be important. I want it to change lives. I want to feel important.* I stopped mid-stitch. *That's it, Jesus, isn't it? I have demanded from You a mission. To serve You, yes, but even more so, to serve myself and my infernal sense of self-importance.*

I thrust the half-finished shawl into my knitting basket and headed for the door. "I'm going out, Marjorie." She peered at me, her brow knit. "There's no need to worry," I assured her. "I just need to think." I grabbed my hat, pausing but a moment to pin it into place. "I shall return in an hour or two."

A warm August breeze greeted me as soon as I opened the door. Soft as a downy chick, it caressed my face and whispered through my greying curls, stopping me in my tracks. I drew in a long, slow breath and closed my eyes. *The touch of my Beloved's hand, the embrace of my Creator. Jesus, forgive me for being so demanding and difficult to please.* Tears welled in my eyes as I shut the door and headed down the walk.

Your value is not in your mission, child. Blinking away the tears before they could fall, I glanced down the road, thankful that no one was in sight. The breeze swirled around me, lifting my skirt, a welcome reminder of my Lord's presence. *Your value is not in the things you do for Me but in the person you are because of Me.* I weighed the words impressing themselves upon my heart. *Your mission is important, but it isn't what makes Me love you.*

My steps slowing, I entered the church yard and approached a glorious patch of violets planted in a shady alcove near an old, stone bench. Though this year's blooms had long passed, I saw them in my mind's eye, swaying gently in the breeze, a lush carpet of velvety purple. I fingered the engraved plaque nestled amid their leaves. Johnny had transplanted them from Mother's garden shortly after her death, a fitting memorial for the woman who had loved us both so dearly. Sitting on the bench, I gazed at their bobbing heads. *Such easy to cultivate plants. They flourish almost anywhere; they multiply like rabbits, they're hardier than a polar bear in winter, and they never seem to die. They even survived the crossing of the Atlantic when Mother first came to the New World, unwilling to leave her most treasured violets behind. Oh, God, would that I were as easily cultivated as they.*

I breathed deeply, inhaling the fragrance of the nearby rose garden. It, too, had been planted in memory of someone dear, though I knew her not. *Now roses... those are far more difficult to cultivate.* I eyed a flowerless bush hidden amid the showy blooms of its neighbours. *They need pruning and soil care, the perfect temperature, and a specific range of light, yet their flowers are big and beautiful, and oh, so fragrant.* I closed my eyes, savouring their glorious scent. *And though they be difficult to grow, and thorns bedeck their stems, they have the power to move hearts in ways no other flower can.* I smiled at the memory of Mother's face the day Father presented her with a single red rose from the garden on the anniversary of Charlie's death. Yes, roses had a power all their own to move hearts. "So, are You telling me, God, that I am a rose in Your great garden, not so easy to cultivate, but gifted with the ability to touch hearts for You?" Sure I heard a quiet chuckle, I turned my head abruptly. Bending forward, I picked up a brittle leaf bumping against the stone bench and shook my head. Autumn would be upon us sooner than I would like. If only the summer could last.

So, I am a rose—thorny and difficult to grow, but fragrant and beautiful and endowed with a mission to change lives. The breeze intensified, wrapping itself around me like a cloak, as if to affirm my statement. I pulled out my notebook and scanned the last line.

Is it not true that the more we have been given, the more deserving we deem ourselves of more and the less happy we become with the blessings bestowed upon us?

Setting my pen to the paper, I picked up where I left off.

Yes, being easy to please is an admirable quality, for a person who is easy to please flourishes wherever he is planted, despite the conditions—rather like the violets in my mother's garden. Uprooted from their home far across the ocean, they endured a long sea voyage only to be transplanted in hostile soil in the early days of fall. They barely had time to take root before the winter snows enfolded them, and yet they survived. Then there is the rose…

My pen scratched feverishly across the page. I glanced once more at the colourful blooms before me and inhaled their heady fragrance. Perhaps being a rose wasn't so bad. True, the rose was more finicky to grow and required far more tending, but its beauty and power to touch the heart could not be discounted. *So many different flowers grace Your garden, O Lord, yet You tend them all with patience and care.* A sparrow trilled in the bushes and another flitted over to join it. *Let me flourish and grow in Your presence, I pray, as I yield to the touch of Your hand. For You are the Master Gardener and, as easy or difficult as I may be, I do belong to You.*

The breeze intensified as if in response, its fingers brushing my face. *I love you, too.*

Chapter 73

SEPTEMBER 1, 1916

Marjorie dabbed her handkerchief to her forehead and fanned herself with her hand. "What a day!" Slipping her hanky back into her sleeve, she adjusted her hat. "Between the crowds and the heat and the demands of our charges, I wonder how we ever made it."

The trolley squealed to a stop and I pulled myself up. Marjorie was right; I was exhausted. "At least we are almost home, Margie. Watch your step." Hurrying out of the car, I stumbled on a misplaced stone, barely catching myself before I ended up on the ground.

"Auntie! Are you all right?"

"Yes. Yes." I bent to pick up the offending obstacle. "Look at this stone. How little it takes to make one stumble."

Marjorie cupped my elbow with her hand and steered me toward the sidewalk, heedless of the revelation stirring in my heart. I held the stone up to examine it more closely. It was an ordinary specimen, not unlike any other rock I'd seen. An inch or so wide, its jagged edges suggested a lifetime of brokenness and abuse, quite unlike that of the stones I used to collect as a child at the beach. I glanced over my shoulder, not surprised to see more scattered along the edges of the road. "You know, brokenness surrounds us wherever we turn, waiting to trip the unsuspecting soul and send it crashing into the dung of hopelessness and unbelief."

Marjorie squinted, shifting her gaze from me to the stone I still held and back again. "Honestly, Aunt Dora, you will find a lesson in everything, won't you? Is not, sometimes, a rock on the road simply a rock on the road?" She smiled broadly and shook her head. "I mean, I've never known anyone like you. You see such meaning in the most trivial of happenings." We rounded the corner onto our street. "I admire that in you, you know, although I confess I don't always understand how you do it."

I tucked the stone into my pocket. "That's, no doubt, because *I* do not do it." I winked, amused by her puzzled frown. "It's like God whispers to me deep within my heart that He wants to show me something, then guides me with clues until I discover it for myself." I blew a stream of air across my face. "It isn't as if I purposely decide to look for some hidden meaning in everything."

"No?" Her eyes danced.

"Of course not."

Home at last, we climbed the stairs to the porch, and Marjorie fitted the key into the lock. The door swung noiselessly on its hinges, thanks to our neighbour, old Mr. Hanson. Knowing that he was always looking for odd jobs to make ends meet, I had asked him to do some light maintenance tasks that neither Marjorie nor I were equipped to do.

"What's this?" Marjorie bent to pick up a thin envelope from the floor inside the door.

The familiar blue markings made my heart race. *A telegram.* I followed her into the house and hung my hat on a peg.

"Who do you suppose it is from?" Margie asked.

"We shall have to open it to find out, I'm afraid. To whom is it addressed?"

She held the envelope toward me. "You."

I hesitated. A telegram could mean many things, but rarely did it mean anything good. Trembling, I extended my hand, grasping the thin paper between my fingers as if it bore a nest of rattlesnake eggs. "I think we had best sit down." I hung my shawl with my hat and proceeded to the kitchen, my stomach roiling. Marjorie fetched a jug of lemonade from the icebox and set out a plate of biscuits while I sat at the table trying to work up the courage to open the envelope.

"So, who is it from?"

I lifted the corner of the envelope and slid the butter knife along its crease. *Who* was *it from?* Pinching the single sheet tucked within, I freed it from the envelope. My breath caught in my chest as I turned it over in my hand.

> Dora Farncomb Toronto
> Come immediately STOP Bring Marjorie STOP
> Alfred.

Marjorie leaned over my shoulder, perusing the message. Silence hung between us for the space of a second. "It's father, isn't it?"

Lemonade forgotten, I rose. "It doesn't say, though the fact that Alfred specifically mentions that you are to come would indicate that it is likely."

"Something terrible has happened to him," she wailed. She yanked out the chair nearest mine and collapsed into its waiting embrace, clapping her hands to her head. "So terrible Uncle Alfred can't even put it in a telegram." Tears sprang to her eyes. "I have to go pack."

I shuddered. Her assessment, tinged as it was by hysteria, was the most likely explanation for the cryptic missive. Returning the lemonade to the icebox, I pocketed the biscuits for later and headed to my room to gather a few clothes. *God, help us deal with whatever news meets us when we get there.* I opened Father's worn, leather valise and set it on the bed. *And fill our hearts with peace.*

A few minutes later, Marjorie appeared at my door, stuffed carpet bag in hand. "I'm ready."

She started to move on, but stopped when I spoke. "Did you pack a black dress?" There it was. A black dress. The one thing neither of us wanted to take, but both knew would likely be necessary.

She nodded curtly. "Two."

My eyes misted as I pulled my own black dress from the closet. "I shall be there in a moment."

・・・

NEWCASTLE

The train squealed to a stop in a cloud of billowing steam. Hefting our bags, Marjorie and I stepped onto the platform, surprised to find it empty save for the usual assortment of rail yard workers. I surveyed the road leading to the station, but it, too, was empty.

"Where's Uncle Alfred?" Marjorie blew a strand of hair from her face. "He always meets us at the station."

I forced a smile, desperate to cover the foreboding simmering in my belly. "Perhaps he wasn't expecting us to arrive so soon." I shifted my bag to my other hand and glanced around. "It's a lovely fall day and it isn't far. Let's walk." Marjorie nodded, her features set in a hard line. "Imagine his face when we arrive on his doorstep," I continued, forcing a cheeriness into my voice that neither of us felt.

She grimaced, then started toward the road. I practically had to run to keep up. *Be honest,* I chided myself. *You feel every bit as afraid as she does and you know it.* "It's going to be all right, Margie," I whispered.

"Is it?"

Her steps slowed, allowing me to catch up. "It is," I assured her. "I know it is. I don't know what we're going to learn when we get to the house, nor the chaos that is about to erupt around us, but I do know that our Lord is in control. No matter what may befall, all will be well."

Marjorie scowled. "Like it was when my brothers died?" Her eyes drilled into mine—hard, dark, imploring. "Or when Uncle Charlie died?"

The words bit into my soul and I winced. A frightened toad emerged from the bushes of my memory, wounded and scarred, his foot dragging awkwardly behind him. He cowered in the shadows, his eyes blinking rapidly, his little chest pounding. "Yes, Marjorie, like it was then." I reached for the arm hanging limply at her side. "Life did not end when Charlie died, nor did it when Jack and Charles were taken from us." Back rigid, Marjorie tugged her arm from my grip and strode on, her pace quickening. Shifting my bag to my other hand, I scurried after her. "It changed forever—and not in a way either you or I would have chosen—but it did not end."

"No?"

I fell silent, allowing the space between us to widen. *Jesus, how can I make her understand?*

You cannot. I stifled a gasp. *It isn't for you to do the work that I alone can do.*

Much as the rebuke stung, it also brought comfort. A wave of relief surged over me. No matter what awaited us, it really was going to be all right. We weren't in this alone.

Marjorie's footsteps slowed, allowing me time to catch up. *Is there nothing I can do to comfort her, Lord?*

Eying the crumpled handkerchief balled in her hand, I sighed. Moisture glistened on her eyelashes and her shoulders drooped. "I'm sorry, Auntie Dora." Her chest heaved. "I know it is as you say. I'm just scared."

"Me, too."

A roadster sped by, kicking up a wayward stone. "I can't even begin to imagine why Uncle Alfred didn't give us more information."

Silence lapsed between us save for the crunching of our shoes on the gravel. *I can.* As we rounded the corner, the house rose before us, dark and foreboding. A lump formed in my throat when I noticed the flag at half mast. Marjorie's hand tightened around mine. *Jesus, help us.*

Chapter 74

"He took his own life?" My mouth could barely form the words. I swallowed hard. "Not Johnny."

Alfred lowered his eyes, hooking his hand around my elbow. "I need your help." He guided me to the stairs and led me upward, each step more difficult than the one before. Stopping one step shy of the top, he turned. I shivered at the emptiness in his eyes. "Forgive me, Dora." He cleared his throat. "I cannot do this myself." Prickles built behind my eyes, but I refused to give way to my grief. I needed to be strong. "I cannot ask the aid of anyone else."

Reluctantly, he led me along the corridor to the door of Johnny's chamber, his head bent nearly to his chest. I closed my eyes, afraid to even think about what I would find on the other side. *Almighty God, grant us strength.* Resting his hand upon the knob, Alfred lowered his head and inhaled deeply, obviously steeling himself to enter. When at last he faced me once more, his eyes glistened in the glow of the gas lights.

"I'm sorry," he whimpered.

He twisted the knob, but I lay a hand over his, stopping it mid-turn. "It's going to be all right, Alfred." I tightened my fingers around his. "We're going to be all right."

"You haven't seen the mess."

"No, but whatever awaits us on the other side of that door, we will be granted the strength to deal with it. We do not walk through that door alone."

He lifted an eyebrow and shook his head. "You'd better brace yourself, sister."

• • •

Fighting the rising bile, I plunged the blood-soaked rag into the bucket and watched the redness seep into the water. *Why, Johnny? Why? How could you do this to us?* I squeezed my eyes shut, hardly able to bear their incessant throbbing. I'd kill the man myself, had he not already done the deed. With a determined sniff, I wrung out the rag and resumed the grisly task before me. Blood had spattered everywhere—on the bed frame, on the floor, on the fireplace, on the wall—and here I was in the midst of it, mopping up the mess. Again. *Was nothing in life easy?* I rose to rub a smattering of dried blood from the bedside table.

"Ever wish it was you instead of him?"

I jumped at the sound of Alfred's voice. I had forgotten he was there. Swallowing hard, I turned to meet his empty stare. I wanted to shout *no*, but I couldn't lie. Not to Alfred. My chin quivered as I glanced into the murky contents of the bucket, and I squeezed my eyes shut. Where was Johnny right now? What was he doing? I dropped the rag and sank to the bed, lowering my face into my hands. For a moment, I could swear I saw him smiling, locked in the embrace of his beloved Jane, surrounded by his two adoring sons. My vision shifted to an older couple and a handsome young man standing off to the side, and I couldn't stop the whimper that rose from deep within me. *Mother? Father? Charlie?* With a gasp, I leapt from the bed when an image of Jesus filled my heart. Warmth encompassed me as He smiled and extended a hand toward a man—a man dressed in Johnny's best suit coat. The man's footsteps faltered as his Saviour drew near, and a look of consternation flitted across his face, but slowly, tenderly, the Lord tipped His head toward my Johnny—for the man could be none other—and beckoned him forward. *Welcome, my beloved, and be at rest. Your earthly sojourn has come to an end; you are home.*

"Dora?"

I raised my head to find Alfred hovering over me, his hands resting lightly upon my shoulders. "He's in a better place, Alfred," I managed. "He's happy now... for the first time since—"

"I wouldn't be so sure, Dora. They won't even bury him in the churchyard. You know what happens to people who kill themselves."

The bitterness in my brother's voice chilled me. "No, Alfred," I whispered. I moved my hands to the side of his face, drawing his eyes back to mine. "I do not know that, and neither do you."

"Oh yes, I do," he spat. "He took the easy way out, Dora. He left us. He ran away."

Tears slipped from my eyes unchecked as I pulled him into a tight embrace. "I don't think so, brother." The force of his sobs thudding against my chest comforted me, filling me with a strength I had never before known. Not when Charlie died, or Father, or Janey, or the boys. Not even when Mother had passed. "I believe he was running toward—toward his loved ones. Toward Janey, toward the boys, toward his Lord. I have seen it." The distant chime of the grandfather clock intruded upon the silence. *Bong. Bong. Bong. Bong.* Four o'clock. "Does Winnie know?" I whispered.

He nodded curtly and turned away. "She and her family will arrive in the morning."

"Does she know the details?" I stooped to retrieve my rag and knelt to scrub the stains from the marble hearth. This room might never look the same.

"No."

The coppery stench of Johnny's blood filled my nostrils and my stomach roiled. "Why don't you go and spend a few minutes with Marjorie, Alfred?" I moved the bucket a few inches to the left and shifted to a new spot. It wouldn't do to prolong this unpleasantness any longer than necessary. "I'll finish up here."

"But—"

"Go, Alfred. I can handle this. You're the closest thing she has had to a real father for a very long time now." It took a minute for him to respond. Daring a glance, I watched his retreating form, his stooped shoulders bearing a weight far greater than any man should have to bear. *Would that we had not been left behind.*

• • •

The pall of shame surrounding Johnny's death kept most people away. As difficult as that was to accept, given the honoured man he once had been, it did ease the stress of accepting the condolences of well-meaning friends who had already doomed the poor man to Hell. *As if the hell he had endured on earth hadn't been enough.*

A rap at the door startled the quiet company gathered about the dining table. The simple ceremony at the site of the interment was scheduled to begin in less than an hour. Alfred rose, signalling the rest of us to stay seated. "Pardon me." He dabbed his mouth with a napkin and placed it on the table beside his untouched plate. Before he could leave, though, Edith appeared at the door with a diminutive man clad in black cassock and collar. Alfred stopped mid-step. "Bishop Maxwell."

The little man cleared his throat. "Greetings to you, my brothers and sisters, on this most difficult day. The Lord be with you." Tears gathered in my eyes. It was a most unexpectedly gracious greeting. He moved to take the seat Alfred offered him. "I, too, loved the Reverend Canon John. He was a friend beyond any other." Again, he cleared his throat. "I could not bear to send him off as if he had never existed, no matter what the circumstances of his death." I studied my hands, his words a balm to my heart. "He was a tortured man whose heart had been torn asunder by sorrows that would have sent a lesser man to his grave long before this." Silence reigned, save for a few quiet sniffles. "I cannot believe that God, in His justice, would condemn for eternity a man whose heart had remained faithful save for a single moment of insanity at the crossroads between life and death."

I looked up, hardly able to see through my tears. "Bless you, Bishop Maxwell, for bringing us this message of hope."

"I only wish I had not had to come alone, dear heart." Our eyes met and I caught in them a glimpse of my Saviour's compassion. "Be at peace and entrust him to the tender mercies of our Lord, who is not willing that any should perish—least of all, one of His own."

Alfred lowered his head into his hands, his shoulders quivering.

He really is in Your hands, isn't he, Jesus? I recalled the glorious vision I had been given of Jesus welcoming my brother with open arms, and I reveled in the peace that engulfed me. *Thank You, Jesus. You remember that we are but dust, and You remain faithful, even when we are faithless.* With each statement, my breath came more easily.

"Come, my brothers and sisters," Bishop Maxwell intoned, "let us lay to rest the body of our dear Brother John and then let us celebrate with him his joy."

Chairs scraped across the floor as we rose in unison and filed out of the room. Life would go on. We would heal, though our hearts would never quite be the same. "We have not been abandoned," I whispered as I pressed into my brother's side. "We'll see our Johnny again." He raised rheumy eyes to mine and nodded, his mouth set. "It's just the two of us for now, but one day…"

Chapter 75

SEPTEMBER 16, 1916
TORONTO

"Are you coming for breakfast, Aunt Dora?"

I flopped backward on my bed, covering my ears with my pillow. *Fight it, Dora. Fight it. You cannot let the darkness claim you.* I repeated the words that had lately become my morning mantra until my heart regained its normal rhythm. *Lord Jesus, by Your mercy, restore my mind and heal my heart.*

"Aunt Dora?" Anxious footsteps approached my chamber door. Tossing my pillow aside, I pushed myself to the edge of the bed and bent to fumble with my stockings. "I'll be right there, Margie."

The footsteps stopped. Mustering a smile, I looked up to find my niece at the door, her hands on her hips. "Do you need some help?"

I shook my head and returned to the task before me. The days and weeks following Johnny's passing had been every bit as difficult for her as they had been for me—perhaps even more so. "Do you ever wonder if you've let God down?"

"Let God down?" Marjorie angled her head, her brow wrinkling. "*You* are afraid that you have let God down?"

"He gave me a mission—to care for my family, to minister to the needs of my parents and brothers—and I have failed."

"Because of Father."

I strode across the room and rooted through the bureau for a pair of pantaloons. "I should have moved back to Newcastle with him, regardless of the work I left behind." I shoved the drawer closed with significantly more force than necessary. "Johnny still needed me, and I wasn't there for him. I was too busy writing and leading Bible studies, directing choirs, and aiding the destitute." I jabbed my feet into the cotton underwear. "I was too busy tending to the needs of others…"

"But is that not what our Lord has called you to do, Aunt Dora?"

I drew the strings on my corset and tied them into place. "Yes, it is." I blew out a harsh breath. "But long before He called me to those deeds of kindness and good works, He called me to care for my family, and He never rescinded that call." Despite the morning sun pouring through the window, the room seemed dark. "I failed Him, Margie—Him and Johnny both."

Marjorie waited for me to button my blouse then held my skirt above my head so I could slip it on more easily. "Do you really think you could have stopped Father from taking his own life?" She fixed the skirt into place and turned me around to face her. "Even you couldn't have stayed with him every moment of every day."

With a grim nod, I followed her from the room. She had a point. Johnny had set his heart upon being with Janey and the boys and had seen no other way out. No amount of preaching or cajoling on my part would have made a difference, yet surely I could have done something. If only it wasn't too late. "So, what is on the agenda for today, Marjorie?"

"Well, we haven't been to see old Mrs. Robson in almost a month, and the attendants at the asylum will be starting to wonder what has become of you." Marjorie set a cup of tea and a platter of tea biscuits on the table before me. "How be we go see Mrs. Robson together, then I'll make my rounds to the widows while you go to the asylum." She sat opposite me and reached for a half-empty pot of blackberry preserves. "Later, perhaps you should work on next month's articles for your column. I'm sure they must be due soon."

I raised my eyes heavenward. *My column.* For the first time since I took it on, I had nothing whatsoever to write about. No insights to develop, no words of inspiration to share, no challenges to issue. Nothing. If Marjorie only knew the emptiness I fought with each passing breath. "Well then, I suppose we should get started."

I went to get up, but Marjorie patted the table. "Not until you've eaten the rest of your breakfast, Aunt Dora." Her tone brightened. "Did you chance to see the newspaper this morning?"

I sighed inwardly. Maybe it would be best if I just went back to bed.

"Our troops have made some headway in the Battle of Courcelette on the Somme. It seems the British forces surprised the enemy by rolling a Big Willie tank into action. Who could have guessed that the Little Willie they introduced last year—with all its limitations—could have evolved into the dreaded machine that made its appearance on the battlefield yesterday. The very sight of it terrified the enemy and resulted in a resounding victory for the allies. The British had done an admirable job of keeping it under wraps until then, or so the paper said. It seems they shipped it to the western front in crates labelled *water tank* and managed to assemble it without detection until the morning of the fifteenth when it made its way onto the battlefield. The journalist suggested that might be the reason the troops started referring to it as a tank." Marjorie reached for a second biscuit. "It looks like this represents a major turning point in the Battle of the Somme."

"You don't say," I responded, hardly registering her words. "We don't hear news like that too often these days."

"But there's more..." Marjorie prattled on, relaying the news of the day.

Where have I gone wrong, Jesus? I've tried so hard to do all that You've laid before me—all that You've called me to do.

But now, because you were unable to accomplish that which I alone can do, you feel as though you have failed Me? I wanted to shout my objection, but no words came. *You expect much of yourself, dear one. Too much. You are not Me. You cannot change the heart of man, no matter how much you wish you could.* I blinked away the tears that threatened to escape. *Nor will I allow you to steal from others the freedom of choice that I, Myself, bestowed upon them. Even when your heart—so very like My own—yearns to keep them from destruction.* Slipping my handkerchief from my sleeve, I dabbed it beneath my nose, dimly registering that Marjorie still spoke. *Just because I call you to a task, it doesn't mean that I am calling you to see it through to fruition or that your earthly eyes will deem the result a success.*

"What do you think of that, Aunt Dora?"

Startled from my Lord's words, I trained my eyes upon my niece. "I'm sorry, Marjorie. It seems I was a mite distracted." I cleared my throat and set my napkin on the table, my breakfast untouched. "What was it you were saying?"

A smile played at the corners of her lips. "It was nothing of consequence." She rose to collect the dishes. "Why don't I head off to see Mrs. Robson while you stay here and do a little writing?" She took my cup and dumped the contents into the sink. "I'm sure that our dear Mr. Wellman would be delighted to hear from you."

A flutter of gaiety winged its way to my heart—the first I had felt since before the telegram had sent my world spinning. "You need someone to set this old auntie of yours straight, eh?" I winked. It felt good to engage in a hint of our old, playful banter. Normal.

"You said it, not me." Marjorie's coy reply begged a playful response.

"Then I have to say that I am quite right. Why don't you head off on your rounds like you said while I write a letter to Mattie."

"Done," Marjorie replied. She helped me from my chair and shooed me out of the kitchen. "I shall let you know when I leave."

●●●

September 16, 1916

My Dear Mr. Wellman,

How are things in New York? Last time you wrote, you were planning to go before the congressional standing committee regarding options to curtail the illegal drug trade in your great city. How did that go? Did anything come of it?

Things have been more than a little overwhelming around here. Thank you for your lovely telegram in response to Johnny's passing. It touched my heart deeply and helped me through some very difficult moments. I wish that I could say those agonizing times are over, but to do so would be to lie. I find myself really struggling these days to make sense of all that has happened. It troubles me that I have failed in that first and most glorious calling God placed upon my life—to care for my family and be for them a haven of safety and strength through times of trouble and despair. And then I hear the voice of God assuring me that just because my earthly eyes deem my mission a failure, it means not that it is so. Things are not always as they appear. It is not my right to steal from others the freedom of choice He has bestowed upon them, no matter how poorly it is being used. Nor is it up to me to heal the heartache of another. He alone is able to change the heart and heal the soul.

My head understands—even agrees—but I fear my heart yet clings to the sense of failure that pervades my soul, Mattie. I want to scream, "Why? Why did You not intervene? Why did You not stop him from destroying himself?" Yet, just as it is not for me to steal from another the gift of free will, neither will He rescind this most marvellous gift from His children. Though I daily remind myself that if He did, He would cease to be a loving Father and reveal Himself to be a tyrant, my heart still battles the devastation of our loss.

Oh, Mattie, I feel so lost. You would think that I would be getting pretty good at dealing with grief by now—Heaven knows I've seen enough of it—but I feel as though I am floundering far beyond my depth on this one. Pray that God would not give me over to the insanity that threatens to wrap its insidious tentacles around my mind. Pray that He would grant me the gift of a sane mind in the midst of the lunacy surrounding me. And pray for Alfred, too. He does not say much, but I know he is struggling.

Well, Marjorie will be back soon and I have a series of articles that must be written, so I must sign off. You could pray for inspiration for me as well, if you think of it. I am afraid I have little to share with my readers these days. Somehow, I suddenly feel very old. My love and prayers are with you, dear Mattie.

Affectionately,
Your Dora-girl

Folding the letter, I spritzed it lightly with lavender water and inserted it into the envelope. Glancing at my time piece, I turned to my typewriter. An empty piece of paper curled around the roller, awaiting my attention. Perhaps my readers would appreciate a break from my usual exposition this time. A story would certainly be a refreshing way to ease my way back into my daily routine. Plucking a pen from its holder, I smoothed a fresh piece of paper over the blotter.

Once upon a time there was a little, brown toad...

Chapter 76

NOVEMBER 13, 1916

Startled into wakefulness, I threw off the covers, my heart thundering in my chest. *I have to get this down.* Heedless of the early winter chill, I bolted to my desk and switched on the light. Already the dream was beginning to fade. Sweeping aside the work of the previous day, I rummaged in the drawer for a clean piece of paper. It had been so vivid—so real. I had to get it onto the page before it disappeared from my mind completely.

> *I thought I stood near a palace fair*
> *In a hot and noisy street;*

I paused to refill my pen. Words dropped from the nib as I pushed it across the page, hardly daring to breathe.

> *And shining doors were opened wide,*
> *So that all who wished might step inside*
> *To rest in the coolness sweet.*
>
> *I was hot and tired and sad at heart,*
> *For everything had gone wrong:—*
> *A kind voice said, "The King is your friend,*
> *He waits within, your cause to defend,*
> *Oh, don't keep Him waiting long!"*
>
> *"But," I said, "my troubles are all so small,*
> *I'm ashamed to tell the King.*
> *He was brave and strong in torture and loss,*

While I shrink back from the lightest cross—
A coward in everything."

Three stanzas lay scrawled across the page by the time I stopped to read the words I had written. Odd how they could resonate so deeply within me, as if they captured the insights and experiences of another, rather than my own.

"Yet He calls for you and for you He cares,"
The voice made answer sweet;
"You want to be strong, and the Cross He sent
Is a gift of love, to strengthen you meant,
Lest you should accept defeat."

Then I passed from the noisy glare of the street
And before the King I stood:
His message of love was for none beside,
I could not repeat it if I tried,
And I would not if I could;

For He waits to strengthen you Himself,
To show you what Pain doth mean;
He calls you to leave the world for a space,
To rest in His Love and to see His Face,—
No stranger may come between.

The Master is come, and He calleth for thee!
Are you too busy to care?
The door is open, He waits within;
You need His help in the fight with sin,
Your burdens He wants to bear.

He calls you to lean on His Heart of Love,
To rest with Him for a space.
I must step aside, for the King is here!
He says, "It is I!" then do not fear,
Look up and behold His Face![3]

As each new verse appeared on the page, I marvelled at the way the words so perfectly captured my dream. *Look up and behold His Face.* Tears bathed my cheeks as I lay down my pen and flipped off the lamp. *I've had it wrong all along, haven't I, Lord? The call You placed upon me was not to care for my family or write for my countrymen or care for the needs of the poor. Your call was to draw near to You—to love You with all of my heart—to surrender myself wholly to Your love.*

Crawling back into bed, I drew the counterpane under my chin. *All those things I've mistaken for my mission in life were simply jobs You gave me along the way.* I yawned. *Jobs along the w…*

• • •

The morning sun peeked through the curtains, casting a rainbow of colour on the wall beside my bed. I smiled at the sight. It was as if I watched my soul, freed at last from the bonds of expectation and good works, dancing with the abandon it was created to enjoy. Leaping from the bed, I drew the curtains, surprised to see a coverlet of white dusting the ground. It must have snowed sometime in the night. The sun sparkled off its surface, sending a shiver of joy up my spine, and I spun across the room like a little girl.

Dressing quickly, I headed to the kitchen, making a mental list of all the things I needed to do. First there was that final article I had to write for next month's column. *The Glory in the Midst,* I mused. A flash of red drew my eye to the window. A cardinal. *The Glory in the midst of the winter. The Glory in the midst of the pain.* I filled the kettle with water and set it on the stove to boil, half wondering if there would be enough coffee left to make a full pot—or enough sugar, for that matter. No matter; I could have tea. I thought of our boys on the frontlines and the sacrifices they made for the welfare of our country and all who lived within its borders. Did they enjoy the luxury of a hot cup of coffee this frosty morning? And what of the womenfolk they left behind? *Hmmmm.* The

---

[3] Dora Farncomb, *The Master is Come and Calleth for Thee*; A Vision of His Face, London, Ontario, William Weld Publishers, 1909, Chapter 18

Glory in the midst of sacrifice... in the midst of service... in the midst of war. It was certainly a most timely topic.

The kettle sang on the stove, and I jumped to retrieve it before it awakened Margie—not that it was likely she still slept. It was, after all, well past seven. Carefully measuring the final grains of coffee left in the tin, I added the water and lifted the lid on the sugar bowl.

"Aunt Dora?" Marjorie appeared at the kitchen door, her lacy night dress peeking from beneath a crimson robe.

"Oh dear," I murmured. "It is as I feared." I wiped my hands on my apron and shook my head. "All of my banging about in the kitchen has awakened you." I poured her a mug of coffee and pressed it into her waiting hands. "I had hoped you might be able to sleep in a little this morning."

She peered at me, clearly confused. "*You* are obviously feeling better."

Cupping my hands around the welcome warmth of my cup, I joined her at the table. "I am."

She lifted a hand and let it drop. "So? Are you going to tell me?"

"Tell you what, dear?" I raised my brows innocently, struggling to keep a straight face.

"Aunt Dora—"

Unable to maintain the façade, I broke into a grin and propped my elbows on the table. "I had a dream."

"A dream," Marjorie repeated.

"A very vivid dream." I sipped the fragrant brew and grimaced. *Ugh. Bitter! At least it is a cup of coffee.*

"Well?" Marjorie demanded.

"Well what, dear?"

"Aunt Dora, you're as bad as Uncle Alfred! You'd think that he was your brother or something."

I laughed. How good it felt to once again be free. Taking another sip from my cup, I set it upon the table then reached into my bodice to remove the poem I had written. "Here, read this." She pushed her cup into the middle of the table and unfolded the paper. "Aloud, if you wouldn't mind."

Smoothing the paper on the table before her, Marjorie cleared her throat. "All right. Let's see... 'The Master has Come and He Calleth for Thee.' Her eyes met mine and she smiled. "That's quite the title."

Without waiting for a response, Marjorie turned her attention back to the piece before her. I closed my eyes, mesmerized by the quiet cadence of her voice as she read each line, my heart leaping anew at the profound truths God had woven into every verse. She slowed as she neared the end of the poem, her voice husky. "Look up and behold His face," she repeated quietly.

A single tear seeped from beneath my lashes. *Look up and behold.* How long had it been since I had truly done that? Silence filled the crannies of the room as I took another sip from my cup. The coffee tasted sweeter than it had before. "I haven't failed in my calling after all, Margie." My voice trembled, though I hardly knew why. "It would seem that I only confused the work God has given me to do with the call that He has placed upon my life."

Uncertainty churned the depths of Marjorie's eyes. However could I make her understand? "He's called me—like He has called us all—to draw near and live each day in intimate communion with Him." She nodded slowly and cocked her head. Encouraged by her obvious curiosity, I plunged on. "He has purposed for me to care for my family and minister to my brothers and sisters both in word and in deed along the way, but His *call* is to intimate communion with Him alone." I paused as comprehension dawned in her eyes. "Knowing that, I've finally found rest. I have not failed in my calling; I just didn't understand what that calling truly entailed."

Her eyes fluttered shut and she nodded. "Amen." Folding the paper, she pushed it across the table. "I wish God would speak to me as clearly as He speaks to you."

Tucking the paper back into my bodice, I drained my cup. "I have no doubt that He does, dear. It takes time for us to learn how to recognize His voice, though." I rose to slice the bread for our morning repast. "Heaven knows, at my age, I ought to have had enough time to do that." I brushed the crumbs from the counter and deposited them into a can on the windowsill. The cardinals would be glad for them once the snow came in earnest.

"Really, Aunt Dora... you're not *that* old."

"I don't know about that, dear." Arranging the bread on a baking rack, I slid it into the oven and noted the time. *Seven forty-five. A few minutes should do it.* "Now what is on our agenda for today?"

Marjorie fetched a list from the sideboard and joined me at the counter. "Let's see. I need to visit the market this morning and drop in on Mrs. Robson on the way home to deliver the headache powder she asked me to get for her at the druggist's. And in the afternoon, I promised to join the women's auxiliary in preparing care packages for our boys. I'm hoping to find a few pounds of hard candy at the market this morning to include in their packages, as I'm told we are running short."

I cracked the oven door to check on the toast. "Now, that wouldn't do. The powers that be say that candy is one of the most important parts of those care packages."

"It's true," Marjorie responded. "The ladies were quite concerned over the deficit this time. After all, candy provides our boys with the energy they require to fight well. They need it."

Wrapping a cloth around my hand, I pulled the tray from the oven and transferred the toast to a plate. "It sounds like a busy day." The toast crunched as I scraped a thin layer of bacon fat across its surface. "I have a few letters to catch up on, and I really need to complete my final article for next month's column, but other than that, I'm free." Marjorie placed a jar of marmalade on the table and topped up the coffee in our cups. "Perhaps I could go with you to the market. I know just the place to go for the best candy in the city."

"But it's Thursday," Marjorie pointed out. She reached for a piece of perfectly browned toast and spooned a lump of marmalade onto it. "What about the asylum? They are going to be wondering what has become of you down there."

I spread a spoonful of marmalade onto my own toast and bit into it, chewing thoughtfully. "Yes... the asylum."

"Do you sense your ministry there is coming to an end?" Marjorie asked.

"No... not entirely." I fingered the crumbs from my plate and reached for another piece of toast, taking the time to fix it to my liking before continuing. "Only I don't seem to feel the same draw to return to it that I once did, not that the need there has diminished."

"Do you suppose that might be God calling you to direct your energy in a different direction?" Marjorie dabbed her lips with a napkin and folded it neatly over her plate. "I mean, you do so much, Aunt Dora—perhaps even more than our Lord has called you to do."

A wave of defensiveness surged within me. "Me? Do more than He has called me to do? Impossible."

"Is it?" Marjorie extended a hand across the table. "There is so much neediness in this world, and the heart of God within you can't help but respond with compassion, but do not the scriptures tell us that God has a pre-ordained purpose for each of us to fulfill?" I nodded slowly, troubled by the direction her words were taking. "He has also, as you have just reminded me, given us free will which He refuses to rescind. He will not force us to comply with His purposes for us, yet neither will He stop us from pursuing other avenues of service, though they be bound to wear us out and keep us from fulfilling, to the best of our ability, the work He has created us to complete."

I took another sip of my coffee. "Are you suggesting that in my lifelong quest to know the call of God, I have worn myself out by purposing to do every good thing that touches my heart rather than concentrating on that which God has truly called me to do?" Marjorie collected the plates as I drained my cup, but didn't say a word. "It is, I suppose, something worth thinking—and praying—about," I conceded. I wobbled as I rose, thrusting a palm onto the table to steady myself. Marjorie looked at me oddly, but I laughed it off. "Nothing to worry about, Margie. I just rose too quickly. Your auntie's getting old, I'm afraid." The last thing the girl needed was to be worried by the increasing episodes of wooziness I had been experiencing lately. She was right, of course. Perhaps it was time for me to let a few things go. *The Master has come and He calleth for thee. Are you too busy to hear?* The words ricocheted through my mind. "You are a wise woman, Marjorie. You've given me much to think about. Perhaps it is time for me to let some things go, beginning with my work at the asylum." I headed toward the door. "I shall pray about it."

She wiped a cloth across the table. "I will, too, Aunt Dora." Shaking the cloth into the trash can, she spread it over the faucet to dry. "When do you wish to leave for the market?"

"You name the time and I shall be ready."

"Shall we say half-past nine, then?"

"Half-past nine it is." Leaving Marjorie to clean up the kitchen, I headed to the sunroom. *The Master has come and He calleth for thee. Look up! And behold His face...* The words of my poem drummed within me. *Help me, Jesus, and show me what it is that* You *want me to do.*

•••

November 13, 1916

My Dear Mr. Wellman,

I pray that this letter finds you well and that the ailment you suffered from last time you wrote has resolved itself. You will be pleased to hear that the darkness clouding my soul since Johnny's passing has finally lifted. I had a dream last night, so vivid it could only have come from God alone. You know the type of which I speak. It was as if He stood by my side describing the ebb and flow of my entire life, begging me to step out of its eddies to join Him atop the waves. Words do not exist to express the glory He revealed to me in that dream, but I did the best I could to capture it in the poem I have included with this letter. I am sure I shall never be the same again.

I have decided to decrease my time at the asylum in the coming weeks, settling upon one day per month rather than the four I have given them since Janey's death, and I also plan to scale back my work at the church. I will continue to lead the women's Bible study each week, though, while I groom a capable assistant to take over sometime next year. My writing is enough to keep me busy, along with the charitable work it entails. I tire so easily these days, it seems. This aging process really is no fun. I watched Mother go through it and I recognize the signs. Who would have thought it would happen to me?

Marjorie, too, seems to be doing much better these days as she comes to grips with the tragic events of her own life.

I lay my pen aside and rubbed my temples. If only this infernal headache would subside. Perhaps I should ask Marjorie to get some of that headache powder for me as well. I moved to rise, but fell back into the chair, my head whirling. *What is wrong with me?* Rising more slowly this time, I steadied myself on the desk and let my head settle. *More coffee. Perhaps that would help.* Returning to the kitchen, I lifted the lid on the coffee pot and scowled. It would have to wait.

"Shall we go?" I jumped, startled to see Marjorie at the door, basket in hand, clad in her warmest woolen cape and muffler.

"Is it that time already?" I glanced at my pocket watch. *Nine thirty-five.* "Where does the time go?" I chuckled self-consciously, trying to ignore the look of concern flickering in Marjorie's eyes. "I shall be but a moment." Turning a little too quickly, I stumbled into the counter.

"Aunt Dora!" Marjorie exclaimed. "Are you all right?" In a trice, she was at my side, her arm around my waist, her hand grasping my elbow.

I shook her off, determined to be gracious, yet feeling anything but. "I just turned a bit too quickly, dear, that's all." I stepped past her to don my woolies.

"Are you certain that's all it is?" Concern laced Marjorie's voice.

I pushed aside the urge to rebuke her. "I'm fine, Marjorie. There's no need to hover so. You're not a fruit fly." I strapped on my boots and bent to retrieve the basket by the door. "Shall we go?"

When she didn't respond, I turned, my hand balled on my hip. "Well? Shall we…" The words died on my lips. What had I been thinking? Marjorie gaped at me, the pain in her eyes almost more than I could bear. "Oh, Margie…" I rushed to her side. "Forgive this old girl for hurling such thoughtless words." She blinked rapidly. "I suppose I'm feeling rather old and infirm this morning, and your loving attentions managed to inflame my impatience with this aging body of mine." She lowered her head. Cupping her face in my hand, I waited for her to look up. "I ought not to have spoken to you so rudely. You didn't deserve that."

Marjorie dabbed her handkerchief beneath her nose. "I know you didn't mean it, Aunt Dora. I'm sorry for making you feel inept." She leaned her head against mine, her arm encircling my shoulders. "My concern got the better of me. Will you forgive me?"

"Of course I will, dear." I squeezed her affectionately. "I really am fine; I promise. Shall we get on our way?"

• • •

Grandpa Annett's Candy Kitchen lay a mile or so past the church, in the block just south of Eaton's department store. Despite the snowfall of the night before, the sun shone brightly in the blue sky, warming us as we walked. "We could take the trolley, if you'd like," Marjorie said.

"But it's such a lovely day for a walk." I hooked my hand through her elbow. "With winter on our doorstep, we'll be yearning for a walk like this before long." The milk cart rattled past as we neared Yonge Street, and we waved.

"Mornin', ladies." The milkman doffed his hat and nodded. "Beautiful day."

"That it is." I responded. Amazing what a little fresh air could do for a person.

A bell rang as we entered the candy shop. "Be right with you, ladies," the shopkeeper called. Rubbing my hands together, I perused the shelves laden with sweets. *Caramel taffy, bars of smooth milk chocolate, Turkish delight, licorice pipes.* I stopped before a tray of fudge, my mouth watering. Sixty-five cents a pound.

"How may I help you today, ladies?" An elderly gentleman entered the shop clad in a chocolate-smeared apron. The neatly-trimmed beard framing his face stood out in bold contrast to his balding head.

"We're hoping to get a supply of candy to send to our boys in the trenches," Marjorie responded. "What would you suggest?"

The shopkeeper slid his apron over his head and hung it on a hook behind the counter. "Ah, yes—such a worthy cause. Come right this way." He led us to a set of three open kegs in the far corner of the store. "It seems to me that lemon drops would be your best choice." He reached into the first bin, allowing a handful of bright yellow candies to sift through his fingers. "That, or these horehound squares over here." He gestured to the bin next to the hard candies. "Then again, there are these butterscotch patties." He pointed to the third keg. "They're always a favourite."

I leaned over to peer at the horehound candy filling the second bin. Father had always loved horehound, though I personally preferred the fudge.

"All three travel well and provide a rich source of energy," the little man continued, "and all are made right here in this shop by me. I would be most happy to sell them to you at cost, or even, perhaps, a little less. Anything to help our troops."

Marjorie eyed each bin in turn. "Let's see. If we take five pounds of lemon drops at fifty-six cents and five pounds of horehound at ninety-seven—" She pointed to her fingers, enumerating each item.

"Nonsense," I broke in. I turned to the shopkeeper. "We'll take five pounds of each—and two very small pieces of maple fudge," I added quickly.

Marjorie grinned. "Fudge?"

"Of course, dear." I picked a ball of fluff from her cape. "We, too, need to shore up our energy reserves if we are going to cart all of this candy home." I nodded sagely. "Do you not agree, Mr. Annetts?"

Deep dimples dented the shopkeeper's cheeks. "'Tis a fact, ma'am." He weighed out the candy and divided it between four large paper sacks, then turned to the fudge. "Would you like the fudge wrapped?"

He selected two small pieces from a tray behind the counter. "No need." I winked at Margie. "I believe we shall be enjoying it right away."

He handed a piece to each of us. "Thank you," Marjorie said.

"Yes. Many thanks, Mr. Annetts." I nibbled a corner of my piece and closed my eyes. *Heavenly.* "No one makes fudge like you, sir." I took another bite, savouring the mapley flavor. He smiled, obviously pleased.

"How much do we owe you?" Marjorie interjected.

"Let's see." Taking a pencil and pad from beneath the counter, he did a figure or two then turned to the great gold cash register. His fingers flashed across the keys. "Fifty-six plus ninety-seven plus a dollar eight for the butterscotch patties is two sixty-one minus seventy-five cents for our boys equals... How be we say a dollar seventy-five." He looked up. "How does that sound?"

"What about the fudge?" I asked.

Again the dimples danced on his cheeks. "The fudge is on me, dear ladies." I moved to object, but he hushed me with a finger to his lips. "Just say thank you." He nodded encouragingly as if speaking to a child.

My objections died on my lips and I sighed, returning his grin. "Thank you, Mr. Annetts. You are a kind and generous man."

Walking around the counter, he placed two sacks in each of our baskets. "You do me great honour, Miss Farncomb. God grant you a glorious day."

The bell tinkled behind us as we stepped into the street. "Shall we take the trolley home?" Marjorie asked.

I weighed the basket in my hand. "I suppose that might be a good idea." I checked my pocket watch. "It won't come by for another twenty minutes, though. Is there somewhere else you would like to go?"

Marjorie glanced down the street. "We could go to Eaton's for a look-see. The streetcar stops there every half hour."

I shifted my basket to my left arm and slid my right hand through the crook of Marjorie's elbow. "Lead on."

• • •

With a yawn, I returned my pen in its holder and set the article I had been working on aside. *What a day.* If I didn't retire to my chamber soon, I'd be spending the whole night at my desk. Rising, I paused just long enough for the whirling in my head to subside then glanced at Marjorie, breathing a prayer of thanks that she hadn't noticed. Ensconced in a blanket, she sat by the fire reading the latest novel by that great Scottish bard, George MacDonald. I bent to kiss her on the head as I passed. "I think I shall turn in, dear. Enjoy your book."

"Aunt Dora?" Setting her book on the coffee table, Marjorie straightened in her chair.

I held up a hand. "No need to get up."

She raised an eyebrow. "It can't be much past seven." She glanced at the clock on the mantel. "Are you feeling poorly?"

I patted her shoulder reassuringly. "Not at all, Marjorie. You need not fret so. It's simply been a long day." I felt her eyes following me as I walked from the room. There was no need to worry her with the fact that I remembered watching her grandmother struggling with these very symptoms before being struck by apoplexy so many years before. I stepped out of my skirt and sagged onto the bed. *I'm tired, that's all. A good sleep will restore me to my usual vigour.* I lay back on my bed and snugged the counterpane around me. I only needed a good night's…"

• • •

"Aunt Dora? Aunt Dora!"

Violent shaking drew me from my slumber. Had a whole night passed already? I struggled to open my eyes, but only my left would cooperate.

"Aunt Dora, wake up!"

I forced my mouth to open, pushing it to form words it couldn't say, alarmed by its inability to respond. A series of unintelligible sounds issued from my throat. What was wrong with me?

Marjorie's face blanched. "I shall be right back. You–you just rest." Like a hare pursued by a coyote, she shot from the room. I raised my hands to my face, shocked when only my left arrived at its intended destination. *Breathe, Dora. Breathe.* I might not be able to speak, but at least I maintained the sanity of coherent thought. Something was terribly wrong.

"Mr. Hanson has gone to fetch the doctor." I lurched my head up at the sound of Marjorie's voice, every movement an effort. When had she returned? "He is going to stop at the telegraph office on the way back to contact Uncle Alfred as well." Marjorie sat on the edge of the bed, her breath coming in ragged bursts.

I reached for her hand, chagrinned to find it already firmly clasping the fingers of my right hand. "I ca-a-a-a-a-no-aw ee-eel m a-a-a-n-n-n-n-d." Unearthly sounds issued from my lips. *O Lord, what is happening to me?*

Marjorie drew my left hand into hers and squeezed it gently. "Everything will be all right, Auntie Dora. Just rest." She stroked my hair with her free hand, her voice rising in song. "When peace like a river attendeth my soul, when sorrows like sea billows roll—" Her sweet voice soothed my spirit, and I forgot for a moment the terrifying paralysis that gripped my body.

"It is well…"

It is well. I fought to make my mouth form the words, appalled by the series of grunts I emitted instead. *Lord God, what is wrong with me?* I tried to push myself up. *I can't speak; I can barely move. I can't even feel my writing arm.* I wrenched my good hand from Marjorie's and flailed it in the air in a fevered attempt to rise, ignoring her pleas to lie back and relax. *Relax? When nothing within me functioned as it should? When my body refused to respond to my command? When Mother's insidious decline haunted my every thought? Relax?*

"Sh-h-h," Marjorie soothed. "Lord Jesus, bring peace to Your servant, Dora." I drew in a sharp, short breath and let my good eye flutter closed. "Let her feel Your presence and find security in the knowledge that You are in control—even in this." My breathing slowed with each word and the stiffness in my limbs began to subside. "She's scared, Jesus, and so am I. Send Your Spirit upon us and imbue us with courage to bear this cross, whatever it might be."

I managed a wobbly nod.

A quiet knock at the door startled us both. "Dr. Turner." Marjorie crossed the room, extending her hand in greeting.

"I hope you don't mind," he responded. "Jeb Hanson let me in." She beckoned him to follow her. "He indicated that it was urgent."

Marjorie drew a high-backed chair up to the bed, urging the doctor to sit. "I had a difficult time awakening my aunt this morning, and when I finally succeeded, I found her unable to speak, or even move parts of her body, particularly on her right side."

"I see." The doctor pushed his spectacles into place and smiled into my eyes. "Good morning, Dora. Can you hear me?" Again I managed a wobbly nod. "Fine, fine," he answered. "Now don't you worry, Miss Farncomb. We're going to take very good care of you." My eyes filled as I looked from him to my niece. "I recall you once told me that your mother suffered from that which we used to term apoplexy."

"That is correct," Marjorie interjected.

"In the language of today, we would say that she had a stroke."

A stroke? The word sent shivers up my spine. I had heard of such things.

The doctor reached for my hand and patted it gently. "Such maladies of the cerebrovascular system tend to run in families, I'm afraid." I took a shaky breath, turning my face away. "It looks like that is what we are dealing with here," the doctor continued.

We *are dealing with?* I drilled my eyes into his. *We?*

"People do recover from strokes—at times." Deep lines creased the doctor's kind face. "In fact, as in the case of your mother, Dora, a person can live many years after its onset."

A vision of my mother sitting on the lawn in her wheelchair came to mind, her angelic smile inviting me to hope. *But she could still speak.*

"What can we do to aid Aunt Dora's recovery? Is there a medication you could prescribe that might help her? Should I be taking her to the hospital?" Ever practical, Marjorie fired questions at the doctor in rapid succession, barely stopping to breathe in between.

The doctor eyed her, clearly warning her to cease her interrogation. "Perhaps you and I could talk about those things later, Miss Farncomb." He turned back to me and wiped a crease from the counterpane. "Right now, I would like to examine our patient. Would you be so good as to make us both a cup of tea? I shall meet you in the kitchen when I am through." Marjorie nodded submissively and backed from the room. "Now, let's have a listen to that heart of yours," the doctor said. He positioned his stethoscope over his ears and held the bell to my chest. "Don't you worry a bit, dear Hope." The use of my pen name warmed me, reminding me of the One in whom my hope was found. "I do not believe you are ready to leave us just yet."

Chapter 77

MAY 25, 1917

"Aunt Dora, you'll never guess what I have!" Marjorie burst into the kitchen waving a letter. "It's from Mr. Wellman."

I blinked my eyes a few times, forcing my sight to cooperate, and held out my hand to receive the precious missive. Cradling it to my chest, I sighed, annoyed by the tear that slid down the side of my nose. This hyper-emotionalism was starting to get on my nerves. *As if I wasn't emotional enough before this blasted stroke.* I forced the letter into my right hand and, with an undignified grunt, ripped at the flap with my left.

"Here," Marjorie said. Reaching for the envelope, she wedged the tip of a butter knife into the gap I had opened and slid it across the fold. "How's that?" She tugged a thin piece of paper from the envelope and unfolded it carefully before handing it to me. "I'll go get your spectacles."

Even with my glasses perched on my nose, I had to squint to make out the words, and my head began to pound. "Yo-o-o-oooo rrrr-ee-ea-d." I thrust the letter toward Marjorie and lowered my head into my hand.

"Of course." She took the proffered letter and pulled out a chair. "Let's see… Dearest Miss Farncomb, How are you doing, my love?"

I sniffed back a sob, stubbornly refusing to give way to the rain of tears threatening to overwhelm me.

"I can only imagine the way you must feel cooped up in that chair all day, unable to do the things you have always done and hardly able to speak. Remember your mission, my dear Dora-girl. It is as you so keenly saw in your dream—to draw near to our Lord and live in communion with Him—though we have always deigned it to be found in acts of service."

I dabbed awkwardly at my nose. He was right, of course. From the moment I began to seek the mission God had appointed me, I had always thought of it as something I had been given to do. *God forgive me, not once had I considered it might be something I was to* be.

"That is not to suggest that acts of service are not part of that mission," Marjorie continued. "Acts of service flow naturally from the soul that knows true communion with our Lord, as you well know, for his heart—or hers, I might add—is one with the King of Love."

May it be as he says, Lord Jesus. I raised my head, my mouth contorting as I strove to respond. "Bu-u-u-u-d I-ai-ai-ai cccca…" I struck the handle of my wheelchair with my fist. *I cannot serve; I cannot speak. I…* Snatching a notebook and pencil from a pouch on my chair, I leaned toward the table. Twice I had to use my left hand to reposition my right on the paper to keep the notebook from moving as I laboriously scratched out the words with my left.

Can't serve!

Angry tears tumbled from my eyes as I shoved the paper across the table.

"No." Marjorie's voice, as soft as dew drops on a summer's morn, washed over me. "You can no longer do the things you used to do, but your mission has not come to an end. The truth is, you continue to serve Him and His people in ways you've never before considered." She pushed the notebook back, stopping it just before my eager fingers could grasp it. "You have no idea of the wondrous things God is teaching me through you, even now." I grimaced and shook my head, but she pressed on. "Not through what you do or what you say, but through who you are." I turned my head away, too lost in the throes of self-pity to listen to her senseless prattle. "You know, this may not be the mission that you would have chosen for yourself, Aunt Dora, but did you not long ago surrender yourself to accept with joy whatever mission our Lord would commit into your care?"

I swallowed hard. *Is it possible, O Lord, that this, too, is a mission from You?* Marjorie pushed the notebook into my hand, urging me to respond.

Mission of suffering. Of weakness.

I paused to add two more words before nudging it back across the table.

Like His.

Tears gathered in Marjorie's eyes. "Yes." She nodded. "Exactly."

A familiar peace enveloped me—a peace that I had sorely missed over the last three weeks. "Llli-iek H-i-i-i-i-is."

"Look up and behold his face," Marjorie intoned. The words stung, yet heartened at the same time. "Shall I finish reading the letter?" I nodded and leaned back in my chair, closing my eyes.

"There is little to report about life here in Times Square. Redmund, the gentleman I told you about who lost his wife and two sons to the influenza epidemic last year, is now my right hand man in working with our youth. To many, he has become more of a father than a mentor, and he has taken on a role in their lives not unlike that which you played in the lives of the young men of your own parish after Charlie's death. The boys had all been good friends with Redmund's boys prior to the young men's passing and have gravitated to him in their grief. The fact that the attraction is mutual makes it all the more beautiful. I am convinced that God has brought them together for the healing of all their hearts. Do you ever wonder how your boys are doing?"

Marjorie paused, lifting her eyes from the paper. "You know, last time I was at the newspaper office downtown, I saw Byron and Cecil." I raised my left brow, hoping she would continue. "They still work together, you know, though Byron, much to Cecil's chagrin, is the head honcho. Some things never change."

I inclined my head, recalling the incessant scrapping between the two in their younger years. "G-oo-oo-oo-d b-b-b-oe-oeys-sss-s."

"You're proud of them."

I nodded. I had loved those boys as my own. Of course I was proud of them. I was proud of all my boys. I looked pointedly from Marjorie to the letter before her, circling my fingers impatiently in the air.

She laughed. "Are you trying to tell me to get on with it?" I nodded emphatically and she laughed. "Oh, my dear, dear aunt, you may not be able to say much, but you surely haven't lost your ability to communicate." I drew my lips into a tight moue, determined to keep my amusement from reaching my eyes. "Okay. Okay." Marjorie laughed again, throwing both hands into the air in mock surrender. "I'll read on." I clasped my right hand with my left and closed my eyes to listen.

"Alas, I digress and it is time for me to go. I pray for you often, my Dora-girl. How I wish I could be by your side as you walk through this most difficult valley, but God has ordained it otherwise. It cheers me to know that I leave you in good hands, though." Marjorie's cheeks coloured and she stumbled over the words. "Your dear Marjorie is as devoted to you as I and loves you every bit as much. Take heart, my beloved, and be of good cheer. 'The Master has come and He calleth for thee.' Is that not what you told me? It is true for us all, dear Dora. For every one of us. 'The Master has come and He calleth for thee. Look up, and behold His face.' Affectionately, Your Mattie. P.S."

Marjorie stopped reading abruptly. I drummed my fingers on the table. "Oh, that last part is just a little note thanking me for keeping him abreast of the news and imploring me to take good care of you and see that you remember the reality of your true calling."

I sighed. *Dear Mattie. My dear, dear Mattie.*

"How about a cup of tea?" Marjorie handed me the letter on her way to the sink.

Eyes blurring, I folded it awkwardly and clutched it to my chest. *Jesus, how long? How long must I endure the heartache... the frustration... the pain... of separation from him whom my heart desires?*

Marjorie puttered around the kitchen, making sandwiches and slicing cucumbers to go with our tea. I watched as she arranged four cherry-topped shortbread cookies on a plate, my heart swelling with gratitude for the wonderful gift God had given me in her—the daughter for whom I had so yearned, a daughter not of my womb, but of my heart. Tears seeped from beneath my lashes to trickle down my cheeks. *You are so good to me, Jesus. Forgive me for harbouring resentment toward You in my heart for allowing this body of mine to fail as it has.* Marjorie set a plate before me and tied a towel around my neck. "Th-tha-a-an-y-y-ou," I managed, unable to meet her eyes. *Let me live what days remain to me on this earth in the spirit of gratitude, not merely in word, but in humility of heart and soul.*

"Are you hungry?" I jerked my head up to find Marjorie seated across from me, her hands folded before her plate. "*I* certainly am." She continued as if I had spoken, hardly missing a beat. "Let's pray." She bowed her head and waited, giving me time to do the same. "For what we are about to receive, O God, may our hearts be truly thankful. Let us feed not only on that which sustains our bodies, but even more so, on You who sustains our souls. In the name of our Lord and Saviour, Jesus Christ, who was and is and ever more shall be, world without end. Amen."

"M-mm-m-mmnnn," I repeated. *May it be so, precious Lord. May it, indeed, be so."*

Chapter 78

JULY 19, 1924

"Aunt Dora, you have visitors." Marjorie slid a pillow behind my back and folded the counterpane around my waist. "They can hardly wait to see you." I gazed at her, barely able to keep my eyes from closing. "It's Uncle Alfred, Cousin Helen, and those two young lads of hers." She nodded enthusiastically. "You remember them, do you not?"

My eyes drifted shut as I leaned my head upon the pillows. *Helen... Helen—that was Alfred's youngest, and her two boys—did she have two boys? Oh yes. Young Farncomb and Balfour, was it not?* I opened my eyes, but Marjorie had left. *Why could I not shake this confounded tiredness?*

Snippets from a whispered conversation in the hall drifted through the door. "It's been days, even weeks, since she has spoken and longer yet since she's left her bed, but her spirits remain good and her face glows as if she spends her days basking in the presence of the Almighty." A man's voice mumbled something I couldn't hear and Marjorie responded. "No–no... although perhaps, at times. The other day, I could swear she laughed when I reminded her of how Uncle Charlie had convinced Grandfather to let him keep that old mutt, Samson." Another voice joined the conversation, followed by Marjorie's hushed response. "Her body weakens with each passing day and it's difficult to entice her to eat, but her heart yet beats for our Lord alone, and she is at peace. The other day I even caught her with pencil in hand, laboriously committing a word or two to her notebook as she does from time to time."

The man's voice returned, so like that of my father. "A-a-a-llll-fr...." The word died on my lips, the effort too great to maintain. I gasped for air, my chest heaving from the exertion, and let my eyes close. *This is my chance to say goodbye, isn't it?* A comfortable silence reigned within my soul. *However will I make them understand?* A shuffling of feet. The creak of a floorboard. My eyes snapped open. "A-a-aaa—"

"Good morning, Dora-girl." Alfred's eyes misted as he bent to embrace me. I had forgotten how big he was. "I hear you're doing pretty well these days, all things considered." I locked my good arm around his neck, wishing this moment could last forever. "Have you missed me?" he asked. I released him from my grasp and nodded, my eyes boring into his. "But there's more you want to say, isn't there?" he probed. Again I nodded, surprised by his insight, not that I should have been. He was, after all, a doctor. "Are you trying to tell me that the time has come for us to say goodbye?" He hooked a finger beneath my chin and nudged it upward. "Are you afraid?"

"N-n-nnn…" I closed my eyes and relaxed into the pillows, unable to sustain the effort.

"More like exhausted, eh?" With a weary chuckle, he bent to sit on the edge of the bed. I peered at him gratefully, jerking my hand up to rest on his chest. "Me?" He glanced away, a battle raging in his eyes. I let my hand drop, fighting the urge to press him for a response. "I only wish it was me instead of you." His words barely stirred the air.

Words bubbled within me—words of comfort, of understanding, of encouragement—yet try as I might, only one word escaped. "S-sss-ss-ss-ooooooooooo-n-nn."

He turned to face me, running a hand down my cheek. "Will you say hi to Mother and Father for me… and give my little Alfie a big hug?" He paused, blinking away the water that had gathered in his eyes. "Tell Charlie I miss him, and Johnny… please tell him that I forgive him… that I understand now in a way I never could before."

I drew his head awkwardly to my bosom. *Oh, big brother. Jesus help you to endure the heartache of losing yet another so close to your heart.*

• • •

My eyes fluttered open. The gas lamp on the table cast a feeble halo of light about the bed, but the room seemed somehow brighter. No matter. There was something I had to do. Now. I reached for the notebook and pencil on the bedside table. I had one more letter to write. Propping myself up as best as I could, I flipped to an empty page and positioned my right hand on the fold to keep the pages from turning. Seizing the pencil in my left, I dug it into the page, carefully drawing each letter.

My dear, dear Mattie,

I paused, resting my hand. Words whirled around in my head, too numerous to record. I had to keep this short.

The time has come for me to go home.

I closed my eyes, my fingers quivering from the exertion. *Lord, give me the time and the stamina to complete this final letter to my love.* Forcing my eyes to open, I gripped the pencil between my thumb and forefinger. A sentence or two more and I would be done.

The light in the room intensified as I wrote, imbuing me with a strength I hadn't felt in months. *I love you, Mattie. Please don't be too sad at my passing.* I signed my name as best as I could and let my hand fall to my belly. It was finished. I rested my head on the pillows, my breath rattling in my chest. A moment later, my eyes popped open. There was one more thing. Once again I seized the pencil, laboriously etching a final sentence into the page. *There.* The pencil fell from my hand as the book clattered to the floor. A figure emerged from the light—a man so bright, I could barely stand to look upon Him. "I am rr-eady, Ll-ord."

Come, thou, my good and faithful servant; enter into My rest. I held up my good arm as if I were a child once more, and He gathered me into His arms, lifting me from the bonds of my failing body. *It is time for us to go home.*

Epilogue

AUGUST 12, 1924

Winnie slid the broom beneath the bed, determined to capture every last dust bunny before the room was handed over to her daughter. "What's this?" The broom hooked something solid and she bent to pick it up.

"There it is!" Marjorie exclaimed. "I've been looking all over for that." Winnie raised a brow as she handed it to her sister. "It's Aunt Dora's notebook." She flipped through it, stopping at the final entry.

> *My Dear, Dear Mattie,*
>
> *The time has come for me to go home. Please do not be too sad. Our Master has come and I am with Him. I love you Mattie and will miss you dearly.*
>
> *Until you join me here,*
> *Your Dora-girl.*
>
> *P.S. Do not be long.*

Marjorie closed the book and hugged it to her bosom. "She's got her dancing shoes on, Winnie; her calling is complete."

"And what of yours, dear sister? What will you do now?"

"Oh, God will reveal that to me in time, I am sure," Marjorie answered. "In the meantime, I shall don the mantle our dear aunt left behind and follow her example in living a life of communion with our Lord. Then one day, when the time is right, I shall get my own dancing shoes and join the grand celebration."

"May it be so," Winnie whispered. "May it, indeed, be so."

Author's Notes

This is not a true story. While it has been inspired by real people and—in many cases—by real events, the story itself is a work of fiction, as is the timeline it follows. If you would like to learn more about the real Dora Farncomb, please read the following article, adapted from a piece first published in the *Newcastle Village and District Historical Society Newsletter Issue 126* in winter, 2017. Dora Farncomb was a gifted and dedicated woman; I look forward to one day meeting her.

Back Row Left to Right: Thomas, **Dora**, William, Frederick, **Jane**, **John**
Front Row Left to Right: **Alfred**, **Jane (Mother)**, **Frederick (Father)**
Missing: **Charles** (1865-1879); The children are John and Jane's two eldest, **Winifred** and **Charles**

Photo Taken Approximately 1884

DORA FARNCOMB: AUTHOR, MUSICIAN AND TEACHER
BY KATHERINE J. LE GRESLEY

Born on May 11, 1863, Dora was the fifth-born child of Frederick and Jane Farncomb of Newcastle, Ontario. Besides her four older brothers (William, Frederick, Dr. Alfred, and Canon John), she also had two younger brothers (Charles and Thomas). Little is known of her early years until she began her studies in 1878 at Bishop Strachan School for Girls in Toronto. Sadly, Dora had only completed one year of her studies when her younger brother Charles drowned in a horrifying swimming accident in September, 1879. Needed at home, Dora was forced to put her formal education on hold for a year to aid her family during this unexpected season of grief. She did, however, manage to keep abreast of her studies in her year away, enabling her to rejoin her classmates the following year and graduate with her form. She was a good student and was honoured to receive the "First Religious Subjects (including Scripture) Award" at Prize Giving in 1881.

Returning to Newcastle, Dora devoted herself to service at St. George's Anglican Church where she played the organ at times, helped to decorate the sanctuary for special events, and ran a Bible study and social club (more like a service club) for the young men of the village. In time, the young men she taught—most of whom went on to become prominent, service-oriented citizens in their own communities—became known throughout the area as Dora's boys.

Many tragedies were to befall the Farncomb family in those days. Frederick, Dora's father, died in 1893, and only a few years later, her mother, Jane, fell ill and was confined to her bed. While it would appear that Dora may have moved to Toronto by that time, where she had begun writing for *The Farmer's Advocate and Home Magazine*, she immediately returned to Newcastle where she nursed her mother until Jane's death in 1905.

It was a difficult time for Dora. Demands at *The Advocate* had increased exponentially. She had gone from writing guest articles for "The Quiet Hour" segment of *The Home Magazine* to writing weekly articles under the pen name *Hope* for her own column, now entitled "Hope's Quiet Hour". She also wrote regular articles for "The Children's Corner" for several years. As her devotional column grew in popularity, money started to pour in from across the country for her to distribute to those who were in need. An unanticipated blessing, the offerings added to Dora's workload, but were always gratefully received and directed to families who would benefit from the financial support. Between caring for her mother, the demands of *The Advocate,* and her continued work at church, there must have been few quiet moments for this kind and dedicated young lady, but she was not one to give up or feel sorry for herself. God had given her a job to do and she would do it, despite the cost.

The turn of the century came and went, bringing yet more tragedy for the Farncomb family. In 1901, Dora's brother John's two teenaged sons (not actually twins) drowned at the harbour in a swimming accident reminiscent of the one that had taken their Uncle Charles years before. Heartbroken, John's wife, Jane, was committed to the Toronto Insane Asylum. Within a month of their sons' deaths, John transferred his rectorship at St. George's Anglican Church in Newcastle to St. Matthew's Anglican Church in Toronto where he could be nearer to his wife. With no calm to follow the storm, Dora stayed in Newcastle to continue nursing her mother. Yet the tragedies were not to end. In 1905, her mother succumbed to her long-standing illness.

Undecided as to where she should go or what she should do after her mother's death, Dora set off on a new mission. Being alerted to a great need (probably by her childhood friend, Bishop Charles Brent), she moved to Boston to help the poor and needy who lived on the streets of that great city. Tragedy, however, brought her back to Canada once more when in 1907, her brother Alfred's ten-year-old son died of pneumonia. Knowing her family needed her, she settled in Toronto, determined to help the underprivileged of her own land while doing all she could to support her brothers and their wives who still struggled to cope with the loss of their sons.

Claiming John's church as her own, Dora once again immersed herself in the life of the parish. She taught Bible studies, directed Christmas concerts, ministered to the less fortunate and helped her brother in any way she could, all while continuing to write for *The Advocate* and expanding her ministry to the poor. Marjorie, John's youngest daughter, joined Dora, becoming her trusted and devoted companion, but when Marjorie's mother died of pneumonia in the asylum in 1914, Dora once again found herself surrounded by grief. John, able to handle no more, moved back to Ebor House in Newcastle leaving Dora to continue her ministry of service to the people of St. Matthew's and the surrounding community on her own. A strong, determined and practical woman, full of compassion and self-sacrificial love, she took up the task before her with a passion that no amount of tragedy could dampen. Her life was not easy, but nor did she expect it to be. Her goal was to serve Her Lord and be His hands to every person she met, a mission which she took very seriously. When her brother John died suddenly in 1917, her life was rocked, but her foundation remained sure. She had a mission to fulfil and she would not rest until it was done.

Dora outlived all but two of her brothers (Frederick and Thomas). She lived through the confederation of Canada, the First World War and the Great Depression. She witnessed the birth of my grandmother, the marriage of my grandparents, and lived to see my father turn twelve years old, not once letting go of her mission to serve. Her final article in *The Farmer's Advocate and Home Magazine*, entitled "Glory in the Midst", appeared in January of 1938. While it had been written in the final weeks of November—just prior to the stroke that left her bedridden and eventually took her life on August 23, 1938—it almost seemed as if she knew that it would be her final farewell. Her passing was a peaceful one as she stepped from this life into the presence of her Lord. She had touched many lives. The author of three books and numerous articles, she was lauded as an author, a musician, and a teacher by her alma mater and as an inspiration and beloved friend by her faithful readers across the nation. Few women of her day had what it took to make it on their own, but she did, for although she never wed, her Lord was her husband and in Him she was content.

MENTAL ILLNESS IN THE EARLY TWENTIETH CENTURY

The concept of mental illness has evolved greatly in the past 150 years. While the terms used to reference it in this book are far from politically correct and may seem utterly offensive, they reflect the terminology used to describe mental illness, and the limited understanding of it, common to the people of the time. While the very idea of the historical lunatic asylum—or even the hospital for the insane—conjures horrifying images of deplorable conditions and unspeakable abuse, it must be noted that historical records, including letters written by inmates themselves, suggest that life on the inside may not have always been as bad as it has been portrayed, at least in the time period addressed by this book. Sanitary conditions were not always good and there were definitely reports of abuse by inmates and attendants alike, but in the years of moral therapy during which our Janey was an inmate—when restraints were frowned upon and before insulin shock therapy and electric shock therapy were invented—life may not have been as bad in the asylum as we have been led to believe. That leisure activities like weekly dances, walks in the gardens, and periodic excursions to places like the exhibition were arranged for the patients seems surprising given the images etched in our modern minds of such institutions, as do reports that refer to solid friendships between residents and their attendants. The doctors, in particular, really did seem to care for their patients and, working with such knowledge as they had at the time, did their best to cure them of their insanity.

That many inmates feared to leave the safety of the asylum is evident in more than one letter written by those on the inside, at least when it comes to the Hospital for the Insane in Toronto. Conditions within the asylum varied greatly, however, according to whether or not the patient's family could pay for his/her care and how much the family could pay. One cannot deny that life within the mental asylum was far from ideal, and too often, utterly deplorable, yet, it was not so for all. Still, to be declared insane in those early days of the twentieth century—when the only options for "treatment" were life in prison or in an asylum—must have been terrifying both for the person being committed as well as for his/her family since lunacy was firmly believed to be a genetic trait. Nor did it take much to be certified a lunatic, especially for women. Few who were committed to the asylum ever returned to their regular lives. If you would like to learn more about life in the Toronto asylum in the late nineteenth and early twentieth centuries, I would encourage you to read Remembrance of Patients Past: Patient Life at the Hospital for the Insane, 1870-1940 by Geoffrey Reaume, ©2000 by University of Toronto Press. As difficult as it was to read in places, I found myself in many ways relieved. Perhaps my Great Grandaunt Jane's life there wasn't quite as bad as my imagination had made it out to be.

SUICIDE IN THE EARLY TWENTIETH CENTURY

Suicide is never a comfortable subject. It has touched far too many of our lives in some shape or form and, even now, carries a stigma all its own. In the early twentieth century, suicide was something nobody spoke about, though we can be sure that it happened more often than we know. Considered an unpardonable sin, it was deemed that the soul who dared to commit suicide was doomed to an eternity in Hell. The funeral, if the deceased was given one at all, was not attended by those whom he had once called friends; his body could not be interred in the churchyard; his name was no longer spoken for the shame he had brought upon himself and his family. Should the deceased be a member of the clergy, so much the worse. To even attend the funeral might make it appear as if a priest or bishop condoned the actions of the dead in opposition to the teachings of the church. A lot has changed in our understanding of suicide over the years as our understanding of mental illness has evolved. While some continue to view it as an unpardonable offense, more have come to see it as the result of a physiological imbalance, an illness. And as our understanding of mental illness has grown, so has our compassion for those who fight it all their lives and for those who have lost that battle. Dora's response to her brother's suicide in this book is quite progressive for her time, as is the response of the bishop who attended the interment, yet the still-changing attitudes of a century later had to begin somewhere. It is my prayer for any whose life has been touched by the grief of suicide that God would renew your heart with hope and healing and joy. If suicide seems to be your only way out, please reach out to someone you love and share with them your battle, or call your local suicide hotline. You are not alone and you are greatly loved; there *is* a better way.